Little Bastards in Springtime

Little Bastards
in Springtime

A Novel

KATJA RUDOLPH

STEER
FORTH
PRESS

Hanover, New Hampshire

First published in Canada in 2014 by HarperCollins Publishers Ltd

For information about permission to reproduce
selections from this book, write to:
Steerforth Press L.L.C., 45 Lyme Road, Suite 208,
Hanover, New Hampshire 03755

Cataloging-in-Publication Data is available from the Library of Congress

ISBN 978-1-58642-233-2

First U.S. Edition

1 3 5 7 9 10 8 6 4 2

for Ali Drummond
nine hundred years and counting

When the leaders speak of peace,
The common folk know
That war is coming.
When the leaders curse war
The mobilization order is already written out.
—BERTOLT BRECHT, *War Primer*

The duty of youth is to challenge corruption.
—KURT COBAIN

Prologue

Baka told me the story of how she walked up into the mountain forest to join the partisans so many times that I can write it down without hesitation in ten minutes flat. All the words are already there, I don't have to think up a single one. It's a good place to begin. Sava, this is for you.

Autumn 1941

THE GIRL SQUATS BY THE ROADSIDE, ARMS resting on knees. She can see far out into the valley, a haze of green and rust punctuated by dabs of oily black smoke. Beyond this rise mountain peaks capped by snow. She has all she needs with her: food for several days, a change of underclothing, a knife she took from the kitchen just before slipping away. Directly below, where the road enters the mountain forest, the Italians are burning her village and along with it, she prays, her father, her uncle, her brothers, and her loathsome husband-to-be.

The girl has been waiting without stirring since morning, savouring the stillness, the solitude, how the sun moves inexorably across the sky. The harsh white of noon is replaced by a golden afternoon, which, following an interval of fading light, blooms into a luminous pink sunset. With dusk, the girl calls her prayer back from the changeable sky. She no longer wishes for her father and the others to burn to death within earshot of fascist curses. She is satisfied to be up in the mountains away from them. Let them live their lives, let me live mine, she thinks.

As the sun sets she hears footfalls. Indistinct on the loose edge of the road, their soft crunching and sliding might be the sound of an animal burrowing but for their purposeful regularity. The girl listens with anticipation. She was told to expect a man when night fell. She knows what he will say to her once he comes upon her. She knows how she will respond.

The man is at her side. She senses him as much as she can see him. He is a dense breathing presence undulating in the blue and purple night. She can feel warmth radiating from his body, smell his cigarette breath, his sharp salty sweat.

"Do you wish to continue with me?" he asks her.

He speaks in a dialect that the girl has not heard before. She feels a shiver rush from her lower back to the crown of her head and arches her spine with pleasure, knowing the gesture will remain invisible. This is the marriage ceremony I choose, she thinks, this is my special day. Up here, on a moonless night, bathed in forest scents, no witnesses to steal the moment from me. A man from a distant region whom she has yet to lay eyes on asks her a question she can with all her heart say yes to. There is a tremor in her voice when she replies.

"Yes, let us continue together to higher ground."

The man and the girl walk side by side through the night. They say nothing more. Occasionally, he reaches out and touches her arm; occasionally, she reaches out and touches his. In this way, they stay within three feet of each other as they move quickly into the mountain. After some time, the girl takes notice of her body, the way her muscles propel her forward in a complex sequence of contraction and relaxation, the way her ligaments secure her joints, the way her arms swing rhythmically at her sides and her breath steadies and deepens despite her exertion. It does all of this of its own accord, the girl notices, leaving her mind free to wander, for the first time in her life, in an immaterial world of its own making. In this state of entrancement, time and place no longer fetter her; she conjures up a hundred diverse futures for herself, none of which include the vile man her father intends her to marry, or the house in the village to which she would be tied for the rest of her life. She would like this night march and its visions of the wide world to go on forever.

Eventually, however, light seeps through branches and morning arrives. The girl looks outward again. She sees a narrow path through pine trees. She sees mountainside thrusting upward beyond the treetops. She sees the man, who is tall and wiry and leans forward to counterbalance the weight of his pack, walking next to her.

"Day is breaking," he says. "We are almost there."

"I like walking distances in the dark," the girl responds. "It's the first time I've done it."

"Well, that's good," replies the man. "There's going to be a lot of that. We conduct our raids and ambushes like bee stings, quick, sharp, painful, then we melt away into the forests, hills, and sometimes high, high up into the mountains where there is snow and the enemy and all his machinery cannot follow."

The camp is a peasant farm. There's a barnyard, several tall hay cones, a stone farmhouse to the left, a wooden barn and several smaller sheds to the right. The girl sees the farmer leaning in the doorway of one of them, his anxious eyes on the road; he could be one of her uncles, one of her neighbours. She knows his wife and children are in there, waiting for their uninvited guests to leave. The girl and the man follow the sound of raised voices into the farmhouse and to the kitchen. Fifteen soldiers are squeezed tightly into its dim confines—thirteen men, two women, each talking loudly over the others. Their faces are swarthy and slick with an oily sheen, since the kitchen is stuffy and hot, and their hair minus caps is matted and stringy. Propped up next to each is a rifle, different from the guns the girl has seen hunters carrying in the village. All at once all present turn, look at her, raise their mugs, and shout, "Welcome, Partizanka!" Then the girl is jostled to the end of the long table.

"We'll take you to training camp from here," the man says. "For now, meet your comrades, eat and drink."

A mug of tea, a boiled egg, a slice of sausage, a piece of bread are placed in front of her. There is no plate. She takes a sip of tea.

"What's your name?" asks the partisan next to her. He has a scraggly beard, a cigarette tucked behind each ear, and round spectacles emphasizing soulful brown eyes. He's wearing a uniform the girl does not recognize.

"I haven't decided yet," she says.

"Oh?" His eyebrows rise, his forehead wrinkles.

"I'm going to choose my own name." The girl says this with a deep feeling of joy.

"Well, Yet-to-Be-Named, you are about to learn everything we know about resisting and terminating the occupation. Harassing the enemy, cutting communications, guerrilla operations like that. And active offensives. I am the political commissar here, by the way."

He reaches out a hand. The girl shakes it.

"I know why I'm here," the girl says.

"The occupiers are not our most important enemy," continues the commissar. "Our most important enemy is all that stands in the way of a united Yugoslavia and a just and equit-able society."

"Yes, I know," says the girl.

"The Germans and their Axis are superior in weapons and equipment, but we have—"

"—knowledge of terrain, speed of mobility," the girl finishes for him.

The commissar squints at her, then smiles. "That's it," he says. "You've heard our lecture in the village. You children learn fastest."

"Yes, I did. In the village."

"The children will all be ruined by war, that's the truth of it," the commissar announces, not to her but to the table in general. "Yet some will rise arduously from the ruins to change the world for the better." No one is listening to him. "And when the next war breaks out, the same will happen," he continues. "When this cycle has occurred enough times, the ruined children of war will have changed the world sufficiently to eradi-cate the benefit of war to any man, venture, nation, or empire and there will be no more wars. You see, progress!"

"Maybe it will only take one more generation," the girl says.

"Maybe. That is our intention," says the commissar. "Death to fascism, freedom to the people!"

He turns to talk to the man beside him.

The girl chews her bread. She peels her egg. The food is good. After this brief exchange, no one pays attention to her, so she sits and concentrates on tasting and lets the hubbub of voices envelop her. In this way, she finishes eating, then turns her attention to the two partizankas at the other end of the table, strange lumin-ous creatures in the girl's eyes, wearing men's uniforms, gesticu-lating boldly with their hands and jumping out of their seats as they talk. One of them has cut her hair short, the girl notices. A dark lock has fallen down over her forehead and stays there, stuck down by sweat. The girl is thinking about this, whether she will cut her own hair short, when the room falls abruptly silent. She looks around wide-eyed. For a heartbeat everyone is motionless, heads cocked, listening. And there it is, gunfire at the sentry's post a hundred yards down the road.

The soldier at the head of the table barks, "Go," and "Now," and a cacophony of chairs tipping over and guns being picked up and mugs smashing as they're swept off the table accompanies the scramble for the door. The girl is dragged out of her seat, the kitchen, the farmhouse by the two partisans sitting closest to her, the commissar, and an old-man soldier with a head of grey hair and a gaunt, pitted face. She is aware of a bruising grip on each upper arm, of her head dangling awkwardly on the stem of her neck, of her knees dragging along the floor, then banging on the ridge of each step down to the farmyard. And there she is set on her feet and pushed hard toward the back perimeter of the farm.

"Run," the commissar shouts. "It's a raid. Follow us."

The girl runs, following her comrades out of the farmyard and into a field beyond it. There she observes them fanning out, each one heading to the forest at the edge of the field. Gun- and mortar-fire echo against the mountainside, and raised voices too, the orders of the enemy officers, the pleading of the farmer, the cries of his family, the shrieks of animals. When she reaches the edge of the forest, the girl stops to look back. The farm buildings are on fire, the animals are being slaughtered. She turns, enters the forest, and chases after the officers' whistles. When they are all together, running in single file, the whistles stop and they move silently but for the rasp of their breathing, ever uphill, off the path, ducking between trees, jumping over roots.

Part One

Spring 1992

———

Mayday, Mayday

1

IT'S CLOUDY BUT WARM FOR APRIL. WARM AT least in the huge crowd of people. Thousands of bodies pressed together, all breathing on each other.

"It's an unpredictable month," Mama says, looking at the sky.

There is mist on the hills surrounding the city and trees are wearing haloes of green. I've seen swallows making their nests in the roofs. I struggle to take off my coat, I hand it to her. She tells me to put it on again.

"You'll get a cold," she says.

I swear at her, but she's distracted by the crazy energy of the marchers. Everyone's mouth open, shouting, whistling, singing. There are signs. There are flags. I can hear drums up front, and next to us is a big group of miners from Tuzla who sing, "*We miners, we don't drink wine, we only drink the smoke coming out of the mines.*" There are old men and old ladies too. And lots of students in leather jackets and scarves. They're chanting, "We don't want cantons," "Resist nationalist propaganda," "Fuck the World Bank," "We want to live together," "Yugo, we love you." Things like that. And there's a beggar on the sidewalk with a sign that reads, My wife refuses to cook for me, I want changes. I think it's funny, but Mama and Papa aren't laughing.

We're all walking in the same direction down from Maršala Tita to Obala Kulina Bana. Everyone ignores the shops and cafés, the food smells and coffee smells. The water-hungry Miljacka is close and I want to stand on the bridge to watch the brown water and beer bottles and deflated balls go underneath, but we can't get out of the crush, we have to keep going. Papa is somewhere in front of us. Every now and then I see his hat bobbing along, the black hat he likes to wear. His hair is very long these days, gets curly when it grows beyond his ears. He knows many people here and wants to talk to all of them, one hand grabbing the back of their neck and the other waving in their face. He walks sideways so he can look into their eyes the whole time. He's very intense, Mama says.

Mama knows people too. She is always calling out to someone. "Yoo-hoo, Milan, yoo-hoo. Over here!" "Hello, Zlatko, let's meet for coffee soon."

I recognize that tone in her voice. She's on the edge of a meltdown. It's how strongly she feels about this. She's very passionate, Papa says.

"This is our chance," she said to Papa over and over again this morning when we were getting ready to leave the apartment. "This is our chance. We must take back the moral leadership."

"Yes, yes. Do you have to shout in my ear? I'm standing right next to you. Standing, waiting."

Mama, rushing around the apartment as usual, looking for something. "But this is our chance. We can't be complacent now. We must be heard." Her umbrella, in her hand, finally.

"Yes, for Christ's sake, you know I agree with you." Papa, rubbing his face with impatience. Papa hates to wait. He wants to be in the action right away.

"This is our chance to take hold of history. We are the majority, we must drown out the fascists once and for all."

"Sofija, I know all of this. Can we just *go*?" Mama, suddenly crying, trying to get her raincoat off the hanger in the hall closet, which has too many coats in it. Crying is something she's doing more of lately.

Papa, holding her in his arms, rolling his eyes at me and Dušan over her head. *Women*, he mouthed at us, then waved us out the door. But he's a crier too.

By the time we got to where the march started, Mama and Papa were walking hand in hand, all calm and collected again. I turn and there are Amir and Edin elbowing their way through the marchers, chasing after someone. Maybe it's someone else from school.

"Can I go with Amir and Edin?" I ask Mama.

"Are you crazy?" she says. "We'll never see you again. Can't you see how big this is? So many people." She grabs my hand. I yank it back. She shouts Papa's name. "Lazar," she yells. "Lazar. Where is that irritating man?"

Then he's right here at our side. He's wearing a big smile on his face. He hugs Mama, then lifts her and swings her around. I don't know where Dušan is. He's sixteen and goes wherever he wants. He met up with his friends at the beginning and they're probably drinking beer somewhere. Papa's lecture in the elevator on the way here didn't suddenly change him. "Progressive grassroots politics is vitally important, Dušan. Now more than ever. Pay attention and participate in the democratic process." Stuff like that, which Papa likes to say.

"Hasan is here," Papa says. "And Juka and Raif and Ivo. Anyone who's anyone. This is the real Yugoslavia, the true

Sarajevo. Artists, writers, professors, journalists mixed in with everyone else. All nationalities, no nationalities. Demos triumphing over ethnos."

"Yes, yes." But Mama looks like she's going to cry again. That strange pull around the edges of her mouth.

Papa winks at me.

"Put him on your shoulders," Mama says. "Let him see the size of this demonstration, this people's rebellion against the fascists. Jevrem, read all the signs you see. Read them aloud to us."

"He's ten, he's too goddamned old," Papa complains, but he grabs me by the hips and heaves me up, groaning and staggering around. I knock off his hat by mistake and he calls to Mama, "Quick, quick, pick it up, pick it up."

"I'm eleven," I shout into the noise. "I'm eleven."

From his shoulders I can see the backs of thousands of heads. They're floating all the way to the government building, which stands so tall and shiny in front of us, and the parliament building next to it. I turn and look behind us. I see thousands of bobbing faces edging forward, staring at me. My heels bang against Papa's soft belly. I haven't been up here for years. I remember when my legs stopped at Papa's collarbones. I remember placing my dirty paws in front of his eyes, pinching his nose, pushing my face into his hair, the smell of his warm scalp.

"There are some signs in English."

"Well, read them to us," Mama says.

"I don't pay attention in English class. It's boring."

"Well, you should."

"*You* don't speak English," I grumble, but I try to sound out the words I see. "Our-nation-is-Yugoslavia. We-are-one people. Three-Lunatics-Milošević-Tuđjman-Izetbegović, Resist fascism." I'm yelling to be heard.

Papa laughs. "Could you have a thicker accent?" He does speak English.

"When will I ever need that crappy language?" I cry at him.

"You never know," Papa says. He cranes his neck for someone else to discuss important issues with. "That crappy language runs the world. If you don't want to lead a narrow life, you're going to have to learn that language, now that everything's changing."

I look up. The clouds are thinning out. The hills surrounding the city are dark green. I see blue sky. Sometimes I wish I were a bird and could take off whenever I wanted. I'd fly high above all these noisy people, all trapped together in these narrow city streets. I'd soar into the mountains where there are trees and rivers and foresters' cabins.

CLOUDS move in again over the city when evening comes. But the sunset shines through, painting bright red streaks in the sky and turning the hills purple and grey. I stand on the balcony with my Walkman plugged into my ears, watching the lights come on in the apartment opposite. I'm not listening to music, I just like to be alone sometimes. I listen to Sarajevo sounds. Cars, trams, muezzins from the minarets, bells from the churches. The shouts of kids playing in the courtyards.

Our apartment is full of Mama and Papa's friends and some depressed relatives. The blare of their voices mixes with Rachmaninov blasting from our stereo. Mama listens all day long to the composer of the piece she is rehearsing. The twins Aisha and Berina are carrying trays of snacks. Their skinny eight-year-old arms can hardly hold them up. They keep bumping into people like bossy waitresses and saying, excuse us, let us

through, exactly at the same time, like they do. Dušan is the bartender; he's allowed to have three beers and he's already drunk
them. Now he's taking slugs of vodka from the bottle. My baka is
pumping her fist into the air. She's telling partisan war stories, I
can tell by the way people are looking at her. Kind of proud, kind
of pitying, kind of bored. They think she's old-fashioned, all
that tired old communist stuff from the past. She thinks they're
pathetic wimps, and says so to their faces. She made up her own
name when she was a girl. She invented the life she wanted to live.
She tells me that quite often. Soon she'll say, "About our beloved
leader . . ." and launch into a Tito story, her favourite kind.

"All the good people today are passive, too passive. In my
day, we fought the fascists as soon as they descended upon us,"
she shouts. "About our beloved leader, our Joza . . ."

And she's off. The group around her begins to turn away,
embarrassed little smiles on their faces.

"Kumrovec, his village, is in Croatia, so what? His ancestors
lived in those hills and valleys for hundreds of years, so what?
Did this make him a narrow nationalist? No, it did not!"

Only one of Papa's students is still listening, and he's blinking hard and rocking back and forth on his feet. Tipsy people
are easy to spot. Baka doesn't care, that's the way she is, she
keeps right on shouting.

"The important point is that we and Tito fought the Ustasha
and Chetniks, those terrible nationalists back then, as much as
the Germans and the Italians. We didn't care where anyone came
from, what religion, what home village, what region, we knew
them by their politics alone. That's all that mattered at that
time. That's all that matters still. It was death to fascism, freedom to the people! We fought on principle, not tribe. And now
see what's going on. You younger generations are a disgrace."

Ujak Luka, my wild uncle, mimics Baka behind her back. He's tipsy too and he's got a girl with him who is very pretty and young, maybe only seventeen. He drives Baka crazy, but they love each other, even though he's irresponsible, a theatre person. Mama says he's still a little boy, with all his different interests and ideas, his actor friends and their illegal ways, like smoking pot in front of the police headquarters and I'm not sure what else. Mama says he plays with fire, he rocks the boat, he's always walking on the edge. Maybe he's a criminal of some kind, but no one will tell me.

He sits down next to me and points at my Walkman. "What are you listening to, little Jevrem, my favourite eleven-year-old nephew?"

"Nothing," I say. "I sometimes put earphones on so people won't bug me. Then I can daydream without being bothered."

"What do you dream about?"

"All kinds of things. What I'm going to do this afternoon, what I'm going to do when I'm a man, that kind of thing."

"That's good, little Jevrem. A man without a dream is a dead man. Everyone should dream. Don't say anything to anyone, but I've got my dreams too. I'm going away. Far from this nightmare, far from these zombies that have taken over our country, stumbling along our streets oozing dying brain cells out of their noses and ears."

I laugh, I can't help it. Ujak Luka is a funny guy.

"It's like we've forgotten we're a sophisticated, civilized country; we've sold our souls for a worthless idea that's never worked for any nation in any time. We've let the losers take over."

Ujak Luka is not tipsy, he's completely drunk, his eyes shiny red marbles, his breath smelling like fire. "Don't tell anyone, Jevrem, but I'm going away with my girlfriend; this place has become ridiculous. Even my oldest friends avoid each other, from one day to the next, infected by this deadly illness called nationalism. It's pure bullshit." He sighs, rubs his eyes with one hand.

Papa is lecturing a group sitting around the dining room table. His voice bellows when he drinks and drowns everything else out. Ujak Luka points at Papa, pokes me in the ribs with his elbow.

"See, he thinks he's immune to the spreading plague," he says, rolling his eyes, lighting a cigarette. "Do you want a drag?"

"The media, it's our only hope," Papa proclaims. He's chain-smoking today. I guess he's decided to put off quitting until life is less tense. "We must gain the upper hand on the airwaves again, and in print, change the tone of the discourse, eclipse ethno-nationalist politics, forge a post-communist democratic citizenship, maintain communities of affinity over communities of biology and tribe. There are journalists who will write anything for a bribe, but there are more of us who are ready to write the real story—but no newspapers or magazines will take our pieces, not even abroad."

Ujak Luka repeats each of Papa's words into my ear, with a high whispering voice. "Do you know what all of that means, Jevrem?" he asks me. "All those big, fancy words?"

"Yes . . . no," I say.

"Do you know that it's all been said a thousand times and not made any difference?" Ujak Luka's face is red and sweaty.

I nod my head, then shake my head. Dora, Orhan's wife, is talking with Mama in the corner, their heads bent together, their faces serious and pale. I wish they'd brought their son Zijad along. He's my age. I'd have something to do.

"*Ethno-politics, democratic citizenship, communities of affinity ver-*

sus communities of tribe," Ujak Luka repeats. "As if those words will reach people. Where is the talk about bread and jobs for every human body? That's the point." I feel drops of his spit on the side of my face. "The other side is telling unemployed men how their jobs were stolen by hostile neighbours, how they're going to be wiped out as a people if they don't take up arms and fight. Who do you think they're going to listen to?"

A group of men stand by the window. They talk over each other and gesture at the city.

"It was a terrible mistake, a criminal mistake, of Germany and the U.S. to recognize secession so soon, that's been the biggest mistake. But it wasn't a mistake, was it. The destabilization tactics were intended." Papa shouts over them all, and next to me Ujak Luka rolls his eyes again, sighs, twitches his face, shrugs his shoulders, picks at his fingernails.

"No safeguards in place to manage the fall out over minority rights. They know it's all going to explode and end Yugo and socialism, which is what they want. Small free-market states, ownership of our resources, access to cheap labour." Papa is standing up now, throwing his arms in the air. "Just another move in the neoliberalization of the world."

I know it's serious what Papa is saying but he looks silly.

"Just keep on talking, talk, talk, talking," Ujak Luka sings quietly into his glass. "If the richness of countries is measured in words, our Yugo would be on top. But it's not going to help, it's way too late for that."

"The Balkans, as wild and savage." Papa looks like he's about to climb on the table. "Our ancient hatreds, and all that crap. That's the Western media's story and the whole world will believe it one hundred percent after reading the newspaper for two minutes."

"Hypocrisy, injustice, imperial bullying, the Congress of Berlin," a lady pipes up.

"Friends, calm down, come back to earth. We must talk about how to protect ourselves now as individuals, that's all that's left us," a tall, skinny colleague of Papa's says. "We're surrounded on all sides by weapons shipped from Israel, South Africa, Europe, America."

"He's right," Ujak Luka whispers to me, pointing. "That one, he's nailed it. It's going to happen, the whole place is going to burn like a country-size incinerator. Where would you go, if you could?" He puts his arm around my shoulders and looks at me like he really wants to know.

"I wouldn't go anywhere. Sarajevo is our home," I say. "Only cowards leave when they're scared."

"I'm not scared." Ujak Luka gulps from his glass, then burps into his hand. "I'm disgusted. It's so ugly, do you understand, Jevrem? It's the ugliest way humans can behave, and it's all been orchestrated for cynical ends. My people against your people, acting in frightened herds like animals. Have you ever asked yourself why you haven't seen your other grandparents these past months? Why your other uncles don't drop by and surprise you with chocolate anymore? Why you don't go to Ilidža for visits?"

I think about it for a moment. He's right, we haven't been over for Sunday lunch in ages.

"We used to visit them all the time," I say. "Stric Ivan and Stric Obrad are fun guys, big guys, not like you. They're much younger than Papa. They throw me around and play soccer with us in the backyard. They're soccer-crazy, it's their religion. They come to watch me play in my school league."

Ujak Luka smiles, nods. "Yes, big guys, fun guys. But they're on the other side now, my smart little dude. Let's see how much fun that turns out to be. Doomsday has been set in motion by the powers that be. I think that sometimes you just have to pull yourself out of the muck, there's nothing else to do."

Mama clicks over on her heels, sits on the armrest. "Luka, stop scaring Jevrem," she says. "Please. Jevrem, it's time you and the twins go to bed. Who's that girl with you, Luka? I've never met her before. And why haven't you visited Mama this month?"

I actually want to go to bed for once. They're all giving me a headache.

"Izetbegović stole the presidency," someone calls out. "We're standing between Islamic fundamentalism and Western imperialism."

I give Ujak Luka a hug. "Good night," I say. He squeezes me against his chest for ages, until I can't breathe.

"I love you too, Jevrem. Keep your distance from the zombies." His eyes are even redder than before. "If we see each other again it means the fascists haven't won. I hope we see each other again."

I go to Papa and tap him on the arm. "Divide and conquer always works," he's trumpeting. "What is it, Jevrem?"

"Good night," I say.

Papa grabs my head and pulls it against his chest. "The end-game of the Cold War. As soon as they dismantle us, everything will be owned by multinationals, with the lowest wages in Europe as our reward." His words are thunder in my ear, rumbling to the beat of his heart.

"Hey," I mumble into his shirt.

"Good night, Jevrem." Papa gives me a loud kiss on the cheek. "Where are the twins?" He looks around for them, but absent-mindedly. He doesn't care about bedtimes tonight.

I know where they are. They're in the kitchen sneaking sweets. I saw them go in with their trays and innocent expressions. They'll eat sugar out of the bowl if that's all there is.

Rachmaninov is still rattling the windows. And Mama is rushing around like crazy, using that strange, tense, happy voice of hers, talking to everyone for half a second. But she looks so beautiful in that silk dress, her red lips, her sweeping hair and glittering eyes, smelling so sweet of lilies. When the record ends, she sits down and plays the piano. More Rachmaninov.

"This music is universal," she cries, her fingers going wild on the keys.

"It's so German," says someone. There is loud laughter.

"This isn't German, you ignoramus," says Mama, "it's French."

"No," says someone else, "it's Jewish."

"That's ridiculous," says Mama, "he wrote this as a Frenchman, not as a Jew."

"Maybe he wrote it as a European?"

"Or a man."

"Or a romantic."

"Or a revolutionary."

"Or an internationalist."

"Or a lover."

They go on and on, with big bursts of laughter. Adults think they're so clever. Nerds. Then there's a moment when no one talks, they just stare into the air listening to Mama's playing.

"Jevrem, put the twins to bed," Mama calls over her own notes with her singsongy mother-voice.

I go to the kitchen and see the twins are spooning Nutella out of a jar.

"We have to go to bed," I say. "And no, you can't take the jar with you."

They scurry ahead of me, giggling into each other's hair. In their bedroom, they just stand and look up at me with their big eyes. I can see that Aisha has snuck something from the kitchen under her shirt. I don't search her. They should have whatever it is. They were stuck with old Safeta all day long while we got to go to the march.

"Put your pyjamas on and go to sleep," I say.

"What about a story?" they ask with one breath.

But I shut the door and go to my room, I'm not in the mood for a story, for all their little questions. I fall onto my bed and put the pillow over my head.

When I wake it's dark outside. The party's still going, but it's quieter now. Most people have gone home. Now, someone is reading from a book or magazine. It sounds like poetry.

". . . gashes across the landscape . . . red earth exposed, like a wound . . . who sees the sly farmers of disunity? . . ."

They'll probably go all night with that kind of thing. I stare out of the window at the small square of night sky that glows with reflected light from the city.

MAMA has a hangover. "What a depressing day," she moans. Drizzle is spraying the window with tiny droplets. She plays scales in her nightgown every morning.

Papa is in his office. He's trying to get his latest article into a foreign magazine.

"But the spring flowers love this weather," I say, hopefully. That's what she usually says.

"What?" Mama barks.

"The spring flowers . . ." But Mama isn't listening.

"But they don't want to hear from actual Yugoslavs on the ground." Papa is talking loudly into the phone in his office, a pencil in his mouth. He does that, he chews pencils all the time. "No, that would be too much information. That would be too much like real journalism. They say it to my face. Too convoluted, your piece. Too complex, too technical, readers can't follow. They want a dramatic narrative, they want simple-minded theology. Good against evil."

Papa can get so mad at the stupidity in this world that his face turns purple and the veins in his neck bulge out. Maybe I'll be a journalist like he is when I'm old enough. Then I'll know what's going on too. I go into the kitchen and Dušan is there. His eyes are little slits, his face all swollen from sleep. He's got the cereal box and empties it slowly into a bowl right in front of my face.

"You pig," I say.

He sniggers. "Here, eat the box, it's good for you. Extra fibre."

"Dušan, give me some cereal."

Dušan holds the bowl above my head. "Sure, take what you can."

"*Dušan.*"

"Enough," shouts Mama from the living room. "No fighting in this house. There's enough of it outside."

Dušan slouches to the living room and eats on the couch. Mama stumbles to the bedroom to get dressed. Instead of cereal, I make toast with jam, two slices. Then I throw myself on the armchair next to the couch and listen to the radio on my Walkman while I eat. It's the usual music that's everywhere, evil '80s technopop, that's what Dušan calls it, making vomiting sounds. But it's better than the horrible folky polka music the old people love.

A whole Saturday stretches in front of me. I can't decide what to do. There's always soccer in the yard, which is usually the most fun. Pero, next door, wants to play a game of chess. But even though it's morning, I feel very tired. I can hardly sit up.

Mama returns, sits at the piano, breathes deeply.

"I'm practising all day. Dušan and Jevrem, go outside and play with your friends. Aisha and Berina, be very quiet in your room."

Play with my friends, Dušan mouths, rolling his eyes. Punks like him don't play with their friends. They lie around, drink their faces off, smoke, get high, listen to Nirvana or whatever.

I'd rather lie on the couch and stare out the window, dream about the summer, my favourite season. I love hot sunshine and swimming in rivers and lakes. But I search for my shoes without complaining. Mama and Papa aren't normal these days, they're like crazy people, talking too fast, too loud, fidgeting, pacing the hallway, mumbling under their breath, shutting themselves in the bedroom, the office, whispering fights they think we can't hear, snapping at us kids before we've even done anything wrong.

WE'RE all in the courtyard. Everyone's feeling lazy and trying to decide what to do. Cena, Nezira, Zakir, and Pero sit on the half-wall that juts out from our building. I say "Let's play a game," but nobody moves. I miss my practices, I miss the league. I kick the ball against the wall over and over again, trying to hit the same place with the same force every time. I'm a good striker. My thigh muscles have the same shape as the professionals', just smaller.

"You kick like a girl," says Pero.

I hold the ball in my hands, take a good look at Pero, then shoot really hard right at his chest. He catches the ball, teeters, then falls backwards off the wall. There's a thump, then a gasp, then swearing.

"You little bastard," he shouts. "That hurt."

Zakir laughs, then falls backwards too. "Ow," he whines, "ow, I'm hurt." Pero punches him, then they're rolling around wrestling, swearing, grunting.

Cena and Nezira cheer them on. Their voices are high, like a song, like foxes barking in a pine forest. They have the same straight wheat-coloured hair with a metallic glint. Dry, fly-away. I know what their hair smells like. Like outdoors, like charcoal-grey sky.

We hear thunder and look upwards, but the sky is clear blue.

MAMA and Papa come back from another demonstration. They're strangely quiet this time. I think they're really scared, I can see it in their faces, in the way they move around, bumping into things, standing for no reason in the kitchen or living room, like they've forgotten what a day is for. I wasn't allowed to go to this one even though I whined and begged. But Dušan went with a bunch of his friends—it's not fair, he gets all the action. He's still not back.

While they were gone, I leaned over the balcony railing, trying to see what was going on, but our building is too far away. I could hear pops and loud bangs, and other new sounds that must be weapons, guns and artillery. Every now and then, Baka came out and stood behind me muttering, I can't believe it, I can't believe it. I wanted to sneak out of the apartment with my bike and go all over the place like I always do, me and the others, flying down the steep narrow streets like little thunderbolts, even down the ones with stairs, bumping all the way, our heads coming loose on their stems and all our bones jangling together like sticks in a sack. We weave around all the walking people, their shopping bags and baby strollers, past the shops, their awnings and curved windows, the market stands with fruits and vegetables, slaloming the tables and chairs of the cafés, old men shouting at us, crazy boys, go home!

"The war's started," Papa says. He lights another cigarette. He has one smouldering away in every ashtray in the house. "Fifty-one years to the month since the Nazis invaded, forty-seven years to the month since we kicked them out, sacrificing a whole generation in the process. And for what?" He grasps his head and shakes it.

"Shh," says Mama. "Please, Lazar. The children." She sits on the chair in the hallway that no one ever uses. "Things can still be resolved."

"They shot real guns at us." Papa isn't listening to her. "As thousands of us were chanting, *Put down your arms*. The Chetniks are back. People were killed. *Killed*. On the bridge."

Mama is shivering; she's cold from being outside in the street for so long. I go to the bathroom and run her a bath, boiling hot the way she likes it.

"You can't take a country apart with all this fear and fascist rhetoric around. What are the Germans and Americans thinking, it's total insanity. Civil war was sure to follow—did they *want* that?" Papa holds a bottle of vodka. He pours big slugs into a glass, then hurls them into his mouth.

I'm not worried. I've heard a million stories about war. It makes life interesting, tests your courage and your cleverness, and you get to defeat the enemy. When Baka was a partisan, fighting the Nazi and Italian invaders during World War Two, they also fought the bad Serbs called Chetniks and the bad Croats called Ustasha. That's the thing about the partisans, they were a mix of everyone, and they fought and vanquished the internal and external enemy all at the same time. Now the leaders tell us we should forget what we did together and stick with our own people, Catholic, Orthodox, or Muslim. A while ago kids at school started asking each other that new strange question, What are you? Because we really didn't know. But lots of people don't have a religion and are a mix of everything, like us. What should they say? I say what Papa tells me to say: I'm a boy. Anyway, I'm not scared. Adults are always getting upset about the news.

But there's something funny about Mama's face when she comes out of the bath. She has this blank terror look, the sort of look people get in scary movies when it's nighttime and they've just seen a face staring in the window at them. And they live in an apartment building like ours, ten floors up.

‡ ‡ ‡

BOSNIA IS NOW INDEPENDENT, THAT'S WHAT EVERY-one is saying. The EC recognized us as a country yesterday, and the Americans today, so it must be true. But nothing's changed as far as I can see. There are forests covering the hills surrounding the city. Often they're filled with fog. It's strange how fog makes sounds quieter and sharper at the same time.

Branches crack, birds twitter, water drips, animals call out to each other. In April, the forest floor is covered with tiny flowers, ferns, mosses, fungi, shoots of all kinds. It smells delicious, like the first day of the world.

Last summer, we all went on vacation up in the mountain forest. It's like a fairy tale up there. Real life goes away and you walk forever along a path looking for things that are invisible. I saw ancient baba yagas, trolls, fairies, talking wolves. They all waved to me as I passed by. And partisans, lots of partisans, quietly marching in single file, guns over their shoulders, just like in Baka's stories. She told me about the child guides from the local villages who led the partisans along the mountain pathways. It was probably fun for them, all that adventure, running around the forest, doing what they wanted, looking after themselves, feeling so useful. Without them, the partisans couldn't fight, because those children knew about enemy positions and manoeuvres; they could lead whole units to perfect hiding and attacking places and then go back to their villages innocently, carrying school books and doing their chores and things like that. They knew those mountain forests like the back of their little child hands.

My baka always carried a rifle and had a grenade attached to her belt with a piece of hide—I've seen photos. And she knew how to set explosives too. She always starts her partisan stories with "Once upon a time, high up in the green, mountain forests smelling of black earth, pine needles, fallen leaves, there were bands of patriots who defended our country from the invading enemy and from the fascism within." And then she says, "Did I ever tell you, Jevrem, about our beloved leader, our Joza?" And I say yes, yes. And she says, "Well, about our beloved leader, little Joza loved animals, nature, and spent his childhood roaming mountain and forest. He knew every rock and tree. One day, he and his gang were raiding a neighbour's pear orchard when the neighbour caught them. Our Joza dropped from the branches right onto the man's head, knocked him out cold. He was a terrible nuisance, Joza was, but so what?"

I didn't know the man. He died before I was born.

Mama and Papa's idea of heaven is hiking every day, so that's what we did on our vacation. The lodges we stayed in were full of Austrian and Slovenian hikers, all up at 6 a.m. Aisha and Berina were slow and whined a lot, Mama nagged everyone, Dušan pulled branches from living trees and argued about how early we had to get up, and Papa lectured about all the revolutionary movements around the world that we needed to support, like the working classes and the Natives in South Africa, Latin America, North America, how everything is linked in this world, especially injustice. But we were all happy, I know that now. The sun was hot every day and we had snacks with us. And after the first ten minutes everyone stopped complaining and talking and then everything was quiet, except for the forest noises. We just walked and walked, staring at each other's backs or through the columns of tree trunks at the sun coming through the green leaves, until we came to a place where there was a good view. A view of a valley with white mountain peaks in the distance, where Croatia is and where Baka came from. Then Mama and Papa, Aisha and Berina, exclaimed about how beautiful it was. Oh, they said, over and over again, oh, it's so beautiful, oh, it's so breathtaking.

But in my mind, I was slinking around the mountains with Baka's partisan comrades. We were eluding German patrols by moving position, walking single file along the forest paths, pack mules behind us, everything we owned on our backs, liberated

German Lugers in our belts, rifles over our shoulders dropped by the Allies onto a mountain meadow in the dead of night. I was a child-courier escorting American OSS officers who'd just parachuted out of the sky with their precious wireless radio set, asking questions about partisan numbers and victories to tell their commanders back home.

I begged Mama and Papa to let me sleep a night outside alone, like Baka did for years. A sleeping bag, that's all I'd need. And maybe a knife. Dušan laughed at me, but I just walked down the steps of the lodge and into the forest. It's a lonely place, but also crowded with something, you get that feeling, but you don't know what it is. Maybe it's just all the animals tucked away where you can't see them. I followed the trail, passing through sun shafts that shine down into the green forest-world like beams from a UFO, and it felt good to be just me. You can hear your own breathing loud and clear when you walk alone, it whooshes like wind in your ears while you think of many things. Will you turn into a wolf-boy if you get lost forever? Will you be able to smell your way around? Will you know which animals have just passed, how healthy they are, the state of the vegetation in spring and summer? Will you have no more thoughts or words at all after a while, just senses, using your nose, eyes, ears to get around and survive? Will you lose your human mind and gain an animal mind?

Baka said hunger is the only thing in the world that doesn't have words, it grabs so deep inside you, deeper than your soul. When it got dark, I was hungry, but I had eaten the sandwich Mama had forced me to take along. I lay down and heard my eyes blinking in the dark. The dark was like moth wings caressing my face, my hands, neck, wrists, crawling into my ears, nostrils. The forest is alive in the night, things move in every direction.

And up in the sky is outer space with its gazillion galaxies. Space has its own sound, a huge silent sound that you can feel vibrating in your bones. I lay there wide awake in my sleeping bag and imagined partisans all around me, sleeping in hollows, or up in treehouses. Maybe my baka was up here too, only a few years older than me, with her new name, wearing ski pants before she got herself a uniform off a dead German soldier, a small one. Beautiful, tough, happy, a hardened killer. Maybe we were on our way to blow up a bridge, a railway line, or a road. Maybe we were going to ambush an enemy company. Maybe we were waiting for an airdrop. Sometimes we had to wait for days until the conditions were right, no clouds, moonlight. Sometimes we waited for weeks.

The birds were loud early in the morning and when I woke my hands smelled of dirt. The light was grey and flat at first, but the sun came up after a while and I trudged back along the trail. Papa says different generations of people, in different places on the earth, get to experience different kinds of lives. Baka got to spend three years in the forest worrying about life and death. You, he says, get to watch sixty-five channels on TV, ski in winter, swim in summer, study in Germany or France or England. But, I tell him, I will never go away, I will never leave this country with its mountain forests. Maybe this country will leave you, he says. He's always turning things around like that, to be clever.

That was last summer. This summer's going to be different. We probably won't go on a vacation, Papa says.

‡ ‡ ‡

THEY ARE SHELLING THE AIRPORT REGULARLY now. Also Baščaršija, which is full of mosques, minarets, souks. The television tower was hit, and some of the markets. I hear this from the old men in the lobby when I hang around to see if anyone will come out to play. They used to go to the park to play chess with big chess pieces, but now they can't, they're stuck in here with their stories and their pipes. They list all the next targets because they know about war; they were in the last one. The *Oslobodjenje* newspaper building, the Holiday Inn, the public transportation system, the presidency and parliament buildings, the flour mill, the bakery, the brewery, and the Olympic complex, of course. The post telegraph and telephone building, Alipasin Most, the Jewish cemetery, the Lion cemetery. The tobacco factory, the Dobrinja apartment complex, the central district, Stari Grad, New Sarajevo, Maršala Tita, the shopping district at Vase Miskina. To me it sounds like the whole city is one big bull's-eye. They say the train and bus stations are jam-packed with people, all desperate to leave the city. They've packed a toothbrush and left all their stuff behind, even their cats and dogs with a huge pile of kibble and the toilet seat up.

Fighting is noisy, that's something you don't think about in peacetime, the non-stop rumbling and thudding and exploding. I hear machine-gun fire rat-a-tatting and grenades going boom all day long. Sometimes I think I can hear high voices screaming with fright, girls and women as they run through the streets. Snipers fired on another bunch of peace demonstrators in front of the government and parliament buildings yesterday. More than ten people have been killed, and those are the ones we know about. They're still whispering about all these things, Mama and Papa, trying to protect our little ears. As if we kids don't know what's going on, as if our little ears can't figure out what's loud and clear every minute of the day.

Papa's trying to write an article about a siege. It's coming, he says, Sarajevo totally surrounded and cut off. The Serbs in the hills around the city don't have the numbers to match our defenders, so they won't be able to capture the city, only imprison it. But I see him looking out of the window all the time, pacing up and down the hallway, making himself more coffee, fiddling with an electric pencil sharpener that stopped working ages ago, not writing a single word. He's very stressed out, I can tell by how he rubs his fingers through his hair all the time and pats his chest and his trouser pockets with the palms of his hands, like he's looking for lost keys.

Mama is teaching at the conservatory. Music must flourish now, she says, even more than before. Papa calls the receptionist a hundred times all through the morning asking about conditions in the area. Schools have closed for now. Mama and Papa told us to stop cheering when we got the news, it's not a good sign. We still have to do our homework, they said, we still have to practise. Aisha and Berina play scales and violin duets for a while but Papa isn't paying attention so they stop pretty soon. When we're hungry we fish through the fridge; when we're bored we listen to music or half read whatever's lying around. We're not allowed to watch TV; it only broadcasts the war back at us like it's a TV show and that is freaky and deranged. The twins steal halva from the kitchen, Dušan pours rakija from the sideboard into his flask. It's a weird kind of holiday.

When evening comes, we all sit at the table without Mama, who is late, eating whatever we feel like, Papa smoking like a demon. Dušan says he heard that the tobacco factory is about to stop working, then sniggers at Papa's horrified expression.

Just joking, he says, but now Papa is even more stressed out than before; he's scratching his chest really hard with one hand like he's got a rash.

"There have been firefights all day long," he says. "Between Muslim paramilitaries, Croatian paramilitaries, the JNA, Serbian police, and irregulars. It's a real shitty mess. They stormed the police academy yesterday."

He jumps up and bangs dishes around. Aisha and Berina are pale and tiny, they look more exactly like each other when they're tired and scared, with their long black hair curving around their faces and all the way down their backs. They want Mama, I can tell by the way they slouch in their chairs, blue smudges under their big eyes like bruises.

"What does that mean?" Aisha and Berina whisper. Papa doesn't notice them. He doesn't remember to be a father when he's talking about politics.

"We're so fucked," Dušan says. His face is an oily shade of green, and he's got a huge pimple under his nose.

I look at Papa but he hasn't heard Dušan either. I guess we can all swear as much as we want from now on.

"What does that mean?" Aisha asks again. Berina pushes a spoon around the table. Sometimes when she's scared and tired, she lets Aisha do the talking.

Papa ignores us all. I've never seen him this way. He throws back more shots of vodka.

"Well, we're going to have to fight for the city. Unbelievable. I'd never in a million years have ever imagined I'd say those words."

We stare at him like he's a crazy person. He's telling a story about some other people in another city in another time, Baka's time.

"Goddammit, where's an ashtray?"

Papa's rummaging around in the cupboard above the stove. We all stare at the two ashtrays on the kitchen table, his favourite Zippo standing next to them like a loyal friend.

"Explain to them what's going on, Papa," Dušan says. "So they can understand."

"How can you not know what's going on here since every possible shit is going on?" Papa yells. "There are newspapers spread all around this apartment." And it's true, Papa is a newspaper junky. He's reading one all the time, at breakfast, at lunch, on the toilet. He even walks places, his office, to meet a friend, to the dentist, with one rolled up under his arm.

"They're six," I say.

"Some"—Papa glares at us—"*some* of these states, Croatia, Slovenia, us in Bosnia-Herzegovina, are declaring independence from Yugoslavia, prematurely in all cases, I might add, illegally in at least two, with the prodding of Germany and America, and are becoming their own countries; but not everyone in them wants to break away, they will be the minorities in their own country and they don't feel safe because no one feels safe in someone else's backyard. Because that's what nationalism does, it creates insiders and outsiders, enfranchised and disenfranchised. The Serbs, the largest group in Yugoslavia and spread all around in all the different states and provinces—"

Aisha slips down in her chair and hides her face in her hands.

"What?" sighs Papa. "Okay. How about this? A few terrible fascistic people are stirring up grievances and myths from the past, that's always how it starts, as a way to grab power, reconstructing ethnic identities, dividing us from our Yugoslav identity, our humanistic identity. There is a spreading of fear, there is a revival of national symbols and flag-waving, scapegoating, there is a manipulation of the media, of foreign actors. It's all incredibly stupid and dangerous and fascistic and it's not what any progressive Yugoslav wants—"

"They can't understand that, Papa," Dušan says, his voice all hard and serious. I've never seen him care this much about the twins. "This is how it is, you two." He stuffs some bread in his mouth—he likes to chew and talk at the same time. "In our country, there are these people, the Croats, the Serbs, and the Muslims, who've lived together forever and are all basically the same, except for some little things, like maybe cuisine and religion, you know, food and prayers, but their asshole leaders have been getting power by setting everyone against everyone else. Basically, it's like kids arguing about what's better, roast lamb or cabbage rolls. If people are fighting about that stupid stuff, the politicians don't have to sort out the real problems."

I stare at Dušan. I didn't think he ever thought about this stuff.

"The Serbs in Bosnia are scared that when we separate, the Muslims will take over and put them down, like in Ottoman times," he continues.

"What are we?" Aisha whispers.

Berina is sneaking huge spoonfuls of sugar, then looking at Papa to see if he notices.

"Aisha, that's exactly the main issue here. *It doesn't matter.* We're citizens." Papa rubs his face very hard so it gets all red.

"It matters now," says Dušan. It's weird that he's even here sitting with us. Usually he takes off right after we've eaten. "Papa's family is Serb and Mama's is Croat. That's how it is. Half of us can escape to Serbia, the other half to Croatia, just cut us right down the middle, blood and guts spurting everywhere—"

"Dušan!" Papa shouts, and Dušan looks down at his hands, his lips kind of quivering. He looks like he's going to cry.

Mama comes home finally, and everyone sighs with relief and looks a bit happier. She's windswept, rattled. Her eyes are squinting as though she's travelled for days through a sandstorm.

"A state of emergency has been announced," she says, standing perfectly still in the middle of the living room, with her purse still over her shoulder, a plastic bag in one hand.

I'M IN Dušan's room, sitting on his floor, half listening to the Kovacics argue in their bedroom right above. Dušan's lying on his bed looking through a magazine. There's a 10 p.m. curfew now, and he's pissed off, he wishes he could be out. He says that the Muslim Green Berets are out guarding our neighbourhoods, standing around on street corners, men and boys both, with their automatic rifles cocked. He wants to be out there too, holding a gun. And so do I, but I'm not sure who I'd be shooting at.

"At the Bosnians Serbs, you moron, the Chetniks, in the hills and in the suburbs," Dušan says. "They like Yugo the way it is, they say they're defending themselves, defending their life the way it used to be."

But I'm still kind of confused. Those Chetniks are Papa's whole family—Baba and Deda, Stric Ivan, Obrad, and Pavle—and their neighbours who we know quite well, so how can we shoot at them?

"Baba and Deda won't be fighting," Dušan says. "Of course not, they're old. It's their militias that are attacking us."

Who are their militias, I ask, and Dušan says, their militias are their men and boys. Our uncles? I ask. Yes, maybe our uncles, probably our uncles. But why would they shoot at us, I ask, they know us, they know that we're nice people, that we like them. But Dušan gets annoyed with all the questions. He pulls me up, shoves me out of his room, and bangs his door shut.

We're all meant to be asleep, but I crouch in the hallway and listen to Mama and Papa talking. Defended by Muslim paramilitary militias funded by Iran, Saudi Arabia. Juka's wolves. The nationalists on all sides armed for months now. Petty criminals selling weapons in front of Hotel Europa in complete fucking openness. Papa is saying that word a lot now. Fucking kalashnikovs, fucking bazookas, fucking sniper-rifles fucking weapons pouring in from the four corners of the fucking hypocritical world. In the countryside arms dealers went everywhere, sat down with village elders and said the next village over would definitely attack, so the men bought weapons. What could they do, stay unprepared? They sold livestock, furniture to raise the money, then surprise, surprise, every village was suddenly armed to the teeth, and a few people were getting very rich. You see, that's how they got us, Papa says. That's how propaganda works. When you fear the worst and prepare for the worst, the worst comes.

I can hear their glasses clinking against the table. They get louder the more they drink, that's how it is with adults. Warlords, Papa barks, local and international. Now the extremists will start moving populations around to strengthen their negotiating position, to match on the ground the new ethnically determined maps they want the EU and UN to recognize on paper. Geopolitical engineering. Cartographic final solutions. Our very own apartheid. Mama's and Papa's words keep pouring out of their mouths, they do this every evening when we're in bed, sentences they fling at each other even though they agree about most things. It's the stress, Baka says.

I feel tired and lie down on the hallway floor for a moment, trying to remember what Mama and Papa used to talk about before all this independence stuff, what we used to do on holidays and weekends. When I wake up, Mama and Papa are standing over me and staring down.

"Jevrem, what are you doing out here, lying on the floor?" Mama says. "My love, you have to sleep."

Papa picks me up and carries me to my bed. "Don't worry about all our yacking," he says. "Let us do the worrying; you just go on being our little Jevrem-full-of-dreams." Then he puts his big hand on my forehead and sings to me, his voice so deep and rumbling and his breath smelling bitter of cigarettes and alcohol. *"Sleepyhead, close your eyes, father's right here beside you. I'll protect you from harm, you will wake in my arms. Guardian angels are near, so sleep on, with no fear."*

MAMA's all twitchy today because a concert was cancelled and she's mad about that. All those things should keep going, concerts, plays, readings, lectures, she says, that's how the civilized people will defeat the barbarians. The university is still open, that's something, anyway, Papa says. And *Oslobodjenje* is publishing every day.

Mama pounds away at the piano like a demented witch for hours, her hair flying in all directions, like she's trying to make enough sound in our apartment to reach the roadblocks and barracks, the militias and their commanders, the foreign leaders far away in their fancy government offices. I go downstairs to Baka's apartment to get some chocolate and to comfort her because Mama said Ujak Luka's gone; he did as he said he would, was gone one night with the pretty young girl, not a word to anyone. "He's a good-for-nothing," Mama shouted when she found out. "He's selfish, just a degenerate playboy, worse than the thugs, smugglers, pimps, and criminals who have stayed behind to fight. He's leaving to make a comfortable life for himself getting up to no good, while we suffer and die defending our city." Mama was so angry with him that she broke down and cried for an hour after she'd finished calling him names.

"Oh, him," Baka says. "A disgrace. What if every able-bodied man picked up and left?"

I think about this for a minute. "There'd be no war," I say.

"But one has to defend against the enemy," Baka says.

"I mean, if *no* man wanted to fight, even the enemy men."

"But you have to be prepared to fight in case the enemy wants to fight."

"But, let's say *no* man on the whole planet ever stayed around to fight when the politicians told them to." To me it's just a matter of logic.

"That's not how the world works, Jevrem," Baka says. "There are always men who want to fight. They think they can conquer the world. They get frustrated and angry about their little lives and need to create mayhem, just to feel like men. This happens when things aren't going well in the economy— that's the most dangerous time for any society."

"You just asked," I say, slowly and patiently, because sometimes adults are idiots, they just don't use their brains, "what if *every* able-bodied man picked up and left? And I'm telling you, Bako, there'd be no war, that's what would happen. Isn't that a good thing? Isn't Ujak Luka doing a good thing?"

"Oh, Jevrem." Baka shrugs her shoulders like she's shaking off an irritating hand. "Sometimes you're just like your father."

"Right all the time?" I mumble under my breath so Baka can't hear.

I like Ujak Luka, I don't think he's a coward, I don't think that's why he left. I think he left for good reasons, but I'm not exactly sure what they are. And Baka's not that sad, I can hear it in her voice; she's secretly happy he's safe, somewhere out there in the normal world.

"He's always done his own thing," she says. "He's always been a rebel. Don't tell anyone, Jevrem, but he called me. He's in California, America. He's doing crazy things, as usual."

"What crazy things, Baka?" I ask. I picture him robbing banks in the hot, dusty afternoons like in westerns, a big glinting gun on each hip, and then in the evenings throwing parties for Mafia dons and movie stars in tuxedoes who stand around drinking champagne beside gleaming blue swimming pools full of girls in tiny yellow bikinis.

But she just shakes her head; she doesn't want to talk about him and his outlaw behaviour. So I ask her about the criminals and gangsters here, and Baka says, at least they're doing some good for once. Standing up for their community, their city. She thinks our new defenders are scum, but that's all we have right now to stand up to the scum on the other side. I feel happy about the criminals too. It must feel nice for them to be doing some good for once, getting some respect. Maybe it will turn them into better people. I tell Baka I overheard Mama saying they're just in it for the money, so they can carry on their shady deals, smuggle, take over the black market, drive fancy cars, get all the girls they want, and basically get rich and have a lovely time while the rest of us are tormented and trapped like rats. Baka says, as long as they save us from the fascist mobs I don't care why they're doing it. Sometimes you just have to be practical-minded, Jevrem. She wags a finger in my face. Sometimes you just have to do what needs to be done to survive, and not worry what everyone else thinks about it.

I play with my Transformers on Baka's kitchen table. She does the crossword puzzle. She lets me help sometimes and I'm quite good at it. *Grateful? A-S-H-E-S.* She brings out half a chocolate cake, which her friend made for their weekly get-together, and we each have two big pieces.

I GO home at suppertime, but no food has been prepared. Mama's friend Olga is over, the one with a man's haircut and bright red glasses who plays violin in the symphony. They're sitting at the table drinking coffee, talking about the usual thing.

"Barricades. Everywhere," Olga is saying. "The First Corps Sarajevo are very badly armed, compared to the Serbs and their Territorial Defense Forces. But we have more men."

"Men," Mama says. "Always men, men, men and their violence. Wearing stockings over their heads so their neighbours won't recognize them at the barricades. Women set up counter-barricades and serve meatballs. That's what the women do. They feed people. Lazar, did you hear that story? Women *feeding* people, men *shooting* at people."

Papa appears in the hallway, irritated. "What?"

"The men have guns to shoot each other with, the women have meatballs. I want to see a day when meatballs are more powerful than bullets. But where are the women tonight? Oh yes, they can no longer go out because it's too dangerous."

"Oh," Papa groans, "it has nothing to do with that. Women can be just as nationalistic and fascistic as men." He disappears back into his office.

"Jevrem," cries Olga, finally seeing me standing in the kitchen door. "There you are. I don't see you for a few months and what do you do? You grow big and handsome."

Here it comes. I remember her now, she's a hugger.

"Come here. Let me give you a hug."

I don't move. Mama laughs, then rescues me by pulling me onto her lap. "Jevrem is our soccer star. He runs like a cheetah." I love sitting on Mama's lap. She presses me against her chest like I'm her most precious possession in the world.

"Tomas is organizing the ten-part series," Olga says. "Bach, Scriabin, Rachmaninov, Prokofiev. How is your piano playing, Jevrem? Your mama tells me you have promise."

"Okay," I say. But I haven't practised for days. Now that I think of it, I kind of miss it.

"That's wonderful," Mama says. "What is the venue?"

"The Academy," Olga says. "Tomas goes on and on about Leningrad, their endless siege, how the city's musicians dropped dead from starvation in the middle of performances. This he thinks is terribly romantic, an example of the noble human spirit, how music overcomes all worldly evil. But I think it's sentimental horseshit, Sofija. No, actually, I think it's sick."

"Shh. Please, Olga," Mama says, and nods her head at me.

"Oh, he has to hear these things, Sofija. Real life is already harsher for him than anything we can say. We must keep playing, but we must never pretend that playing until we die means that we've won some kind of moral victory. We will win when the men in the hills are driven away, when our fascist leaders are driven out of office."

"Who can live with themselves, shooting at women and children and old men?"

"It's just a tactic of war." Olga is fidgety. She twists a corner of her scarf round and round her forefinger. "They're told it's essential to their survival, for their children's survival, that it's necessary. Twentieth-century war is waged against civilians, all of it, siege or no siege. There is no ethical and unethical war anymore, it's all a massacre."

Mama shivers and shakes her head. She doesn't want to talk about this anymore. "I hear Ponthus is coming to give a concert," she says, and walks her fingers up and down my arm.

"Oh yes, just watch. All kinds of international artists and personalities will suddenly pour into our city to cheer us up by feeding our poor, savage souls."

"You're so cynical, Olga. People need to be uplifted."

"People need this war to end. The negotiators are just protecting their own interests." Olga knocks back the rest of her coffee.

"Well, what can we do about that?"

Olga shrugs her shoulders, lights another cigarette. "The process has been hijacked by all the wrong people telling the wrong stories."

They sit in silence, staring off at nothing. They never have an answer past this point: why the wrong people are in power, who let them get there, how to get rid of them. I fiddle with the bracelet on Mama's wrist, I steal a sip of coffee.

"Well, on a more cheerful note," Mama says suddenly, "shall we get Papa to go out and find us some pizza?"

"Yes, yes," I say.

"It's still safe in your mahala," Olga says. "But I wouldn't stay out too long."

I want to go with Papa, but Mama says no. I slouch to my room and stand in the middle of it, not knowing what to do next. Boredom feels like a terrible flu. My bones hurt. I knock on Dušan's door but he ignores me. He just wants to be out with his friends. Aisha and Berina are in their room. I can hear them through the door talking in high chipmunk voices. They're lucky, they have each other to play with all the time.

"Do you want to play with us?" Berina has suddenly opened the door. She has this way of looking up at me, her head tipped to one side, that is hard to say no to. "No," I say anyway, just so they know they can't push me around, but after a few minutes I go in and lie on their floor.

They run in circles around me, giggling, and making up little poems that don't make sense. Then I read *Snow-White and Rose-Red* to them. I like sitting on the bed with one of them on each side of me, the way they lean against me and hold hands across my stomach, the way they breathe on my neck and stroke the pages with their little fingers. When they were tiny babies they sucked each other's thumbs—that was funny. There's a photo of it in one of our photo albums, which I sometimes look at to remember the past.

I WAKE up in the dark and hear voices murmuring in the living room. I can't stand that sound these days. Mama will start crying, Papa will shout, Mama will shout. I hear the clink of bottle against table, ice against glass. We aren't allowed to drink; what can we do to get through this shit-time? I pull out the pack of cigarettes from under my mattress. I bartered for it with one of my comic books.

Dušan is at the door, he always knows when I've got something he wants, it's like a sixth sense.

"Can I have one, Jevrem? Where did you get them?"

"I got them from Konstantin. For my Wolverine comic."

I light a cigarette and Dušan and I sit next to each other on my bed, smoking. It reminds me of the time before Dušan became a teenager, when we played together quite a lot.

"They never stop talking," I say.

"They don't know what else to do. We're all so fucked. I'm going to score some weed tomorrow, lots of it, and get baked every single day. Going to sell some of it to make back the cash. Too much bullshit around to stay straight all day long. U.S. soldiers were high during the whole Vietnam War."

"Didn't they lose?" I ask.

Dušan picks up one of my comics and I wander into the living room feeling dizzy. Mama and Papa are slumped on the sofa, their clothes rumpled. The room is blue with smoke.

"What are you doing up, Jevrem? Go to sleep."

I sit down in the armchair and pretend to read *National Geographic*. I flip through the pages. Black people with spears, black people with painted faces, black people with no clothes on, poor black people in slums. Giant, weird-looking sea creatures at the bottom of the ocean. I put down the *National Geographic* and stand up. I hover over Mama and Papa, staring right at them, but it's like I'm not here. They're totally blind they're so tired; they've had so much to drink. But they can't get themselves to bed. I wander back to my room and there is Dušan fast asleep on my bed.

"Dušan, come on." I grab his arm and shake. "Go to your own room." I bend over and put my ear to his nose. I can hear his breath, faint and even, I can see the pulse jump in his soft white neck. He's so skinny and tall. Without a shirt on he looks horrible, like a starving guy who's about to die even though he eats all the time. That's why he has weights under his bed.

Every evening he stands in front of the mirror and tries to pump up his muscles so they hide his bones.

He doesn't hear me or feel me. I shake him again but he doesn't move. Maybe he's high already. Or maybe I somehow got killed and I'm a ghost, the first child killed in the war. I float into Dušan's room feeling dizzy and see-through and curl up on his musty, twisted sheets, wondering what it feels like, the moment you don't belong to your body anymore, the moment you know that all the ordinary days are over, nothing more than dim, hazy dreams.

‡ ‡ ‡

FROM THE BALCONY I WATCH THE TREES OPPOSITE our building. They just stand there. The sound of explosions doesn't seem to bother them. Some of them might be hit too, but they're not worried. In our forests, the foresters often cut down trees. They use them for firewood, but the reason for felling them is to keep the whole forest healthy. Now the trees are a light hazy shade of green. Soon their leaves will grow to full size. In the breeze I catch the smell of pine trees and apple and lilac blossoms, or maybe I imagine it. I love this time of the year because the days get warm, spring flowers bloom, summer is just a month away. But I also hate it sometimes. All the rain, the heavy mists and fogs, the low, angry sky. Baka says that during her war, weather was very important. It could be a fierce enemy or a powerful collaborator. Spring was unpredictable in the mountains, friendly one moment, deadly the next.

I look up at the hills. Death is coming from up there, and everyone has stopped looking at them like they're a nice piece of scenery. The pine forests still stand, like before, but what is lurking in them? And the sweet chestnut trees. They're still there, and the rivers still flow, fed by cold springs and mountain snow. We went fishing once for brown trout and soft-lipped trout. Papa wanted to try it for an article he was writing. He wanted to see how it felt, hurting a little creature for fun.

I sit down at the piano and begin my scales. It feels good to let the notes come out, to watch my fingers moving fast. I race through scales and exercises, fudging the bits that are hard, since Mama isn't here to yell at me. I really want to learn the piece that I'm practising now, the Chopin Fantaisie-Impromptu, because it runs out of your hands all by itself, like water rushing down a hill toward a lake.

My friends are at the door. They crowd in, making faces.

"I'm going out," I yell over my shoulder.

Mama's hand pinches the back of my neck. She moves fast as an athlete sometimes. "You're not going out," she says. "It's too dangerous."

Everyone looks innocent, eyes big. "But Mrs. Andric, we're all going out. Our parents say it's okay."

"My papa heard on the radio that it will be okay today. Our neighbourhood." Nezira looks sad when she lies.

"Please, Mama." Mama's hand is touching me, in public, holding me in place. They will all laugh later. They'll copy me. Please, Mama, please, Mama.

Mama hesitates. I duck away and am out the door.

"Be careful," she shouts after me. She'd like to keep me home forever, where she still thinks it's safe.

We move like one lumpy breathless animal down the dark hallway. In the yard, we kick a ball around. Cena and Nezira share a cigarette they stole from Cena's mother. They hold it awkwardly, but they're cool anyway. They look identical, but they're not even sisters. They even wear the same clothes. Adidas, Puma, Levi's. Both their mothers like to shop, in Zagreb and Vienna. The boys always crowd around them, listening to what they have to say but pretending not to.

"Let's get a game going," says Mahmud.

"Yes, yes," I say.

But no one else can be bothered. We sit in a group beside the swings in the playground insulting each other, laughing, throwing pebbles at the see-saw. Cena and Nezira turn the skipping rope, chanting a high singsongy weird poem they know off by heart, while Raza skips. She's good at it, she could keep going for a thousand years, her feet hardly touching the ground. Mahmud takes a plastic pistol out of his pocket. He aims it first at Cena, then at Nezira, then at Pero. Right at his temple. *Pow. Pow. Pow, pow*, he shouts. Pero turns and punches Mahmud in the arm.

"You're a fucking idiot, Mahmud," he hisses and walks off. He's actually angry. We stare at his back until he disappears around the corner of the building.

‡ ‡ ‡

THE PHONE RINGS AND MAMA ANSWERS. "OH no," she says. "Oh no. Oh no. Oh no."

I go into my room and close the door, then sit on the floor against my bed. There is nothing to do. I feel like I have asthma or something. I can't breathe.

Emira was killed, Papa tells me when I come out again. Emira Subic. I remember her, a lady with fuzzy hair who always smelled of cigarettes and laundry detergent. She came to dinner sometimes, and they talked about writing articles, which magazines paid well, which had nationalist editors, who was giving in to the fascists, that kind of thing. She's dead? Who would want to kill her? Dušan wants to know exactly how she died. Was it a shell? A sniper? What part of town was she in? Where was she hit? Why didn't she know to stay off the street?

"Stop it," Mama says to him. She doesn't want to talk about the details. "I'll light a candle for her tonight." As if that's going to make things better.

The radio says that a ceasefire agreement has been reached. The EC made it happen. And it's true, today is quiet. What a relief, Papa says. He has bursts of happiness all day long even though his friend just died. "Wow, that was scary, eh, kids?" he says. He makes us all pancakes in the middle of the afternoon, for a snack. Even Mama has one. We open the windows and let the fresh air in.

I WAKE up from a strange dream about the men in the lobby. They are selling chicken fat in Coca-Cola cans, and they try to force me to buy a dozen, but I don't have any money. Your family will die without it, they shout at me, it will all be your fault. Baka told me how valuable animal fat was during the war. It was the best part of the meat. You'd eat it by the spoonful if you could get it, that white, congealed fat like creamy honey or paraffin. You'd get as much of it into you as possible. I wonder what it would be like—if I could keep it down or would puke all over the place.

I hear gunfire. I can see by the sunlight that it's early morning. I get out of bed and walk into the living room. Papa and

Dušan are standing at the window, looking out. It started again at six fifteen this morning, Papa tells me. He looks suddenly unfamiliar, old and bent and dishevelled. The JNA, our national army, has taken up new positions in the suburbs, the newspaper says. They say they're creating a buffer between the Serbs and the Bosnian forces, but Papa scoffs at that, bangs the window with his knuckles, lights another cigarette. "The JNA are Serb controlled," he shouts. But the JNA command says that political leaders have lost control of well-armed paramilitary forces, therefore the army has to step in. And there are a lot of paramilitary forces, a crazy number, something like 150,000. I read this in yesterday's newspaper. The command says that these forces are terrorizing people, looting and destroying property, and spreading fear, tension, panic among citizens.

"Why can't we trust the JNA, it's our army?" I ask Papa, but he doesn't answer. He's looking at the city like he's never seen it before.

It's now almost impossible to get to Baba and Deda and the uncles in Ilidža across the river. I hear Mama and Papa talking about it. Not that we've been trying. I miss them all. The uncles didn't move into the city like Papa did when he finished high school; they go to college in different towns and still come home to Baba and Deda on the weekends. They go to soccer games together, and Baba makes delicious krofne, palatschinke, and chocolate tortes, and Deda lets me take drags on his pipe and shows me what is coming up in his vegetable garden. Papa must be homesick for his Mama and Papa and his younger brothers, but he doesn't mention it. He and Mama whisper about the Ilidža house, what to do about it and Baba and Deda. He calls them sometimes, not as much as before, and afterwards he always looks sad or angry, he always shuts his door. Dušan says it's because Baba and Deda want us to go live with them, because it's a Serb neighbourhood, because it's on the outskirts of the city. But Mama and Papa say no, they won't go, they're Sarajevans, they won't join the cowardly exodus.

The day goes by so slowly I want to scream. I feel headachy and a bit ill from doing nothing but sitting inside and playing cards with myself. Aisha and Berina have been fighting, shouting at each other about who gets to draw in the colouring book, who gets to read the comics, who gets to play with the Barbies they share. They have small red eyes today like they've been crying hard for hours, but it's just because they're tired. Mama says they crawl into bed with her and Papa every night and I secretly wish I could too; it's hard to sleep with the new sounds outside, rumbling and booming and sirens and cars screeching around corners. But I'm too old now, Dušan would laugh.

Mama's and Papa's friends and colleagues are coming and going from our apartment all the time. They slouch on our couch for a few hours, or sit on the edge of chairs. They give each other the latest news, even though everyone knows it already, have a drink or six, get drunk, laugh hysterically, cry into their handkerchiefs, leave when the next shift arrives. Like waves, in and out, on a stormy coast, Baka says, timed around the curfew and the amount of shelling. Sometimes people stay over, but they never sleep. They're exhausted but they just sit there and gab non-stop, or stare out of the window at the city.

"Can't we please tell people not to come so much? Can't we please have some normal time together as a family?" Mama asks. "I still have to practise, I still have to focus."

"Normal?" Papa says. "*Normal?* People have to get together as much as possible now. Alone in our apartments, we lose courage. And then people just leave. People are leaving the city by the thousands, sometimes in secret, without telling their friends. People are scared to stay, ashamed to go. This city's glue is the best of human relationships, not family, not tribe or clan, friendship. *Friendship*."

It's true. Some apartments in the building are empty now, and neighbours have been asked to watch them. Pero and Mahmud and I want to break into one and just hang out there, to see what it feels like poking around in other people's things. We wouldn't take anything, at least not anything we didn't really need.

‡ ‡ ‡

THE CITY WAS A HUGE CARNIVAL LAID OUT between hills, that's how I thought of it in my mind when I was a little boy. All kinds of sounds, songs, prayers rose from it like echoes close and distant. And the stones and domes and minarets and spires were many shapes, fitting together like a completed puzzle in colours of white, sand, orange, copper green. Trees were brown and black in winter and dark green puffs in summer. And the narrow, twisty streets of the old town flowed with strangers as familiar as friends. They gabbed, they joked, and birds flew in fluttering flocks around the Turkish Square. At night, a wash of lights like jewels filled the valley, and the river reflected moonlight when it was in the mood. Even the crappy parts were beautiful, because of the grandeur of our geography, Papa said, with hills and mountains on three sides, always visible no matter where you look, the frame to the picture. When I was little, delicious smells pulled you into bakeries and fishmongers and restaurants and the kitchens of friends' mothers. Hookah, ćevapčići, pizza, burek. The bazaars, markets, souks had everything in them from all the countries of the world. And the city had many sneaky corners to be discovered when you became a teenager, like bars and discos where the punk bands played that Dušan told me about, the underground city painted black. And in Ilidža, there were nature walks by the wide river, the Roman Bridge, the waterfalls, Big Alley with the fat old trees on either side like giant living columns, the fields that Deda walked over in the autumn reciting poems about peasants. And there are other places that I will know about when I am a man. I'm vague about them, but they're there, I know they are. I've already been to three concerts that Mama played, one in the National Opera House with the whole symphony. I had to wear a tie to that one.

Now it's a small and dangerous cage, our city, completely surrounded by rocket launchers and maniacs, with all of us trapped in our houses and apartments, remembering how it was before. And it's only been two weeks. We're so bored, Dušan, the twins, and I, and all our friends, everyone wanting to be outside so badly, like we've never wanted to be outside before. Dušan puts on earphones and dances wildly in front of his bedroom mirror. He has his bale of weed under the bed. His room smells of jungle, skunk, field grasses in summer. I chase Aisha and Berina around the apartment pretending to be a wolf. I throw them to the floor, I pretend to eat them. They love the thrill of fear, they want me to play this game all day long for the rest of time.

"In the forest, packs of wolves sniff the earth to pick up the trail of your scent." I say. "They follow it all the way into the city, and at night they wait panting in the stairwell, drooling with the need to eat you up. One of these days they will find their way in here, right into our apartment, right into your bed."

In my room I pull my stuff off the shelves, I kick it around, I trample it underfoot. Stupid, shitty stuff, locked up with me in this jail. I lie on my carpet and stare at the ceiling. I know all the cracks in it, and the little spiderweb that grows in the corner. The spider is a friend of mine. She's tiny and clever, catching little bugs that I never see anywhere else in the room. The afternoon changes to evening but I don't notice. When evening comes, I build a marble run. It starts way up at the top of my window, the tip of Mount Triglav in the Slovenian Alps. It runs all the way down to the Adriatic, that one place where Bosnia meets the sea.

MAMA and Papa are crying in each other's arms. They press close, grasp each other's hair, neck, back, make moaning noises. I can't watch, it's horrible. Someone else they know died, someone they liked a lot, a musician named Marko who played flute in the symphony. Mama played with him just a few nights ago, and she was so happy when she and Papa came home, she woke us all up. The hall was packed with people, she told us, they're not intimidated, they're partaking in culture, they're continuing to live their civilized lives.

They don't notice me standing in the hallway, they won't notice if I leave. So I slip out of the apartment and pound down the stairs, the palm of my hand burning on the railing. The basement has been prepared for direct hits. The ping-pong table is gone. The old couches have been pushed to the edges. There are signs on the wall saying, Don't cook in this room, and Don't leave your stuff down here, bring it back up with you at the end of the raid. The teenagers are hanging out, smoking pot, kissing in the corner. Two of them look like they're both girls, one has very short hair, but I can't tell for sure. I stare. They tell me to get lost.

In the lobby, the old men are huddled in a tight little circle. Cena and Nezira are playing cards on the bench. I sit down next to them and see that Cena has a bandage on her hand.

"What's that?" I ask, as though I don't care that much, but I do. Her hand is so small and pretty.

"Oh, just a cut," Cena says.

"One of their windows shattered yesterday," Nezira says, slapping down a card. "And a piece of glass flew through the air."

"Yes, it flew through the air all the way across the living room and stabbed my hand, then lots of blood ran down my fingers. It's exactly the temperature of skin, you know, so you can't feel it, but there's still a ticklish trickling feeling. It felt like my skin was melting off my bones." She says this like she thinks it's kind of cool, like she's describing a chemistry experiment.

"Oh," I say. "Does it hurt?"

"Not anymore. Mama gave me some painkillers. The stuff she got for her back last year."

"Now we feel great," says Nezira.

"You took some too?" I ask.

"Of course," says Nezira. "I can give you one if you want."

"Where are Mahmud and Pero?" I ask.

"We don't know," says Cena.

"Probably in the courtyard playing soccer. That's all Mahmud wants to do." Nezira is fumbling around in her pocket.

I hope she finds a painkiller. Maybe it'll make me feel great too.

"Mahmud's such a little boy," Cena whispers. "He doesn't even like to kiss."

I do, I want to say, but I'm afraid to.

"Here." Nezira puts a little white pill in the palm of my hand and winks. "The first one is free," she says, then she and Cena laugh hysterically.

I feel sleepy and dreamy all afternoon and time doesn't go by so slowly, or I don't mind that it goes by slowly, I can't tell which one. After supper, Dušan lets me have puffs from his joint. He can't go out with his friends so I'm all he's got. Just don't talk to me, he says, so I lie next to him on his bed while he listens to his music in his headphones. I think about all kinds of crazy things, my mind roaming around the city, the countryside, my memories, my daydreams and fantasies, like it's a camera that I can send wherever I want it to go just by flicking my thumb on a remote. The room is a helicopter, the moon is a lighthouse, clouds are sponges dabbing the earth's surface, trees are partisans coming down from the mountains to fight. Gunfire is popcorn popping over a crackling fire. Dušan is a large dog that scratches its matted fur with giant human hands.

I wake up blinking through a fog. Someone is at the door. Papa comes in, his hair all ruffled and standing up, which is how he looks after hours of writing. He sniffs the air and tells me to go to my room. I get up, sway, then wobble slowly to the door. Papa watches me with a frown, then closes the door behind me. Dušan is going to get a talking-to. I listen in the hallway, but Papa doesn't shout and Dušan doesn't shout. This is a good sign for the weed. Papa comes out, stares at me, shakes his head, leads me to my room, and lies down next to me on the bed. He doesn't yell, he doesn't say anything. We lie side by side for a while and stare at the ceiling.

Then Papa reads from *Oliver Twist*, which is what I've been doing all day, his arm around my shoulder, pulling me tight. As

I listen, I watch his chest moving in and out, his mouth forming the words. I stare at the hairs curling out of his ear. Mama is at the door, watching us with shiny eyes. After a while, she comes in and sits down, one hand on Papa's foot, one hand on mine. She listens all the way to the end of the chapter with eyes that are far away, then she leaves and comes back with a candle. She lights it, switches off the lamp, and pulls the blankets up to my neck. She kisses my cheek, she kisses my forehead. Mama and Papa sit next to each other on the bed like they did when I was little and tell me a story from the olden days, like they used to when things were normal—the story of when they met way back when.

In those days they dressed like hippies and were students at the university, and there's a funny photograph of Mama with long straight hair next to a sign saying Proletarians of all countries, who is washing your socks?, which always made us laugh. They went on a university trip to Prague and fell in love. In those days, they tell me, our dreams were as big and sparkling as galaxies and one of those dreams was you. And here you are, you came true, you are as big and sparkling as a galaxy. They sing one of their favourite songs, which is my favourite too, and while they sing, they smile at each other and sway back and forth in that silly way they sometimes do. The song is about the moon, the seventh house, Jupiter and Mars. It's about harmony, understanding, sympathy, and trust. Peace guiding the planets, love steering the stars.

IN THE morning, Mama is all tense again, I can tell by how high and fast she's talking. When I come out of my room, she makes me a bowl of cereal and tells me to go back in. But I leave my door open a crack. I can hear everything they say.

"We should go," Mama says. "Olga is leaving. She's taking her two daughters."

"Go where?" Papa says. He's tense too because he's writing an article on the Yugoslav-wide peace movement, why it was ignored by the international press, the EC, Germany, and all the other stupid foreigners who are somehow involved in sorting us out.

"We should just go."

"Go where?"

"Just GO."

"Go where?"

They're prodding each other with their worries, Baka says. She tells me to just ignore it, they'll be okay eventually, when they get used to how things are, that's the way of war.

"The children, anyway, should go," says Mama.

"*Go where?*"

"What does it matter where? Away."

"It matters where. They are our children. We're going to send them to complete strangers in Germany or England?" Papa says.

"They are shooting at us."

"That's why we are needed here." Papa's voice gets louder. "It's a matter of principle. They want us to run away."

"Shh, please, the children," Mama says, but she's not any quieter. Her whispers can pierce your eardrum. "We're needed here as, what, as targets?"

"No, to show them they can't terrorize us into going."

"But what are you going to do about it, just sit waiting to be hit?"

"No, fight back."

"You Serb men, all you think of is fighting," says Mama.

I creep out of my bedroom and crouch in the hallway. I want to get closer to them, to get them to stop arguing, to tell them that I don't want to go anywhere. I won't.

"I don't believe my ears," Papa shouts, "why are you saying such ridiculous things? We must all stand strong and stick together, especially now. To fight Serb extremism and Croat extremism and every other kind of nationalist extremism as well, that is the goal. Why would we leave now? It makes no sense."

"I love you," Mama says in a low voice. "I won't survive without you."

I suddenly feel like I'm going to choke, like an invisible hand has grabbed my throat and is squeezing hard. I lie on my back on the hallway floor and pant. I can hear Papa's lighter. He's lighting his thirtieth cigarette of the day, since he's been up a couple of hours. I know, I've counted how many cigarettes you can smoke in an hour if you're my dad and you don't take a break.

"You don't have to. We are here together, we *are* the city. I am not going to run off without a word, like Bozic and Jokic and Zec. I'm a journalist."

Aisha and Berina come out of their room. They stand at their door and stare at me with their big round eyes.

"A dead man is no good to a woman." Mama sounds like she's going to cry.

"Women, always so melodramatic." Papa is suddenly standing in the hallway, looking at the three of us. "Come in here," he says to us. "I thought I heard breathing and snuffling."

I get up off the floor and the three of us trail in after him. Then Papa hugs Mama tight, kisses her on the forehead, cheeks, mouth, chin.

"You keep playing and I'll keep writing, it will count for something, it has to, goddammit." He breathes her in like she's a forest breeze in springtime. "You three," he says to us. "Want to play a game of quartet? Want to wipe the floor with your old Papa like you always do, with your sharp, cunning little minds?" He doesn't seem to be annoyed that we've been lurking in the hallway, watching them, listening to them, that we follow them around the apartment like shadows.

‡ ‡ ‡

THE SHELLING IS PART OF THE CITY NOW, ONLY A couple of weeks after it all began, and there's a pattern to it. We know when the men in the hills go home for dinner, when they get washed up to go to their workplace or tend their farm, when they're fresh from a full night's sleep in their beds and in the mood to pound the living shit out of us. Our neighbourhood has not yet been hit, but it shudders and quakes with the hundreds of hits farther away. In Baka's war, the Germans swept down from the north and up from the south, occupying all our major cities in less than two weeks. Like now, everything changed in such a short time.

Baka is at our place making us lunch. Mama is out rehearsing with her ensemble and Papa is at the Holiday Inn trying to sell an article to a Western newspaper. Papa is obsessed with this. He paces the apartment day and night thinking about it, he yells hysterically into his phone about it. Those Western journalists are telling lies, he shouts, they're telling sentimental sob stories, they're repeating the propaganda of our fascist leaders. If the West doesn't understand the complexity of what's going on here, how can they help?

Dušan is suddenly talking history. "The Serbs fought the

Nazis during the war," he tells me, "and the Croats and some Muslim groups collaborated with the Nazis. So, you see. People forget that."

"Some Serbs collaborated as well," I say. "The Chetniks. And anyway, the partisans were made up of everybody, all religions from all different parts of the country."

"The partisans murdered collaborators after the war, they're not all heroes. And Tito hoarded money, houses, jewellery, Playboy bunnies, famous people, even though he was a communist. He's not a hero either, whatever Baka keeps telling you."

Dušan hasn't bothered to get dressed today. He's wearing the track pants he sleeps in and a torn undershirt. He's now hanging out the window to smoke his weed—maybe that's the rule Papa made, or maybe Papa wanted some too to help calm his nerves, and it's their big secret from Mama. Dušan's eyes are stoner slits. He's so bored he's started to carve his initials into his thigh.

I wander into the kitchen. Baka says to me, "Jevrem, did I ever tell you about our beloved—?" and I nod and say, yes, many, many times. "Well, our beloved Joza fell in love with a Russian girl when he was hiding from the Whites in Omsk, but so what? She was beautiful, and young, and a Bolshevik. Polka was her name. Did he care where she was from? No, he did not, because he loved her in particular, and all of humanity in general, that's how enlightened the communists were."

I think about how to escape into the mountains, like Baka did when she was a girl. She just picked up one day and ran away from her parents, her brothers and sisters, her husband-to-be, her village, to fight with the partisans. That's how she invented her new life—she somehow knew that there was a better way to live, that her whole future would be changed by that one walk into the mountains, I don't know how. There has to be a way for us too. If we kids could just slip up into the forest, we could get organized and take out the Chetnik firepower in the hills around the city. Kids are small, agile, fast. They can learn how to work any machine, like guns, rockets, mortars, grenades. And they don't eat as much as adults, another advantage. The best part is kids are the future, they have no past or prejudices except the ones you teach them. That's what Papa says. I can think of fifteen kids right now who I could recruit in this building just by knocking on doors. They're not just from Sarajevo, their parents come from everywhere in Yugo, and from Germany, Turkey, Iran. We'd end the war in only a few days because the enemy wouldn't be looking for us, hundreds of platoons of little kids storming their positions with guns in our hands. If we're old enough to get shot at, why aren't we old enough to fight?

After lunch, I think about practising the piano. Mama mentions it every now and then, and I try, but the noise of guns and shells outside makes me lose the feel of the keys. Instead, I take the elevator to the top floor, then walk along each hallway all the way down to the ground floor, keeping a mental list of where all the kids live and what they'd each be good at in a battle.

I GO to Baka's apartment and knock on the door. I like to visit her. She has opinions, stories, and a weird collection of food. For years she's been hoarding tins all over her apartment.

Baka stands at her window looking at black plumes of smoke rising slow motion in the distance. She shakes her head.

"They're destroying all our good work," she says. "For centuries, engineers have made a work of art of this city. It takes intelligent people years to build it all up, and idiots and vulgar imbeciles only weeks to tear it all down."

I like to think of Baka barking orders at construction workers, a hard hat on her head. Baka bustles around her kitchen, doing dishes. She lives here alone, but she has many plants growing on her balcony and friends used to come over all the time. In the summer months she lies on the balcony in her bright yellow bathing suit. She's a sun-worshipper, and a forest-worshipper, and a mountain-worshipper, those are the things she trusted when she was in the war. But what she worships most of all is Yugoslavia, our country. After the war, you could join a brigade and rebuild everything that was destroyed. You could build railroads and highways, subdivisions, schools, factories, city buildings. You could build them with your bare hands with thousands of other young people and spend months living together, playing sports, sitting around campfires, putting on plays, singing together in the evenings. That's what Baka told me. Mama says the communists knew how to get work out of people back then without paying them, how to make it feel like a fun thing to do.

Baka says, "If we could just get us old partisans together, we would sort this mess out in no time. We'd clear out the dead leaves, branches, animal carcasses from the cave bunkers. We'd find our old ordnance depots. We'd choose a leader to organize us. You know, when I was very young, I walked into the mountains to join the partisans. In doing so, I made a new future for myself, it's that simple, a whole new life. I remember the exact moment when I knew everything would be different. How I felt a tingling all through my body, like I was being anointed by life itself. I was squatting by the roadside, my arms resting on my knees. I could see far out into the valley, a haze of green and rust punctuated by oily black smoke. I had all I needed with me: food for several days, a change of underclothing, a knife I took from the kitchen just before slipping away."

Her hand trembles as she lifts it to her face to brush back her hair. When she walks these days, she's unsteady sometimes, like the floor is moving under her feet. But I can still picture her scrabbling around in the underbrush preparing a bunker or charging down a hill with gun in one hand to ambush an enemy convoy. Baka is bored by my grammar homework that Papa says I have to do, school or no school. "You know how to speak, so what's the problem?" she says. So we play cards. She likes belot and poker, I like gin rummy. Today it's her turn. We play texas hold'em, and place our bets with the small, smooth white pebbles she collected from the beaches of Istria.

"Your djedica took me there when we were young, a few years after the war. We spent days exploring secluded coves and drinking crates of wine. The light is breathtaking there, bright, warm, clear. Beautiful like you can't imagine. He said he'd show me paradise, and he didn't break his promise."

"I know," I say. "Remember, we were there last year." Hot sun, white houses, bright blue water, fishing boats, ice cream, pizza.

Baka bets hard, never folds. She loses more than she wins, but that doesn't matter to her. It's toughness that matters. The westerns we watch on TV, she plays like that, eyes squinting, blank face. Scary, that look, her face rigid like she's paralyzed, but any minute she'll jump up and pull a huge old gun on me.

"Your djedica spoke Italian and tried to teach me, but I was a bad student. His family moved from Italy to Istria after

World War One, when Italy took it over. They were winemakers and bought a small vineyard that overlooked the Adriatic. The family did not turn fascistic when Mussolini's army invaded during World War Two. But after the war, they still had to flee back to Italy because the Croats chased them out. They couldn't prove their patriotism. Even a partisan hero for a son didn't help."

"They had to leave the vines?"

"Yes. Picked up and left it all. But Haris—Horatio is what his mother called him—he didn't leave with them. He knew he was a true Yugoslavian, a fierce fighter for our nation. He wasn't going to be chased anywhere by anyone. So that's why he came here, to Sarajevo. We came together."

I know the story. He was a city engineer, just like her. Baka gets up and goes to the kitchen. I listen to her rummaging. A shell lands somewhere north of here with a deep thudding sound. The vase on the windowsill shivers, then jumps sideways a fraction of an inch. Baka comes back with bags of chips and cookies, all opened for some other card game or visit, then carefully rolled up and sealed with a neat row of paper clips. But still everything's stale. Baka doesn't notice. Her taste buds disappeared in the forest during the war. Anything with fat, sugar, salt in it tastes good to her, even if it's a hundred years old. She grabs fistfuls of chips, shoves them into her mouth. She munches, while studying her cards, glaring up at me occasionally to see what she can read on my face.

"We floated down the Krka River in a small boat, we camped in Dalmatia," she says. "Swam in clear pools. Picnicked on the shore with bottles of delicious wine. Splashed in the clear water, looking for shells. During the days we dove into waterfalls, lay on rocks in the hot sun, hiked hand in hand along the magnificent coast. He was courting me, you see, your djedica. He paid so much attention to me, it was a dream. I knew life would be wonderful after the war, Tito building our great country up from the ashes, a handsome, dashing man to love me, a beautiful city to call our own. But it was better than wonderful, it was heaven. Studying all day long, evenings with friends, drinking and discussing the future late into the night. And to think my parents were going to force me to marry an ugly old man in the village before the war. And have his ten ugly babies."

She tells stories to distract me, but I win three hands in a row. Baka finds a box of chocolates and opens it slowly in front of my nose. Each chocolate is white with age. Baka says there's nothing wrong with them, just fat or sugar, the best parts, coming to the surface, so we eat every one of them with tea while the building rumbles and shivers around us.

"Istrian olives. Istrian oysters. Ancient coastal towns, clusters of red roofs on white buildings, small, shapely ports, schools of fishing boats. Grilled fish and truffles. Sunsets like the light of God's eyes." And Baka doesn't believe in God. "Your djedica, he had the vitality and devilish wit of a prince." And Baka doesn't believe in princes.

I never knew the man. He died of cancer in 1981, a month before I was born.

There is a rattle of gunfire not too far away, but I can't tell which neighbourhood. A deep rumble of shells landing farther away vibrates in my chest, and my teeth buzz like I'm getting my hair clipped. Baka cocks her head, listens, then barks, "Airport."

"The man I loved so much now dead and gone," she says. "And the other man I loved, too, dead and gone. But I don't complain. 1941 to '81. Forty years of pure happiness and good, hard, productive work. No one imagined that at my birth, in our poor village hut, just a ragged peasant girl." And Baka puts her hand on her chest and sings a bit of a song, like she sometimes feels like doing. "*Arise ye workers from your slumber. Arise, ye prisoners of want.*"

"Do you know that I chose my own name? The day I chose the life I wanted to lead?"

I nod my head, yes, yes, I know, I know, you've told me a thousand times.

"I was very young. It wasn't a very special name, Andjela, but it was my very own." Baka looks at me meaningfully. "Sometimes one has to begin life again, somehow. It's not easy, but it's possible, always remember that."

2

BLACK SMOKE IS RISING FROM FIVE PLACES IN the city. It billows upward slowly in tall snaking columns, way higher than the rain-filled clouds that brush their bellies against the hills. Sometimes the columns don't seem to move at all. Papa says they're like sculptures hanging over the apartment buildings. Like some crazy art-piece, he says, like that guy makes, the one who wraps buildings and islands.

I run down the stairs to the lobby in the early evening. The old men are standing around talking loudly. The Chetniks have captured the radio station. Or maybe they are about to capture the radio station, shut down the transmitter. Or is it the hospital? The electricity is down in some of the suburbs, no one is sure which ones, and there are rumours of looting. I think of Baba and Deda, then force myself not to. There are tears stored up in the back of my eyes and I don't want them to come out. JNA soldiers are the ones who are looting, the old men say, and criminal gangs. Ordinary Sarajevans would never loot their neighbours, their own city.

Nezira, Pero, and Zakir are sitting in the stairwell. I sit down next to them.

"Three children wandered across the front line while trailing a wounded bird," Nezira tells me, fast and breathless. "And they were raped and killed and strung up on lamp posts, dripping blood like butchered cattle. The old men just said so."

"No, Nezira. They said they were taken prisoner and transported to a camp in Serbia," Zakir says. "You didn't hear right." He has a small rubber ball and he's bouncing it against the grubby wall.

"No, you guys weren't listening," Pero says. "They were returned with notes pinned to their shirts telling their parents to watch them more carefully. You see, they ran into their uncle, who's fighting with the JNA, and he brought them home after his shift on the front and they ate a big family dinner together."

"No, that's not what happened," Nezira cries, and the three of them begin to argue, as if it matters what we think. Those three kids are either dead, in a camp, or at home by now, and arguing about it won't change anything.

I ask the old men on my way upstairs and they say each version could be God's own truth, and each version could be a deliberate evil lie, there's no way of knowing, that's the problem with this cursed war. You'll tell the version that makes the most sense to you and makes you and yours look innocent, like victims, they say, that's how war stories work.

I slip quietly into our apartment. I can tell the moment I'm inside that Mama and Papa are in a bad mood. They're trying not to look out the windows at the columns of smoke, at the fires that flicker brightly at their base now that it's almost dark. Mama is banging pots around the kitchen. Papa is pacing the hallway. And Aisha and Berina are awake in their bedroom. I can hear them singing a sad song to themselves like they're little orphans in an orphanage. Dušan is in the stairwell two floors down, smoking up with friends. I passed them on the way up and he told me to get lost.

"This city," I tell Mama and Papa, repeating Baka, "has survived eight hundred years of foreign occupation, fires, bombardment, and other bad things. It's not going to be destroyed now even if some of us have to die."

"Please go to bed," Mama says, as though it's way past bedtime. But it's only eight o'clock.

In my room I lie on my bed and hang my head over the edge. I peer underneath and am face to face with clumps of dust and some old junk. Two toy cars from when I was younger, an elastic band, a sock, a chewed-up ballpoint pen, some candy wrappers, a comic book, the cover torn. I'm meant to clean my room, but I never do the places no one can see. I hear the TV in the living room. Mama and Papa watch it sometimes just to see how bad things are. I crawl under the bed and lie there to see if it helps me fall asleep. I'm jittery because of doing nothing all day long. We sit on our beds, slouch on the sofa, loll on the floor, like the bones in our bodies are dissolving and we're turning to jelly. I want to be outside so badly, I think about jumping off the balcony. The few seconds down would feel so good, the cool fresh air, the wind in my hair.

The forests of Yugoslavia are mixed, deciduous and coniferous. They cover the mountainsides like a shaggy fur. Oak, birch, beech, pine, that's what the encyclopedia says. Foresters for centuries walked the pathways, cutting and pruning and clearing as their ancient knowledge told them to. Early farmers cleared fields and pastures as far up as one thousand metres. Their descendants still farm the upper meadows. They raise sheep, goats, cows, chickens, pigs. They cultivate large vegetable patches. They harvest apples in hardy orchards. Without the peasant farmers, the South Slavs would not have gained their independence from imperialists and invaders. The partisans would have starved to death. Or maybe they would have turned into wolf-men and wolf-women, those partisans. Maybe they would have stopped fighting fascist invaders and disappeared into nature, hunting in packs for rabbits, pheasants, foxes. I hunt with them in my mind, the wind and rain on my face, smelling the ground with my nose, while the city shakes and crumbles.

I LEAVE the apartment early in the morning and wander through the building for no reason, listening to people's morning sounds, smelling coffee and toast. There are no egg smells or meat smells anymore, people ran out of those fast. On the fourth floor, I see Nezira walking slowly along the hallway, hugging the wall. Her clothes look crumpled, dirty. I walk fast until I'm next to her.

"Are you okay?" I ask her.

"Yes, I'm okay."

"Where is Cena?"

"She got hurt."

"Again?"

"It's much worse this time." Nezira suddenly grimaces weirdly, one of her eyelids fluttering like she's winking at me over and over. "She might be dead."

"Oh," I say, like an idiot. It doesn't make sense to me, Cena getting hurt twice. It's not fair. "What happened?"

"I don't know."

"Where is she?"

"I don't know."

I go to Cena's apartment. The door is open. People are huddled in the living room, eyes wide, lips pressed tight together.

"Where is Cena?" I ask. "And her mom and dad?"

"We're waiting to hear," a woman I don't know tells me.

"They'll call from the hospital when they know."

"Know what?" I ask, but no one answers.

I go in and sit down on the floor by the couch. I hunch over, feeling kind of sick, and pretend to look at a magazine that's on the floor. They're talking about a shell that exploded yesterday in the marketplace.

A TRIP to Hungary, in the glorious '50s, when Mama was little, this is what Baka wants to tell me about today. Baka, Djedica, Mama, and Ujak Luka, all four of them driving in an old Yugo car, which was new then, the kids sitting on top of sleeping bags, pillows, towels, and clothes. Hungary was very beautiful, the food was very good. They camped on the shores of Lake Balaton, floating on the still water all day long, sitting around a campfire at night, sweating in the hot breezeless night air. They sang revolutionary songs and tried to forget that Hungary invaded Yugoslavia with the Nazis. I picture the whole family in geothermal baths, soaking up Mother Earth's mineral gifts. And when Baka lost a ring in one of them, I see them spending a happy, fun-filled afternoon diving for it, the other bathers scowling at them and turning their backs.

I try to imagine Mama and Ujak Luka when they were little, how they lived in the same home all the time like Dušan, Aisha, Berina, and I do now. How they shared a bedroom and went to school together in the mornings, how they ate dinner in the evenings with Baka and Djedica, how they all told stories about their day. It's hard to picture, because now they hardly spend any time together, and when they do, he's always teasing her, and she's always frowning at him. He says, "Lighten up, Sofija," and she says, "Grow up, Luka." I guess one day the six of us won't live together anymore, and maybe the twins and Dušan and I won't visit each other much, and Mama and Papa will get old. But that's a long time in the future, so far I can't see it at all.

Some kids in the building are allowed outside today even though there's shelling. They're playing soccer in the court, I can hear their cries like hungry seabirds over a fishing boat. Not too far away, buildings go boom, but it's cozy in here with cards, snack food, a sip of slivovitz if I'm lucky. And the droning, crackling sound of Baka's voice as she tells her stories.

Done with Hungary, she says, "Did I ever tell you about our beloved leader, our Joza?"

I nod my head and feel dizzy because I'm very tired. I didn't sleep at all last night, the city was so wide awake, shaking and twitching and moaning more than usual.

"Well, for centuries, South Slav freedom fighters who perched in mountain strongholds tried to get rid of conquerors, the Turks from the south, the Austrians from the north, because, you see, our region has always been cursed with imperialist invaders. This went on right up to World War One. When our beloved leader came home from Russia after that war, he found that the Serbs had fought courageously against the Austrians, empires had crumbled, and a union of South Slavs had been born. Peace, happiness for all? Well, not quite, because the Serbs took control, and the Croats and Slovenians didn't like that. But our hero didn't care about any of that. He was a communist, and his loyalty was to a cause far bigger than nation and tribe, his loyalty was to universal human dignity . . ."

One minute I'm sitting at the table listening to her, the next I'm lying on Baka's bed and she's draping a blanket over me.

"Shh," she says. "It's okay, Jevrem. You sleep, my boy, this terrible time is exhausting our young, it's depleting our future. Down with fascism, freedom to the people! May the ideals of your elders live in your heart."

It's daytime, so I sleep with my eyes open, the ocean of my dreams swimming around me in Baka's cramped bedroom.

‡ ‡ ‡

DUŠAN BEGS MAMA TO LET HIM GO AS WELL. HIS face is white, his mouth twisted into an O, ugly with wanting. Papa has decided to join up, and there's no way Dušan will stay cooped in this apartment with Papa on the front line somewhere, shooting guns from a muddy trench. Papa leads the girls to their bedroom, his face stony and hard. Then he stares at me like he's never really seen me before.

"You," he says to me, "will help Mama from now on."

"Okay," I say, and feel light-headed.

"Everyone decent hates war," Papa says. "I am a pacifist. But now there is no choice. When they are at your doorstep, there is no choice. The government is desperate for fighters. It needs to form a proper army, take control of the paramilitaries and the criminal gangs who are defending us now. Am I going to sit here and simply wait for other men to do the hard work, to make the sacrifice?"

Mama shouts, "*Noooo, noooo, noooo . . .*" She cries, she covers her face.

"The draft will come soon enough, anyway," Papa says quietly. "Please. Sofija, you must understand. I don't want to live in a Greater Serbia, I don't want to live in a Greater

Croatia. One has to draw the line somewhere, and mean it, and fight for it."

"They don't want a child, Lazar. They don't want someone of Dušan's age." Mama's voice is a high sob. I want to hide somewhere, but I can't move. "They don't want Serbs, Croats, they only want Muslims, you'll see."

Papa stares at her, but his mind seems elsewhere, probably going over all the things he needs to do before he leaves.

"I can't believe it's actually come to this, either," he says slowly. "Years of watching the political situation, raising alarm bells, protesting with friends, family, colleagues, and now off to fight in my hiking boots."

"I know we all have to help," Mama whispers, "but there has to be something else you can do. You have skills, you're educated. And Dušan . . . ." Mama begins to cry again.

"That's true of everyone here in the city." Papa is calmer, quieter than I've ever seen him.

He shifts his gaze to Dušan. Lots of teenagers are fighting, girls too. Everyone knows that. "It's not civic-minded to protect your own, Sofija."

I stare at Dušan. He suddenly looks like someone else. How could he be a soldier? He'd have to get up early, obey orders, keep neat and tidy, run around with heavy things on his back. Mama knows he will go with Papa, she can't keep him at home. Her face is an open book, she wants the old Dušan back, the pot-smoking slob who was out with friends all the time, his torn shirts, his grumpiness in the mornings and most of the rest of the day too. Well, if he goes, I will take his place. It won't be so hard to be like him, if that's what she wants—it won't take that much effort at all.

"Just please stay together," Mama cries. "Surely they

don't put young ones like this at the front. Or old ones like you, Lazar."

"Everywhere is the front, Sofija. Our front door is the front. They'll put us where we're needed."

IT ALL happens so fast. A week of Mama dragging herself around like she's suddenly sick with a terrible disease, of Papa and Dušan running around getting their stuff together all hyper-focused and excited. And then they're leaving. They've chosen warlike clothing from their bedroom closets, dark button-up shirts with pockets on the chest, pants with pockets on the sides, jackets with as many pockets as possible. But it doesn't matter that much what they choose, the old men in the lobby say the T-shirt-and-running-shoes war is coming to an end already; now there will be a uniformed war, with official ranks, exactly how it happened with the partisans. The government is seeing to it.

Dušan forgets to say goodbye. He just walks out the door, down the hall, and pushes the button for the elevator, fingers drumming his thighs, his pack dragging on the floor. His face is rigid like he's in a very tense dream. Aisha and Berina cling to Papa's sleeves. Where are you going? they ask. Why are you leaving? He hugs us all. He cries. He says they'll be back soon, in a few months when training is done. Then much more often. That's the one good thing about this war, he says, we soldiers can come home really easily and rest and be looked after by our loved ones. What other soldiers can do that? He lugs his gear to the elevator, grabs Dušan by the back of the neck, and marches him back to the door of the apartment.

"Say goodbye like a human being," he says quietly into Dušan's ear.

Dušan seems surprised that he's still here. I can tell by the look in his eyes that he's at the front already, sitting in his trench, having a smoke, fiddling with his machine gun.

"Wait, wait," Mama shouts. She pulls us all back in, closes the door. The twins are sobbing in that silent way they do, their faces getting redder and redder. I just stand there looking at everyone, like I'm watching a movie with weird pointless scenes that make no sense.

"What are you doing, Sofija? We have to go."

"Lazar, for all the years that we have loved each other, just take a moment for me, for the children. Everyone, come sit down in the living room."

So we sit in the living room and wonder what's going on. Papa starts to cry quietly, his cheeks are wet, he blows his nose. Mama picks up the phone. "Baka, come up, please," she says. "As fast as you can." Then she sits down at the piano, her back to us, her face to the window.

We wait without speaking, listening to each other breathing. The door opens and Baka comes in. "What's going on here?" she says loudly. "I thought you two were gone already."

"Mama," Mama says, "they're just leaving. Please sit down. I want to play for us all."

Baka perches on the edge of the couch, and Mama begins to play. She plays for ten minutes, maybe, or an hour, it's hard to say, but Baka makes clicking sounds in her throat, and Aisha and Berina sit slumped on our laps, chins against their chests, and Papa holds my hand, and I put one finger on Dušan's wrist, so lightly that he doesn't bother to flick it off. The music Mama plays is not sad and not happy. It says, *terrible sad things happen but we go on, that's how human existence is.*

After she plays the last note, we all sit there for a moment listening to the silence it leaves behind, then everyone gets up at the same time and Papa and Dušan are suddenly at the door, then down the hall. The elevator comes with a ping. I stand by the apartment door, watching them pick up their bags in the greenish light of the hallway. I think of the hundreds of times Dušan and I have raced, checking and grabbing each other, from where I'm standing to where he's throwing his pack into the elevator. How every single time he won.

"I love you," Papa shouts, and walks into the elevator.

The doors close. They are gone.

One second later, the apartment feels like it's been abandoned for years. All the nice things Mama and Papa have collected, the paintings and sculptures, the rugs and books and glass bowls, seem ratty and thrown together randomly. I suddenly see that the place hasn't been cleaned or tidied in a while and the windows are streaked with city dirt. We look at each other, Mama, Aisha, Berina, Baka, and I, the leftover ones. Everything feels strange and muffled. Already I can't think about them, Papa and Dušan, because it makes me want to sob like the girls.

I go to my room and lie on my bed. I sleep.

Dusk creeps over the city. I wake. My room is filled with eerie half-light. Supper smells are wafting under my door. I picture the food and feel sick. I curl up into a ball. Mama calls my name. Her voice is too high, too clear, it echoes through the apartment. For once, the stereo is not on, there is no piano music blaring from the speakers. Mama is at my door, her head a dark blob against the frame. I can't see the expression on her face. She doesn't say anything. Then she's gone. I get up slowly. We're eating tonight?

At the table, Mama still looks like she's sick with a terrible kind of cancer. Her face is yellow and sags like warm wax. Her eyes are small and black, set back in her head. They reflect no light. She sips some tea. She hasn't bothered to put a plate out for herself.

"Eat your food," she says quietly.

My sisters look small and dishevelled. Aisha whines that she can't cut her potato. Mama asks her how old she is. Aisha begins to cry, pursing her mouth in that way the girls do, in that way I thought was so cute when they were babies. Berina sits still and silent, staring at her plate.

So this is war. It's completely different from Baka's stories. There isn't any action for me, nothing to do, no way to help, just waiting around for bad things to happen. It's going to be hell. And it just crept up on me. Yesterday I was happy, I know that now.

‡ ‡ ‡

MAMA IS MOANING INTO THE PHONE AGAIN. I can't stand that sound she makes. "Oh no, oh no, oh no." Someone else has been killed. I think about Papa and Dušan but it can't be them, they've got guns and it's safer on the front than in the city, that's what Pero says. I run out of the apartment in my slippers, my heart pounding, blood pulsing in my temples. I fly down the stairwell, jumping from landing to landing so hard my skull snaps back against my spine, past the women and kids who spend their days in the stairwell now, scared of the booming and rat-a-tatting that's coming so close, of exploding glass and the lottery of flying shrapnel, past the whores who sit on the stairs smoking cigarettes and picking at their fingernails all day long, waiting for customers to come by.

In the lobby, I feel dizzy and stunned, so I sit on the floor and listen to the old men. Rations are sure to come, they're saying. Flour, rice, milk, sugar, salt. And these Chetniks, why don't they just go back to Serbia if they don't want to live with us? Instead, they are raping Bosniak women in Grbavica, so many terrible stories, those poor girls. The old men turn to me. I think they're going to yell at me, at my Serb half, but they don't, they ask me a question.

"Do you know what rape is, Jevrem?"

I nod my head uncertainly. "Yes," I say.

"You tell us, what is it? What is it that these animals the Serbs are doing like the animals they are?"

I feel winded, like I've been playing soccer for ten hours, and there's more blood flooding into my eyeballs. I see red, jumping to a steady beat.

"It's, like, a kind of war," I say.

"Yes, yes," the men say. "He's a wise boy. It is like a kind of war. It's a war on our future."

I jump up. I don't want to hear any more of their depressing talk, but I don't want to go home either. Mama is crying all the time now, stumbling around the apartment, her eyes seeing nothing. She's sleepwalking, I tell the girls, that's why she's so strange. She's probably having a nightmare, we should wake her up, Aisha says. Berina doesn't say much since Papa and Dušan left, Aisha does the talking for both of them now.

I walk up the stairs to Baka's apartment and knock on the door. She waves me in as perky as ever but she looks wrinkled and tired. We eat tuna out of a rusty can, and for dessert, toffee that's as tough as old tires. I stare out the window at the afternoon sky. I haven't been outside for days.

"Well," Baka says, "the men have gone off to fight, Jevrem.

That's what men do in a war, there's no avoiding it. And in my time, when we were more enlightened, also the women."

I nod my head. I don't know why she's telling me these obvious things.

"Let me cheer you up with a story," Baka says. "In the time between the world wars, the Triune Kingdom dominated by the Serbs went after communists and threw them all in jail. But our beloved leader Tito still managed to agitate in the countryside where he was the mechanic for a mill in the small town Veliko Trojstvo. Do you know where that is? It's in Croatia, but so what? So what that it's in Croatia, to him Croatia wasn't a country of Catholics, it was a country of exploited working people and peasants just like all the other South Slav countries. He had long talks with the peasants waiting to mill their grain, talks about their pitiful conditions, about the greedy capitalists sitting rich in the cities. He knew that security is what human beings need the most in life, physical and social security, everything else grows out of that. So, our hero showed us that great good can come of hard times, that new worlds are built from anger. You remember that, Jevrem, when you're feeling sad, when you're feeling angry—"

Suddenly I want to go outside more than anything else in the whole wide world. I say goodbye to Baka before she gets to the end of her sentence. I say, I'm going up to see how Mama is. I run out the door without looking back and plunge down the stairs for the hundredth time today. The lobby is strangely empty now, the men gone. I stand by the front door for five minutes, then I walk out. Just like that. It's a warm evening, with a hint of early summer. May is almost here. The light is fading, the shadows are black and long. I hear the breeze rustling around the front door like a dog sniffing for garbage. I feel my lungs open wide as butterfly wings, sucking it in. I stumble around the front court, giddy with oxygen and smoke, the smell of green things growing and man-made things burning.

Then I walk down the street. It's deserted, like it's been abandoned for decades, shop windows shattered, glass everywhere on the sidewalk. The sun is setting. It's dark around me, but bright red on the western horizon. I can still see smoke rising in dirty puffs from four places in the city centre. I get to the corner, look for the tram. The main station has been hit by shells, and most of the trams are destroyed, but I peer up and down, anyway, like a man who's late for work. Only a few cars race by, driving crazy fast like bank robbers escaping the scene of the crime.

I decide I'm going to go see what shelled buildings look like up close, what their skeletons are like, are they wood, are they metal? What happens to brick and plaster when it's shot to hell, it's a good question. So I begin to walk, why not, there's nothing else to do. Then I have an idea, I stick out my thumb. A few minutes later, a car squeals to a halt. It's banged up, with black ragged holes all over the side, and it's full of our soldiers.

"Where are you going, Little Man?" someone shouts.

"Can we fit the little man in?" There is laughter. Cigarette smoke billows out the windows like there's something on fire in there.

"I'm very small," I say.

Then I'm sitting on a soldier's lap. He smells metallic, also of sweat. His breath is hungry, and bitter with cigarettes. But they're all laughing and joking.

"Where are you going, anyway, Little Man?" the driver asks.

"Where are *you* going?" I ask.

"To Stari Grad. We're stationed there. We're meant to stop the shells with our bare hands."

"I want to go to Vrbanja Bridge," I say. "The old men say that's where our soldiers are stopping the Chetniks from coming over. Do you know a man named Lazar and a boy named Dušan? They are my papa and my brother. They might be there with their unit. Can I have a cigarette?"

"He's fearless, our little man," one of the soldiers says. "This is good. We need little men like him. We'll drop you off close by. The challenge is not to get killed, do you understand? Give him a drink for strength and good luck."

"Where do you live?" I ask. Someone hands me a lit cigarette and a glass bottle. I inhale the smoke and feel invincible. I drink and gasp for breath. I love the feel of my burning stomach, then warmth spreading all over my body.

"We come from the suburbs, Little Man, from Vogošća, but we can't get to it. There's no way. We're in exile a mile away from our own beds."

"What about your moms and dads?"

"And brothers and sisters and cousins? Haven't seen them since the war started. We're fighting so that we can go home for Sunday lunch."

The car lurches to a halt. "Here, get out here," the soldiers shout. The cigarette and slugs of brlja make me feel funny in the head. I sway when I get out, then I fall to my knees. The soldiers laugh and point. "He's wearing his slippers," they call out to the night sky, "he's wearing his slippers, long live our children." Then the car squeals away, its headlights off.

It's completely dark now, no street lights, no lights from windows, or cars, or shops. The gunfire is so loud my ears explode, my bones vibrate, my heart skips beats. I see nothing but fast-moving streaks of fire nearby, and glowing surfaces in the distance. I know I'm inside the war zone and the war zone is inside me. Just like Papa and Dušan.

I sit for a long time in the middle of the street, my legs stretched out in front of me, my hands gripping pavement, each cell in my body vibrating inside this timeless vortex of noise. Then I raise my head, I see water. The Miljacka River glitters orange. I'm not far from the bridge, it's a dark line across the fiery water. Streaks of light flash as guns fire from both sides. I get up, I move closer on shaky legs. The air hisses with bullets. I watch the bridge and think of Baba and Deda on the other side. I want to go to them, but there is no way over, so I move away from the river, up one of the streets, looking for Ulica Maršala Tita. Our street branches off from it, but nothing is familiar, the city's shape is disappearing, there's only rubble, shattered glass, fire, smoke, noise. Concrete shattering sounds like the end of the world.

A man calls to me, he's very close. "Who goes there? Make yourself known." He must be a soldier.

"It's Jevrem," I say. I look around, but I can't see him.

"Jevrem who?"

"Jevrem Andric."

"Which Jevrem Andric?"

I laugh very loudly, it's like we're playing a game.

"Stop that, boy," the soldier shouts. "You're out after curfew, it's the front line, the enemy is just over the river. Are you crazy?"

I move away from him into blackness. If I keep going, I'll run into another street eventually, that's how cities work. But two minutes later I hear, or maybe I feel, footsteps right behind me, so close I think I can sense hot breath on my neck, a hand on my shoulder. It's the soldier, he's coming to arrest me. Or a criminal or a thug or a mafia killer. The city is full of them, that's what the old men and Papa and Mama say, full to bursting. Outlaws running wild, murdering their rivals, running their rackets, making millions off our misery. I walk faster, but there is that breath in my ear this time, those fingers clawing at my shoulder blades. So I start running fast and keep running for a long time, around corners, between buildings, falling over debris, scraping my hands, knees, nose, forehead, banging into walls, falling into shell holes, panting, gasping, panic squeezing the air out of my lungs. I'm trapped in a maze in a deep black cave, in a nightmare that has no waking. I'm blind, I'm deaf, I lose all sense of direction, what's up, what's down, what's in the four corners of existence. My mind stops thinking, my body takes over. I feel it beating its way through space. And still the footsteps keep coming behind me, still the hand is almost around my neck.

‡ ‡ ‡

WHEN I WAKE, GREY LIGHT IS GLIMMERING ON me, the reflection of a cloudy day in a mirror propped up against a chair. I'm on a bed, but the house around the bed is gone, except one wall and half the ceiling. I see past the mirror into the neighbour's house, which has no walls either, just jumbled furniture, shattered doors and windows. I see a bookshelf, and books spread evenly across the floor like they've been deposited by receding flood water.

I sit up slowly. My hands are smeared with dark sticky stuff, and I hurt all over, like someone beat me everywhere with a stick. The floor is covered with plaster and broken bricks and glass. I try to get off the bed, but I see that my slippers are gone. My stomach aches, a deep, weirdly numb pain, and my head, and my hands and arms look strange, blue from cold and covered with scrapes, bruises, splotches of bright red smears, more dark sticky stuff. And I wonder, how long have I been here? I lie back and breathe. I close my eyes.

When I sit up again I find I'm stuck to the mattress, I'm welded down, I can't lift myself up, I can't pull free. I must be in a dream. I look around for Mama, I look around for Papa. Suddenly I see there's blood everywhere, all over the mattress, in splashes on the floor. I bend my legs and strain and pull, I need to get off this mattress, I need to go home. Mama. Mama will be worried about me. And then I see where my shirt is torn. The blood, fresh, warm, is spilling like a miniature fountain out of my belly.

A voice is calling. I hear it in the distance, echoing from another world, but then it gets closer and louder. Then it's just downstairs.

"Anyone in here? Is there anyone in the building?"

I want to call out but my voice doesn't work. I try not to sob, but I do, a pathetic little animal sound that I've never heard before.

"We're coming up," the voice says. "Hold on, we're coming up."

My feet are cold, my head feels hollow. I hope they don't find me, I'm a wreck, I don't feel well, I shouldn't be here. But they charge in, three huge men wearing dirty white jackets. I can smell their clothes, their hands, their hair, fresh air and cigarettes and sweat. I can feel their warm breath on my face.

"Careful," one of them says, "the floor looks unsound."

"It's just a young kid." One of them has got his big hot hands all over me, feeling here and there, pressing rags onto my belly. "He's just been dumped here."

"Oh shit. We need to stop this bleeding."

"Where do you live?"

I think about home, my bedroom, the kitchen table, the living room couches, our kettle and fridge, cereal, how I'd like some, the piano and the coffee table, how far away they all seem, another life, a daydream. I don't want to tell them where.

"On the other side."

"We're medics, we'll get you out of here. How did you get on this side of the river?"

"I don't know," I say. "I was running, then I woke up here."

"You must have run over the bridge. A big fucking miracle you survived that."

Suddenly I think of Mama all strange and absent-minded. Even she's going to notice this. I fight back more sobs. There's a hole in my belly, I saw it where the blood was seeping out. The ambulance men haul me down the blown-out stairs on a stretcher. I don't know where they're taking me, they could take me anywhere. I have to tell them that I have to get home.

"I'm okay," I croak.

"You're not okay," they say.

"Are you Chetniks?" I ask.

"We're citizens of Yugoslavia," they say.

"Where are you taking me?"

"To the hospital."

"I don't want to go."

"You don't have a choice. A bullet glanced your stomach. You're very lucky it didn't go right through. And you may have hit your head quite hard. Concussion."

"But I have to go home. I can't breathe."

"You'll go home after the hospital."

"I can't breathe."

"He may be having some kind of asthmatic episode."

"He's scared we're going to take him somewhere and do bad things to him. They think we're all animals."

"We're medics, boy. We save lives. We're taking you to the hospital to get your wound fixed. Okay?"

I don't want to listen to them anymore, I just want to sleep again. Maybe I should tell them that Papa is one of them and Baba and Deda and the uncles in Ilidža too, and half of me as well. I just won't say that Papa is fighting on our side of the river, that he calls himself a cosmopolitan Sarajevan of the world community. Maybe they'll take me to Baba and Deda. I picture the front door to their house, how it smells inside, the kitchen window looking over the garden, the roughness of Deda's wool vest when he hugs you hard. But I can't lift my head, I can't even open my mouth, and anyway, Papa would not be happy with me if I did; we're all just human beings, a complex multiplicity of aspects, he said over and over again, big words I used to ignore. I hear his voice in my head. We don't use ethnic labels reductively even as shields, it's disgusting, it can only lead to evil.

I'm lying on the floor of a school gym, I can see basketball nets on either side, and a scoreboard in the middle. Hundreds of people are pressed around me, breathing and talking and coughing and sighing, dazed and wondering what's going on, just like me. The thing is, there is no air, it's too hot, there are too many people and no windows. The whole place stinks of shit, piss, puke, blood.

My belly has a wide bandage on it, and I'm wearing huge old track pants and girls' sandals. Some old lady next to me is rocking back and forth, talking to herself, her head resting in her hands.

"The boy is awake," she's saying. "The house is locked up, the boy is awake. The house is locked up, the boy is awake. Maybe he'll live. Tarik is in Italy, thanks be to Allah. I don't know where Emira and Fadila are. I don't know where Abdulah and Mirsad are. Maybe they'll tell me tonight. Bobo ran into the ravine, I saw him go. He knew to run away into the ravine. What do dogs eat in the wild? My patients will miss me. I have to follow up. Who can I call? The boy is awake, the house is locked up."

A man hisses at her, *shut up*, but she doesn't listen.

"Guards, we need water," she shouts. "The boy has to get out of here. I don't know where Emira and Fadila are. Water, please. We need *water*. This boy has a wound. It's seeping. He needs more attention. Guard. *Water*. Tarik is in Italy, thanks be to Allah, Bobo is in the ravine. I'm asking you, what do dogs eat in the wild?"

A young soldier with a gun shouts at her from the small door at the front. "Be quiet, lady! No talking!"

"There is no medical treatment here, boy," she whispers. "Your wound will get infected. You must leave. You need to get more help. I'm a doctor, I know."

She reaches for my bandage with trembling hands. I jump up and move away, stumbling between bodies, stepping on people's fingers, forearms, ankles. They snarl at me. I fall down, I wrench my wound, my bandage suddenly has a patch of red on it. For a while I sit and hold it with both hands. Then I cover it with my shirt.

"I want to go home," I say to the soldier at the door. "I'm a

Serb from Ilidža, I just got lost, my name is Jevrem Andric, I'll give you my grandparents' address." When I say this the room spins around me, like I'm on a ride at the fair.

WHEN I wake up I'm not in the gym anymore. I'm in the back of a moving truck with wooden sides and a canvas top that makes loud flapping sounds in the wind. It feels like we're going crazy fast along twisty roads, up and down hills, around steep corners. It's murky in here but I know it's full of soldiers, they're laughing and swearing and I can smell damp clothes and sweat and alcohol-breath. I'm leaning against one who is holding me up with one arm, like I'm his little brother, but he doesn't say anything to me and I'm too scared to ask where we're going. The thing is, they're not our soldiers, they're Chetniks, but they sound and smell like our soldiers. I think of saying, is anyone here Pavle or Obrad or Ivan Andric or any of their neighbours, but for some reason no sound comes out of my mouth so I just press my belly wound and try not to puke. It seems like we're driving for hours in all different directions, and when we stop and the back gate opens and two soldiers jump out, I expect to be way up in the mountains somewhere, with only trees and mountain silence surrounding us.

"Come on, Little Man," they say. "This is your stop."

It's a sunny afternoon and I see houses. I blink as the soldiers help me out.

"Get home safe," they say as they pile back in. "And stay home, don't wander off again. Life is a dangerous motherfucker right now."

I look at their faces and not one of them is my uncle, but they could be.

The truck roars off and I look around me and I know exactly where I am. They've put me down at the end of Baba and Deda's street. I'm so happy my legs wobble and I can hardly walk. But somehow I get down to their gate and I open it and I'm in their garden, so cozy and green and bursting with spring flowers, and I run up to the front door not caring that my belly hurts. I try to open the door but the door doesn't move. In all the years I've visited, it's never been locked.

"Deda, Baba," I call out. "Deda, Baba."

There is no answer. I know right away they're not here, the house has that empty feel hovering all around its windows and walls. So I sit down on the front step and wait and shiver and shake because I'm not wearing a coat. I look at my bandage and it's completely soaked, bright red in the middle and brown at the edges. It's weird to sit on these steps with a wound, hungry and sick and dizzy with a headache, waiting for Baba and Deda to come home while time goes by. They've always been here when I'm here, and Mama and Papa, and the uncles, and Dušan and the twins, they've never been somewhere else.

After a while, I decide I'm going to get into the house even if the door is locked. Baba and Deda wouldn't mind, they'd want me to if things were desperate. I get up and check the back door and all the windows. Everything is locked. I find the garden shovel and bang it against the small side window. It feels both terrible and exciting at the same time, trying to shatter their window, trying to break in, like all the rules of ordinary life are gone and anyone can do whatever they like. My heart beats fast and for a moment my belly doesn't hurt. It takes a few times before the glass breaks into shards and falls to the ground, tinkling like the sound of a piano's high notes on the stone below. I get my hand in and open the window, then I pull myself up and over the sill, my belly wound burning like crazy. But then I'm standing in the house, and it's all silent and dim and warm around me.

"Baba, Deda," I say quietly, in case for some reason they're asleep in their bed in the middle of the afternoon. But only quietness echoes back at me, and peacefulness. Then I walk into every room on the first floor, one after the other. They're all empty and neat like no one has lived here for ages. There are no coats hanging by the front door, no shoes and slippers tucked into the shoe rack. I walk into the kitchen and it's empty and tidy, like I've never seen it, no Baba bustling around cooking up a storm. But Baba's aprons are still hanging on the door handle, and I go up to them and smell them and they still smell of her breakfasts and lunches and dinners, all of us squeezed around the table in winter, or out in the garden under the tree in the summer. Then I look in the drawer for halva and chocolate and dried fruit, but it's empty, with just a few mouse droppings where crumbs used to be. This makes me think of Fidel the parrot and I run to his cage in the living room, but the door is open and Fidel is gone.

There's a noise at the front door. The door is opening. I hear scuffing of feet on the door mat. They've come back from a walk, from shopping—they're here, they're here.

"Baba, Deda," I shout, feeling the tears at the back of my eyes and a sob revving up in my chest. I run into the hallway but stop suddenly. It's not Baba or Deda, it's Mr. Petrovic from next door. He stares at me with his mouth open, like he's trying to remember who I am. He's looking scared with his rifle under one arm, half crouching like he's getting ready to shoot or run, like he's expecting a sudden blow on his head.

"Mr. Petrovic, it's me, Jevrem," I say.

"Jevrem. What are you doing here? What happened to you?" I look down and see that blood is flooding through my shirt and down my pants.

"I got lost at night in the dark and was wounded and lying on a mattress in a ruined house and they brought me to a gym with all these other people and then they brought me here," I say.

"Oh my good God, Jevrem. We have to get you to a doctor. I heard glass breaking and thought some hoodlums were in here looting. Your grandparents have gone to Belgrade."

Mr. Petrovic picks me up, as though I can't walk, as though I'm a baby, and carries me huffing and puffing over to his house. Mrs. Petrovic looks at my wound and says, oh dear Lord, that's terrible, you poor boy, what is happening to our world, then cleans it out with lots of cloths and liquid that burns and I shake, I shiver, sweat drips down my scalp. We have to go to the hospital, they say, we must leave right now. But I don't want to go to a hospital, not over here, I want to go home. So I scream and I cry and I call out for Mama, I call out for Papa.

Mr. Petrovic is on the phone with Mama. His wound isn't deep, he says, but it's long. I can hear Mama's voice very loud on the other end. There are stitches, it was treated, he says. And more of Mama's muffled words, and he says, yes, yes, I will, I will. You should leave, Sofija, he says. Come here. I'm telling you, things won't get better. It's difficult now, but soon there will be no way to get into or out of the city. They're going to blockade it. I'm telling you, Sofija, very soon, in a week, maybe. No way to get in or out at all, do you hear, like a siege. You must leave now. Pack some things, come here with the girls, and we can get all of you to Belgrade. I'll drive you, if there's no other way.

I sit on a chair in the kitchen and sip soup that Mrs. Petrovic gives me. It's warm and delicious but I can only eat a few small spoonfuls before feeling weak and tired. Mama's going on and on to Mr. Petrovic and he's frowning and shaking his head and pacing up and down the hallway, the phone cord bouncing behind him. When he hangs up he rubs his face and looks sad.

"Your mama wants you back home," he says.

"What?" Mrs. Petrovic says. "Is she crazy?"

"Shh." Mr. Petrovic points at me. "She has her reasons, Grada. Lazar and Dušan have joined the civil defence. Can you believe it?"

I can hardly hold my head up anymore. I think of Baba and Deda packing up, all by themselves, locking the door, getting on a train. In ordinary times, we'd have come over for a fare-well lunch, we would have helped them to the train station, we would have prepared food for their trip and given it to them in a cloth bag. I wonder when I will see them again.

Mr. Petrovic tells me I'm going to sleep for a few hours and then he'll find a way to get me home. He's a truck driver, so he can get anywhere. I love truck drivers, they travel all over the place, through all kinds of terrain, over mountains, along valleys, through night and day, thinking, picking up hitchhikers, seeing the world. Mrs. Petrovic leads me by the hand up the stairs to their bedroom. I lie on the soft bed in the still, sunny room, listening to a fly buzz against the windowpane and feeling my body vibrate like an engine. Then, suddenly, I'm very heavy, I'm very dizzy, I'm falling down a black well toward the centre of the earth.

‡‡‡

THE BOYS OF THE NEIGHBOURHOOD PLAY WAR whenever it's safe to be outside. They have guns of their own, some of them real. I have one too, but it's not real. Mine is a perfect likeness of a Tommy gun, made of plastic. I traded two cans of beans and my Adidas jacket for it. I stole the cans from the kitchen. Mama cried for an hour when she found out, then didn't speak to me for a day. "There is no food in this city, don't you understand, Jevrem? When we've eaten our last reserves, we'll have to stand in line for hours to survive each day, we'll have to beg from the religious charities, we'll live off humanitarian-aid lunch packets if we're lucky. All for a plastic gun!" But the jacket was way too small, she didn't care about that.

I long for a real gun. I want to shoot the person who put the hole in my belly. I look down the gun's sight and press the trigger. I could hit Mahmud right between the eyes if I had a bullet. I feel a shiver running over my shoulder blades and up my neck. My body shakes itself, suddenly, violently. I want to be a sniper. The sniper gets to kill people from the safety of his little nest. I want to be the killer, not the loser scurrying like a hunted rabbit through the city streets waiting for the sting of the bullet against the side of his head.

We talked once on the phone with Papa and Dušan after they left, then nothing. They sounded far away, even though they're just a few miles from our apartment. Every day we wait for news. Every day, Mama plays the piano for them. It sends out life energy, she says to me, it'll help protect them from harm. That's obviously not true but it makes her feel better.

In our war games, no one wants to be the Chetniks, but I volunteer, I don't care. When we play, the Chetniks always lose, which means I get beaten up. When I feel the boys' fingers in my hair, their knuckles against my ears, I relax a little, the worst has come. The blood in my mouth tastes like the ocean, and I'm with Papa and Dušan in a trench somewhere, because maybe they've also tasted blood, no matter how hard Mama plays. After they're finished thrashing me, the boys are always in a good mood, it's a law of human nature when victory has been claimed.

Mama leaves us with Baka when she goes out to play or teach. She's out every day, even though it's dangerous, even though she vomits in the toilet before she leaves. I know, I can hear everything through the bathroom door. Lots of people want her to accompany them, ensembles, soloists, dancers, actors in their plays. And she's doing it, because she can't travel to give her concerts, she can't be a star on the stage. We're making music as an act of resistance, she says, all of us together, that's what Papa wants me to do, he'll be proud. And in between she hunts for food like a beggar on the street, like a hunter in the forest, like a scavenging animal, going to all the places where food could be, lining up, waiting and seeing.

Sometimes Mama asks me where I went that night on the other side of the river. And what happened when I got there. But I can't remember anything, except stepping out the door and how nice it was to walk across the square of ragged grass and feel the breeze, to smell it, how loud it was and the streaks of light in the sky, the fiery water. How I ran and ran. And something about men's shiny red faces, their drunk breath and loud shouting voices. And some girls were there too, they were screaming, crying, moaning, but maybe that's all part of a nightmare, the men standing over those girls, holding them down, banging into them like crazed, frenzied zombies, grunting, swearing, and twitching like they were being electrocuted.

Baka asks me too. She says, you don't have to have secrets from me, you know that, Jevrem, you and me, we're friends. I know everything that happens in a war so you don't have to protect my feelings. But I still can't remember anything, except for the feel of the cool night air on my face and the sound of things shattering close by, the stench of things burning, those sweaty men, those wailing girls, their straining, grimacing faces, the pain in my belly, the room with no walls, lying there waiting, the three huge medics coming to get me, how they looked sad and angry when they saw me, how cold my feet were. I remember those things, or maybe I've created them in my mind when I daydream, those visions that start out happy and end up all twisted and weird, overrun by savage wolves and dead ends, places I've run to but can't get out of, like a jail. So I say nothing to either of them.

Mama has to change my bandage every day, and when she does sometimes she cries. She tries to hide it, but I know.

THE shells are hitting here now. Even the air shatters apart in the blast, and the floors go soft and spongy. The foundations are too rigid, Baka says, these buildings aren't built for war. A week ago, Mama and I dragged everything away from the windows and outer walls, we put the valuables in the bathroom. We covered the windows with Dušan's mattress, a bookshelf, some carpets, piles of Papa's books stacked high.

Air-raid sirens go off, like they do in wars in movies. Our ears go numb, then ring for hours. Mama shouts instructions, runs around looking for things, though everything is already packed in a big bag in the hall. Food, water, knitting, books, cards. We wait for her at the door, like Papa used to. The stairs are crowded, everyone shuffling downward past the stairwell dwellers. We get Baka on the way and she complains. Like a herd of animals galloping off a cliff, it's a disgrace, she says. We should be fighting back, she says. All of us, women, children, everyone.

Then there we are, in the basement with all the same people, some freaked-out mice, and a few long-tailed rats. Berina sleeps in Mama's lap, and Aisha hums a song that has no end. It's dark, but we have flashlights and small lamps and people murmur, sigh, wonder how long we have to stay. I can feel them moving around the room, I can feel them trying to get comfortable, rummaging around in their bags, turning pages of books. When the building shudders and shakes, the murmuring stops, and everyone waits for the plaster to come down in big chunks and suffocate us all.

Baka sings a song. Some old people join in. They know all the words. Others grumble, old communist stuff, see where that got us. But Baka enjoys herself. She remembers this, huddling together in the dark, waiting for one violent thing or another to happen, waiting to spring into action. "If our Joza could only see us now," she tells them. "You should all think about how we've let him down, this man who fought so hard for our better selves. When I was very young I walked into the mountain forests to join our righteous cause. The camp was a peasant farm. There was a barnyard, several tall hay cones, a stone farmhouse to the left, a wooden barn and several smaller sheds to the right. I saw the farmer leaning in the doorway of one of them, his anxious eyes on the road; he could have been one of my uncles, one of my neighbours. I knew his wife and children were in there, waiting for their uninvited guests to leave. Fifteen soldiers were squeezed tightly into the kitchen, thirteen men, two women, each talking loudly over the others. Propped up next to each was a rifle, different from the guns I had seen hunters carrying in the village. All at once, all present turned, looked at me, raised their mugs and shouted, 'Welcome, Partizanka!'"

The people in the basement aren't that impressed with this story, some turn their heads away and pretend they can't hear. They know it as well as I do from their parents own lives, or from their grandparents, and they're too freaked out about being stuck here in this fucked-up present situation to figure out why she's telling it, what it can possibly mean now. Baka has a windup lamp, packs of cards, knitting, sewing, some old engineering magazines, lots of candles. She's brought a whole suitcase of stuff, a blanket, some pillows, extra clothes, bread, cheese, her old knife from the war. She says she's not going to rush up and down those stairs every time they throw a grenade in our direction. She sits on a pillow with her legs stretched in front of her, a plate on her lap, like she's at a picnic on the beach. I sit next to her, and when I feel like screaming and panting, when it's hard to breathe, when the dark edges of the room press in on me, she reaches over and holds my hand. Just before sleep pulls me out of the basement, out of the city, carries me high up to snowy mountain peaks where there are no people, no words, no stories, no booming, only clouds, birds of prey, fierce winds, I feel happy that Baka is mine.

THE war just keeps on going and all the adults are somehow shocked about that. Nothing gets better, everything gets worse. And it feels like there are no more days, weeks, or months, just flat time passing, passing, passing, and bad things happening, one after the other, and everyone talking about a siege, about other cities that went through it, all the terrible things you have to do to survive. The twins and I are staying in the basement to be with Baka. She won't come up ever, even when it's quiet, when they're concentrating on shelling other parts of town. She likes it down here, it's like being in a cave in the forest, or a dugout, or a well-made trench. Much better than being in a concrete box way up in the air, she says, like a sitting duck, like an easy mark, like an idiot who's lost the will to live. But the truth is, going up and down the stairs gets her wheezing, and she has to stop to catch her breath, and she wonders what's wrong with her soldier body, why it's betraying her with weakness, why she gets dizzy and feels pain in her chest and arms and head.

And Mama has stopped coming down, she says it's ridiculous, walking every night into your own grave. What if everything catches on fire, she asks. Then we'll roast to death like lambs on a spit, like potatoes in an oven. And what if the ceiling collapses. We'll all be crushed to death like cockroaches hiding from the light. Baka sends me upstairs sometimes to keep Mama company, so I sit on a chair or lie sleeping on the floor in the hallway of our dark jumbled apartment where it's safest, while Mama practises non-stop for the Shostakovich recital. She's the only performer left. Two escaped the city. One was wounded. One is dead.

Both places make me think of prison and people who are caged for years, looking out of small windows at the sky, a few treetops, dreaming about their old life.

Asleep or awake, we're thinking of food, the feasts we had before, the weird meals we'll have today, made from old stuff from Baka's apartment, random things Mama gets from the empty markets with Deutsche Marks she saved in her concert suitcase. Asleep or awake, we're floating in an ocean of dead air. Like in an underwater dream, there is no oxygen, but we do not die. We open our mouths like fish, and we keep on existing.

‡ ‡ ‡

MAMA IS TELLING US THAT PAPA IS DEAD. SHE'S sitting on the chair trying to light a cigarette, the three of us lined up on the couch in front of her. She looks like someone I don't know, so skinny, with bony hands that shake. What I notice is how bright the cloudy sky is beyond the dirty, broken windows. So bright I have to squint and shield my eyes with my hand. I notice that the old camera Papa was fiddling with is still on the coffee table, that his coat is still hanging on the back of the door, that the ashtray he stole from the Holiday Inn is still on the coffee table. I notice that the building is shaking, that Aisha and Berina are crying. I watch as fine dust seeps down from the ceiling.

Mama's not finished. "And Dušan is missing," she says. "Not dead, but missing."

My arms and legs won't move, like they're someone else's, and I feel very tired, and my stomach wound hurts. I want to slide down onto the floor and go to sleep right here in front of them all. I stare at Mama, waiting for her to do or say something more, or go away. But she can't get off her chair. She too wants to lie down on the floor, I know, I can see it in her eyes. Lie down and close her eyes and never get up again.

I can't think about Papa. "Dušan is missing? What does that mean?" I say. Dušan has always been everywhere I've been, listening to his music, stinking up his room with smoke, guffawing on the phone with his friends. The way he used to shove his dirty clothes under his bed, smell his fingers compulsively, eat ten pieces of toast in one go, with butter and jam, or cheese and peppers. He's too unimportant to be missing.

"They just don't know where he is."

"Why is he dead?" Aisha asks.

"He's not dead, he's missing." Mama's voice is a whisper.

"Papa," Aisha says. "I mean Papa."

"He was killed on the front. There will be a funeral on the hill."

"What hill? Where?" I ask. We all stare at Mama, but she can't seem to say more.

"Did it hurt?" Aisha asks.

Berina sits slumped over, fiddling with her fingers, as though she's bored, as though she's not heard a single word.

But Papa is not dead, he's in the room. I can feel his presence, tight, tense, wound-up, his big body always moving, legs jittering like springs, arms like wild branches in a high wind, hands playing with anything that happens to be sitting in front of him. Mama telling him to stop. The salt shaker, the butter dish, knives, forks, spoons, jar lids, jars, spinning them around on napkins, clinking them against each other. I can see the shape of his fingernails. They are round and even. His fingers are thin and long, but strong. He can open cans, glass jars, bottles, no matter how tightly shut they are. He fixes mechanical objects, like the blender, the DustBuster, the camera. He takes them apart to see how they work.

"When are they coming back?" Aisha asks. Mama is trying to get up from the chair.

"We don't know when Dušan is coming back," she says. "We just don't know."

"Maybe tomorrow?" Aisha asks.

"Yes, maybe tomorrow, but maybe also not till the next day. Or next week. We have to be patient." Her voice is just breath now.

Mama gets up from the chair, then stands in the middle of the room. We watch her. She stands there for a long time, looking at nothing. Then she walks to her room. I hear the bed creak.

We don't move. We sit on the couch. After a while I notice that the girls are asleep, their arms intertwined, their eyeballs moving behind their eyelids. And I remember that beside them, it's just me, and I'm meant to be Dušan, to look after things, and I wonder what he would do in this moment, but the answer isn't clear. He never had to do that much around here, he was just a regular teenage kid. So I ask Papa what I should do and he says, *cover the girls with a blanket and go and see how Mama is.* So I find a blanket for the girls and then I go into Mama and Papa's dim bedroom and there is Mama lying on the bed, very still, a scarf over her face. I get on the bed and curl up against her and try to keep her warm.

THE scab on my belly itches like crazy. Sometimes I spend whole mornings scratching it, very lightly at first, and then sometimes harder. When I'm upstairs, Mama doesn't nag me to stop, she doesn't notice, her eyes don't see and her ears don't hear ordinary things anymore. In the basement, Baka searches through her suitcase for a soothing ointment, but she never finds one.

Upstairs, I stand for hours by the covered window and look through a crack. All I see is dirty grey sky, puffs of smoke here and there, the place where a shell landed in the fourth floor in the opposite building. A bed, a wardrobe, some flapping clothing, it's all in the open for everyone to see. I try to think about nothing, I try to keep my mind high up in the sky somewhere, with clouds and birds and a vast open view, but it always circles around closer and closer to the place where Papa lies dead. When I'm just above him, I hover there on currents of nightmarish feelings, staring at his body until it stops looking like anything I recognize, until it's just another lump of rubble in the wreckage.

I've read all the books in the apartment that I can understand, and in other people's apartments too. There are no strangers' voices or musicians in our rooms anymore, no radio, no television, no singers, or famous pianists. Even when the electricity works, Mama doesn't play records or tapes, doesn't want to hear the news. She shouts, no, when I try to turn something on. She says, turn it off, leave me alone. I guess she likes silence better now, the silence of guns and shells. I wander along the hallway of every floor of our building, working my way from top to bottom, hunting for smells of cooking, picking through ruined apartments. I carve my name over and over again in the plaster of the stairwell. I gouge round hollows that look like shrapnel craters and bullet holes.

In our apartment, when Mama's gone out for food, I go through piles of our stuff that used to look so good arranged on bookshelves, hanging on walls, everything in its right place. In Papa's study, I sit on the floor and pick up one thing after the other just to hold it and touch it. Things that used to be on his desk. A notebook, his pencil holder, his small Buddha carved from stone, his carved wooden box with the little frog wearing a crown on top, his stapler, erasers, hole-puncher, pencil sharpener. The four perfect seashells, each a little bigger than the others, just like us, that we found on the beach of Istria and gave to him. The big map that used to be on the wall behind his desk. It has the whole world on it and Papa used to give me cities to find when I was bored and he was busy writing, cities and rivers and seas and mountain ranges. Sometimes he forgot I was there because he had to concentrate, and sometimes he forgot he had to concentrate and told me about history. How the Ottomans took over half of our country before it was a country, and the Austro-Hungarian Empire took over the other half. How we, the South Slavs, struggled for hundreds of years to kick out invaders and imperialists, how we had to get together to do that. How imperialism starts wars.

I take his fancy new laptop that cost a fortune from its case, take a notebook, a pencil, one of the books from the windowsill, and place them all on his dusty desk, standing crooked in one corner. I find him an ashtray, I get him a mug from the kitchen. I drag his chair across the room to the desk and he's all set up to work. He says, *where are the drawings you kids made, I taped them all on the wall, those are what I want to see the most*. And I know where they are. Mama took them down and put them with Papa's tower of papers as high as my chin in the closet. She took everything off the walls, for some reason, and off the shelves, the tables, all surfaces of our home.

It's a thick stack of drawings, and I bring them to Papa, and he lays them out one next to the other on his desk and on the floor around it. *That's better*, he says.

SOME kids were killed playing in the court of their apartment building, so we're not allowed to go out anymore, but no one is watching so I can do what I want.

Sometimes when it's safe, when I'm up visiting Mama, I lean over the balcony railing and stare at the city. It's still there, but it looks like a drunk man who's fallen down a few times on his way home from the bar. Fallen down and scraped some skin, bruised a knee, blackened an eye, shattered a bone or two. He looks bloody and dishevelled and disoriented and everyone wonders how his body can take all that abuse. But he manages to get up the next day and get drunk all over again. The thing is, people still go out, they're still running from one place to another, even if they sometimes get hit, even if they sometimes get killed. You have to, Baka says, or everyone would starve to death safely in their own homes. Sometimes you have to risk everything for all time to get what you need in the moment.

When Mama's not out finding food, she sits on a mattress in the hallway with papers spread all around her, everything from her filing cabinet and Papa's filing cabinet, from the closets and boxes under their bed. Sometimes she just sits and stares at them all, sometimes she reads through each page carefully, going over the same one for hours like she's in a trance. None of it matters, she says, except a few for the future. Sheet music for us, our report cards, passports, that's it. When Mama's sorted a pile, she gives it to me to take downstairs to burn in the stove. She says, make sure Aisha and Berina are warm, never let them get cold. When she's not looking at papers, Mama sleeps, even if it's daytime. She sleeps and sleeps, without moving or making any sound at all, and I sit beside her if she lets me and cut up *National Geographic* magazines and glue photos together into collages that look pretty good. I stick them up on the walls but the tape doesn't hold. They slide to the floor and land in piles of plaster dust. Everything in the apartment is covered in fine powder. Even the piano, which Mama never touches anymore; she's done with it. Just an ordinary piece of furniture now, it's pushed into a corner, random stuff dumped on top. I don't touch it either, Mama hates the sound, but sometimes my fingers itch for it.

BERINA is asleep, her head lying on Aisha's lap. Aisha is reading a book and writing down words on a piece of paper. I squat down next to her.

"What are you doing?"

"Homework," Aisha says, without lifting her head.

"Why? No one's going to look at it."

"Yes, they will. One day. I'm doing Berina's for her too."

"No, they won't, they don't care about that stuff anymore."

"Yes, they do."

"No, they don't." I stare at Aisha, and she turns away from me and keeps writing words on the ragged piece of paper.

"Let her do her good work," Baka says. She's playing solitaire on her suitcase. "All three of you must go back to school soon. War schools are opening up, just like during my war."

I leave the basement and go upstairs to see if the old men are there. There are just two left, Mr. Ibrahimovic and Mr. Beganovic. They look depressed and sick. They hunch their shoulders over their sagging stomachs and chew empty air with their flabby jaws.

"Papa is dead and Dušan is missing," I tell them.

"Poor boy." Their faces don't change expression. "Poor, poor boy."

"He wanted to save the city," I say. "He wrote articles about politics and history, he had notebooks full of notes." When I say this I feel terrible, it doesn't describe him at all. "He was good with little machines," I add. "Like hair dryers, electric can openers, drills, cameras. He could fix them all."

"Is that so?" says Mr. Beganovic.

"Yes, and he was always looking for an ashtray."

"Is that so?" Mr. Beganovic repeats.

"Where can I go to look for my brother?" I ask.

"You shouldn't go out there," Mr. Ibrahimovic says. "It's not good today."

"But if it was a good day, where would I go?"

"I don't think you can look for him, Jevrem. If they don't know where he is, you will never be able to find him. It's a big war out there. A big war, with big money, big weapons, big stakes. People in Bonn, Washington, London, Paris, and so on are watching. They're not just watching, they're pulling strings."

"And we're doing the dance," Mr. Beganovic says, picking at fluff on his vest.

"The dance called falling-down-dead," says Mr. Ibrahimovic.

Outside, the yard is empty. The kids who are allowed out are scrounging for fuel and wood, carrying water, waiting in lines, begging at the hotel, playing in ruined buildings. Clouds are scudding by, grazing the tops of apartment buildings. Shells are landing not too far away. I can see a plume of smoke rising just beyond the next building. Then I see Nezira, Pero, and Mahmud running out the side door, along the crumbling pathway. They're probably not meant to be out, but they're going to see what happened anyway, to see if they can find the tails of exploded grenades to collect. I head toward them, trying to catch up with my fastest sprint.

Another shell hits, very close. I'm not running anymore, I'm on my hands and knees, staring at scraggly grass and lumps of earth. Then I'm standing at the corner of the building. There is a big hole in the middle of the parking lot, sand underneath the stone, black earth underneath sand. Nezira is jumping up and down shrieking.

"What's wrong?" I ask. "What's wrong?"

"Look," Nezira shrieks. "Look."

There are two strange lumps next to the car. Then I notice a head. And a foot.

"It's Galib and Konstantin," she cries, "from the other building."

They're moaning, writhing. Some parts of their bodies are moving, other parts are still as stone. I walk closer, and can see all of Galib's teeth on one side, and a bit of his jaw. One of his arms has come off. His belly button is full of blood. Konstantin's legs are crushed below the knees. I can see splinters of bone. His Puma track pants are completely ruined, and his running shoes too. He was very proud of those, relatives in England sent them to him, he couldn't live without them. They're both covered in dirt, like they're already buried.

"Do something." Nezira grabs me by the shoulder and shakes hard. "*Do something. Do something.*"

Pero and Mahmud are running around in circles, their arms outstretched like they're pretending to be birds, like they're playing some kind of strange flying game.

Konstantin is twisting his head from side to side. *Help*, he's saying. *Help me.* I want to do something, something must be done, it has to end. So I crouch down, pick up a piece of paving stone, grit my teeth, raise my arms above his head. From a far distance, I hear adults shouting on balconies. I hear a siren. Then the world goes soft and dark and my body turns into air.

I wake on Mama's mattress in the hallway, my head in her lap. She's stroking my hair in a strange way, *you're safe, you're safe, you're safe*, she says. My sisters are up in the apartment, which is unusual. They stare at me with bottomless eyes.

"What's wrong with him?" Aisha asks. "Do something to fix him."

"I had a strange dream," I say.

"It's all a strange dream," Mama whispers. "It's all a terrible dream."

‡ ‡ ‡

AISHA AND I RUN ALL THE WAY TO OUR WAR school in the basement of the house on Marije Bursac Street, zigzagging and hugging walls along open stretches. Mama said okay without even thinking about it for a minute after I told her that Baka told me to tell her that we had to go, that otherwise our brains would begin to rot. She said, yes, yes, Jevrem—but I'm not sure she really heard what I was asking. Berina can't come, she's too weak.

Whenever you're out, always make sure something is between you and rooftops, windows in buildings, anything two or three floors up, Baka says. Look for the shields that the soldiers have built, out of buses and cars piled up and other city wreckage. Never stand still. She keeps on trying to sound like a tough old partisan, but sometimes she can't even stand up from her chair in the basement. She wants to take us to school, but her bones hurt, and so does her chest, her lungs, her heart.

The room is stuffy and dark. All the students in the rows behind the first fall asleep soon after class starts. There are only four rows. Nezira sits in the front row and points her face at the teacher. She says she can sleep with her eyes open, like I do sometimes too. Aisha sits next to her, but she's alert, back straight, eyes wide. She knows the answers to all the questions, she does the exercises and tests twice, once for herself and once for Berina. Zakir sits next to me. He has an eye infection that looks terrible. He keeps touching it with his dirty fingers, then leaning over and putting his hand on my shoulder while he whispers into my neck. And at the back of the room, Papa sometimes stands in the door listening to the lesson with his head tilted to one side, his chin resting in one palm the way he does. Whenever I look back at him, he steps into the hallway so I won't be distracted. So I face forward properly and pay attention.

The teacher doesn't ever get a good night's sleep. Some days she doesn't have anything to eat. She hates living with her husband's parents now that her husband is dead. She feels sad they didn't have a baby. She feels tormented they didn't leave together the way he wanted. She looks at their photo albums every night. She tells us these things every morning when class starts, then writes some words on the small homemade blackboard and tells us to copy them. The lessons have no beginning, middle, or end, her words are as tired as the men who sit in the lobby. Baka says I should be polite to her, it's hard to be a teacher even in good times. She's probably not getting paid.

We add up fractions.

We take apart sentences, looking for verbs or nouns or adjectives.

We study the festivals and traditions of the Masai tribe in Kenya. Our teacher once went there. Her husband was an anthropologist.

‡

NEZIRA and I sit side by side in the first-floor stairwell after school. There's a lot we could do, like search for useful things, because Mama doesn't keep track of me anymore, she's too tired all the time, like someone put a spell on her. But we're tired too, so we're taking a break. The door is open a crack. Outside, it's a sunny day and flowers are blooming like it's a normal spring in a normal year. Inside, the light is dim, the steps smell of pee. Nezira's looking at me and I know what she sees. I'm thin as a twig, and so is she. I didn't know how little time it takes for a city to empty of food, for people to get hungry and cold, to feel desperate to eat, to feel shaky and fragile and panicked. It takes only a few days, really, if you think about it, no trucks coming in on the highways, no trucks stopping in the markets, in front of the shops; if you think about skipping one meal, how it puts you in a terrible mood, then another meal, then another one, how soon you feel really ill and weak, how quickly the fat ones get thinner, the thin ones get skinny.

And then those days drag on and turn into a week, into two weeks, and three weeks, and you feel nauseous and hollow, just like Baka told me, then desperate, and you don't want to talk about it, you don't have the energy, there are no words. Your mind stretches and stretches because it doesn't know when being hungry will end, and the mind doesn't like that, not at all. You want to eat anything, grass maybe, drink your own blood from your veins. You curse the smugglers who lurk in your lobby, who could get you food if you had the money. You hate their evil guts. And then there are more days, and more. And it feels like forever. *But the human body can survive on very few calories, don't you worry, Jevrem,* Papa tells me. *Baka and her comrades did it, you only have to persuade your mind that it's okay, that you will live.* I see him getting into the elevator every time

I'm in the hallway of our building. The door opens, he goes in, the door shuts. He tells me things I need to know. He whispers them right into my mind.

We're a fine pair, Nezira and me, like the animals in the zoo, no one there to feed them, no one to let them go. I lean over and kiss her on the mouth. Her lips are dry and hot, her breath tastes of earth. She lets me. I kiss her harder. She doesn't seem to mind, or at least she doesn't stop me. She doesn't move at all.

Part Two

Spring 1997

―――――

When the Smoke Clears, Here I Am

3

I LOOK OUT OF THE KITCHEN WINDOW AT BRANCHES moving in the dusk. April has made the garden green, but it's raining ice pellets. Welcome to Toronto. I try to remember when spring came at home. It's absurd that I can't, it's only been a year since we left, but that year feels longer than the whole freaking four-year siege, which just kind of went on and on bitch-slapping us until we all got numb and time stopped moving forward. Suddenly, I desperately want a cigarette. Behind me, Mama moves slowly between sink and stove; Aisha whisks plates and cutlery around like a circus performer.

Baka shuffles up to me. She says, "Why don't you boys do some good for once?" I look down at her, she's so tiny and frail these days it makes me crazy. She says it again. She knows I'm not really paying attention even though I'm looking her right in the face. She's been nagging me like this for months. *Why don't you do some good for once?* With that pained look of hers. Sometimes it washes over me, and sometimes it makes me angry. I sit at the table and stare at my fork like I've never seen one before. Or a spoon, or plate, or glass. Everything glows eerily in the dim overhead light, a single sixty-watt bulb covered by a dusty paper shade. Sometimes, the table gets smaller and smaller until it's a tiny circle the size of a bottle cap. Mama, Aisha, Baka, Milan, and Iva, maybe some distant relative or family friend, cling to its edge like strange little creatures, slugs maybe.

Baka thinks I'm a smart boy who fell in with the wrong crowd. But she's wrong, I'm the wrong crowd, and the others, those poor fucking bastards, fell in with me.

Downstairs in my bedroom after supper, I smoke a joint, then a cigarette, play with my computer, smoke another cigarette, smoke another joint. Do some good? To her, doing good is dressing neatly, getting a buzz cut every two weeks, studying lame old textbooks about a past that is dead and gone. Saying please and thank you, following orders given by your superiors: teachers, doctors, politicians, priests, the ones who will lead you into the next disaster. By her definition, the Nazi SS did some good just by keeping their uniforms clean, washing behind their ears, standing straight, modelling good posture to the rest of the world.

Lie. Lie. Lie. Baka isn't like that at all. I'm describing someone else's baka. Mine doesn't give a rat's ass about posture or haircuts, never has, which is why when she looks at me in that disappointed way, it feels like daggers in my heart. You see, if you were a partisan in World War Two, lived in the forest for years, kicked the shit out of the Nazi and Italian invaders, you'd be the definition of good too, it doesn't matter what you did with the rest of your life. How can anyone compete with that shit? *Our* war was just a bunch of maniacs killing each other, and people in faraway places watching and making the decisions. They say that Sarajevo was a lie. But Sarajevo was the truth, it was multi-religious for hundreds of years. Then the lousy lie that it was a lie and all was ruined. And here I am rotting in a basement in a city a world away. It's so flat here. No mountains, no river valley, no spring.

My room is freezing, but I've got a space heater, one of the first items I ever liberated, from a huge creaky house in Bloor West Village with a hundred rooms. I go over to it and crank it to high. I think about that space heater quite a bit, and also about the word *liberate*. The space heater, just that little box, plus just a couple of hours of electricity each night, makes a big difference to the outcome of things, a life-and-death kind of difference. People don't think about that stuff enough, how people need just a few basic things to keep on living. It might have saved Berina's life, that little shitty box of a space heater and two hours of motherfucking electricity. That's all it would probably have taken to keep her from fading away as the war years piled up. One day, she just didn't wake up in that rank basement, she just lay there unmoving on her mattress, her little hands curled at her side, like a wax doll on display, everyone wailing and moaning over her. I think about all those people crowding around her, how no one could believe it, a little girl dying in her sleep in this day and age. I can hardly remember what she looked like, which is strange since she looked exactly like Aisha. I don't remember her funeral either. I was there, they say, it was a sunny day, not a cloud in the sky, remember? But they must be wrong.

And *liberate*, well, that's just another word for "steal" in the English language.

Outside, a vicious wind makes the tree branches crack. What was the sound of the wind back home? What was the smell of April, of May? What I recall is the stink of burning furniture, tires, metal, brick; the stench of smouldering clothes, shoes, curtains, sheets, books. What I'm forgetting is the feeling of buildings jammed close together, of walkways, cars, parks, markets, statues, fountains all jig-sawed into place, every square foot tended over centuries, every square foot accounted for. Now there's a new feeling for a new city. The feeling of the space between things, of structures standing solitary amidst weeds, of millions of square feet of concrete sidewalk, of vast lawns that no one uses. The relief of that, so much emptiness for everyone to breathe into their lungs without getting on each other's nerves.

DUŠAN shows up from the front, and strange things happen. That's the dream I have over and over again, about once a week. He's eating dinner with us in his dirty uniform, and then he drags me out of the apartment building and around the city looking for jars of honey to take back to his comrades. We find some jars of honey, but when we open them we see that the honey has gone bad, it's scaly and brown and smells of crap. I want to throw the jars away, but Dušan says no, he says we should bring them up into the mountains and leave them for the wolves. He says the wolves are starving because of the war. He says, *the animals don't deserve to suffer because of us.* And I think, of course, Dušan is genius: we can leave the city and give the jars to the wolves.

That's one of the dreams. But sometimes the dream is a nightmare. Dušan shows up from the front and he's just been badly wounded. A leg is missing, his guts are hanging out, half his face is gone, something like that. I turn away, I can't face the flesh, the blood, the jagged ends of his broken bones. He screams at me to look at him, to not be such a fucking coward, but I wander off and get distracted by some unimportant thing like finding my school books or a pack of smokes. Everything is such a mess in the apartment, all our stuff thrown together on the floor, that I spend forever picking through books and clothes and random objects before I remember Dušan and go back to where he is lying and find there's a loud party going on. Ujak Luka and his girlfriend are hosting it, and a hundred people have shown up in tuxedos and fancy dresses, all laughing and drinking and shouting happily at each other. And there is Dušan, propped up in a corner soaked in blood and bleeding out, a bottle of beer standing in the black sticky pool around him. He's talking and joking with a girl, but I can tell that he's in agony, he's sweating and shivering, his hands are white-knuckling his thighs, and between bursts of conversation, he pants softly like a little dog. It's an eerie sound, a sound that follows me when I wake up, when I'm trying to get through the next day.

Dušan did show up one day, standing at the apartment door a few months after he went missing. He looked like someone else, someone much older, with deep, pimply lines from his nostrils to the corners of his mouth. He chain-smoked and told us about trenches filled to the knees with water, about boredom and cold, but left out the fighting parts, he didn't want to talk about that, not in front of Mama. He told her he hadn't really disappeared, there'd just been some confusion about what sector he was meant to be in.

When we were alone, just the two of us huddled in his bedroom smoking our faces off, I asked him again, where did you go missing to? I want to know. But he wouldn't tell me either. He said it doesn't matter. I asked him what happened to Papa, how did he die, was he there when it happened? And he snapped, *Papa got shot, Jevrem, what do you think?* And I tried some other questions.

What was it like at the front, what was it like to actually fight in a battle? Has he killed anyone yet? What was the food like? Where did they go to the toilet? I thought he'd want to tell me all the gory details, he always liked to freak me out. But now he said nothing, he just fiddled with his Walkman, turning the dial, listening, turning the dial. I whined and begged, I wanted to know, it wasn't fair. Finally, he turned on me and grabbed me by the throat and crushed my head against the wall. He had a weird expression on his face, like his head was about to explode, and his eyes were squeezed shut tight. *Shut up*, he hissed. *Shut up, shut up, shut up.*

The evening before he had to leave again, when we were sitting with Mama on her mattress, he told us about seeing our uncle, Stric Pavle, on the other side, that Stric Pavle held his gun in the air and waved and smiled, that he shouted something that Dušan couldn't hear. This story made Mama cry and turn over to face the wall for the rest of the day. I think about our uncles quite a bit now, wondering where they are, if they feel bad they fought against us, if they're pissed off that we fought against them. I think about Stric Pavle's motorcycle, a good one from Germany, how he raced up and down the hillside roads with us on the back after Sunday lunch. Maybe the motorcycle is still sitting in my grandparents' garage on the other side of the river, maybe the people who took over their house use it now. After the motorcycle ride, we would lounge around in the backyard with all the colourful flowers my baba planted and they'd smoke pot and cigarettes, take swigs from a flask, crack jokes and laugh so hard they'd cry. Sometimes they gave me a puff. Those were good times. The garden was full of butterflies.

I think about it quite often, Dušan hissing *shut up* at me over and over again. How strong his hand was, how I couldn't breathe at all, that terrible look on his face. The morning that he left I really wanted to say something to him, something nice, I wanted to bring up some funny story about when we were younger, but I couldn't think of any funny story. All I could picture was watching soccer on TV with him, with Papa there too, how we jumped up and slammed our palms together and shouted every time our team scored, which wasn't really funny, or much of a special story, since we had watched games together about fifty thousand times. But Dušan ate breakfast with his head down, his eyes focused on his hands, and I couldn't find a way to break his bubble. Mama sat silently at the table, watching every move Dušan made. When he left, he dragged me with him down the hall to the elevator. When the elevator came, he dragged me into it and as it descended we watched the light travel down the numbers over the door. At the front door, Dušan finally said something to me. He said, "When all of this is over, let's do some things together again, okay?" And he sort of ruffled my hair with one hand in a way he'd never done before.

But then, a week after he went back to the front, Dušan was killed too. Mama told us. It was like a punch in the face. When the ringing in my ears stopped, the whole world was changed forever. There was another funeral on the hill, in the rain, people sobbing and wailing, I can't remember who. Mama was frozen like a statue, and Aisha and Berina faced the wrong way, their little chalky faces staring across the valley at who knows what. And everyone thinking about snipers aiming at their own skulls, that was the problem with funerals on the hill. And me? Well, I couldn't concentrate on everyone's pitiful sadness, it seemed pointless and pathetic to me, it made me furious. What did everyone expect would happen if you send a kid off to war? What was wrong with all the fucking stupid, sobbing, bullshitting adults? Making wars, then wailing about the dead children. They were ridiculous, absurd. They made me sick. Instead, I was thinking about other things, about food and the things people need to live a proper life, how stupid and humiliating it was to be huddled in this little city, burning our furniture, our socks, our underwear, our sports equipment, pencils, art projects, everything we own, for heat, hungry all the time, while the rest of the world went right on living their normal happy piggish selfish ignorant lives all around us in every direction, not giving a damn, buying cool new stuff, throwing half of it away again, going on vacation, playing soccer, swimming in lakes, having barbecues with neighbours, watching crappy TV shows for six hours every night, maybe watching us on the news for five seconds. Well, I wasn't going to sit around crying my eyes out like a moronic little bastard, I was going to look after myself in this city full of smugglers and thugs and movers and shakers, and when I got out, I'd look after myself some more, no matter what.

I wake up suddenly, my hand numb, crumpled against my cheek. I'm lying on my bed. They're still at it upstairs. Coffee and rakija, voices shrill, everyone sitting on shitty furniture in our second-hand living room. You could almost say they sound happy, like in the old days when Mama and Papa sat around forever after the plates were cleared talking, talking, but I see how Mama prepares for these Sunday dinners, dragging herself out to shop with the money Milan gives her, moving around the kitchen in slow-motion, her face expressionless and pale, her shoulders slumped forward. She invites Milan and Iva over because she has to, because they rescued us and sponsored our start in Canada, because they're old friends from university back home, because it's the right thing to do. And other friends and distant relatives too, to show we made it out in one piece. But it's a lie. She wants to crawl into bed in the afternoon, pull the covers over her head forever. She wants to let herself come apart in a thousand separate pieces, each sharp as a shard of glass. I know because I read her like a book, I hear her sobs every single night, and every morning I see her crumpled face, I see her washed-out eyes and everything that's gone. I know Papa and Dušan visit her in her dreams. And little Berina too.

As for the rest of the family, Ujak Luka never shows up for a visit. He's in L.A. with a tan, a fast car, some teenage porn star on his arm, living life big like a movie director or a pimp or a criminal mastermind, or that's what I imagine, anyway, from the way Mama and Baka talk about him. He's a hedonist, Baka says, which sounds like a pretty good solution to life's bullshit, but no one knows how he makes a living. Does he ever do any acting or producing? Does he run a gaggle of whores? We don't know because Mama won't talk to him. He's a coward, she says, he's a traitor, he's a bum, and she doesn't even want to hear his name. And no one from Papa's family made the big move over the Atlantic. Baba and Deda never left Belgrade, never saw their house again, Stric Pavle is in Australia, Stric Obrad got killed right at the end, after four years of fighting. We don't know what happened to Stric Ivan, if he's dead or alive. Milan's reliable source back home says Ivan, Papa's own brother, was one of Arkan's bodyguards, making him a member of the worst bunch of crazy vicious killer Chetnik motherfuckers around. I think about this quite a bit. I know brothers can be different. I think about Dušan and me, how much I'm like him now, how close he is to me when I'm asleep, how the feeling of him is with me all the time. How I would let him come out with us at night sometimes, if he was here.

I sit up feeling dazed and look around the dim room strewn with junk. The others will be here soon. Then I hear someone creeping slowly down the stairs. And there is Aisha poking her head in the door.

"Jevrem," she says, "can I come in?" She's almost as tall as I am, and thin as a runway model. She stopped eating when Berina died.

"No," I say, "go back upstairs."

"Oh, Jevrem." Aisha's head droops.

I stare at her, feeling sorry, the kind of sorry that rises up and chokes your throat like a nightmare.

"No, I don't have time. My friends are coming over soon."

"Oh, Jevrem, you never say yes." Her eyes are two dark pools of feeling I don't want to see.

"On the weekend," I say. I lie. I know I won't hang with her then, or any other time; she reminds me of the others, of the way things used to be.

"Okay," she says, "maybe we can play chess or something." She turns slowly and walks back up the stairs.

The school social worker, Ms. Markowski, says I'm a patho-logical liar. Well, maybe she doesn't use those exact words but I know that's what she means when she says I tell stories to protect my inner self. She gets a kick out of digging around in my life, asking a thousand nosy questions with her eyebrows raised to show how much she cares. She asks about Mama, Papa, Dušan, the twins, back home, the siege, what it was like, why I don't care about school. Do I do drugs? Am I in a gang? How do I feel? Do I have flashbacks, bad dreams, frightening thoughts, sweaty palms, a racing heart? Do I feel on edge, angry, numb, disconnected, sad, or constantly in danger? Can I get to sleep at night? She says, you can tell me, it helps to talk about it. She really wants me to tell her all about the war; she keeps asking, almost salivating for those blood-soaked sob stories. I see her wet lips and gleaming eyes. But I tell her I have a brain injury from being dropped on my head as a baby, that's my problem, the war was nothing, that my father, brother, and sister live in a mansion on Lake Constance, the Swiss side, my parents are separated but not divorced, that I have a trust fund waiting for me when I turn eighteen. From the tobacco fortune my father smuggled out of the country just before the war. And a whole bunch of other things that feel like they could easily be true, that become truer and truer the more I talk about them, while she raises her eyebrows, nods her head, writes her notes.

The thing is, I leave her office looking forward to visiting Papa on Lake Constance during school vacations, to drinking cocktails with them on the family yacht on sunny Sunday afternoons, to partying all night with rich slutty German girls, to water-skiing drunk and doing lines of coke off the hood of a Rolls-Royce. I can picture it all, Papa, Dušan, Berina all tanned and preppy, wearing Ray-Bans and topsiders, jumping off the boat for a swim twenty times a day, playing cards anchored out on the lake under a huge full moon. The thing is, a deliberate liar knows when he is lying, but a pathological liar may not. I looked it up. A pathological liar lies all the time, without cause, which after a while could get really confusing and disappointing.

I get out of bed and brush my hair with my hands, take a gulp of warm beer from a bottle that's been sitting there for days. The thing is, I paid attention after she told me I was a liar a few months ago, and sure enough I walked out of that office and told my first lie half a second later to this guy Chris who was on his way to lunch. He asked me where I'd just been because I wasn't in English class and I said I was in the car with this girl Marni.

I mean, why didn't I say I was with the social worker? It's not like I'm ashamed of it. Everyone knows I see the social worker. Everyone sees the social worker. Chris sees the social worker. It's cool to see the social worker, because it means that you're fucked up, and being fucked up is cool in this country because it means that you've lived a little. In this country, the worst thing is to have a boring life, but everyone does—they don't know what excitement is.

I lied for no reason this afternoon when I sat down in the cafeteria with the gang and Madzid asked when we're going to get that guy Andrew who called Madzid a rag-head and sand-nigger right to his face because Madzid asked that girl Silvia or Silvana or whatever her goddamn name is out for a drink. And I said, I don't know, what dude called Andrew? But that wasn't true. I did know. I knew exactly.

When someone lies it tells the truth about them, about their psychological state, so it's not really a lie. That's what Sava says, and Sava's truly smart. Last year she had a zine called *Propaganda* and in it she told lie after lie but each one was also the absolute truth, if you looked at things from a different angle. She was trying to make some kind of complicated point, but we're too busy for that kind of nerdy stuff now. Most nights we're out roaming the city, taking what's necessary, seeing what's to be seen, looking after ourselves.

The thing is, I didn't appreciate the way Ms. Markowski said pathological lying is connected to other bad behaviours like conduct disorder, antisocial personality disorder, inappropriate aggression, destructiveness, and serious violations of rules and laws. Apparently, this condition is caused by either "challenging situations in the home" or a lack of serotonin in the head, in which case Prozac or Zoloft can help. And maybe psychotherapy. That's what she said. I told her I don't have any of those bad behaviours, not one. But of course, I was lying. And I don't tell her how I often see Papa early in the morning after a long night of drinking and hunting and gathering. He's walking along the street, hands in his pockets, head down. He's about to duck into a doorway, or turn a corner, or disappear into a park and be lost from sight. Or he's fixing things on the driveways and front lawns of strangers' houses. Bikes, swings, porch railings.

My room is in the basement, the story of my life. There's fake wood panelling, peeling paint, a mildewy old carpet, a mattress without sheets, what's the point, I've got my old sleeping bag from when I was a kid. There are clothes and garbage all over the floor, and random crap stuffed in the closet, CDs, magazines, some broken toys from when I was young that we brought over for some reason no one can think of. It's a complete mess down here, everything's junk, except for some of Papa's things that I picked out of the rubble in the apartment before we left. The old camera he was fixing, his old hat, which still has the alive smell of his head, his Holiday Inn ashtray, a couple of stubby pencils with his tooth marks on the end, the wooden box with the frog on top. It held coins and paper clips and thumbtacks then, and still does today. And two of his notebooks, one filled with his handwriting and one almost empty. It has only one line in it: *Camus wrote: 'There are causes worth dying for, but none worth killing for.' Can this really be true?*

I'm hungry again, but I don't want to go upstairs, to face that sad scene. I check chip bags for crumbs. I light a smoke. Ms. Markowski asked me about Papa's things, if I've made a shrine out of them, and I said, why would I do that, that's creepy fucked-up shit. He wasn't a god. But I lied, I did make a shrine out of them, sort of, all his things arranged on a milk crate beside my bed. She said, use his notebook to write about the war and about life now, what you're feeling and doing every day. It will help you make sense of life, it will make things easier. As if a few scribbles could do so much. I never write a single word. And that's a big fat lie too.

Mama didn't bring much from the wrecked apartment, only some clothes, a few papers that didn't get burnt, Papa's old typewriter from the early '80s and his favourite lighter, which stands on her chest of drawers like a tiny solitary tombstone in a big unfriendly field. When we moved in, Baka put out her framed photos and blankets and tablecloths to make the place less depressing. But Mama said no, she didn't want to see the photos, the one with Papa holding Dušan and me up in the air by the straps of our life jackets, a river flowing behind us; the one with the twins curled up together like newborn puppies in a little basket the day they were born; the one with Mama and Papa after a concert, their fancy clothes and their flashy, superstar smiles. She said, please Bako, take them to your room.

I look at the clock and it's 8:20 p.m. Where are those motherfuckers? They're late. We call ourselves The Bastards of Yugoslavia, as a joke. We like the word *bastard*. It's got a ring to it, and has a lot of different meanings. It's what the nationalists who took over our country called us, the offspring of women in mixed marriages. They meant it as an insult, but we feel proud. It's why we're here, together, in this flat, endless city next to an abnormally large lake. They didn't want us back home, not really, in all their new separate little cleaned-up countries, Slovenia, Croatia, Serbia and Montenegro, Macedonia. And Bosnia, split completely in half, Croats and Muslims on one side, Serbs on the other. Where were we beautiful mongrels meant to fit?

They still haven't left the kitchen table upstairs. In my mind's eye, I see Mama sitting stiff and silent at the table, a cigarette in one hand, the smoke rising slowly above her head, her face pointed at whoever is talking, but her gaze somewhere else, seeing some other scene in some other time. And Aisha, hovering over the table, serving food, mixing drinks, arranging dessert on a plate, making coffee, doing dishes, like she always does. Every weekend it's the same depressing thing. Don't Milan and Iva and their friends get bored? Don't they notice that Mama can't wait for them to be gone, for their yacking to stop? Every time, it's the same old gossip about other Yugo immigrants. Who insulted who, which fascist bastards are keeping the war alive on this side of the ocean, who are still old Tito communists, who were undercover agents for which side, who appeared with whom at which Sunday service at the Croatian parish, or the Serbian diocese. Mama's not interested. She wasn't into that stuff back home, why would she be here, like we're in some tiny peasant village in the countryside? But the guests can't get enough of it. They go on and on about the lovely folkloric dancing at the hall. Oh my God, Mama sometimes says very quietly, please, not folk music, we're cosmopolitan people, let us live in this century. But no one listens to her, they just keep on yapping—what's happening at the pavilion, the hall, in the Serbo-Croatian newspapers. What famous people are actually Croats or Serbs but have changed their names? Who gave the most money to which side during the war? Who was in the arms-smuggling business? And, they say, I should join the Serbian community theatre group, or a Croatian choir. Are they fucking out of their minds? You'll love it, they say, giving you a wholesome connection to your people and your homeland. I'd rather be burned on the forehead by a thousand shitty wartime cigarettes.

At some point in the evening they always ask Mama to play for them, and she always makes some excuse. I think of how gorgeous she was sitting at her baby grand back home in her satin dresses, with her sweeping hair, red lips, glittering eyes, a sensation in our living room and on the stage. But the truth is, she hasn't played at all since we landed here, even though Milan and Iva put a lot of work into finding her a piano, raising the money to buy it, moving it into our cramped little living room. This old church-basement wreck, Mama said when it arrived, tears streaming down her cheeks. They're so generous, I'm so grateful, but what do they think I can do with this pile of kindling? Mama was going to break into the North and South American orchestra and ensemble scene, she was going to teach at the conservatory. Or that's what everyone thought. But the conservatory doesn't need another teacher, her agent isn't calling, her old contacts have lost touch. The thing is, if you don't perform for four years because you're trapped in an exploding city, it's easy for everyone to forget about your genius. And anyway, how is she meant to play the most beautiful music ever composed when her soul is hollowed out by death like a rotten tree, when her playing would bubble up from somewhere deep under a stagnant, filthy lake of corpses.

And in my mind's eye there's Baka sitting opposite me ignoring the ridiculous table talk, looking at me in that way, like she wants to catch my attention, to say something really important. Like she wants to repeat it one more time: why don't you boys do some good for once? She can hardly lift her fork these days, let alone her voice. She wouldn't go to the hospital during the siege, even though she had a hard time breathing, even though she couldn't walk up a single stair. Hospitals in wartime are for soldiers and wounded civilians, she said, that's the first rule of war. So now her heart is damaged beyond repair, and without a working heart you begin to fade away, like houses in war zones that look like shit, grey and stained and abandoned-looking, even if fifteen families live in them, after only a couple of years or so.

She was so much younger back home, and so was I. She was a warrior, I was "open and enthusiastic." That's what my grade four report card said, anyway. I know that because Mama saved our reports and brought them over and I read through mine after Ms. Markowski told me I'm a pathological lying fuck-up. I wanted to see when that lying thing slithered into my life, when it got a hold of my mind. Probably it was only a year ago, when I was fifteen, soon after I got off the plane at Pearson International, when I told my grade ten class, in my ridiculous English, that I was a survivor of four years of war and the longest siege of a capital city in the history of modern war, and my teacher told me not to exaggerate, and I told her it was the truth, I was shot in the stomach, a big long wound needing thirty-seven giant spidery stitches. When I said that, all the kids rolled their eyes and sniggered, which I thought was weird, but the thing is, they thought I was telling the most stupid kind of lie, the kind that couldn't possibly be true. And I said, I have a scar to prove it, and I pulled up the itchy second-hand sweater they hassled me about along with my name, which no one can pronounce because of the *j*-like-a-*y* sound, *Yevrem*, and showed the scar on my belly, which was still kind of shiny and purple back then. There I was with my white stomach exposed to the teacher and all the students with their smallish, red-rimmed eyes, and for a moment I thought I was going crazy. I thought, maybe I'm wrong, maybe World War Two was the war-to-end-

all-wars-two, maybe my own war happened in my head somehow, that it came out of my own filthy imagination. So I said,
okay, I didn't get the scar in a war, I got it falling off my bike
going down a steep hill. We've got steep hills back home.

Later, the teacher told me she was sorry she'd put me on the
spot, but it was too late for me. The kids had already laughed,
I'd already lied my first lie.

THE BASTARDS have no discipline, it's a sad fact. Where are
they? We've got stuff to do. Baggies to fill, boys to bring into
line, livelihoods to make. Specifically this Andrew motherfucker who called Madzid a rag-head, we'll drag him out of
his parents' house and beat the crap out of him, then do a
house ten blocks over while we're at it. I need more plun-
der to get more cash to give to Mama, which she'll refuse to
take. Maybe Baka needs something nice. A blouse or slippers,
a pearl necklace or whatever the fuck someone old and sick
like her would want. I have no idea. But that's a lie. I know
what she wants. She wants to spend time with me like when I
was small, tell me her stories, sing some communist working
songs. I loved her then because she was fierce, like a woman
should be. Now she sits on the living room couch all day staring at nothing. Now she shuffles and shakes, now she nags at
me with accusing eyes.

They're finally here. They clatter down the stairs, Milan,
who's sitting at the kitchen table with Mama, calling after
them, "Hey, aren't you going to say hello to your elders?" in
that half-joking, half-serious way of his. He tries to get me
to go out with him, to be my male role model or some such
ridiculous horseshit. He even bribes me with beer, as if that's

a huge thrill for me, so he can sit me down and tell me how things are with my family. Your mother repressed her grief the whole time she worked to get you and Aisha and Baka here to Canada, and now it's coming out, now she's suffering so much. She needs your support, Jevrem, she needs you to be considerate. Can you do that for her? But Mama's got Aisha to be the perfect child, she doesn't need me for that. She needs me to dig in the grime, even if she hates me for it, because sometimes you have to do what you have to do to get what you need, whether people like it or not.

Geordie, Zijad, Madzid, Sava, and me, that's our gang of little bastards. The five of us spend time together, time and energy and other people's money. We lie around and dream, we go out into the night and do things. They're all Yugo too, speak the same language, share the same memories of humanitarian lunch packets, water pills, rice and beans, smelly stoves, lineups, noise, dirt, rubble, feeling sick and weak and bored and terrified. Of death everywhere. But we're more than that, we're nomads of the world, that's what Zijad says when he's in a dreamy, philosophical state, when he's snorted some random pills he's found in a rich person's bathroom cabinet. Ethnicity-is-destiny is bullshit, the biggest lie, that's pretty obvious everywhere you look around the world, he says, but we know each other's background anyway, it's impossible not to since the war. That's how the fascists ruined things for us.

"I've got the stuff." Geordie sits down on the floor, takes off her ski jacket. She lived pretty close to us back home but I didn't know her there. She's Croat one hundred percent, which means mixed in with a bunch of bloodlines, Italian, Austrian, Hungarian, Gypsy, Albanian, ones that can never be mentioned, so she's still a bastard to us.

"Roll us a few," says Zijad, and makes himself comfortable on my sleeping bag. He's the son of Dora and Orhan, Mama and Papa's friends who didn't make it out of the city. They were killed on their way to a concert one day, so much for culture. He doesn't talk about them. He's also a dog's breakfast of Bosniak, which means he's Muslim, with traces of Turkish and German and Macedonian, staying with his Bosniak aunt and uncle not far from here. The three of us met at some lame Yugo event just after we landed in Toronto.

"Here, I'll do it, pass it here." Madzid is huge, with long dark hair hanging in his eyes. He's a Bosniak on one side, a Catholic Croat and Italian on the other, with a Serb grandfather lurking somewhere in his closet too.

"Hey, Andric," says Sava, "you motherfucker." She slumps down against the wall. She calls me by my last name, I don't know why. She's Serbian with Slovenian and Jewish and Hungarian mixed in, so what?

A year ago, when we started grade ten, we found Madzid and Sava wandering the hallways of our school, a skinny pair of pale homesick Yugo kids looking for some action.

"Hey," I say back. I think of adding *you cocksucker* for half a second but I can't say the words out loud. Putting Sava's mouth on some random cock even just in all our minds as a joke is impossible, that's how proud and untouchable and glorious she is.

Sava is gorgeous in a rough kind of way, combining fearless strength and agility with crazy curves and long, supermodel legs, an unholy combo for any warm-blooded onlooker like me, especially when she flicks her blond fuck-you hair over her shoulder while staring you down with mountain-grey eyes and an angry pouting mouth. I could stare at her non-stop for the rest of time, but she walks like a fighter and growls at me when

I do, so I only look when she can't see, when she's distracted by being pissed off with the rest of the world. Whenever she's around, I feel okay, like there's one upside to life, like at least one glittering ray of sunshine is making it through the murky fog of existence. I wish I could grab her and kiss her for ten thousand years, but that's not how she rolls.

"It's fucking crazy outside," says Zijad. "It's raining and snowing at the same time. And there's lightning. Total weather overkill."

Geordie pulls a huge bottle of vodka, a bottle of Jack Daniel's, a large plastic bag of weed, and a scale out of her knapsack. Madzid begins to roll. The rest of us sit on the carpet in a circle, smoking cigarettes and bagging weed into small, super-locking Ziplocs. We don't speak, we're on a schedule. It's in moments like this, when we're all together, before the action begins, that I sometimes think of Pero and the others. Mahmud, Zakir, Cena, and Nezira, how we used to hang out in the same way, the younger-kid version of us Bastards, with a soccer ball, skipping ropes, with our first cigarettes and our first kisses. I know they're alive somewhere, except Cena, breathing in and out just like us, scattered across the world, figuring things out, finding stuff to do, forgetting and remembering, trying to get by.

After a while, Mama comes down and stands in the doorway, speaking very quietly.

"Jevrem, it's Sunday evening, we have guests."

I say, "Sorry to disturb the endless family reunion, Ma, I'm going out." I know Mama has smelled the pot, but that's not what bothers her, and she doesn't care that I'm not entertaining the guests. Her main goal in life is to keep me at home safe, to keep me from walking out the door. "I'll be back soon," I add, a completely pointless lie.

We leave by the side door. Outside, ice is slicing down at an angle, but we don't feel it because we've just smoked a bale of weed, downed a bottle of cheap vodka, and our faces are numb. We run down the cement walkway and jump into Madzid's car, which is parked on the road. We love to drive all over town, weaving between evening commuters, zipping along deserted late-night roads, coming home early in the morning when the sun begins to rise. Gas is cheap here, gas is easy, you just go to the pump and buy it, no need to steal it, or bribe U.N. forces with cheesy Yugo porn to get it. Once, at 3 a.m., we raced all the highways of the city, up the curving Don Valley Parkway, across the sixteen-lane 401, down the 427, and across the Gardiner Expressway perched on its concrete pillars at the edge of the lake, flying like devils unleashed from hell, all the cops parked, eating doughnuts.

Zijad drives because Madzid is cracked, he snorted some blow, but Zijad is stoned and drives so slowly it feels like we're floating like exotic birdwatchers in a rubber dinghy along a swampy river of buckling asphalt. The icy rain makes the night seem darker, so we can hardly see the bedraggled little match-box houses of my neighbourhood glide by, with their tiny front lawns and crumbling cement steps, their short driveways and uneven walkways. C'mon, we say, step on it, but Zijad pulls out onto St. Clair in a wonky slow-motion arc, cars honking all around us. Jesus, we say, and observe with curiosity as he straightens out and begins to weave all over the road, bumping up onto the sidewalk, scaring the uptight pedestrians. It's funny watching the pedestrians scamper so awkwardly, but we aren't going to get to Andrew's place anytime soon, and I'm an impatient guy, so we stop and Sava gets in the driver's seat. When she drives the car is a heat-seeking missile.

Andrew's place is a small, rundown bungalow, just like mine, but there's a big old tree on the front lawn and pots of spring flowers on each side of the front door, so it looks more cheerful. By this time, it's only 9:20 p.m., and the lights are still on everywhere.

"Hey, his parents are around, what the hell?" says Sava. "Look the dad is at the door with a garbage bag. I thought they were meant to be out." She looks at me and frowns. "And it's only just past nine, we can't beat the crap out of him on his front lawn when the whole street's awake watching *Law and Order*."

"Losers," says Madzid. "It's the same show over and over again. Don't they realize that? Don't they get so bored they want to rip their eyeballs out?" He sighs. He has high standards when it comes to TV.

"It's escapism," says Zijad.

"Whatever," says Madzid. "What do these people need to escape from?"

He has a scraggly Ayatollah beard, a nose ring in his left nostril, and never wears more than a T-shirt and a jean jacket, even in deepest winter, to prove that there's only mind and no matter.

"Not escapism," I say. "All humans like to hear stories about other humans. We watch each other, we listen to each other, it's how we figure out how to act and feel. TV, movies, plays, they're all part of that."

"Yeah," Madzid says, "books, plays, opera, sitcoms, commercials, gossip. Stories for smart people, stories for dumb people."

So there we are sitting in a car in front of Andrew's friendly house having a ridiculous uninformed conversation about what makes the human mind and heart tick. I scowl at everyone.

"We're going in now anyway," I say. "Did he call you a fucking rag-head when everyone was asleep in their beds? No, he did not, so we won't give him the same courtesy."

We pull our scarves up over our faces and we pick up our weapons of choice. I have a gun, as always, the sniper's rifle I got from that creepy weird place way up in Maple. Lie. It's not really a sniper's rifle, that would cost a fortune. It's just a plain old crappy hand gun, the kind you can buy for a hundred bucks south of the border. The others have baseball bats, hunting knives, their fists. We get out of the car, march up to the house, open the front door, walk in. The front hallway is bright. There is a smell of bland food, chicken with rice, maybe, and some kind of air freshener. The TV is booming in the living room. Mom calls out to us, "Hey, who's there?" Then she appears in the hallway, goes pale, staggers backwards. With the scarves we probably look to her like battle-ready Mohawks. The poor freaking Indians, too nice and polite for their own good, and still the scariest motherfuckers she can think of.

Geordie and Sava are the ones who do a lot of the shouting and directing. Sava is as tall as I am, Geordie the opposite, small, dark, quick, and vicious as hell when it's necessary. Back home, they grew up in different neighbourhoods, their families on different sides of the roadblocks, their fathers and uncles shooting at each other across soccer fields, one-way streets, laundry lines, wading pools, rose gardens, and farmers' markets.

Sava slaps Mom across the face to get the ball rolling. Mom shrieks and falls to the floor. That's when Dad finally turns up in the hallway. I always like the part where the man shows up, when he tries to confront us, tries to take charge. Because he's always scared out of his mind, knowing he should save his women and children, save the day, but not knowing how to do it. The thing is, he has no tools or techniques, no plans or strategies or strength or fitness. He's always counted on his Y chromosome, like it can be heroic for him without any practice or thought at all.

I say to him, "Hey, Dad, where's Andrew?"

Dad says, "Get out of my house. Get out."

I say, "We're just looking for Andrew, and we want your TV too."

Dad says, "I'm calling the police."

Sava says, "No, you're not."

Dad says, "This is an outrage, young lady." I'm not lying, that's really what he says.

I say, "Go find Andrew."

Dad says, "Get out of my house."

Mom is crying in a heap. Her body looks awkward, broken. Like she hasn't sat on the floor in forty years.

Sava walks up to Dad menacingly, in that way she does so well. Dad sticks out his chest and steps back at the same time.

"Call Andrew," says Sava, softly.

"This is an outrage," says Dad again, more hesitantly.

So Sava punches Dad in the gut. Dad collapses slowly, then he's lying next to Mom, gasping and moaning and holding his stomach. It's so easy to hurt people, I think, just a small jab and they're writhing at your feet. While they're down blubbering and sniffling, we search the house. There's a bright yellow kitchen, a neat guest bedroom, a large beige master bedroom that smells of musty sheets. The living room has too much furniture in it, its large TV blabbing on about the massive amount of energy it takes to get a barrel of oil out of the ground. This stupidity depresses me, so I shoot the TV instead of taking it. Zijad is in the bathroom searching for the pills he likes the best, and the rest of us take slugs from the whisky on the sideboard, which burns nicely all the way down. There's a pipe on the mantelpiece but we can't find tobacco. I like the smell of pipes. They remind me of the old men back home, their wool vests, their non-stop chatter, the way they could sit on the bench for a whole day, not moving an inch. I wonder if they're still chattering now, or if they froze to death or got shot in the head one fine morning.

Andrew's probably downstairs. He'll come up in a couple of seconds. A gunshot catches people's attention, even the attention of a teenage boy connected by headphones to a stereo, lying on his bed, watching TV, playing games, jerking off, sleeping, dreaming, believing he's alpha dog.

We hear him shouting up, "Mom? Dad? What's going on?"

And here he is, wearing a sweatshirt, torn jeans, his longish hair matted at the back.

He sees us, freezes, then sprints for the back door. But Geordie is standing there. Small Geordie, with her bat. One swing and he's sprawling on the floor.

"No, no, no," says Andrew.

"Yes, yes, yes," we say.

We drag him outside onto the front lawn, then across it over purple and white crocuses to the tree. We surround him and begin our work, beating him up with rhythm. For about a minute we go at him, bats, the butt of my gun, fists, boots. Blood and snot fly out of his nose. His face twists and crumples. He begins to cry. We hear neighbours shout from across the street. We wave. "He's an asshole," we call to them. Then we hear hoarse shouts from Mom and Dad. Stop, we've called the police, the police are coming, they shout from the safety of their front door. When we've made our point, we sprint for the car, hop in, squeal down the street.

The cops will arrive in four minutes. They're always four minutes too late.

WE DRIVE north on Dufferin, east on St. Clair, then park on a side street for a few hours of drinking, toking, and smoking our faces off. It's after 1 a.m. when I direct Sava to the street that I've chosen, our diversion. The rest stare silently out the windows at the occasional dog walker, the overachieving jogger at the end of a long day. And there is Papa walking down the street, his hands in his pockets, his head down, his shoulders hunched over like he's deep in thought. I say, look, *there he is, the one with the newspaper under his arm*—but he turns a corner, he disappears into the night.

"What?" says Sava.

"Nothing," I say. One day they'll see him too, and they'll hassle me for not pointing him out sooner.

We turn onto a Forest Hill street that I've marked on my map as a perfect score. The houses here are mansions, pampered, tricked out, strangely close to Andrew's low-rent neighbourhood. We choose the house with the birch grove on the side, two fake marble lions guarding the front door, no lights showing inside. "Quick in and out," I say. The others ignore me. They know what to do. We spring up the pathway. I break a small side window and glass falls to the ground tinkling like high piano notes on the stone below. I shiver weirdly, like I always do at this part, then I open the window, slide through, and I'm inside. A comfortable gloom greets me, and good smells, wood wax, after-dinner coffee.

I open the door for the others and we search the first floor. Heavy velvety curtains. Persian rugs. Dazzling vases. China in display cases. The light bulbs in the lamps are still warm, the family has just gone to bed. Madzid and I sprint upstairs to see what's what. We hear a woman's shrill, breathy voice from the upstairs hallway.

"Who are you? What are you doing? What do you want? Who are you?"

Why does a grown woman's fear come out in the voice of a small girl? We see her standing in a shiny nightgown in the dim lights that illuminate greasy paintings in heavy frames, and behind her a man of medium height with tussled hair in his slippery dark blue PJs. He croaks, "What the hell? What's going on?" as we charge toward them for a flying tackle.

Geordie and Sava have followed, they've checked all the rooms. "We have a silk and satin couple in this house," Geordie sings out. "And a couple of flannel kids."

Madzid, Geordie, and Sava look after Mom and Dad in their room, so I visit the kids. The girl's room is a fluffy pink nightmare and she's Aisha's age. She's sitting perfectly still on the edge of her bed staring at me and Geordie with big shiny eyes. I feel huge and wild in with her stuffed toys and lace curtains and frilly cushions. I want to say, I'm not going to hurt you or rape you or anything fucked-up like that, I'm not a fucking barbarian, I'm only here to redistribute some wealth so we can all get on with our lives. You see, my mom the artist is cleaning toilets for rich people, the bullshit war that brought us here was everyone else's war too, your parents are a couple of spoiled, ignorant mofos, and, so, to conclude, what goes around comes around. But there's no time for informational or sentimental speeches of that sort. Geordie asks her if she has brothers and sisters.

"Yes," she whispers, "a brother."

"Call him," I say. "Go stand by your door."

"Zac, Zac, Zac," she calls in a soft, scratchy voice. Her lips are quivering. In a few seconds there is Zac, a big boy, about twelve, face pale, eyes wide and darting.

"Look after your sister," I tell him, even though it's a ridiculous thing to say. He may be big, but he's just a kid.

"Don't follow me," I tell him. "Stay in this room."

In the master bedroom, the silk and satin couple are duct-taped together on the bed. "No, no, no, no, no," the woman cries. They've probably not been this close in years. They buck and writhe and we all watch, it's impossible not to, these two struggling without any hope of success.

Madzid empties out the jewellery cases. We hear Zijad crashing around downstairs.

"The basement's loaded," he shouts up to us.

We race down to the basement and are amazed. It's an electronics superstore, every kind of entertainment equipment known to man, most of it still in boxes, arrows pointing up.

‡ ‡ ‡

WITH MY SHARE OF BOOTY PILED HIGH IN MY bedroom, I lie on my bed, light a joint, drift into dreamland, to the place where wolves roam, sometimes as big as horses, sometimes tiny as rats, their furry wolf-heads bristling with teeth sharp as shrapnel. And there is Baka's face hovering right over mine, like it does when I'm tired, when I'm still, when I crash after a fix of adrenaline. Her teeth are out, her thin hair held in that net she used back in the first weeks of the siege when we had to rush down the garbage-strewn stairs to the basement every two minutes. Why do people stop cleaning in a war? Even a little sweeping would have made things better.

Now, hovering over me, she is whispering, *why don't you boys do some good for once?* She's hovering there, whispering into my ear, like she used to do. Telling me how much better the world was when she was young, singing a Dalmatian folk song about taming a pigeon. When I was a little kid in the basement, I liked that song with the pigeon. I danced with her when she was singing, we danced and sang and the pigeon cooed and pecked and burst into flight and flew up into the clear blue sky.

Golube golube pitomi
Proleti proleti kroz selo
I reci mojoj dragoj
Da stoji veselo.

Baka's songs were like a witch's spell against the shells that just wouldn't stop raining on the city from the hills around, wouldn't stop ever, not for an hour, or half an hour, or a quarter of an hour, or five minutes, even if you screamed and cried and threw yourself on the floor. On those endless nights, you closed your eyes, you clenched your teeth, you prayed to ghosts and martyrs floating around in the sky, and none of it changed anything. Baka's voice didn't bewitch the men in the hills and quiet their guns, but it made me feel better. It probably saved my mind.

Now Baka is singing to me again, "*Bad deeds breed bad deeds . . .*"—a new song she's invented in English, a language she never bothered to learn when we arrived here. I'm too old, she cried, when Milan suggested English-language courses, I don't want to be here, I want to be at home, in my own country. That's why Mama got Milan and Iva to find a Bosnian doctor for her, because she didn't sound like herself—she, the big warrior adventurer—she sounded like a sick person. That's how we found out her heart was shot, that's why Mama forces her to take the pills. Because she's only seventy-two and that's not too old these days to learn a new language, to start a new life. I guess she only had one new self in her.

Those are really bad lyrics, I say to her, I must be dreaming. But she brings her finger up to her mouth and says, shh. She sings the words again, this time using a different tune: "*Bad deeds breed bad deeds . . .*" Stupid old communist, stupid, ridiculous saying, I've seen how the world works. Nice, law-abiding people lose everything, criminals and warlords take what they want, ignorant motherfuckers believe what they see on TV. It was on television that we all first heard how much we hated each other, and the rest of the world believed it in an instant because they're lazy, spoiled, stupid idiots who know nothing and don't bother to find out. And now some other family lives in our apartment in Sarajevo and I wonder who they are, did they come into the city from the countryside after the war, can they hear Mama's piano playing in their sleep? I picture the details of the apartment, all our little knick-knacks, the ones we picked up on our vacations, the ones that were precious and not to be touched, the ones that belonged to our ancestors. I see our books and pictures, where the scissors were kept, the elastic bands, string, glue, batteries, tape, and ball-point pens, where the sunlight fell on the wall at certain times of the day. I smell the different smells of food Mama cooked, of perfume and soap in the white bathroom. I run from room to room, and I see that everything's still here just like it's always been. And outside, on a sunny afternoon, Sarajevo is like it's always been, a fairy-tale city with birds flying up in clouds, smoke rising from chimneys, clay tiles lying unbroken on roofs, narrow streets filled with strolling people, green domes nestled comfortably next to skinny spires, trees flowering triumphantly like the first spring. That's what my mind does sometimes when I'm drunk or stoned out of my mind and drift into sleep. It fixes everything.

‡

SAVA, my Sava, is reserved and powerful. Her face is always composed. Even when she's delivering a vicious left hook to the jaw of some surprised-looking guy, or binding arms to the back of a chair with duct tape, she has this stony face that tells you everything you need to know. I dream about her almost every night. Sometimes we're driving really fast in the car, squealing around corners, accelerating through mountain bush, getting away from the cops, or from bombs falling like hail from the sky. Sometimes we're in an apartment looking for something and there are strange, shady characters there with us, Celo's mafia goons who have looted every store in the city and are busy selling food to starving people at monster prices. Sometimes Sava is wrapping her arms and legs around me, and I'm so big inside her, moving so slowly and rhythmically like waves on Paradise Beach. And she's saying, yes, yes, yes, oh yes, oh God—that kind of pornographic thing. But it isn't like porno, it's like choirs of angels singing songs that make your heart explode over and over again and fly in a million different pieces throughout the universe..

I wake to find Mama standing over my bed, it must be morning. Jesus, I wish she wouldn't do that. I check to make sure I'm covered up. Then I look out my small high window at a patch of white frozen sky. I'm sick of winter, and spring in Canada is winter part-two, with icy nights and snow-squall days. When I was a kid, winter was fun and short and not too cold, and we had mountains close by, and we went skiing whenever we wanted. Trees fluffy with snow, a clear view across the valley, a basin full of glittering holiday lights. I frown up at Mama.

"Get up, Jevrem," she says. She stands over me rubbing her

hands the way she always used to, to loosen them up for playing, to bring creative blood into her fingertips.

"What do you want?" I say.

"Where were you last night?" She stops rubbing, and puts her hands on her hips. Even when she stands tough like this, she looks thin and empty.

"Out with friends."

"Because I got a call from the father of a school friend of yours," she says in that quiet, flat voice she uses these days. "And he was shouting at me that you went over there and did terrible things to him, his wife, and his son. What is wrong with you? You're lucky they're not going to press charges. You'd be deported."

Mama should be angry, she's trying to be, but she's standing over me like an uncertain ghost, fading in and out of my sight. There is so much she doesn't know about me and the gang it's ridiculous. As if Andrew would let his parents go to the police. He probably begged them not to on his knees, he probably said it was his fault, that it would all come back to him, that he'd be thrown in jail, or some stupid shit like that. That's the power of power—he'd admit to all kinds of things he didn't do rather than piss us off again. I think about being deported, I've never considered that before, how I'd fit back in that old, fucked-up city now that there's peace. I look up at Mama and realize I actually feel something for Toronto, for this country, this continent, for how you can get lost here, in the streets, on the open road, how you can sense the emptiness, the vast swaths of land where no people have ever lived. I'd probably feel suffocated back home, and that would be a real problem.

I sit up. I wish Mama would go away. I don't like it when she sees me in bed, just waking up. It reminds me of when things were different, when she smiled in the mornings, when she held out her arms and kissed me on both cheeks, when she played scales and arpeggios and exercises for hours, her gusts of music mixing in with the toast and coffee smells, with the church bells and muezzins echoing up into the sky.

"Mama, that's ridiculous," I say. It's a good lie, protecting her from the hard realities of life. "I mean, why would they think that?"

Mama sits down on my bed. She's not elegant anymore, not glittering after a night of performances, conversation, drinking, and laughing. She's bony and stiff all over, her clothes are every-day clothes, clothes to endure waking nightmares in.

"Jevrem," she says quietly, voice tense. "I know that you're a hoodlum, roaming the streets, stealing, lying. I know it, and I'm ashamed. What would Papa think of you now?"

I look around quickly but Papa isn't here, standing in the door's shadow, listening thoughtfully. I'm happy because I don't want to bother him with this crap.

"I'm proud of you too, Mama. Housecleaning. Very good. Your pianist's hands in a stranger's filthy toilet."

"You know why I'm doing that," Mama says. "I'm sup-porting my family. My English is not good enough yet. We have to eat, to pay rent, pay off loans. Milan and Iva and the other families can't lend us much anymore, everyone's generosity has limits. They gave so much when we first got here, Jevrem, you know that. Everything we have."

"I've got money," I yell. I'm sick of this endless debate. "Lots of it."

I get up and march to my closet. There's a coat in there stuffed with money, the pockets and two bulging sleeves pinned at the bottom. I grab a handful of colourful Canadian bills and hold them up for Mama to see. Sometimes you have to do whatever it takes to survive, fuck whatever anyone else says.

"Why don't you ever take any of it? It's here for you. It's for real stuff, you know, food, rent, those loans and bills. It's a fucking disgrace what you have to do for shit pay." I feel my lower lip trembling, I know she can see it.

"I must be employed, those are the rules, and I'd rather clean rich people's dirty bathrooms," Mama says so softly I can hardly hear her, "than take money from a hoodlum and a bully. We left Sarajevo to get away from people like that."

I drop the money on the floor, march back to the bed. "That's the problem with your generation," I shout. Mama's quietness can't shut me up. "All these principles, all these big fucking ideas about life and art, and then you end up turning on each other, just like the leaders want you to, and killing each other. *Killing each other.* But you won't take my money so you can feed us, so you can play your music again? Oh no, because that would be bad. *That would be wrong.* Well, I'm not going to sit around waiting to be saved again, waiting for cast-off shit and embarrassing handouts. Tell that to Papa."

"What's going on?" Aisha is standing in the door, a pen in her hand, a wary look in her eyes. It's Saturday, which means she's spending the day in her room, sitting at her desk, doing giant piles of homework. She'll sit there all day and into the evening, with a break in the afternoon to practise violin for hours.

"Nothing," I say. "Don't worry about it."

"I do worry about it," Aisha says, her face completely serious like she's a fifty-year-old nun praying for my soul.

"It's okay, Aisha." Mama sighs. "It's between Jevrem and me."

Aisha looks back and forth at us, then turns and walks back up the stairs. Now I feel bad. I get back into bed and lie face-up, staring at the ceiling. There are tears running down my temples into my hair. I pray Mama can't see this, I close my eyes, turn my face to the wall, wait for her to go away. But she doesn't. She sits down beside me again and puts her hand on my cheek, my forehead, pulls on my arm so I'll turn toward her. But I don't turn, I feel tired, I have nothing more to say, I have nothing more to give her. The little shit that I am.

I SIT in class and stare out of the window. The teachers take one step forward, two steps back. That's how they walk through a lesson over here. The other kids seem to be used to it, which explains why they're a bit stupider every day. During the two steps back, I watch the houses opposite the school. Some have clapboard or vinyl siding, others the original, orange-brown brickwork with some frilly bits along the eaves. They're big and primped, with Yuppie families floating around inside like astronauts in all that space. I see them coming and going with their new cars and shiny bikes and fancy strollers, I see them clearing dead leaves from their pretty front yards, digging in their gardens, planting their flowers and bushes. Not like our tiny falling-apart house north of St. Clair, with its rotting front porch and small patch of matted, cratered lawn. Nurseries are expensive, that's the difference between poor and rich neighbourhoods. I know, I checked it out because Baka liked planting on her balcony back home, and Mama used to garden with Baba and Deda in Ilidža on Sunday afternoons. I thought I could buy them some gardening happiness, but Mama shouted, no, no, I don't want anything from you, when I mentioned it, really freaking out and acting like I'm the number-one criminal of the whole fucking universe.

Afternoon sun turns brick houses into big chunks of red rock lined up straight by some highly motivated ancient people, like with Stonehenge. I follow the mailman with my eyes as he walks up to each house, goes up the stairs, stuffs paper in the mailbox, goes down again. Then I slump low in my chair. My brain is suffocating with boredom. Sava, Geordie, and Madzid are breaking into lockers in the west corridor. All the students here are rich. Lie. Not all of them are, that's just what we tell each other to feel better about robbing them, but a lot of them act like they are. Their parents give them money for nothing, an allowance just for existing. We know because they spread it around every week like they've won the lottery. They go to movies, to the mall; they buy CDs, cigarettes, pizza, pop, new clothes, and weed by the truckload from me and the gang, like every day is a big party.

I didn't have new clothes when I arrived in this city, one of the problems with my first day of school. The second-hand stuff from our sponsors was a pile of rags from the '80s, fished out of someone's mouldy attic. Acid-washed, padded, pleated, baggy, neon, I looked like a little Eastern bloc freak, like a bastard refugee from the past. When Mama dropped me off, she waved and tried to act upbeat. She said, just look, listen, and copy what the others are doing. Well, that was bad advice because people were doing all kinds of random things in the classrooms, and going in all different directions in the hallways. The stuff on the blackboard didn't look familiar even in math class, and the teachers spoke fast, and I couldn't follow them even when they remembered to slow down. And when I learned to speak in sentences, I was attacked by a thousand creepy questions. Tell us, Jevrem, teachers asked in every class, where are you from, what is your background? Share with us, it's important, your roots, your culture, your people, your flag, your food, your God. I said nothing, I pretended not to understand, I didn't get why they wanted to know, why it mattered so much, because this is how it started for us, with questionnaires and sorting everyone by religion and teaching us who were our own kind and who were the others, forcing us to decide, to choose a side, and next came interrogations, beatings, house-torchings, evacuations, transports, concentration camps popping up all over the countryside. So I got depressed—what did they all expect? Couldn't they ask me some fucking normal questions, like what music I liked, what sport I was good at, what books I read or television I watched, who my friends were back home, Pero and Zakir and Mahmud? About Cena and Nezira? I could talk about them, how much I missed them, how we played soccer in the courtyard all the time. But no one asked me about those things, so I put my head down and began to think of other ways they could get to know me. How I could show them the force of my brilliant personality, shining brightly all on its own.

OUTSIDE the school entrance, I stop in the noisy crush of students, light a smoke, think about what I'm going to do with the rest of the day. I hear someone calling my name. I look around. The music teacher, Mr. Green, is walking down the entrance steps. He's looking at me and waving. I wonder what they're going to haul me to the principal's office for now. I pat my pockets to assess what criminal goods might be lurking there. But when he's standing in front of me he doesn't looked pissed off at all, he looks really freaking happy to see me.

"I just realized that your mother is Sofija Andric, the wonderful Yugoslavian pianist. That's fantastic. I heard her play in Vienna when I was there on a trip in '89."

He has this huge smile on his face. I just stand there and stare at him, cigarette hanging from my mouth.

"I bet you play an instrument too, then. All children of musicians take lessons, isn't that true?"

"Nope," I say. "Not me. My sister plays the violin really well, though."

"Do you think your mother would come and play for us, for my music students? I'd organize a concert."

Mr. Green has a neatly trimmed beard and wears John Lennon glasses. He's looking at me like he's found a long-lost friend. I want to tell him that she's not here, that Sofija Andric the Pianist never made it out of the ruined city.

"We'd be very grateful and honoured," Mr. Green continues.

"She doesn't play anymore," I say.

"*What?*" His eyes pop out, he looks really upset. I agree with him, it is very upsetting.

"Why?" he asks. Then he takes a sharp breath in, puts his hand to his mouth. "I'm sorry, was she injured in the war?"

"Yes," I say. "She was very badly injured. Both her hands. And her head. And her chest."

Mr. Green looks like he's going to burst into tears.

"I have to catch a bus," I say, and move off toward the street, though I've never been on a Toronto bus in my life.

I walk away fast and don't pretend even a little to catch a bus. I head down Oakwood toward home, but I don't want to end up there. Mr. Green has made me think about Mama and her music, and that's pissing me off a lot, a feeling that grows and grows in my throat like a hard knot of food that's not going down. I light another smoke and think about whose place I'm going to crash at, what kind of mayhem we'll get up to once night sets in.

‡

VEILS of white fog rise from the grass, which turned from brown to green at ten fifteen yesterday morning. That's how it seemed, anyway, or I'm not getting enough sleep. I was walking to school and I saw it happen right in front of my eyes, which was kind of mind-blowing and trippy. But today it's still green, so uniform it looks painted on, so I guess I just happened to be looking at exactly the right moment. Spring has finally arrived.

I'm standing at the back door inhaling my cigarette after being away for a few days, looking at the trees fading in and out of sight. I see Mama at the far end of our weirdly long, narrow backyard. She's on her knees facing the back fence, near the scraggly red-twigged bushes, where she's built three little mounds, where she sits with our dead. Papa's has a fist-size stone on it, Dušan's has a piece of driftwood, and Berina's has a seashell from the Croatian coast. Mama says they're the elements that make up human bodies. They came over from home in a suitcase. Even in winter months she's out there, on a blanket in the snow, wearing two coats, shivering, praying, lamenting, cursing, forgiving, who knows what, because we all keep clear, Baka and Aisha standing at the kitchen window, whispering and worrying.

I keep watching her even after my cigarette is done. She can kneel completely still like a statue for half an hour, an hour, two hours, half a day; it's amazing, freakish, like she becomes the tombstone holding them all in place. Sometimes Papa is out there with her, standing a few feet away in the shadow of a tree, a puzzled expression on his face, like he's surprised Mama is the type to turn into stone. I think about tombstones and waiting and if I have Mama's patience, if I can suffer like her, full time, with total commitment, not hearing or seeing any other god-damned thing, just floating without struggling on an ocean of misery and pain. But of course I can't, I'm not strong like her, I don't have the guts, the loyalty, I'm the pussy who scrounges around for pleasure wherever I can get it, I'm the asshole who gets pissed off instead of sad.

‡ ‡ ‡

WE MEET AT ROGERS ROAD AND OAKWOOD, smoke up in the alleyway with the Jamaican kids, their skateboards, bikes, cat-calling, and chatter. Then we drive to the filthy twenty-four-hour Coffee Time on St. Clair, drink nasty coffees and inhale a thousand stale doughnuts. After that, we drive around town endlessly, parking here and there to drink and smoke our faces off and talk and kick cans around on the sidewalk. Hours go by in a haze this way and we're pretty happy doing nothing, just existing. We drive to Zijad's when the city is deserted, every street like Sniper Alley, making this the most fun time to try to get from A to B, just you and the cops and a hundred temptations. We fly along Dundas Street, over the highway, past the strip clubs and whores, the junkies and homeless guys like piles of rags on benches, across Yonge Street, past the Eaton Centre, through Chinatown, where we sometimes eat late at night, blinking in the bright light sur-rounded by drunken clubbers, back to the west end and straight up Bathurst Street to the underground parking lot of Zijad's apartment building. We stare at ourselves in the elevator mir-rors as the elevator bings up to the tenth floor. We're vampires in the dim light, lost souls in a cruel world, with dark circles under our eyes and yellow, splotchy skin.

Inside the cramped apartment, we eat leftover potatoes and chicken stew from the ancient fridge and through the rest of the night we talk and laugh and smoke and toke and drink some more. We don't feel like sleeping. The sun's first light is shining in our eyes when finally we fall asleep in Zijad's closet-size bedroom.

‡ ‡ ‡

WE WAKE UP TO ZIJAD'S AUNT SCREECHING AT US from his bedroom door. Zijad scrambles up, looks confused. The sun is shining at a late-morning angle into this tiny concrete box in the sky. It seems we're late for school.

She says, "Get out of here all of you good-for-nothings. Zijad, I don't want to see any of these Chetniks here again. Never. Never again. Do you understand?"

Zijad just stares at her and doesn't say anything.

"Have you no shame to bring people like this into our house? Respect your grandparents and your dead parents.

"Her," shouts Zijad's aunt. "And him." She points at me and Sava. "And her." She points at Geordie. "You are animals. Animals."

"Hey," I say, "we come in peace for an innocent pyjama party. Remember, we're only sixteen years old. We were just little kids when you adults made your war and nearly got us all killed."

The others nod earnestly. Zijad's aunt lunges toward me over legs, arms, torsos, and crouches down to grab my wrist. Her palm is damp. I can look deep into her wrinkly cleavage and smell coffee on her breath.

"What are you saying? Don't you joke about these matters," she hisses in my ear. "You young thugs, what do you know about pain and suffering. You're just crazy teenagers, you care about nothing."

It's possible that she's just scared of us because we're big, rude kids. It's possible she didn't use the word *Chetnik* at all. Zijad gets up slowly. He towers over his aunt. He looks like he's going to say something, but then he doesn't. He's too nice to tell her to fuck off, so Zijad's aunt stares us down, one after the other. She can't understand how it's possible that we don't care about the things she cares so much about. Here, on her nephew's bedroom floor, Serbian legs over Croatian arms, Muslim heads against Christian torsos, teenage body parts, boys and girls, all nestled comfortably into each other. But it's also possible she just thinks we're pigs, since the last time we were here we drank all the pop and beer in the fridge, seeded the carpet with chip crumbs, and smoked five packs of her cigarettes.

"I'm calling the police if you don't leave," Zijad's aunt says. She sounds sad. "I'll have them charge you with trespassing." She marches out of the room, and Zijad runs after her.

Five minutes later we're outside, huddled and blinking in front of the huge, dingy apartment building in the bright sunshine of an icy April day.

‡ ‡ ‡

AND HERE I AM AT SUNDAY DINNER AGAIN. IT'S the same as last week, and the week before, and the one before that.

Milan and Iva came early with three of their friends and

watched Mama cook. And two of Mama and Papa's acquaintances from Sarajevo, Stefan and Jasmina, arrived from the airport, they're visiting everyone they know. They tried to stay and make it work, they say, but it's too hard. The atmosphere is broken, it's not how it used to be, the wounds won't heal, the nationalities are partitioned, the economy is bad, the politicians are corrupt, the criminals are in charge. It will get better, Milan says, it's early days. Not until they reverse the Dayton Agreement, Stefan says. That European High Representative, ruling us like bad little children, a colonial model without the usual colonial benefits. Like security and employment.

"They're after our coal and oil," Stefan says.

"Yes, the Dayton disaster," Jasmina sings. "A shameful apartheid."

I stare at them all and think strange thoughts. Why is it *these* people I'm eating with today? Why these ones and not some others? Why *this* brand of peppers-out-of-a-can, and *that* kind of bread? Why this table, these chairs, why exactly at 7 p.m., and why this conversation about nothing new? I think, we survived for this? And then I wonder, what else should we have survived for? That's what survival means. So that you can sit around a table with your family and random acquaintances stuffing yourself with peppers and bread, supa and sarma, pickled everything, surrounded by objects you collect and arrange to tell yourself you're home. That's when I lose my grip, I can't help it. I stand up and shout, like a dog suddenly barks. I don't know what I shout, or why. Mama gets up quickly and rushes to my side. She sits me down on the chair and cradles my head in her chest and says, "Shh, it's okay, Jevrem, you're safe, you're safe." Lie. She doesn't do that. She watches me carefully from her chair. She's alert, she's ready to jump.

And then there's Papa, standing by the fridge, patting his chest with one hand the way he did absent-mindedly when he was thinking or gabbing, or when he was stressed. He's telling me that I should get off my ass, get interested in life. He's repeating Baka's endless mantra, *do some good for once, do some good, do some good.*

You have to love something in the world to really have survived, he shouts.

He has other phrases too. Lots of them.

"Jevrem, Jevrem. It's okay," Aisha whispers at me. "Sit down. We're all safe here together in the kitchen."

I notice that everyone is staring at me, forks halfway to their mouths.

Mama looks exhausted. "Yes, please sit down, Jevrem. We're eating. Can we please have some peace."

I sit down feeling a bit dazed, and there opposite me is Baka staring at nothing just to the left of my head, a startled-sparrow look on her face. I want her to get up and rush to my side too, but those days are done. These days she hardly has the energy to breathe. I feel a pressure in my chest, get up, stumble around the table to the stairs, and crash down to my room. I light up my tenth joint of the day, lie on my back, smoke, wait for the shakes to pass.

After a while, I grab my coat and walk out of the house. Mama comes to the back door. Jevrem, she calls, with a small, cracked voice. Jevrem. But I'm already around the corner, I'm already gone. I walk to Oakwood, then down to St. Clair. I stand there, shivering, waiting for a cab. In the cab, I sit back and take deep breaths. I tell the cab driver to drive me around for a while. I tell him to crank the heat.

"It's bloody cold here, isn't it," he says, his English sing-songy like he's from India or something.

"Yes," I say, "it's bloody cold."

"The cold never ends," he says.

"Yup," I say, "it never seems to end."

"Where you from?" he asks me. "Is it Germany? I have relative in Germany. It's good place, Germany. My relative is engineer, he has good life. But Canada is good place too. Toronto is good place, lots of good things, schools, hospitals. But it is cold too much."

"Yes, damn cold, even in spring." I think of my first week here in Toronto, how there was a huge storm and we all went outside and stood in a foot of powdery snow in Milan and Iva's backyard wearing the winter coats they'd organized for us even though it was March. We gazed at the white trees and roofs, at the buried cars, at the orange night sky full of fat snowflakes. Back then I was thinking, everything here is so big and sprawling, the roads, the houses, the city, the suburbs, the sky, even the snow. It's so big it has no shape, it's so big people can wander around forever without bumping into anyone they know.

I stare out of the cab window at the cars, the trees, the storefronts glowing dimly in the night. The streets are mostly empty of pedestrians, everyone's gone home to rest on this moody night. Then I see Papa briefly from behind, head down, shoulders hunched, turning in to a convenience store. I shout, "Stop the cab!" like a man in a movie and the driver skids to a halt at the curb. I run into the convenience store and check each aisle. There is Papa by the magazines, standing with an open newspaper at arm's length, reading intently, his head held back, his eyes squinting without his reading glasses. Papa, I say, and he turns his head, he looks at me in that way he does when his mind is elsewhere. Papa, I say again, I need some advice. What do I do when I can't breathe anymore? And he says, *you're doing the right thing, go for a drive, see some sights, the world is a bigger place than the inside of your head, remember that.* Then his face morphs, and another man is standing there, and this other man is saying, *sorry, what do you want, kid?*

So me and the cabby keep going. We drive down Bathurst to the Gardiner, then up the narrow on-ramp and east across the city. He turns up the radio and we're blasting Bollywood rhythms as we cut through the heart of downtown Toronto on this elevated ribbon of concrete, towering skyscrapers and condos sliding by on either side, all jumbled together, a tight cluster glittering confidently. The CN Tower reaches high into the sky like a giant flagpole, and then we pass it and we're on the other side, going down toward residential neighbourhoods again, the lake somewhere close but invisible on our right. When I'm warm and breathing normally, I tell the driver to take me to Madzid's apartment building. I like it there, his mom and dad don't hate me, I can crash on his floor.

Madzid's parents are out visiting relatives. So we get high in Madzid's room and lounge around eating halva and burek and chips and Mars bars, watching endless bullshit on his tiny TV, the volume turned low. We hear his mom and dad return and get ready for bed, the soft murmuring of their voices reminding me of apartment-sounds back home. I fall asleep late and dream of Papa in his study, of Dušan returning from the front, of little creatures with tiny wolf-heads swarming out of the basement like rats and invading our stairwells and hallways, knocking on our apartment door with little bony hands, shouting, *alarm, alarm.*

Madzid and I wake late, feeling groggy and suffocated and craving adventure. We pile into Madzid's car and shoot across Bloor to get Sava and Geordie, up Dufferin to get Zijad. Sava takes the wheel, muscles up the Allen Expressway, deking in and out among the other cars like the racer she is, screeches around the west ramp to the 401, hurtles west to the 400 in four minutes flat. We manoeuvre onto that huge, straight highway heading north and fly like we're airborne toward the giant supersize lake that lies an hour and a half out of the city, its craggy pink and black rocks, its endless expanse, its wind-swept pine trees reminding me of those paintings that Canadian painters like to paint.

"Let's just keep going," Madzid says. "Let's drive all the way around Lake Superior. Why not? It'd take days, so what? Let's keep going up to the Arctic, or west across those giant wheat fields everyone talks about. You can get to the Arctic from here, it's just straight north through thousands of scarcely populated miles."

We all imagine a road that long, we imagine that emptiness compared to Europe, anyway, and most other places on this planet. We consider driving without turning back, we smoke and toke and think about time going by, people left behind, messy histories, cutting free and moving on, shaping life and being shaped by it. We stop after a while and walk on the beach of a smaller lake ringed by dollhouse cottages and suburban lawns, big shards of ice still in the shallows, enormous leafless trees swaying on the shore, lawn chairs scattered around like driftwood. We look in windows and dream of sunny summer afternoons, fishing in little boats, bonfires, hot dogs on sticks, about summer vacations back home. We each have those memories, we share the same ones. The mountain lake our family went to, the river for rafting, that beach in Croatia year after year, the trees and white buildings and orange roofs and turquoise water and gently rising and falling boats. We all know that feeling of leaving hot dusty Sarajevo behind, pollution hanging like an orange veil over the valley, of driving through the cool green mountains toward timeless days of water and sand and playing that unfold like heaven when you're a kid.

Lake Simcoe is as far as we get; we never reach Georgian Bay, a thousand times bigger than our lakes back home, because we're hungry and the day is fading away. We drive south again through sloping farmland, past brown fields with patches of snow, red-brick farmhouses, wooden barns, stout white silos, to Geordie's house, the one her family just moved into. It's in a brand new suburb north of the city called Dufferin Pine Ravines, a neighbourhood without pine trees or ravines, with construction waste still lying around in bare yards waiting for the landscapers to turn up. Her house is huge, a movie set of a house, all perfect seams, right angles, fake brick stuck to plywood, the kind of house that shady money from the old country can buy, and legit money too, I guess. We have to take off our shoes outside on the front step, not even the front hall can get dirty.

And there is Geordie's mother, standing in the foyer, hands on her hips. Slinky blouse, slippers with heels, pearl earrings, shiny lipstick, she has money carved into her face and smells of an exotic-flower hothouse. She's looking us over with assessing eyes. She doesn't miss an inch.

"So these are your friends, Gordana?" she says. "Welcome to our home. You are very welcome."

We've never met Geordie's parents before, she's always kept us away, maybe because they're rich.

"Thanks," we mutter, looking sideways at expensive vases, fragile side tables, glossy paintings, huge colorful rugs, checking out window fastenings.

She says, "Oh, you all speak our language, isn't that nice. Come in. What do you want to eat?"

We follow her into a kitchen the size of a hotel's with white glistening surfaces and space-station appliances and we know exactly what we want to eat but are too polite to say it, for Geordie's sake. Zijad is dying to make a monstrous sandwich, he has that look on his face, and the rest of us are thinking about steaks and shrimp cocktails. Also, electronics in the basement, TVs in the bedrooms, jewellery in the safe. We can't help it.

"We'll just grab something, Mom," Geordie says. "Don't worry about it."

"But I'd like to cook for your friends." Geordie's mom pretends to pout. "Well, okay. You know where everything is."

Geordie opens the fridge and stares at its contents, waiting for her mom to go away. But Geordie's mom doesn't go away, she leans against the counter looking at us with question marks in her eyes.

"So, where are you all from?" she asks, finally.

Geordie slams the fridge door closed and marches into the pantry, where there's a fridge that's all freezer. I can see it where I'm standing. "Ice cream, steaks, chops, ribs, vodka," she reports.

"Hmm?" her mom says.

"What does it matter?" snaps Geordie. "Leave them alone."

"Well, it's interesting, isn't it?" Mom's smile is dazzling. We don't know where to look, her expression is blinding. "If you can't tell by how they look, how they talk, doesn't that say something? They're all from home, you know that already. Who cares about the rest," Geordie answers.

Geordie's mother laughs gaily. "She is so cynical, my Gordana," she confides in us. "Roots are all we have, my dears. You remember that. That's who you are, your blood. Only your people will stand up and defend you when the time comes. Like with like, that's a law of nature, nothing more or less."

"You can have your swastikas, Ma. We're going to eat something, okay?"

"Oh, Gordana, you'll feel differently when you grow up, just wait and see. When life gets serious, when it's a matter of your very survival, your right to exist as a people in your own land. Don't you think?"

Geordie's mother looks at us, eyes narrowed, waiting for our response. But we say nothing, we pretend we're deaf. Our eyes are glued to Geordie unpacking the freezer.

"Okay. Well. I'll be in the living room watching TV. Your dad is out at a business dinner." Geordie's mom pours herself a glass of white wine and clicks out of the kitchen.

We fry steaks and shrimp, we down a dozen beers, we go through vats of ice cream with giant soup spoons, we blink like overfed lab rats in the blazing light. Later, in Geordie's room, square, dark purple, smelling sour of new carpet, we sit on the floor, listen to suburban silence, feel lost in space and time, and finally understand why we've never hung out here before. Geordie's boxes are still packed, her mattress is on the floor, no sheets, no pillows.

"I'm planning to move out," she says. There's a glint of panic in her eyes, revealing a side of her we've never seen before. Being rich isn't the solution to all of life's problems, it seems. "Next year they want me to go to a school up here, a fucking suburban high school with suburban asshole kids. No more commuting downtown. I think I'll die."

"You can live with me," Sava says.

And I think, I want to live with Sava, she's mine, she belongs in my bed. Maybe we could all live together in an apartment on Dundas or Lansdowne, we're too ruined by war to be children living in homes with our parents. I take a minute to imagine how it would be, how we could trick it out with Forest Hill and Rosedale booty, how we'd have two fridges and a freezer, how we'd fill them with every item in the grocery store, how we'd live so much better on our own. But there's this thing that makes it all impossible: I can't suggest it to Sava. I can't make the first move. Because if she says no, that's it, nothing will ever be the same again, and even the possibility will be crushed.

On our way out we say goodbye, standing awkwardly like eight-year-olds in the plush living room, jonesing for every-thing in it. Designer furniture, gold-framed mirrors, silk car-pets, Chinese vases, sculptures of tall skinny women and round fat walruses.

"Nice to meet you at last," Geordie's mom says, and points at the giant TV she's watching. "See that crowd in Zagreb. Such nice, strong-looking people, so handsome, so pretty. Not a sick person there, you can tell just by looking, they're all strong and healthy and pure."

I see a cultural festival in the heart of a European city. I see ordinary people of all shapes and sizes standing around talking. They could be any people in any city in any country on the European continent. That's the thing about national pride, it's just one big creepy projection.

Geordie's mom stands up. "Where are you going now?" Her smile does not slip, but her eyes are hard. She's looking at Geordie like she'd like to march her upstairs and lock her in her room.

"Out," says Geordie.

4

I STAGGER UP FROM MY ROOM WITH SWAMP-BRAIN
from too much pot and see Mama sitting perfectly still
on the living room sofa. It's a strange sight. Mama hardly
ever sits still like this, like a sack of potatoes, a homeless person
on a bench, as though there's nothing to be done in a day. Her
days are full with dragging herself from one thing to the next
with her grey face. Her cleaning jobs, the laundry, cooking, pretending that life is normal. But now her head slumps forward,
her hands curl on her thighs like little dead birds, she's staring
at the coffee table with unseeing eyes.

"Ma," I say. "Mama."

She doesn't answer. Her cheeks are sunken, and I can see the
fine wrinkles that cover her cheeks like cobwebs. She was young
not that long ago.

"Mama," I say.

She looks up. "Jevrem," she says.

"What's wrong?" I say. "What are you doing?"

"I'm sitting," she says.

"Yes, I know that, but why?"

"I'm tired."

"You just got up."

"Jevrem, you're such a . . ." She doesn't finish her sentence.

I pour myself a coffee. Then I pour one for her and put in half a teaspoon of sugar, that's the way she likes it. I bring it over to her. She can hardly lift her arm to take it.

"Mama, did something happen?"

"Baka came into my room last night and told me that in the morning we'd all be going out to the countryside. To Veliko Lake."

"Oh yeah?" I say. I sit down next to Mama. I think about putting my arm around her shoulder but it refuses to move. She's got a don't-touch vibe around her like an invisible electric fence to keep the cows in, the wolves out.

"Remember, we went there a few times as a family? And when I was small, we had vacations there often. All summer long. Baka told me to remember to bring my bathing suit this time. *Bring the one with the red polka dots, it's the nicest*, she said."

"I've got an envelope for Aisha's violin teacher," I say, changing the subject. Maybe that will cheer her up. "Paid up for six months, and the back pay she owes too. She can't perform without lessons."

Mama takes the envelope and puts it on the coffee table, but she hasn't heard what I said.

"She's losing her connection to reality." She hangs her head, her shoulders shake.

I look around for Papa, but he's not here right now. Mama crying reminds me of him crying. He'd cry over movies, books, commercials, soccer matches, when he was outraged by a newspaper article, only for a few minutes and then from one moment to the next he'd snap out of it and be all boisterous again. But Mama keeps on going and going. I try to think of something to do for her, but my mind is completely fucking paralyzed. All I can do is stare at my hands, force myself not to turn on the television, not to light the joint in my pocket, not to stand up and walk away. Then Mama suddenly straightens up, blows her nose.

"I'm sorry, Ma," I say. I make an effort and grab her hand. Her fingers are ice cold and stone hard, like they've died on the end of her arms. "I feel sad too." And that's the truth, I guess, if I could feel anything for more than a few seconds. But luckily my feelings are like tiny gnats, they flit around for a bit and then they die.

"She's all that's left of the time before," Mama says. "The good time, the golden time." The shoulder-shaking begins again. "Her and Aisha." I hold my breath for a second. "And you, of course."

Suddenly I'm filled with rage, the kind that's a bursting dam of blood to the brain. "You have your music, too, you have the piano. How can you forget that?"

Mama stops crying instantly and turns to stare at me, her eyes focused and probing.

"You have to play again," I say, breathing deeply, trying to calm down. "You just do. It's the only way." I think maybe it's the only important thing I've ever said, so important that I'll even make a fool of myself in front of Mama. So I stand up and go to the piano. I haven't played since I was little, since the first month of the war. I open the worn lid and sit down. What can I play? Nothing to do with the past, memory, place; everything to do with the wide open space of the future. I stroke the keys silently for a moment, then launch into Vivaldi's Spring, the piano version, in my lurching, faking little-boy style, learned half by ear, half by score, the way that always drove Mama crazy. I play quite well for someone who never practises, with some fudges and bluffs here and there, and after a few minutes I feel the notes surging through my body exactly like the driving energy of spring. I stop, look over at Mama. She's crying again, but she's got a smile on her face, her eyes are softer, she thinks it's funny, she thinks it's sweet, me clomping away like that for her.

SAVA and I are lying on the stained carpet of her bedroom. We're whispering so her mother doesn't hear us. Sava puts in another CD. Hüsker Dü should be played loud but we play it low. I like the way noise buzzes out of the speakers quietly, like a distant thunderstorm. Sava's father coughs next door. Her mother click-clacks across the kitchen floor, no doubt irritating the fuck out of the downstairs neighbours. A seagull swoops by the window in the dark, its belly flashing white for a second in the bedroom light.

"Did you ever go roller skating back home?" Sava asks. "I remember that. That was fun. There was this old disco ball and cheesy Euro-trashy music."

"No, never did that. But I went with Dušan once to listen to this punk group in a grungy pub near where we lived. He was meant to be babysitting me, so he dragged me along. I remember the smell of stale beer and cigarettes, the crazy look on those guys' faces. It was fucking great."

"Sad that he's dead," Sava says, like she's talking about a character in a book.

I stop breathing for a second. Dušan is not dead. Dušan exists in my mind, as flesh-and-blood as every other living motherfucking thing on the planet. A warm body, pulsing, sweating, consuming, expelling, scheming, wanting, hoping. I have the smell of him in my nose all the time, laundry detergent,

ed to love going there, playing in the water for
sculptures in the sand with Papa. In my mind's
standing on the beach, at my favourite spot,
istening, sparkling water.

th sweaty palms and a jittery heart. The closet
just a thin sliver of light seeping in under the
ep, her legs resting heavily on mine. The weight
heaven and I don't move, I don't want to wake
t, have a few tokes, put it out on my palm with
is full of smoke, I cough, lie back, wonder what
e to burn to death. I think about Baka, Papa,
ins, dreams, and the things that people can
y have to. I think about the world, and how it
help, another hero or two, but nowadays heroes
hey get exposed for being fuck-ups right away.

d I come in through the backyard, which is deep
with dawn shadows. I stand by the door, have a
ght seep back into the world. The sun will rise
en we'll all shuffle through another day.

ying around the kitchen looking for something.
r move this fast in months.

ou doing, Bako?" I say.

for something, what do you think?" she says.

hirty in the morning," I say.

our problem? I've lost something at six thirty

ou lost?"

t lost, it's here somewhere."

smoke, cheap cologne, and the feel of his nail-bitten hand on
my shoulder as he drags me around the city and shows me stuff
and teaches me lessons about living life for the moment. But I
forgive Sava. She's an only child, she doesn't know how brothers
and sisters are connected, how they can irritate you, how you
despise them, even hate them sometimes, but how they're yours
like no one else, living with you for your whole life no matter if
they're a continent away, if you never speak to them, if they're
on the other side of eternity. Because they share your childhood
memories, the day-to-day ones, the "eat-your-veggies, two cookies after dinner, cartoons on the floor in your pyjamas, walk to
school, sitting around the Christmas tree" moments that boomerang back at you and hit you hard when you least expect it.

"He was fun sometimes," I say. "When we were much
younger we did things together, like make up all kinds of games
with random toys and objects when we were stuck inside.
On our holidays at the ocean, we sailed boats and caught fish
together. We snorkelled for hours, pretending we were deep-sea
explorers, that we were lost at sea. At night, we slept in the
same bed and he told me stories about aliens and goblins and
superheroes and whatever else he could think of. Later, when
he was a teenager, he always wished he was somewhere else, out
with his friends. He was always jonesing to be out in the city. If
he hadn't gone MIA so soon, he'd have liked wartime Sarajevo,
how some clubs and bars and restaurants opened again after
a few months and stayed open all night, with smuggled food,
booze, drugs, music, craziness, thanks to our very own mafia
godfather, even when it was really bad, even when the city was
shattered, how people sneaked around in pitch-black streets
and still found ways to have fun. He was a badass like that, and
he might have brought me along if I promised not to bug him."

"How did he die?"

I shrug my shoulders, squeeze my eyes shut. "He was shot, what do you think?" I don't want to talk about it, I wish she hadn't asked. A few months after, a friend of his who was in his company came by and told me he lived for hours after it happened and there wasn't enough morphine to go around. This guy thought I wanted to know the truth. I still can't think about it, because Dušan was so skinny and squeamish and he couldn't handle pain at all. He'd moan and swear whenever he got the smallest scratch.

"Five of my cousins were soldiers," Sava says. "They were all under eighteen; three of them were killed."

I don't want to hear about Sava's five cousins either. I know corpse was piled upon corpse in all directions, who needs to be reminded?

"Did you hear me?" Sava asks.

"What?" I say.

"And two of my aunts, married to my uncles in Prijedor, went through Omarska camp. They got it so bad, over and over again, for months—" Sava stops breathing for a moment too, her body goes all stiff.

I don't feel like hearing about that either, how brutal and filthy it was. "And then the rest of the family wouldn't believe them," Sava mumbles. "I couldn't stop thinking about it when I was younger. Every time I went to bed that's what came into my mind."

I look at Sava and feel so bad for her I want to punch the wall. I wonder about the best way to erase memories and thoughts from a person's mind. Mainlining heroine, probably, or some such shit. Whatever it is, I'd do it or get it for her in

a heartbeat. But Sa[...]
need my help.

Sava's mom is c[...]
tiny closet. It smell[...]
it from the "his" si[...]
Bayview.

"What are you [...]
Sava's mother [...]
five-inch heels, hip[...]
pants and tight top[...]
dresses like a fiftee[...]

"I'm lying on th[...]
"I heard voices.[...]
"Probably," say[...]
The door bangs[...]
the hallway. I'm co[...]
dry. I feel like drifti[...]
"Come in with [...]
I think about t[...]
ten, how I stayed at[...]
ning half naked thr[...]
shallow river in ru[...]
loved the Filipovic[...]
ing on the river's e[...]
by the sun. The cit[...]
the hot evening br[...]
pizza when Mama [...]
were exciting time[...]
games, tennis less[...]
ocean is dark blue [...]

the shore. We u[...]
hours, building[...]
eye I see myse[...]
staring at the g[...]

I wake up w[...]
is dark as night[...]
door. Sava is asl[...]
of her feels like[...]
her. I light a joi[...]
spit. The closet[...]
it would feel li[...]
heroes and vil[...]
endure when th[...]
could use some[...]
don't last long,[...]

IT's 6:30 a.m. a[...]
green and filled[...]
smoke, watch li[...]
very soon, and t[...]

Baka is scur[...]
I haven't seen h[...]

"What are y[...]
"I'm lookin[...]
"But it's six[...]
"So, what's [...]
in the morning.[...]
"What have[...]
"Well, it's n[...]
"What?"

smoke, cheap cologne, and the feel of his nail-bitten hand on my shoulder as he drags me around the city and shows me stuff and teaches me lessons about living life for the moment. But I forgive Sava. She's an only child, she doesn't know how brothers and sisters are connected, how they can irritate you, how you despise them, even hate them sometimes, but how they're yours like no one else, living with you for your whole life no matter if they're a continent away, if you never speak to them, if they're on the other side of eternity. Because they share your childhood memories, the day-to-day ones, the "eat-your-veggies, two cookies after dinner, cartoons on the floor in your pyjamas, walk to school, sitting around the Christmas tree" moments that boomerang back at you and hit you hard when you least expect it.

"He was fun sometimes," I say. "When we were much younger we did things together, like make up all kinds of games with random toys and objects when we were stuck inside. On our holidays at the ocean, we sailed boats and caught fish together. We snorkelled for hours, pretending we were deep-sea explorers, that we were lost at sea. At night, we slept in the same bed and he told me stories about aliens and goblins and superheroes and whatever else he could think of. Later, when he was a teenager, he always wished he was somewhere else, out with his friends. He was always jonesing to be out in the city. If he hadn't gone MIA so soon, he'd have liked wartime Sarajevo, how some clubs and bars and restaurants opened again after a few months and stayed open all night, with smuggled food, booze, drugs, music, craziness, thanks to our very own mafia godfather, even when it was really bad, even when the city was shattered, how people sneaked around in pitch-black streets and still found ways to have fun. He was a badass like that, and he might have brought me along if I promised not to bug him."

"How did he die?"

I shrug my shoulders, squeeze my eyes shut. "He was shot, what do you think?" I don't want to talk about it, I wish she hadn't asked. A few months after, a friend of his who was in his company came by and told me he lived for hours after it happened and there wasn't enough morphine to go around. This guy thought I wanted to know the truth. I still can't think about it, because Dušan was so skinny and squeamish and he couldn't handle pain at all. He'd moan and swear whenever he got the smallest scratch.

"Five of my cousins were soldiers," Sava says. "They were all under eighteen; three of them were killed."

I don't want to hear about Sava's five cousins either. I know corpse was piled upon corpse in all directions, who needs to be reminded?

"Did you hear me?" Sava asks.

"What?" I say.

"And two of my aunts, married to my uncles in Prijedor, went through Omarska camp. They got it so bad, over and over again, for months—" Sava stops breathing for a moment too, her body goes all stiff.

I don't feel like hearing about that either, how brutal and filthy it was. "And then the rest of the family wouldn't believe them," Sava mumbles. "I couldn't stop thinking about it when I was younger. Every time I went to bed that's what came into my mind."

I look at Sava and feel so bad for her I want to punch the wall. I wonder about the best way to erase memories and thoughts from a person's mind. Mainlining heroine, probably, or some such shit. Whatever it is, I'd do it or get it for her in a heartbeat. But Sava's face is rock solid as usual, she'll never need my help.

Sava's mom is clacking down the hallway. I dive into Sava's tiny closet. It smells like her cologne, spicy, delicious. She took it from the "his" side of a bathroom in an upscale house east of Bayview.

"What are you doing?"

Sava's mother has opened the door. She's standing on her five-inch heels, hip cocked, stomach showing between tight pants and tight top. That's what I imagine, anyway. Sava's mom dresses like a fifteen-year-old hooker.

"I'm lying on the floor," says Sava

"I heard voices. Are you talking to yourself now?"

"Probably," says Sava.

The door bangs shut again. Sava's mother clacks back down the hallway. I'm comfortable in the closet on top of Sava's laundry. I feel like drifting off to sleep.

"Come in with me, it's like a fort," I say. And she does.

I think about the last summer before the war when I was ten, how I stayed at Pero's mountain cottage for two weeks, running half naked through the forest, splashing up and down the shallow river in running shoes, making up those wolf games. I loved the Filipovics' cottage, the pine needles, the rocks shining on the river's edge, my skin dark brown, my hair bleached by the sun. The city was fun too, that summer, watching TV in the hot evening breeze, all the windows open, running out for pizza when Mama and Papa didn't feel like cooking. And there were exciting times coming up, like grade five, soccer league games, tennis lessons, a trip to the Croatian coast, where the ocean is dark blue on the horizon and the clearest aquamarine at the shore. We used to love going there, playing in the water for hours, building sculptures in the sand with Papa. In my mind's eye I see myself standing on the beach, at my favourite spot, staring at the glistening, sparkling water.

I wake up with sweaty palms and a jittery heart. The closet is dark as night, just a thin sliver of light seeping in under the door. Sava is asleep, her legs resting heavily on mine. The weight of her feels like heaven and I don't move, I don't want to wake her. I light a joint, have a few tokes, put it out on my palm with spit. The closet is full of smoke, I cough, lie back, wonder what it would feel like to burn to death. I think about Baka, Papa, heroes and villains, dreams, and the things that people can endure when they have to. I think about the world, and how it could use some help, another hero or two, but nowadays heroes don't last long, they get exposed for being fuck-ups right away.

It's 6:30 a.m. and I come in through the backyard, which is deep green and filled with dawn shadows. I stand by the door, have a smoke, watch light seep back into the world. The sun will rise very soon, and then we'll all shuffle through another day.

Baka is scurrying around the kitchen looking for something. I haven't seen her move this fast in months.

"What are you doing, Bako?" I say.

"I'm looking for something, what do you think?" she says.

"But it's six thirty in the morning," I say.

"So, what's your problem? I've lost something at six thirty in the morning."

"What have you lost?"

"Well, it's not lost, it's here somewhere."

"What?"

"My bathing suit. We're leaving in a few minutes and I can't go without it. I can't swim naked."

I stare at her, and she looks up at me, and I can see that she doesn't recognize me, not this morning. So I run downstairs, pack my canvas bag, and leave the house again. I walk back along lumpy residential streets with their small shabby houses to Sava's building, which isn't far, just on the other side of Dufferin. I don't care that it's freezing, that my eyes are scratchy and my ears are ringing from exhaustion like I've just been punched in the head. I can't take that Baka's looking for her bathing suit at dawn on a cold spring day in Canada, that when she looks at me she sees a stranger.

I knock hard on Sava's apartment door. There is no answer. Sava is probably still in the closet, stoned out of her mind. I don't care. I knock some more. Then I pound. A neighbour a few doors down opens her door tentatively.

"Shut your fucking door," I shout at her, and she does, quickly, and I hear bolts snap into place..

Finally the door in front of me opens. It's Sava's mother, looking like hell. Her bleach-blond hair is up in a rat's nest. Bags under her eyes bulge pale purple.

"Jevrem," says Sava's mother, "be quiet, for God's sake. You must go home, you must leave us alone. Sava's asleep. You're too much trouble, Jevrem, you're always trouble."

I push past her and walk down the hall to Sava's room.

"You can't just come in like this," Sava's mother yells after me. "You kids are all screwed up, you're just like the imbeciles we had back home."

I go into Sava's room and lock the door. I open the closet. I'm right, Sava is still passed out in there. It still smells strongly of weed. I grab a couple of pillows off the bed and climb in again to be with her. Sava stretches, her long arms tangled in her clothes.

"How did you get past my mom, Andric? Why are you back?"

"My baka was looking for her bathing suit again."

"Oh yeah?"

"Yeah, to go to the lake with."

"Veliko? I loved that lake." Sava is hardly awake. She mumbles, her voice hoarse. "We went there a few summers. My uncle had a summer house nearby."

"Oh, the figs, pomegranates, grapes, kiwis, rose hips, and mandarins, oh, they all grow in sunny Herzegovina," I say. It's our joke, the tourist angle.

"The rugged mountains."

"The woolly sheep."

"The fairy-tale castles."

"The primeval forests."

"The Olympic-sized swimming pool."

"The whitewater rafting."

"The magical skiing."

"The waterfalls."

"And Lipizzaner horses."

"Sarajevo, the European Jerusalem."

"Multicultural since the Middle Ages."

"Where Catholics, Orthodox, and Muslims—"

"—pound the shit out of each other . . . in perfect harmony."

Now we're singing, quietly, out of tune, "*Ebony and ivory live together in perfect harmony. Side by side on my piano keyboard, oh lord, why don't we?*"

It always ends like this. We smile, we don't laugh. Sava puts her leg between mine and rests her head on my arm. The thing is, we know it's true, those tourist ads. Bosnia-Herzegovina *is* a motherfucking jewel, and it *was* proudly multicultural since the Middle Ages. One fucked-up war, and suddenly hundreds of years don't count for shit.

We wake up to Sava's mom looming over us, one hand on each closet door, a look of deep disgust on her face. "Why are you acting like little children?" she asks. "Playing fort in a closet. Oh my God. You'll finish high school soon and you're acting like this?"

I do feel a bit oxygen deprived, but not very much like a child. I have a decently hard erection in my pants that's feeling cramped. Sava rolls over slowly and raises herself onto her hands and knees. She stays that way for a while, trying to wake up.

"I want you out," says her mother, pointing at me. "Please. I want you out. Now. Please. OUT." Her disgust has turned into true distress. I wonder how we can really be bothering her so much when we're asleep in a closet.

Sava's mother is bending down now and trying to grab my arm. "Get up, boy," she says to me, as though I'm some kind of wild animal that's found its way in through a hole in the wall. Why is it that I'm always the animal? She's the one who's behaving inhumanely.

"Get up. Get up. *Get out*." She manages to get my arm, holding her head away as though I might lunge up and bite her face.

This is pathetic, I think, it's time to go. I suddenly feel sorry for us all. I spring up. Sava's mother backs up so fast she falls onto the bed, mouth open, eyes wide, chest heaving. I take her hand.

I say, "Thank you very much for having me, Mrs. B., it was such a pleasure staying in your lovely home."

In the elevator, we watch the light move down from number to number as we glide to earth. Smoking up, remembering, forgetting, dreaming, huddling in closets is important in life, but it can really fog up the brain. Now we're on the hunt for the real world, the one that exists in the here and now. Sava needs a rush of adrenaline, I need money. Mama is broke, the rent is due.

‡ ‡ ‡

SAVA wants a convenience store. I consult with Papa, but he doesn't have much to say on the subject. He never has much advice about my means of raising cash. He sort of looks out at the horizon whenever I ask, as though he hasn't heard me.

"Only if it's a 7-Eleven," I say. "I'm not going to ruin the life of some poor-ass boat-person making five cents on a can of cream-of-mushroom soup and thinking he's hit the high life."

"It's probably more than five cents," Sava says.

"Whatever. I don't like 7-Elevens. The stores are empty, they don't sell anything. You can't even *get* a can of cream-of-mushroom soup. It's irritating. And those bright lights. Late at night it really gets to you."

We walk east along Bloor Street, which is the ugliest street in the history of streets, non-stop shabby, mismatched two-storey buildings with depressing storefronts selling random shit. It's so ugly it's exhilarating, like the wild west with its dust storms, dingy saloons, and wide open space. It's dead at this time in the morning, no more action than small swirls of cigarette butts in the breeze and a handful of cars and bicycles heading downtown. At Ossington we're over the walking, we get in a cab, and five minutes later we're at the 7-Eleven on Dundas Street. We go in and Sava wastes no time. She gets her baseball bat out of her duffle bag and starts whacking away at bags of potato chips. They make a popping sound when she hits them at a certain angle, which is thrilling in a small way. The guy at the counter, from Sri Lanka or Pakistan or Iran or somewhere Eastern like that, yells, "What you doing? What you doing?" I walk over and hold my gun to his head. I feel ten feet tall, invincible, untouchable, like I've just snorted a giant line of blow through a thousand-dollar bill.

"Excuse me," I say, "can you quiet down for a minute? My friend here has something to work out of her system. Her mother is very high-strung."

I lean over and get the register open. I take out a wad of cash. Sava has now worked her way to the ice-cream freezer and has smashed the lid. She fishes out two Popsicles from the glinting piles of shattered glass, the blood on her hand bringing her back to herself in a way that's familiar and comforting. The wreckage is a relief. I can see steadiness returning to her eyes.

"What flavour?" she asks the counter guy. She throws him a grape Popsicle but he doesn't catch it.

I notice that he's breathing very light, very quick, focused one hundred percent on the barrel at his temple. I notice that his face is tight with terror, and something else too, something like despair. Maybe he thinks I'll actually shoot him. It's in this moment that I remember that the evil 7-Eleven corporation makes its money on franchises sold to suckers from poor countries. Which makes me think of all the other immigrants in this city who come from desperate places and drive taxis, wash laundry, sell pop, chocolate bars, magazines, clean houses, look after babies, make lives happen against all the odds. Just like Mama. And my skin burns for a short fiery moment.

I lower the gun. My face feels sweaty, and suddenly I'm

thinking of Baka. I can't breathe, there's a cramp in my chest, my vision blurs. I run outside and stand in the middle of the small parking lot, panting. The sun is popping over the eastern horizon really fast. The CN Tower twinkles happily to the southeast. A light breeze is blowing up from the lake, smelling like it's escaped from a deep cave. The coolness feels ancient, but also alive, that's the kind of spring morning it is.

"Baka's dying," I say, when Sava runs out a second later. "I just got it. She's not just sick, she's not disoriented, she's dying."

"The cops will be here in four minutes, Andric," Sava says.

I run inside again. The counter guy is slumped over the counter, heaving. "No," he shouts when he sees me. "Please. Please. No."

"I'm sorry, man. I'm going to take this pack of gum, and I'm going to give you the cash back and some more to pay for the damage. Okay? You can collect insurance too. Break some more stuff and you can get a vacation out of it."

Lie. I don't say that. I just take the gum and run. But I feel like saying that, I have the urge to say it. It's a strong urge, it's insistent.

‡ ‡ ‡

MAMA'S PLAYING THE PIANO, LISZT'S SONATA IN B Minor, I know it, I know them all, and my lungs are collapsing, I'm on my knees on the living room floor, I'm clutching at my throat, trying to catch a breath. It's embarrassing. Mama looks over at me, but she sees nothing. She's lost in the music. So am I. It's crushing me, this wave of sound, this avalanche of vibrations. The air in this house has been still and grey and dead for so long.

"Why are you praying?" Baka's voice wavers.

"I–I'm not praying, Baka," I stammer. It's only nine in the morning, but I'm exhausted. "Mama's playing again. I don't know what the hell is going on."

"Praying to God does one thing only, Jevrem," Baka says. "It reveals doubt in your fellow human beings."

She is sitting on the couch, a blanket pulled up to her neck, her tiny shrunken head swaying back and forth to the piano. I'm shocked by the sight of her, because now I know what's going on. She's moving on, she's leaving us, she's had enough of this world, she's off to communist heaven. On the coffee table a candle is burning. Mama has lit it. She used to light a candle back home in the evening when someone was killed. After about a week there was a candle going all the time. And then that's all we had, when the power was gone, candles everywhere, our evenings spent in glowing, flickering light that would have been kind of nice if we weren't waiting to die. But now it's morning, daylight. Everything's upside down, something's about to happen.

"I'm not praying, Bako." I get up from the floor and look through the kitchen drawers. I find more candles in with paper napkins and toothpicks. I start dripping melted wax on a plate.

"You know, Jevrem," says Baka, "your mother could have been a concert pianist, she's that good. Listen! Music is the soul of the people."

"Bako, she *is* a concert pianist. And, she's playing again. Isn't that amazing?"

Mama looks blankly over at me again, she's somewhere far away. I'm carrying a plate full of lit candles. I put it on the coffee table.

"Oh, how nice, how wonderful," says Baka. "Candles are so hard to come by."

I turn off the living room light and feel relief. The day has turned soft grey after a vivid sunrise. In this living room, it's a glowing, shifting world. Mama is playing music to die to, Baka seems happy for the first time in years, the wall between two worlds is dissolving, and I'm about to explode into a thousand pieces and disperse throughout the known universe, no way to ever draw me back together again.

"Did I ever tell you, Jevrem, about our beloved leader, our dear Joza?" Baka turns her head slowly in my direction.

"Oh yes," I say. "Many, many times."

"Well," she says. "Those were good times, working hard during the day, evenings full of song, theatre, games, we enjoyed them so. And then, one afternoon, there he was. He'd come to visit us."

"Where? Who?" For the first time, I actually encourage her. I want her to keep talking until the end of time.

"Well, our Joza, of course. That's who. It was after the war and we were volunteers in the youth brigades. Railroads, railway tunnels, highways, public buildings, we built them all. And the evenings in our camps, we enjoyed those evenings so, singing, performing, games, sports, romances—but I was already in love, oh my." Baka sighs. I can see that her eyes are filled with sunny days, brown muscular bodies, pickaxes, shovels, stone dust, red flags blowing in fragrant breezes.

"It was a hot day on the line, I remember that well. We were sweaty, covered in dust, levelling dirt with rakes, when a group of important-looking people in fancy clothes arrived on the narrow-gauge railway parallel to the new one. Our foreman called out, *it's Marshal Tito, it's him!* And we all stopped our work and rushed over to the cars, and there he was. In sparkling uniform, his sunglasses perched on his handsome, tanned face, and he said, *you work hard now, and the nation is grateful, but tomorrow you will live your lives with all the dignity and joy that every working person in the world deserves.* He said some other things as well, and we cheered and whooped like schoolchildren until we were hoarse. Then he was gone again, the train rattling down the line to the next section, and we got back to—"

Baka stops in mid-sentence. She sways to Mama's playing, she hums, she smiles. Her memories have shifted to somewhere else inside her mind.

"You didn't mind doing free work for the government?" I ask. "Like, you know, a chain gang or something?"

Baka hasn't heard me. She closes her eyes, her head tilts forward.

I tap her shoulder. I want to hear more. Suddenly, I feel interested in everything that's in her head, her memories, her thoughts, her opinions. But Baka doesn't answer. Mama keeps on playing, the candles keep on burning.

I go to school, but I hear nothing and see nothing. I have an appointment to meet Ms. Markowski in my free period, but I don't show. She wants me to bring Mama sometime, so we can all talk together about why I'm failing at school, why I'm tired all the time, why I'm such an angry young mofo, and what we can all do about it. I told Mama and she said no, she couldn't go, her English wasn't good enough, that I should ask if the counsellor speaks French, or better yet, that I should ask Milan to go with me instead. As if that's going to happen, as if I'm going to have a cuddly chat about the monumental problem of me with half-joking, half-serious Milan and the nosiest woman on the planet. But it's all an excuse anyway. Mama's English is broken but not that broken. She just doesn't have the energy to go into the complicated intricacies of how life produces a sixteen-year-old asshole like me.

When I come home, I see that candles have been burning all day long and are now sitting in a thick pool of hardened wax. The house smells like a church. No meals have been made today.

"Where's Aisha?" I ask. For some reason today I want to know.

"She's on that orchestra trip," Mama says, and smiles brightly. Mama looks amazingly energized, alert, like someone who's just done five lines of blow in the bathroom. Rosy cheeks, red lips, sweeping gestures, X-ray gaze.

"I've been playing all day," she says. "I had an epiphany. I realized that they loved me, Papa, Dušan, Berina. That they'd hate it if I was in despair all the time, if I lost my connection to the music." Her eyes are like amber lit from behind, they glisten in the way they used to when she was working herself up to perform. "You were so right, Jevrem. You said the words that I needed to hear."

"That's good," I say, feeling pretty fucking proud of myself.

"The past is dead, the past is death. People get swallowed up by it, they step off the path of time, they disappear into memory. All that is ephemeral, you mustn't get sucked into the void with them. Only music is permanent, only music fills the now and moves confidently into the future. Life is music, Jevrem, that's the only way. It's like a white light flowing through me."

"That's good, Ma." I didn't say all of that, but suddenly everything's changed in this house, and Papa's in ecstasy hearing her play again, he's standing in the middle of the kitchen, arms up in the air like a Baptist preacher, face pointing to heaven, eyes closed, a wide sweet smile on his face.

"Yes, it is *good*," Mama sings. "You should find something like that for yourself. You see, I had a revelation. Life is how we choose to see it and live it, even when it strips us bare."

She sounds born-again, but I'll take crazed acceptance over wordless misery anytime. I go into the living room. Baka is lying on her side on the couch, wrapped in a blanket, as small as a child. All I can see of her is wisps of white hair sticking out like silk tassels. I sit down at her feet and stare at the candle-light flickering against the television screen. Mama watches from the kitchen.

"She's not doing well, Jevrem," Mama says. "It's her heart."

"I know," I say.

"Put your hand on her back, lightly."

I hold my hand out. It hovers over Baka's back. I don't want to wake her or hurt her. I settle it very slowly on her shoulder, waiting for her to stir. She feels like she's made of wicker, a sculpture of brittle, hollow reeds.

"When did she shrink this small?" I ask.

"We have to accept that we'll have to live without her," Mama says. "Human life comes and goes, but the spirit lives on."

I stare at Mama. She's standing taller, head up, shoulders back, her paleness a bright hot fire.

"Okay, Mama. Whatever works for you."

Mama sighs, smiles She's looking back at me, really look-ing, like she hasn't seen me in years.. "You have a good heart, Jevrem, a loving heart. I felt it the day you were born. And look what a catastrophic life we gave you."

Mama moves toward me like she's going to wrap me in her arms. I step back, it's all so different, it's all too sudden.

"I'm going shopping," I say. "I want you to play all night long. I'll do everything else."

"Not now, Jevrem. That has to wait."

"Why? There's nothing to eat."

"It has to wait until next week."

"I've got money, I can look after us."

I sprint down to my room before she can say anything more and pull out a nice fat roll from my money coat and stuff it in my pocket. Then I'm out of the house, down the street. I feel strange, torn, kind of happy for Mama, kind of sad beyond describing.

I'M PUSHING a shopping cart. It's 1:20 a.m. The last nine hours just disappeared, I don't know how or where. Something about Sava and a bottle and a lot of pot. I'm drunk and high and have twigs in my hair. The supermarket is as big as an airplane hangar, bigger maybe, a white cube of light hurtling through space at hundreds of kilometres per hour.

I study the carrots, there are big fat ones and little thin ones. I put a bunch of fat ones in the cart, then stand in front of the potatoes, so many different kinds in separate bins. Colour, waxiness, size, shape. I stare at them forever, then move on. The green onions look fresh, but there are also other kinds, small and pink, small and white, bigger and yellow, and the giant red ones. I grab the ones closest to me, and the air throbs around my head like a fever. I'm beginning to feel the challenge of this, I'm beginning to panic, there's too much stuff in this place and I can't focus my mind. I try to picture what's usually in our fridge and cupboards, what we really need, but I can only recall empty cupboards, desolate shelves, cans with no labels shrouded in plaster dust.

I'm standing in front of the spices. Colourful powders, dried, crushed vegetation, they must be important, there are so many of them. I try to remember spices that I know the taste of, Mama using them when she cooks. Nothing comes to mind. There's a high, sharp keening sound coming through the sound system like a call to prayer. It echoes around the freezers, the fridges, the wall of cheeses, yogourts, juices, the miles of chips, sodas, pasta sauces, and I'm back in the old market, I remember the smells, I remember the tastes, I know those foods. I bend over, dizzy, swaying, waiting for the sound to end, but it doesn't, it just keeps calling out to eternity.

After that, there's the cracker section, but I don't even try. It's a wall of cardboard, so many colours and patterns. There must be something we buy regularly. Every household has its favourite. The small orange fish crackers catch my eye. I wonder, why fish?

I leave without crackers and stand outside squinting for a cab. Somehow, I've put two hundred dollars of food in a cart, I've paid for it, I've stuffed it into bags. I feel like I've climbed a very tall unpredictable mountain. And there is Papa on the other side of the street, walking fast, head down, one hand shoved deep in his pocket, a newspaper clamped under one arm. "Papa," I shout. "Papa!" My voice sounds dangerously loud in the silence of night, so many sleeping bodies all around me tucked into their beds inside their houses. Papa looks across at me and raises his arm to wave. I point at the bags of groceries at my feet. He raises two thumbs and nods his head vigorously. *Well done*, he's saying. *Well done*.

IT'S 3 a.m. and I'm drinking a lot of cheap red wine. Every ten minutes or so, I check to see if Baka is still alive. Her breath is like a newborn kitten's, imperceptible. I put my thumb on her neck. All around me there is movement and little glistening flashes of light.

"There are fireflies in this room, for some reason," I tell her. I've been talking non-stop since I got back from the supermarket. It's the amphetamines, a gift from Zijad, balancing the pot, which I've been smoking in giant cigarlike spliffs, filling the room with a grey haze. Baka doesn't mind, she's used to smoke, it's the number one thing that soldiers do.

"April's early for fireflies, it's strange."

But the glistenings of light don't look like fireflies, they look like light shining through heavy material. Heavy material with tiny holes in it, waving in a breeze.

Baka moves, finally, for the first time in hours.

"Bako," I say. "I'm here. Sing me a communist song."

She seems to be trying to turn or sit up. I hear a little grunt. I pull the blanket away from her head so that I can see what is going on. Her face is tiny and white. Her eyes are filmy, her hair matted to her head. She moves an arm. She grunts again.

"Bako, what do you want?" I ask.

"Franjo," she whispers.

"No, it's Jevrem, Bako."

"Franjo, is that you? We have to get up. It's time to get up."

"I'll help you sit up." I place one hand on her back and the other on her shoulder. She rises like an angel ascending to heaven, as light as air, a vague smile on her face. She tries to look at me.

"Franjo, it's so dark in here. Where is our gear?"

"It's because there are only two candles still burning," I say.

"Have we run out again?" Baka asks.

"No, I think there are more in the drawer."

"Those damn airdrops. We ask for candles and we get socks. We ask for explosives and we get pistols. Those British."

I get up. There are no more candles in the drawer.

"You're right, Bako. The candles have run out."

"Look," Baka exclaims, "there are these little flashes of light everywhere, and everything is moving."

"I know," I say, "it's awesome."

I prop her up against the pillows. "Do you want something to drink or eat, Bako?"

She stares at me. "Of course I do," she says. "Are you mad? We have a long march ahead of us."

I think of how she refused to take food aid from Caritas during the siege, how she wouldn't stoop to proving she was Catholic to get it or let some priest bless our home. They should feed human beings, or feed no one at all, she said, over Mama's pleading.

"The part of the track we're going to is more than ten miles away and there are Germans in the vicinity. Are the others ready? Where are the others?" She looks around, blinking. "We can't be late. The political commissar is already on edge about that ambush yesterday, and what's-his-name, the guide, twisted his ankle."

Baka closes her eyes. She's exhausting herself with military thoughts. I go to the fridge and look in. "By some kind of miracle, I managed to buy all kinds of good stuff. Pita, cheese, cold cuts, eggs, pickles, peppers, tomatoes, olives, cucumber, yogourt, cereal, milk, chocolate cake in a plastic box. There are some ćevapčići in the fridge. I can heat them. What do you want?" I speak quietly, in case she's asleep again.

"That's lovely," Baka says brightly, her eyes popping open. "So much. I'll have it all."

I whip out the bread and all the packets and jars. I make her open-face sandwiches, all different flavours, and put a tray of them in front of her, thinking about eating with her at her kitchen table during the siege.

"Get Franjo up," Baka says. "Where is that Marko?"

She tries to get up herself. "I feel so strange," she says. "Like a really old person."

"Just stay there until you've eaten," I say.

"Hamida should be getting up now too."

"I'll wake her," I say.

I walk into Mama's bedroom. Her small night lamp is on, throwing up shadows. I don't hear a sound, but there's a mound in her bed under the blankets. I shake it gently. It moves, Mama's head appears. She moans, then sits up abruptly.

"What?" she asks, gasping, putting a hand to her chest. "What?"

"Sorry. Baka is awake. She wants to eat all this food. Is that okay?"

Mama lies down again. I imagine I can hear her heart going fast in her chest.

"Oh," she says. "Wait a minute. I'll get up."

"You don't have to get up. I'll do it. I just want to know if it's okay."

"Yes. Yes. Of course. Feed her as much as she wants to eat."

I walk back to the kitchen, past Aisha's bedroom. She got back from her trip a couple of hours ago. For a moment, I really feel like waking her, I really want to do this with her, but it's late and I'm too high to be around someone so sweet. I think of her, so scrawny and thin by the end of the war, cold sores all over her face and inside her mouth, bleeding gums, swollen stomach, but still working away every day after school to the light of a candle stub, still practising the violin in the stairwell for hours at a time. Sobbing through the night for Berina. I carried her off the plane and all through the terminal when we landed in Toronto; she was fast asleep, light as driftwood. She smelled of home.

I get food on a plate and when I go into the living room, Baka is on her feet, one hand on the coffee table, one hand on the couch, like someone standing on ice.

"It's all so strange," she says. "I can't seem to stand up straight."

The flame is a creature, I see how it dances with itself in Baka's squinting eyes. Papa says, *just be with her, stay close.* So I squat down next to her. I hold her hand. I have things I want to tell her, but I can't get them organized in my mind. Baka focuses on the food. She shovels it in as fast as she can with her tiny bird hand.

I'M sprawled on the sofa keeping Baka company as endless time drifts by and she refuses to go to bed. There is no label on the bottle I'm slugging from, maybe it's Milan's friend's moonshine smuggled from Yugo, made of rotting potatoes and un-detonated land mines. My eyes are blurry, I'm sweating hard, and every five minutes I'm on the toilet spewing like a sewage pipe at the seaside. I feel like everything on the inside wants to get out.

"Did you hear," Baka says, "about the ambush? It was a mess, with those Croatian planes strafing all over the place."

"Oh yeah?" I stare at her. She hasn't stopped eating. Her mouth is filled with cake, her cheeks bulging like a frog's. She's staring off into the middle distance, the past unfolding before her like a film.

"These German uniforms," Baka says, clutching at the collar of her nightgown, showing me the seams of her sleeves. "They come in so many different sizes, even for really small German soldiers, which is good for us women. Amazing, those fascists, such well-made uniforms, such idiotic ideas. With communist insignias on them, the red star, the commissars' hammer and sickle, it's the best of both worlds."

"You took uniforms off dead soldiers?"

"What are you talking about? Of course we do. And everything else too. Those lousy British and Russians haven't done a damn thing for us yet."

Baka tries to get up again, but doesn't make it past a forward wobble. "Oh, I don't know what's wrong with me."

"Maybe you're just tired," I say. "Maybe you should just sleep a bit."

"But we've got to get going . . . we've got to . . ." Baka is fading, her voice all air and no vibration.

Her head falls sideways. I worry about her neck, so brittle and thin, but when I move in close, I can hear short, light breaths coming out of her mouth.

I light up and smoke and smoke until the room disappears in a deep fog. The one candle left glows eerily like the moon in thick weather. I sit next to Baka while she dreams the dreams of her life. Every now and then she twitches and moans, and I move closer.

SAVA wakes me. She sometimes lets herself in through the back door and slips down the stairs to my room. She says it's morning but I don't remember going to bed. I stare out the window. It's true, the sun seems to be up. The sky is pale blue.

"How is Baka?" I ask, suddenly remembering.

"Your mom says she's sleeping."

I stare at Sava. She has grey circles under her eyes like she's been punched in the face, but I know it's lack of sleep. Sava often stays up all night, reading or watching TV. I sit up, feel suddenly hungover, disgusted, self-conscious. I look around my room.

"Does my room smell?"

"It's kind of stuffy," she says.

"What kind of stuffy?"

"You know, unwashed clothes, bed, hair . . ." she says.

I think about this. "Do you mind?"

"I don't give a shit," she says. I smile. That's my Sava. "As long as I don't have to live in it," she adds. "It reminds me of the war, all those nasty basements. But if you don't mind, whatever."

It does look and feel a bit like a war basement down here. Clothes piled up, bare bed, dusty surfaces, grimy window, crusty plates, cutlery, scrunched-up wrappers, fast-food containers, cans, bottles.

"Okay, then," I shout, springing out of bed. "It's cleaning day." I'm suddenly stamping around picking up clothes and crushed, greasy pizza boxes. I feel rage at myself for being such a pig.

"Jevrem, what the hell? Calm the fuck down."

"No, you're right," I yell, "it's like a fucking war zone down here." I'm totally naked but Sava doesn't seem to notice.

"Shh, don't shout," she says. "Your baka needs her rest. The two of you drank a lot of wine or something last night, your mom said. It made your baka more perky than she's been since you came over."

I pull on boxers and a pair of jeans that I find on the floor. Then I run up the stairs.

"Jesus Christ, relax," Sava calls after me.

I know we have an old vacuum cleaner in the house somewhere, and garbage bags, and cleaning stuff, whatever it's called.

Mama is sitting at the kitchen table with Aisha. I see that Aisha has prepared boiled eggs, soft cheese, baguettes, coffee, a perfect breakfast for Mama. Perfect for Mama on this strange day. And I see that Aisha's ready for school, her knapsack full of books on the table, her violin case against the wall, her hair freshly washed.

"How did it go?"

"We got first place."

"Of course you did," I say. For a moment I stare at Aisha, really see her, her thin, serious face, her genius eyes, her pulse ticking away at high speed where her neck slides into her collarbones. I can see that she's starting to look like Mama, which makes me happy, like something has been saved. I want to pick her up again, to carry her out of the city and into the countryside, up into the mountain forests, to find a cave, a safe quiet place where I can put her forever.

"You're staring, Jevrem," she says, and flashes me a smile.

"Where's the vacuum cleaner?" I ask.

Mama looks at me blankly. "The vacuum cleaner?"

"Yes, the goddamned vacuum cleaner."

"Do you want to vacuum?" Aisha asks. She laughs as though I've told a joke.

"Yes, I want to vacuum," I shout.

"Shh . . ." says Mama. "Baka is asleep."

"But I need to clean." I feel desperate to muck out, like it might change everything once and for all.

Sava might suddenly notice I'm not a freaking little boy anymore, that I'm a decent-looking guy with solid sex appeal, that I'm at least worth checking out, for Christ's sake. I feel a flood rising from my chest through my neck to my eyes, but push it down with a big, jaw-cracking yawn. And maybe Baka would sense it from the limbo she's floating in and see that I'm trying to get my shit together to be a better person, or whatever she wants of me. A lame try, to be sure. But it's all I can do right now, rattling around this house, just fucking waiting for death to come again.

Mama gets up and rummages below the sink. I run down the stairs and begin stuffing clothes into garbage bags. I pull out everything from my closet and cupboards. I've not noticed my jumble of stuff in months, years, but suddenly it's all sickening to me. I feel covered in grime, filth, rot. Sava is sitting in the chair now, reading from my notebook.

"Hey," I say. "What the fuck are you doing?"

"You lie all the time?" she asks me.

"Yes," I say.

"To me too?"

"No, not so much to you."

"Is that a lie?"

"Maybe." Maybe I'll never lie to her again, it would be a start.

"Fuck you," she says.

"Want to go to the laundromat with me?" That place that Mama goes to every Saturday morning, pulling a cart behind her like a peasant woman. I grab my sleeping bag, my pillows, and stuff them in a garbage bag. I pick up all the garbage from the floor, which takes exactly six minutes. Why did I wait so long? It's so easy when you get going. I eye my mattress.

"We're doing a place tonight and we're getting me a new bed."

"Okay," says Sava. "Where do you—?" but I'm not listening, I rush off to have a shower.

I never use shampoo, soap. What's the point except to be liked by the other kids? This time I do. When I'm done my skin feels tight, my head ten pounds lighter. I stop at Baka's open door. The curtains are closed. It's murky in here and smells of apples. She's lying on her back in the bed, her mouth wide open, her cheeks and eye sockets caved in, creating dark shadows. She looks dead. I sink to my knees, crawl toward Baka's bed, put my chin on the mattress. From this angle I can see that her tiny chest is still moving up and down. I wonder whether she can smell the shampoo on me, all those fake nature scents in a bottle.

I say, "Baka, I'm clean."

THE laundromat is peaceful, even with the murmuring and whirling of machines. I like it here, it feels like a train station or a doctor's office, strangers slouching around killing time together with books, newspapers, brooding thoughts, sideways glances, lukewarm sodas. I stare at my fluffy hair in the mirror. It feels straw-like and brittle. I'm wearing one of Mama's turtleneck sweaters and a pair of track pants I found in my closet that smell somewhat clean, taken from some sucker's house in the inner suburbs of the city, someone who has a regular laundry day, Saturday afternoons, maybe, or Sunday evenings, along with popcorn and a movie.

Sava is slumped on the floor, her back to a dryer. "It feels nice, Andric," she mumbles, "it's warm and it vibrates."

There are quarters all over the floor. Sava enjoys using the change machine. She's fed it nine ten-dollar bills and six five-dollar bills, everything on her. My laundry is in four machines.

Now I'm thinking maybe it would have felt better to just burn it all. Outside in the parking lot behind the Dominion. A slug of gasoline, a few matches, a light breeze.

‡ ‡ ‡

A T MADZID'S PLACE WE TAKE OFF OUR SHOES, shake his father's hand. His father is a small, tidy man who wears a shirt and tie, a wool vest, and slippers that look brand new. He traps Sava and me in the hallway with non-stop chatter, cracking jokes, reporting a weird assortment of facts, standing very close to us. His breath smells of almonds. He's a nice guy, one of those people who don't get angry or mean no matter what disaster strikes, and disaster got him good. Robbery, roundups, expulsions, concentration camps, torture, starvation, he was in every ring of the sick, fucked-up circus.

He says, "Did you know there are no clocks in Las Vegas casinos? A timeless fantasyland. Did you know a violin is made up of seventy separate pieces of wood? Absolute geniuses, those violin makers. Did you know that China has more English speakers than the United States? We can all see where that will end."

I nod and look impressed. Sava has a rare expression on her face, like she wants to grab this man and give him a hug.

"Tell your mother I said hello, Jevrem. Such a brilliant pianist. I met her several times back home, once at a book launch in that café. Hmm, which one was it? Can't remember. She was famous in Sarajevo back then, did you know that?"

There's a smile in Madzid's mother's eyes when she looks at us, but she disappears as soon as she can into the kitchen, where she's cooking something that smells like home. We make her nervous, the sound of our voices, Madzid says. Madzid's grand-parents were killed one fine morning of the war when Croat militiamen came into their village to change its ethnicity, or maybe it was Serb militiamen, I can't remember, it doesn't really matter, they were the same drugged-up freaked-out luna-tics trying to prove to foreign eyes that this land was theirs.

Four hours later, when we finally stumble to the front door, numb from lying around for too long and needing to get moving on my very important mission, Madzid's mother brings us a bag of food for the road. I wonder what she thinks we're going out there to do. She doesn't ask. We thank her, but she shakes her head. *No, no*, she says, *I do it with pleasure.*

"A really good mattress," I say when we're in the car. I'm thinking that it should be at least a double, maybe a queen. I imagine Sava sleeping over. I imagine feeding her nutritious porridge in the mornings, nuts and bananas in it, seeds and cream and maple syrup, so that she stops looking so pale, so that she finally falls asleep. I imagine us having sex, both of us naked, in the dark, just flesh on flesh, flesh in flesh. Sweat, sal-iva, tears of happiness, maybe, I'll take it all.

"A queen size," I say. "And the bit that goes underneath."

"The box-spring," Zijad says, dreamily. He's persuaded a doctor to put him on antidepressants because of the war, it's a steadier supply than stealing. They make him feel floaty and untouchable. "But not the metal frame. Takes too long to dismantle."

"Do you know that most lipsticks contain fish scales?" I say.

We're all slumped in our seats. The car's windows are fog-ging up. I can tell that no one is focused, it's going to be one of those nights.

"Do you know that there's a word for the fear of being buried alive? *Taphephobia*. It's actually a phobia." Madzid blows steam onto the window, then rubs it off with his sleeve. "Isn't that the stupidest thing you've ever heard?" He laughs quietly. "I mean, how can it be called a phobia if it's objectively the most fucking scary thing anyone can imagine, and leads to death? I wonder if there's a word for a phobia of torture? Or rape?"

"Or of sticking needles in your eyes."

"Please don't rape or torture me, or kill my children. I have this phobia. It's very distressing. But George over here, you can torture him, and rape and kill his wife and all his children, he doesn't have that phobia, he's cool with all of that."

We drive to a neighbourhood where we think construction workers might live. It takes us ten minutes to spot the kind of van that's good for moving a bed. But once we're in the house and have found the bed, the construction worker who's sleeping in it says he doesn't want to give it up, that he was dreaming something really nice in it when we woke him, a bunch of wild kids in his house. And when Sava tells him that I *really* want his bed, first asking what kind it is and how long he's had it, he says no, flat out, just like that.

What to do? We're at an impasse, all four of us sprawled on the floor of the bedroom drinking beer that we find in the fridge. The construction worker sits in his dishevelled bed like a child in a playpen, staring at us with open mouth.

"I mean," he says, "why should you have my bed?"

"Because mine is old and I slept in it for a long time without sheets. Sava here said my room smells terrible. I want a new start."

"But it's *my* bed. Why don't you go out and get one of your own?"

"With what? I'm a high school student."

"*So?*" he says.

"And my mother cleans houses. She's a brilliant pianist."

"Oh, I see. You're poor. You don't have the money."

"You got it, genius," I say, and offer him a beer.

He shakes his head. "It's the fucking middle of the night, I was asleep a minute ago, I don't want a beer now."

"I like a beer at any time of the day or night," I say.

"You see," says Zijad. "You can claim it on your insurance and then go out and buy another bed. Then we're all happy. That's the thing about life over here. No one gets fucked over for good. There's always a way to make everything okay again. You know, that's not how it works everywhere."

"But then my premium goes up," the construction worker says, making wild hand gestures.

"Yes, but only by a few dollars. I'm sure you can afford it," says Zijad. "You're a construction worker. In Canada."

"But . . . but . . . but . . ." the construction worker stutters. He's very indignant but he can't think of an argument against that. He knows he makes a ton of money compared to most unlucky suckers on the planet.

"C'mon," says Sava. "What are we doing? Let's just take the bed and get the hell out of here. Since when did we start to debate with people?"

"But it's not right," says the construction worker.

"What do you mean, it's not *right*?" I say. "There's lots that's not fucking *right* in the world that you don't give a shit about. For instance, you stole that bed from the workers who made it. They didn't get the full value of their labour in pay."

The construction worker clutches his head. "No, I didn't

steal the bed. The middlemen stole the bed, maybe. I'm just the customer."

"Exactly, that's just it, you're the customer. You know how much evil shit happens in the world because of that attitude? I mean, who got the value of that mattress? If not the worker, who?" I'm channelling Papa. I look around quickly to see if he's here, to see if he's enjoying this moment of political debate.

"You're not helping any," the construction worker says, jabbing his finger in my direction. "I mean, how does stealing this bed from me help all of those, you know, international labour issues?"

"It's like this, fuckhead," snarls Sava. "We're all stealing from each other all of the time. Some of us are just better at hiding this fact, so stop your whining."

As we drive away, with the mattress crammed into the back of the van, Papa's head pops into view in the rear-view mirror. He's crouching awkwardly on the wheel hub. *Capitalism*, he says, *obscures the fact that labour is the source of economic value. Workers are paid much less than the value their labour gives to the product they make. The difference, which can be astronomical, is what capitalists suck into their greedy maws, and they will go to any corner of the planet where the difference is the greatest. Welcome to the former socialist Yugoslavia, shit wages for the people, more profits for the multinationals.*

None of the others pay attention, they stare off into the distance, or shut their eyes and sleep, but to me it's interesting. I say to him, Papa, keep going, tell me more.

BAKA is on her side. Her face is grey as crushed rice-paper, her eyeballs rolled up as though she's peering into her own brain. I'm sitting on the chair in her bedroom, feeling antsy and wasted at the same time. Mama has put a forty-watt bulb in the lamp, draped a scarf over the shade. A candle burns on the night table, and Aisha has arranged a bunch of white roses. Frankincense wafts into the corners, lit by Mama as though she believes in holy spirits. Now it's just me and Baka, and the bedroom like a chapel with trembling light and coiling smoke.

Time goes by and I think and dream and try to figure stuff out in my head because Baka is right, my life is a ridiculous pile of crap, I'm not doing anyone any good, and something's got to give or I'll do something really fucking bad. This possibility makes me truly scared, more scared than back home, because knowing you can terrorize people and get away with it feels worse, if I'm honest, no lie, than anything I felt waiting to die in the city of many religions. Because there is no end to that shit, the sky is the limit, and all you're doing is surviving, you never get beyond it. That's the truth about us Bastards, the family, we haven't made it to the next level of the game.

Baka doesn't make a sound, or even the smallest movement, but after a while I have this feeling that she's looking right at me, watching me, that she's as awake as she's ever been. Her blind eyes are saying, *it takes the same energy, Jevrem, plundering the world as it does uplifting it. Did I ever tell you about our beloved leader, how he, a simple country boy, spent his youth organizing workers, leading strikes, reading works by great philosophers, thinking day and night about how to lift people out of misery, about justice and injustice?*

Yes, yes. I nod. "Many, many times," I whisper.

He could have spent his life drinking, complaining, stealing, adapting to worse and worse conditions, hurting others to get by, dying bitter and resentful at the injustice of life. Or just sat around scratching his you-know-what.

"I get it, Bako," I croak softly. "I hear you."

Near death, she sounds sure about things again, like she's back to believing in the overall progress of humanity, even after our cosmic cluster-fuck back home. Maybe she's even accepted that she has to die in a strange city on an alien continent, that she ended breathing her last breaths in a place that never even existed in her imagination for most of her life. Maybe she even sees some meaning in it. If so, I wish she'd let me know. I wonder what disaster could side-swipe my life now? Where is there to go when you've already escaped to Canada? I try to imagine the last place on earth I'd expect to die. Bhutan, maybe. Or Kiribati.

‡

My head is down on the desk, cheekbone squashed against scarred wood. I'm dizzy and nauseated from lack of sleep, but Mama told me to go to school, to take a break. Somewhere above my head, Mr. Duff, the grade eleven English teacher, drones on like a radio in an empty room about something called *verisimilitude*. My lying mind tries to perk up because it's an interesting idea, how writers use tricks to make things seem real on the page even though they can't possibly be. No real human being ever talks or thinks the way writers write, no book ever captures the actual passing of time. Is it possible, Mr. Duff asks, to determine which false depiction of reality is truest? He paces the room preacher-style, I can feel each footfall vibrating in my skull. It's a problem of interest to scientists as well as writers and philosophers, he says, stopping at the window, tapping a pen against the windowpane. Whether it's possible to determine if one false theory is closer to the truth than another false theory. Degrees of falsehood, so to speak. Because science is one long history of false theories.

I wish I could focus, sometimes it's worth it, and I actually feel sorry that Mr. Duff doesn't have an audience that gives a shit. He really deserves one. But his words fade out and I'm back with Baka, watching her lie still as a statue in her bed. I sat beside her all night, and all that time she didn't move an inch.

"Mr. Andric," Mr. Duff says. He's standing next to my desk, I can feel his heat, hear him breathing. I don't lift my head, open my eyes, or move at all. I'm waiting for his lecture. Instead, he crouches down and says quietly, "I'd like to talk to you after class."

The bell rings and the zombie kids file out. Mr. Duff sits at the desk next to mine.

"You know that you write exceptionally well, even with English as your second language."

Of course I learned it really fast. English is the world's language, Papa was right. It's all over everything in every freaking corner of the planet.

"Or at least, this was my impression of the one half-finished assignment you handed in this term—on torn paper with doodles, I might add. I can imagine you're very talented in your own language. You should take it seriously."

I just sit and wait for the lecture about cultivating your gifts and all that crap to end.

"But that's not why I want to talk to you." He pauses and gives me a searching look. "I want to know how you're doing." He asks me like he actually really does want to know.

"Great!" I say, and wonder why I'm lying to this guy, who's pretty decent, caring so much about verisimilitude in books and nerdy stuff like that.

"Because you seem very tired all the time. Do you work after school?"

"Yes, you could say that."

"Working and going to school is tough. I know some kids have to, but it does interfere with learning. Is it worth it, do you think? Minimum wage doesn't add up to a lot."

"I know, you can't do anything with minimum wage. Pay rent, buy groceries, survive. But I've got a decent job, it pays pretty well."

"Well, that's good to hear, but there are ways to help you and your family find additional support, just so you know, so you can concentrate on school. I can point you in the right direction. Mrs. Bairradas, the guidance counsellor, has information in that regard."

"Thanks," I say, and I mean it, for what does it matter to him if I pass or fail, live or die? I think of telling him about the ten thousand government forms we filled out before we came here, about the thousands we filled out when we got here, about how Mama fucking cried her eyes out over each one of them, how it all added up to so little, how it made her miss our life before so much, how we had to borrow and beg and scrounge from friends and church groups, just like in the war. But what would that change, what could he fucking do about it?

"You know, my brother was over there, with UNPROFOR," Mr. Duff says.

"Over where?"

"In Bosnia."

"Oh," I say. I want to be polite, I like this guy and his sermons about truthlikeness and suspension of disbelief, but his brother didn't do us much fucking good at all. They're all meant to be like Mother Teresa or something, those UN guys from all the different countries, but they're just normal boys, or maybe totally abnormal, since they're soldiers and soldiers are trained to be cranked-up assholes with no morals of their own, getting local girls to suck their dicks and sit on their faces for scraps of food. And they didn't even keep their promises. They couldn't even prevent one single death.

"Thousands of Canadian soldiers were over there. It was hell for them, poor lads. Their hands were tied and there weren't enough of them to deal with the situation. How can you keep the peace when there is no peace to keep?"

Mr. Duff looks at me as if he's expecting forgiveness or something. I shrug my shoulders like I don't know anything about it and glance around for Papa.

"It was an unfair expectation," he continues. "The killing went on anyway, the scale was massive, so savage, neighbour turning on neighbour, such a difficult history, it was like an out-of-control bushfire millions of square miles wide, with a handful of firefighters running around with buckets."

I nod my head. "Thank your brother for me," I say, like an idiot. I don't feel like having this conversation with this do-gooder teacher in this suffocating classroom. I crave fresh air and a cigarette more than life itself.

And all at once there Papa is, bending over Mr. Duff, his face an inch from the teacher's nose. *You idiot*, he shouts. *European, especially German, diplomacy legitimized the fascist leaders and led directly to war in Bosnia. Their premature recognition of independence doomed us to a bloody, vicious civil conflict, and the U.S. promise of intervention kept the war going. The UN should never have intervened. What were they there for? To help a republic secede from its own sovereign state? What bloody business was it of theirs, except that's their MO, they play their neoliberalizing geopolitical games to serve their own interests and hundreds of thousands of people suffer and die, including their own soldiers.* Papa's hands are waving in the air, like they do when he's furious.

"Terrible," Mr. Duff is saying. "Many Canadian soldiers came back with PTSD. So sad, a tragedy."

I stand up suddenly. "I have to go," I say, and crash out of the classroom with cold sweat running down my sides.

"Jevrem," Mr. Duff calls after me. "Go see Mrs. Bairradas. She really can help you."

‡ ‡ ‡

Z IJAD, MADZID, SAVA, AND I FLOP OUT IN MY room, which is weirdly neat. None of them wants to go home, and we all toke up a storm. My bed has sheets on it, a couple of new, thick blankets. Sava slides into them and goes to sleep. I feel a warm wet bubble of air forcing its way up my throat. It's painful, makes me dizzy, I think it could be a small burst of happiness. I got the bed for her, and here she is in it, maybe dreaming something sweet. That was a good thing to do, I tell Baka in my head. But I know it's small-scale good in Baka's world, it doesn't help anyone except me and Sava.

I wake up suddenly, surprised I was asleep. Mama is at the door. She's wearing a housecoat I remember from back home, a deep green silk that shimmers like fish scales in clear water. She wears it like she used to, she's solid and calm and in charge again. There's love and concern, a motherly combo, in her expression.

"Jevrem," she says, "I think you should come upstairs."

I'm now wide awake. The others have fallen back to sleep.

Sava is beside me in the bed, her eyelids sealed, her hand curled next to her cheek. I get out of bed carefully and follow Mama up the stairs.

I stand in the middle of Baka's room. She's making a crazy noise, too loud for her small body. It comes from deep in her throat, or even deeper, deep in her chest, the bottom of her soul. Her eyes are still rolled back, but they're half open now. She's looking up, way up, past the craggy lump that is her brain, into the space beyond the stars and moon, into the space beyond space. Her mouth is a shrivelled hole, her skull shines through thin dandelion hair. It will fly away with the next breeze.

I move closer, stand over her. I put my hand on her forehead and stroke upward. I put my other hand on her chest, and I feel everything, thin blood pooling in her tiny heart, water gurgling like a spring in her shrivelled lungs, windswept, sundried bones ready to collapse into coarse grey powder. But still, a fiery heat comes out of her. I lean down and whisper into her ear.

"It's okay, Bako. You can go now. I'm here."

It's the kind of thing people say in movies, but I really feel like saying it, I actually believe it's true. I'm here to help her go. I take off my shoes and move to the other side of the bed. I sit down on it very slowly, then swing my legs up and lower myself down beside her. She's a small child cradled against my belly, against my scar, my legs pressed against the back of hers, my chest supporting her back. I drape my arm over her, place my palm on her forehead. I feel her shrinking and cooling, and the rattle stops. I lie there, holding my breath, waiting.

Then the rattle starts again.

Mama pulls a chair close. She lays her head on the mattress, close to Baka's, my arm between them. I feel her breath on my wrist, I feel her kiss my knuckles. In the doorway, Papa stands with his hands at his sides, his head down, his eyes closed, like he's listening to distant music, or voices, or thunder. And there we all are, our heads together, remembering Baka in all her different stages, how she looked and sounded, what she did and how she did it. Baka rattles, Mama breathes softly, I drift off to sleep again. I dream we're standing next to the stream, the shallow, swift-running, rocky one, the one up on Mount Igman, where we used to go for walks. Baka is crouched in the underbrush, hunting for mushrooms.

"There is so much in the forest," she says to me, "that can sustain a human life."

The sun is warm. The breeze is strong. I look around for goats and hawks and other wild animals. Something stirs, moves, I wake up. The pinpricks of darting light are in the air again. Mama raises her head. There is silence like I've never heard it before. Baka is gone.

‡

IN THE park, the wind roars through the branches. I can't see much along the winding path through the swaying trees, even though the moon is up, perfectly round, perfectly white, every now and then obscured by speeding clouds. In the forest, there are only shadows of shadows. I walk and walk, blind but with ears, listening for danger. Baka walks beside me in ragged uniform, pack on her back, gun at her side.

I am on my hands and knees, following a scent through last year's rotted leaves. Spring nettle, young shoots, herbs packed full of nutrients, like Baka said. I chew on bark. I search for nuts and ferns. I think about staying here, in the undergrowth, and never going back to my life. I begin digging a hole. But in this climate you can't dig holes in April. Not with fingernails and sticks, not even with shovels. So I lie face up in a surface grave of last year's leaves, the cold rising up to grab my bones, Baka lying at my side. I pull my hood over my head, I wait for the sky to turn pale blue then fade to nothing.

5

I COME HOME SHIVERING, DIRT WEDGED BETWEEN fingernails and flesh. I offered myself to death, but then the sun rose, then a dog found me and licked my face, then the dog-walker loomed over me asking questions, then I got up and headed out of the underbrush as though I'd just been having a little rest. Sometimes life abandons you and sometimes it won't leave you alone. Baka's body is still tucked in her bed, Mama is tidying up, getting ready for the funeral home people. She moves steadily, gracefully, doing one thing after the other with the purposeful efficiency I remember from when I was small. She seems washed clean, like she's cried all night and now that's done, there's only the future stretching before her as straight and uncluttered as a desert road.

She looks at me with clear eyes. "Where were you, Jevrem?"

"I went for a walk."

She brushes leaves and mud off my jacket.

"Why are you always out at night?" Mama asks, like she just suddenly remembered that she can just ask me if she wants to know.

"I feel suffocated indoors," I say. I've never thought about it, but in this moment I know that's the truth.

"Go to bed. You need some sleep. I've called Ujak Luka in California."

Ujak Luka, I haven't thought about him in a long time. I'm surprised that Mama has called him. But Baka is his mother too, Mama has no choice.

Baka's expression is serene. Solemn lines between her eyes, contented curve to her mouth. She looks younger, more like her old self.

"I can wait for the funeral people," I say. "You could have a hot bath or something. I could run it for you."

"Thank you, Jevrem. I would like a bath."

I run the bath, really hot the way she likes it, and throw in all kinds of scented stuff that's in bottles on the edge of the bathtub. I don't want to sleep, I want be awake with Mama until Baka leaves the house. I decided on the walk back from the park that I'll show up at this funeral. The others, the nightmarish ones, were a blur, all of us crouching next to holes in the ground with the crack-crack of bullets echoing around our heads.

When I go back to the room, Mama is pulling a shoebox out from under Baka's bed. It looks a hundred years old. I guess they bought shoes back then too.

"Baka wanted you to have it," Mama says, brushing it with her sleeve.

"What is it?" I take the lid off and inside is a stack of old letters. The envelopes are yellow around the edges, the writing on them brown as insect blood.

"They are her letters from a long time ago. To my father. Just after the war, I think." Mama shrugs her shoulders.

"Oh," I say.

"She wanted you to have them. She was clear about that. And she wanted you to read them too. It was important to her."

"Oh," I say again. The box is not heavy. It smells of dust and, very faintly, vanilla.

THERE are all kinds of people in the chapel of the crematorium, Milan and Iva and all their friends and the old Croatian ladies who tried to get Baka to visit with them, their once a week gossip fest, but Baka refused, she wouldn't meet them even once. Reactionary Catholic housewives, she called them, what would I do with them?

Milan leans on the lectern and gives a eulogy. He says Baka was a nice, friendly grandmother who loved her children and her grandchildren, that she lived a good life, balanced her family and her career. He doesn't mention that she was a soldier, a communist, that she killed a thousand Nazi invaders with cunning and bravery, that she never lost faith in Tito and her Yugoslav comrades. When he's done, when he sits down, everyone waits for Mama or Ujak Luka to get up, but they don't. And neither do I. I have nothing to say to these people, there are no words to explain how it was being Baka's grandson in war and peace, I'm not even going to bother. Then there is Aisha, standing in front of the lectern, holding her hands together, her chin in the air, reciting an English poem from memory in a loud, forceful voice. It's one they studied in school, I guess. *Fear no more the heat o' the sun*, it starts, and she keeps going for quite a while. I catch a few words here and there, *winter's rage, worldly tasks, tyrant's stroke, oak* and *reed, joy* and *moan, witchcraft* and *ghosts*, and lots of references to dust. When she finishes on the word *grave*, there's a moment of silence while everyone wonders what she just said, if it's appropriate at a funeral, and when Aisha turned into a regular Canadian girl with a head full of flowery English nonsense-words.

Then we're all standing waiting for Baka's coffin to be lowered into the floor with the hydraulic lift and shunted off into the flames. I'm thinking of ways to do some good, for Baka, because that's what she wanted, but it doesn't help. No matter how much I distract myself, rows and rows of coffins rise up in my memory, each with the same nightmarish bunch of plastic-wrapped flowers on top, each draped with the Bosnian flag, and I'm kneeling beside one of them, I'm tapping the pale wood, I'm trying to take the lid off. And Mama, grey-faced and stooped, is telling me to be still. She's saying, let's have a quiet moment to be with Papa. But I can't believe Papa is in there. It doesn't even look like he'd fit.

Mama, Aisha, Ujak Luka, and I shake hands with each member of the congregation as they file out. Mama is wearing sunglasses, even though it's a grey day with clouds bursting with snow looming overhead. Ujak Luka flew into Toronto from L.A. last night, but Mama isn't warm toward him at all, there is no family spirit. He's staying in a hotel near the airport, and this morning before the ceremony, he tried to sit Mama down for a conversation, but she kept running off, she said she was too busy.

When it's all over, the funeral, the reception, Ujak Luka takes me and Aisha out for dinner to a little Italian place near his hotel. Mama says she has a headache, so we drop her off at home with Ujak Luka's rental car. At the restaurant, he stares at both of us with glistening eyes, pushes aside the bread basket, reaches his hands over the white tablecloth, grabs our hands with both of his. "You've grown so big," he keeps saying over and over again. And, "What has happened to time, what has happened to us?" Aisha tells him everything about her life, and what she says sounds awesome, her friends at school, her teachers, the subjects she's interested in, her music lessons, what she wants to be when she grows up, a concert violinist and a war doctor. A big smile on her face, like she's the happiest girl in the world.

Ujak Luka has a soft face for a gangster, a pale chin and jaw where he says his beard had been. He shaved for the funeral, for Baka, he said, she wasn't one for hairy men, and I wonder, do L.A. playboys wear beards just like crazy-ass Chetniks? He keeps asking me questions like, How are you, Jevrem? Is it hard settling here, such a different place? Do you think about back home? Who are your friends? Do you like school? Do you have nightmares about the war? Everything's cool, I say, because what's the point of telling him things when he'll be gone in an hour and I'll never see him again? I say, be happy living it up in Hollywood, and he shakes his tanned head, says he doesn't live in Hollywood, he doesn't know how that rumour arose. Such a liar, this warlord of L.A., this crazy Yugo outlaw of the west. Then he tries to speak about his life, about some piece of property on the outskirts of the city, about how Mama won't forgive him for leaving her with Baka, for abandoning his own mother, his city, his country, for not dying in battle like Papa and Dušan. He says she never returns his phone calls, that's how it is, that he tries to make contact all the time, that he talks to Baka and the rest of us every day in his meditations, or some such weird thing.

And he says we should come and visit him, that we'd love it out there, the light is so clear, it's like paradise, we'll see.

But I'm tired, I fade him out, I stop listening to his stories and his questions, I avoid his eyes. Instead, I stare at his
gnarly, rough hands, his dirt-lined fingernails, and wait for the
moment I can go.

BED is my grave. I fall into it, and I never want to get out again.
Turns out that Sava is in there already. The new bed works, she
has slept over every night since we got it, which has made it my
own sweet perfect torture hell since I'm on crazy fire for her, but
there are no more jerk-off extravaganzas for this hungry boy,
except shivering in the bathroom or some such fucking uncomfortable place like a kid, and that's the biggest sacrifice for love
I can think of. But we can sleep the century away together in it,
why not, since Sava seems comfortable with that.

Voices murmur and I wake to find Aisha and Sava sitting
next to me. Baka's old letters are spread all over the bed, like an
ancient, crumbling quilt.

"Her writing is so round and curly," Aisha is saying.

"Like a young girl's. She wasn't very old when she wrote
these." Sava is setting them side by side in an orderly way.

"Jevrem," Aisha says into my ear. "These are an incredible
primary source, the raw data of history. My teacher says that
primary sources are fundamental to the writing of history. Can
I bring them to school to show her?"

"Oh Jesus," I say and turn around, put a pillow over my
head. Since when are Sava and Aisha best friends?

"I used Papa's notebooks, the ones Mama saved, for a history assignment." Aisha is talking to Sava now. "Papa was a
historical materialist. Do you know what that is? People always
look to the superstructure of society, its beliefs, values, ideas,

cultural practices, to explain terrible historical events, when they should instead look at its base, the economic structure of society." Aisha pauses, then adds, "They just need to follow the money and everything will be revealed."

"Jesus, Aisha, how old are you?" Sava asks.

"Eleven," Aisha says. "Why?"

I groan and dive back under waves of sleep and dream that Papa is also sitting on the bed, that he's reading the letters out loud in a language I don't understand. It's Spanish, maybe, or Chinese, though the sounds he makes are more like animal noises, barks, yaps, clucks, peeps, grunts. I can tell that he expects me to know what he's saying, that he's going to ask me why I'm not contributing any raw data to history. I wake suddenly to the smell of food, the sound of clattering dishes. I open my eyes. There are plates on a tray, glasses, cutlery, napkins, but only Sava is here, propped up by pillows. Mama and Aisha are upstairs. I can hear them talking, water running, pots rattling like it's an ordinary day, nothing terrible is happening.

"Look what your mom made, Andric," Sava says, and she sounds pretty happy.

But I'm not ready for a picnic in bed with Sava, even if that is my idea of paradise. Right now, today, I'm not ready for paradise, or any other state of mind.

Sava shakes me. "Listen to this. It's kind of interesting, they're all about those youth brigades, remember that? When the young people built the country up again after the war—my grandfather went on and on about it all the time. But your Baka couldn't really write for shit, no sentences, completely misspelled words."

"Leave me alone." I feel suddenly angry, I want to kick her out. She's taken over my bed, and now my life, when I can't even move close to her, even when we're high together, even when we have no bodies and are floating through space connected by dreams, hallucinations, prophesies, and visions.

"Those are my letters," I say. "Baka left them to me."

"Whatever, it doesn't matter." Sava is strangely perky.

"I'm serious, Sava. Fuck off. Those are my letters."

"Relax, Andric. They're Baka's letters. I'm sure she wouldn't mind."

"What do you know about her? Why do you care? What are you on, anyway?" But I know, she doesn't have to say. Ritalin or Concerta, taken from the home of some tripping little rich kid. "Do you have some more?"

"No. Just get a cup of coffee or something. And listen to this, it's interesting. They're love letters to someone called H. I can't read her handwriting that well, though."

I sit up and look at the letter in Sava's lap. There is Baka's handwriting and I recognize it like she's risen from the dead and is standing right in front of me. She feels so close that goddamned tears start slipping out of my goddamned eyes. I lie back down again and pull the sheet over my head.

"*June 5th, 1947. Samac–Sarajevo,*" Sava translates out loud. "*My dearest H., my love, my* . . . something, I can't read that word . . . *my lion* . . . *I'm sitting on the wooden step of our* . . . um, I'm not sure . . . *barracks*, I think . . . *which were built by German POWs before the brigades arrived* . . . something, something. *Our workday is done and now we have time to write letters or nap or lie in the sun before dinner. The surveying for the line started in January already, done by experts. But the actual building has been going for only a month. The line is organized into 10 Sections, and it's being run smooth as clockwork by our youth organization, you should see. Some young pioneers slipped in, only 14 years old, who act as messengers, and one boy in the*

Triestine Brigade apparently is only 12 . . . something, something. Thousands of foreign youth crossed our borders not to invade us but this time in solidarity to help us build our new country. The World Federation of Democratic Youth sent brigades from many countries, too many to list. The evening sun is still warm, and it's shining splendidly on all of us as we go about our evening tasks and . . . something, something . . . fun and . . . something . . . serious work. Every evening so far we've . . . something . . . other brigades to our camp, or gone to theirs, and there we sing songs, dance the kolo around big campfires. In the first days, our brigade busily cleaned and decorated our camp and our artists painted murals and slogans on the buildings and made five-pointed stars in red and white stones on the ground."

"You see," Sava says, "she was like my granddad, all this Boy Scouts stuff made them really happy."

I sit up, hold out my hand for the letter. "Can I read it? Please, Sava. I want to read them first, maybe there's some secret message in there for me. Then you can read them, okay?"

Sava hands me the letter, shrugs, but I can tell that she's hooked by those tough kids with tanned muscly bodies hauling rocks fifty years ago. "Okay, whatever. I'm going home."

"She was a girl from a village," I say. "You know what that meant? There was no school for her, she was illiterate. That was the whole point of the communists; they taught the peasants to read and write in the middle of battle."

I touch the paper. It's brittle and sand coloured, like it's been baked at high temperatures in an oven.

"I bet she can write better than most morons at school. People here learn to read and write at age five, then are too fucking lazy to ever read and write again," I continue, but Sava's gone. When she leaves, she just goes. No goodbye, no see you tomorrow, just a breeze where she used to be.

I run upstairs and poke around the fridge. Mama and Aisha have been cooking all day. There are containers full of food from back home, all different dishes. Mama comes in all dressed up, looking like an exact earlier version of herself.

"Good morning!" she says.

I look at the clock on the stove. It says 3:37 p.m. There's some colour in Mama's face, more than I've seen in a long time, and she stands a bit more like a pianist again, back straight, chin down, forearms slightly raised. You'd think she'd be even sadder now that Baka's gone too, but I guess Baka was just a reminder of Papa and the good time before everything went to shit. Now maybe there's less to regret and feel bad about, or some such complicated psychological thing. I look at her out of the side of my eyes as I heat ćevapčići in a frying pan, trying to figure out what's going on.

"Now I'm hungry," I say.

"There was a big dinner at Milan and Iva's yesterday," Mama says. "In Baka's honour. We tried to wake you, but we couldn't."

Milan and Iva's condo in North York is the last place on earth I'd want to be, with all those musty old ex-Yugos standing around the kitchen gossiping, but still I feel a sting of regret. I promised I'd be present for this one, that I'd face it head-on. I guess I shouldn't have taken all those fucking benzos, or washed them down with vodka. I make another vow to myself on the spot to clean up, get alert, pay attention, be more of the good boy that Baka wanted.

"It was nice," Aisha said. "There was singing, dancing. Mama played rousing marching songs for them all."

"That's good," I say.

Mama and Aisha fold a tablecloth in exact mirror image,

like it's a routine they've practised for a show. I recognize the tablecloth. It's one of those ethnic ones from Central America or somewhere like that, from the days before I was born when Mama and Papa worked with a committee for solidarity with a revolution, in Nicaragua or something, those times that they told us about. They had a lot of different things going on before we were born.

"Milan set Mama up," Aisha says to me.

"What?" I say, like I don't care too much.

"Milan set her up. There was this man, a musician."

"At Baka's funeral reception?"

"No," Mama says and frowns. "There was no set-up. He's just a friend of Milan and Iva's."

Aisha winks at me. "He's from Quebec. He played the guitar and sang a French peasant song about being oppressed for Baka. Mama cried."

Mama says, tsk, tsk, tsk, shakes her head, and I steer for the stairs because I'm not even going to imagine Mama with some random guy. What would Papa think as he lurks around our house, watching and listening and reading the newspaper?

Downstairs, I turn on the lamp, reorganize the bed, then sit up in it like a school teacher at nine on a school night. I eat the food slowly and begin to read Baka's letters from fifty years ago. I think, what's spelling, grammar got to do with telling a story? She's her old chirpy self in the letters, like I remember, bouncing off the page like she's chatting away at her kitchen table. And she's in a surprisingly good mood describing a camp for labourers. What do they call those? *A labour camp*, which has quite a bad ring to it, kids building whole railroads for free with their bare hands, then singing and dancing and feeling good about it in their spare time.

June 7th, 1947
Samac–Sarajevo

My H., my love, my warrior, I miss you, I wish you were here, I want to feel you holding me, kissing me softly like horse nibbles the way you do, I want to listen to your dreams and visions, your heartbeats against my ears. I wish you were here, not over there, but we're both contributing to this great work in this optimistic time, so I feel good, I feel better than ever. How is it there? Write me soon. I want to know everything, if you got your place at the university and how your building is going, will you meet your target? Is the morale as high as it is here? Have you heard from your family? Will they go to Italy? We can vouch for them, they don't have to flee, our people in Dalmatia and Istria can speak for them, they will be safe, why should they go? It's wrong, they are true patriots and anti-fascists, and with a son like you! I hope you are not worrying too much. Don't carry on with any other beautiful partizanka girls, you dog, or you know what I'll do, you can imagine it well, because there are plenty of handsome boys around here to play with me, no matter what the rules say. Last night, some of us stayed up very late around the bonfire, after the singing had stopped, and discussed endlessly what makes a good life. I'm bringing this to the mail depot right this minute. I love you completely,

Your A
We build the railway, the railway builds us.

I lean back against my pillows, stare at the stained ceiling tiles, think about railway ties, crushed rock, steel tracks, about dust, diesel fumes, ear-splitting noise, about the massive coordination effort, so many hundreds of thousands of kids, each with a specific task or skill. No government on earth could get me to work on a railroad, I know that for sure, I'm not a sucker, or sing songs and play games around a campfire like a freaking kid at a summer camp. But some little part of my mind feels sorry about it, that it would be kind of thrilling to have something useful to do with my time, with life. I imagine building something real, something usable, with my breathing, sweating body, how it might feel satisfying at the end of the day. In Canada they had peasants from China build our railways across this huge country. That's free enterprise for you, I guess, getting foreigners to do your back-breaking dirty work for pennies.

‡ ‡ ‡

I'M LATE FOR SCHOOL, SO I STAND WITH THE OTHER smokers by the front steps until Period 2. It's a warm, sunny day for a change and all kinds of kids are outside standing and sitting in clumps, mostly sorted by colour and language like they do over here, Blacks and Asians and Portuguese and Italians all hanging with their own kind beyond the classroom walls, what they call multiculturalism, I guess. The school is huge, solid, red brick, with giant windows framed by moulded concrete, lots of trees scattered around, a Canadian flag flopping on a white pole.

When the buzzer goes, everyone shuffles inside and along the hall to their classroom. There they slouch back in their seats and try to find a comfortable way to doze off. Our room is stuffy and damp from the last group of teenagers herded together to learn some stuff in a forty-five-minute slice of time. It's English class again, and Mr. Duff starts pacing and speaking right away—that's what he loves to do the most.

"One of Canada's most well-known and well-loved writers . . ." he begins, and I stare out the window, wishing someone would open it since it's impossible to breathe in here. How do they expect us to learn anything without oxygen? How do they expect our minds to open when we're trapped in buildings against our will? I feel an old kind of panic rising but I try to focus on him, what he does with his hands when he talks, fiddling with his glasses, shoving them in his pockets, playing with a pencil. He reminds me of Papa, how he wants to put that pencil in his mouth and chew, how he cares so much about things that happen in the world and on the page. Yesterday, I gave Mr. Duff a fat present in an unmarked envelope for trying to help me, since they don't pay teachers enough here. I asked the secretary to put it in his box, I told her it was from someone else. Now, I take a moment to imagine how his mouth opened and his eyes popped out of his head when he saw the contents, how he looked furtively over his shoulder in the faculty room, how he threw the envelope in his briefcase like it was hot to the touch, how he sweated all night deciding what to do about it. I hope he kept it.

"After she graduated from Winnipeg's United College in 1947," Mr. Duff sings, "she married John Fergus Laurence, who was an engineer. She travelled with her husband to Africa . . ."

As much as I want to support Mr. Duff's storytelling efforts in this fucking airless room, he fades out fast and I'm back with the thousands of tanned teenage labourers sweating and grunting together in the open air on the Highway of Brotherhood and Unity, singing and calling to each other in the construction zones of New Skopje and New Belgrade. I'm with them as they set explosives and shift giant boulders, as they haul pieces of track and cart thousands of pounds of gravel to where it's needed. I'm with them at night, when they sit around large campfires and tell stories about the war, and I'm with them in their memories of war, the thousands of girls who harvested, threshed, and transported wheat, potatoes, and beans for the fighters and civilians in the liberated zones, the tens of thousands of young men and women in the mountains who tracked the invaders' movements, who waited to pounce, who pounced over and over again. All these kids, doing so much, risking all. And they believed that it was right, it was good. And so I ask myself again, watching Mr. Duff's winding progress up and down the aisles of tables, what Baka thought I should be doing all those times she said, *why don't you do some good for once.* But do something good now, here, today, by myself? How? Where? These are questions I would like answered in school, but they never come up, so no one even tries. Baka had fascists to fight, Mama and Papa had fascists to fight. What do we have, us Bastards, and the rest of these loser kids?

The chair is not comfortable at all. Sleeping here takes concentration and endurance. I thrash around, sticking my legs out to one side, then to the other. I want to scrabble at my collar, my tie, but I'm not wearing a collar or a tie. I'm just wearing a sweatshirt that says *Run for your life* on it, as a public service announcement to all who come near. Mr. Duff has a high singsongy voice that is good to daydream and fall asleep to. Sava and Zijad have managed it, they are out cold, heads down, hoods up. It was a late night last night. And I think about that, how busy we were, how little we slept, how we hunted and gathered for the greater good, how Baka wouldn't agree, how she's got something else in mind for me.

There were more people in the house than we expected. Three of them were giant men with meaty arms sticking out of their shoulders like extra legs, a father and his two sons. Then there was the mother, the grandparents, three teenage daughters, a male cousin, three cats, a very small ridiculous-looking dog. These are facts we read about in the *Toronto Star* this morning. It was chaos, pandemonium, a fun challenge for us all. There we were checking out the basement stockpiled with enough electronic equipment to outfit a large and bored platoon. Three huge TVs, three VCRs, five computers, five very good quality sound systems, extra speakers, amps, a keyboard, headphones. We were dazzled, mesmerized. Then the big men came charging into the room, all flexed in white wife-beaters, massive necks holding up puffy, creased faces. They couldn't believe their eyes: five skinny teenagers, two of them girls. So it goes. *What the fuck*, they kept screaming over and over again. *What the fuck you think you doin'?* The women wailing upstairs, and someone calling the police.

Mr. Duff is standing next to me. "Prose fiction narrative is one of the most powerful human inventions. In my humble opinion, anyway," he says. "Along with various things engineers have come up with. It has the power to transform the world, because it has the power to transform you. How you think and feel, the extent to which you understand and empathize with others, and therefore how you act in the world."

The thing is, our exit was blocked. First rule in a situation like this: grab at least one thing. It's a point of pride. Second rule: don't waste time talking to anyone, especially each other. Third rule: bring out the heaviest weapon you have and use it fast. So, Zijad popped the tear-gas canister, we dropped to the ground, the men stumbled around coughing, we slithered past them, the men swore and wheezed, we sprinted up the stairs, the men shouted at each other, we flew past the women, burst out the back door, and ran like wild dogs for the car. The police were wailing down the street as we threw our loot into the trunk. We squealed out of the driveway, doors still open, and burned the engine in the opposite direction, with a whole half-minute to spare. We love this part of our escapades, when we're almost caught. With adrenaline sluicing through our veins, Sava, Madzid, Zijad, Geordie, and I feel like Buddhist monks perched on the craggy peak of a remote mountain, minds free of tormenting thoughts, hearts free of sadness and fury. We're so Zen our heart rates drop, our breathing slows, our third eye opens to see all of reality sparkling brilliantly in every direction of existence, and in the midst of chaos, we feel normal for a few sweet moments of our day.

"Read a book cover to cover, and you will become a more thoughtful, interesting human being," Mr. Duff says, thumping his hand hard on the pile of books he's going to hand out, trying to get our attention. "And that—" The buzzer goes and his voice is drowned out by thirty chairs scraping backwards.

SAVA and I walk home, moving slowly along the cracked sidewalk, not caring if it rains, sleets, thunders, or blows a typhoon, we need the fresh air. In the houses, fridges open, milk is poured, chips are eaten, TVs are turned on, kids rest their brains from badgering and sudden revelations, women throw pots and pans around, drink glasses of wine, try to remember which children go where, when, what happened to the last ten years of their lives, were they good, were they bad, and think about life's simple pleasures like melted cheese on broccoli and precut fruit. That's what I think is going on in those houses, anyway. In my house, there is pealing piano music and waiting to see what the future will bring.

"We build the railroad, the railroad builds us," I say.

Sava says, "My grandfather told me they also went on expeditions together, like up to Tito's war headquarters, or to his village in Croatia, and places like that. They went all together, in trains—and guess what they did on those train rides?"

"They sang," I say.

"Yup."

"And discussed vital issues of the day."

"Yup."

"Laughed and joked and slapped each other on the back."

I scoff. Sava scoffs.

"Whose village would you want to visit now, on a train full of singing people?" Sava asks.

I can't think of anyone's village I'd want to visit.

"The Dalai Lama's?" Sava suggests. "Kurt Cobain's? I don't know."

We think about it and watch the clouds race by above our heads.

"Do you ever think about politics?" I ask Sava, Madzid, and Zijad, who are lounging on my floor in the late afternoon, smoking up a storm like a bunch of nervous soldiers in a trench. People were paid in cigarettes during the siege, they were an essential of life. Now we inhale a hundred dollars and four pounds of flour every day without a thought.

"What do you mean?" Madzid asks.

"Oh, you know, about the way things should be, justice, injustice."

"Ah, no, not really," says Zijad.

"You know, what you believe in, what form of government."

"Like what party? Liberals, NDP, Conservatives?"

"No, you idiot, like socialism, communism, liberal democracy, capitalism, that kind of thing. Which is the best way to live, for individuals, for society, you know, the good life."

"Never. They're all fucked."

I take one of Baka's letters out of the box and read it aloud to them. "Listen to this," I say. "There was a time where this is what you did if you were kids like us . . . *Railroad fever has really spread, whole school classes are here together on their summer holidays, no one wants to be left out of this hundred-and-fifty-mile-long adventure. Everyone feels strong and enthusiastic, there are no stragglers, everyone works double-fast time because we want to better the target date for finishing, we're like one body, that's how it is, and some of us do it all on the run. Oh, the constant rattle and whine of those squeaky wooden barrows along the line, day and night. But the government has supplied us with some big machinery as well and that will make us lay the miles down faster than ever, you should see them, giant tractors and steamrollers, and when we come to excavating the tunnels there will be explosives and of course many of us know exactly how to use those, that's one good thing about the war, we have so many skills to give our new country. And there is special training, some are going to be civil engineers, they're being trained on the job starting with surveying, and it looks so interesting, I want to do it too. I see sunshine and happiness in our future, maybe we'll have surveyors' tools and hard hats too, or desks with blueprints and technical drawings on them, you and me waving our pens around sounding knowledgeable about sewers and bridges and important things like that. Write me soon, all my love to you (I love you so much and miss you), my H.*

Your A
We build the railway, the railway builds us."

I look at the others and they're staring at me like little children listening to a fairy tale.

"She wasn't that much older than us, that's the thing," I say, feeling depressed for us all.

Mama is calling me from upstairs. When I burst into the kitchen she's got a look of determination on her face. She tells me she's going out with Aisha to get her some new clothes, Aisha is growing tall and nothing fits her anymore. Okay, I say, whatever. But Mama stares at me with a message in her eyes. She wants to tell me something, but she doesn't want to say the words out loud, she's ashamed. Suddenly I understand her loud and clear. For a moment I feel light as a balloon, like my whole body has suddenly filled with helium and I'm floating in space like a moon-walker. I waft downstairs and get the cash that Mama wants. There's enough here to dress Aisha for all seasons, and all her girlfriends too, the ones who never come over to stay because Mama's ashamed of our house as well.

‡ ‡ ‡

ZIJAD'S COUSIN WHO IS HUGE AND ROUND BUT looks about thirteen is in the living room when we enter Zijad's apartment. He's slouching on the sofa, eating chips, his big white-socked feet pressed up against the wall. He says,

"Heya, Zid" when we pass to go to Zijad's room. "You hanging out with your filthy Chetnik friend?"

I say, "You're an ugly kid," and walk into the living room menacingly, but he doesn't flinch. His hair sticks straight up and is dyed blond, a home job that's left dark patches all around his ears.

"You're animals, you just kill and kill and kill," he says.

"What are you talking about, I've never killed anyone in my life." Which, as I say it, I suddenly, sickeningly, have doubts about. Those two kids lying in the parking lot in front of their building, the ruined Pumas, the limbs that didn't move anymore. And me, my arm raised.

Zijad says, "Get a life, Johnny, you're such a loser sitting around with these old people listening to the same old mentally ill stories. Find some friends. Play some video games. Watch American movies. Buy stuff. Anything but that depressing old-country bullshit. Move on, for Christ's sake."

Johnny says, "Someone has to stand up for our people, Zid, otherwise we'll be, you know, dragged down forever. It's not our fault that we're the best and had to cut the rest loose."

His voice is deadpan, and he hasn't moved an inch during this exchange, except that he's still eating the chips and crumbs are accumulating on his chest. The living room windows reveal a huge dark-blue sky and downtown Toronto glittering optimistically in the distance. I stare at it for a second and think that life is surreal.

"You be respectful to Auntie and Uncle, Johnny. Do you hear? You shut up about this stuff around them or I'll fucking kick your ass."

"Ha ha," says Johnny. "You're so lame. It's a free country, I can say anything I want."

I sigh. The only response to a stupid point of view is to punch the person in the face, because reasoning will never help. Or walk away. And since beating this boy up isn't going to make him grow a brain, we turn our backs and walk down the hallway that smells of fried oil to Zijad's room, banging the door shut behind us. We light up smokes and spliffs and sit around decompressing in a five-alarm cloud. Zijad grumbles about Johnny and his other cousins, how the family was ripped apart at home and over here, how relatives still don't speak to each other, and all that fucking pathetic stuff.

To cheer him up, I tell Zijad about thoughts I'm having, thoughts about doing something real for once, something useful, thoughts that are obsessing my mind and won't go away.

"You know, for Baka, because that would make her happy."

He says, "Oh yeah, sure, man. That's good. I like that, I get where you're coming from. It's worth a try. Whatever."

"There's this old lady two blocks over," I say, sitting up, a plan suddenly sprouting in my mind like a little pea shoot. "I see her all the time sitting on the retaining walls at the bottom of the lawns on our street. Sitting there, with her grocery bags and cane lying in front of her, as though she can't carry them one more step. When she isn't sitting, I see her stop every twenty feet or so, stand panting, wiping her face with a handkerchief."

Zijad nods, lets a thick white puff of smoke hover at his lips for a moment, then inhales hard. He flicks ash into a Coke can.

"I know what she buys, Zijad," I say. "I see it in her net bags every time she passes. She has milk, cereal, white bread, margarine, cigarettes, and a bunch of cans. Do you know what that means?"

Aisha reads aloud to me.

June 6th, 1947
Samac–Sarajevo

My dearest H., my love, my warrior, how I miss you, even in this summer of happiness and adventure. There is nothing I can write that you aren't also experiencing, but so what, I will still write. The shock workers of our nation's youth must also spread the word, that is part of our job. Soon this railroad will be transporting goods made in factories being built in every region, and Bosnia will rise to the standards of the other republics, of Europe, of America. Our Section is already ahead of schedule, our works foremen and the Chief Engineer made a big announcement, and so we had a celebration on Sunday to congratulate ourselves and hand out badges to those who've worked especially hard. Of all the brigades, the Albanians are the best as they have had days exceeding the norm by 400 percent, and they are cheered up and down the line. We had a full band, a sports competition, then a huge meal in the warm dusk, with wooden tables set in a wide circle and tins of gold and purple wildflowers on them, singing and folk dancing, a giant bonfire, and a generous supply of alcohol, and lots of us got drunk and fell about in the middle of the night trying to find the right bunk. A photographer was here and took several photos of us in our groups holding a flag for the newspapers—this was in the day of course, before we got drunk! I am so happy that you have your place in the university. I want to come and join you, let's live together there, in that beautiful city. I will apply to study in Sarajevo as well, we will make our dreams come true there, that is my plan from now on and everything I do here will go toward

*that plan. Imagine me, going to university! I love you. Long
live Tito! Long live our socialist Fatherland and the Five-Year
Plan! We build the railroad, and the railroad builds us.*

"People wrote to each other a lot back then," Aisha says.
"We did a unit on letter writing in school, in the time before
people had access to a telephone and cheap long-distance and
electronic mail. And we looked at epistolary novels too." Her
mind is like Sava's. It's as quick and hungry as a clamp trap.
We're on my bed sorting the letters by date. Mama is in the
living room practising a light, airy, tinkly piece. Chopin. It
sounds like a summer afternoon in a park in Paris, or that's
how I imagine it. I'm hanging with Aisha, because it's the right
thing to do, it would make Baka happy, and Baka is on my mind
every minute of the day.

"I've never written a letter in my life," I say.

"We don't have the same need to express and understand
ourselves," Aisha says in her teacher voice.

"Oh yeah?" I say.

"Unfortunately, it makes us less precise thinkers. Letter
writing requires keen observation of the world around us, and
of ourselves."

"Oh yeah?" I repeat like an idiot.

"Baka had so much to express. Life was exciting, meaningful
for her with so much going on. And she was in love with our
djedica." Aisha's eyes are fixed on my face like I might have
something interesting to add. But I don't.

"She wanted me, us, to know that her generation did great
things," I say, trying at least to fake it.

Aisha is sitting as close to me on my bed as she can get, her hand resting on my leg. I look at it and realize it's as familiar to me as my own.

"Why aren't we rebuilding our country from the ruins of our war now?" she asks.

"It's not the same now, our war was a different kind of war. There was no Yugo left to rebuild after, everything fell apart, that was the whole point. Especially the idea of Yugo. Their war pulled it together. The communists did."

"Do you ever see Berina and Dušan in the night?" Aisha asks me.

"No," I say, unless dead people can visit you in your dreams.

"I do, they sit at the foot of my bed and play cards."

"Do you talk to them?"

"Yes, I've tried, but they ignore me."

"What game do they play?"

"I don't know," she says.

"Take a closer look next time."

Aisha rolls her eyes. She wishes I were more serious, a thinker like her and Papa.

"Do you think it was a good thing that youth worked together in the brigades to help build the country?" she asks.

"It depends who you ask. A communist will say yes, an anti-communist will say no."

"Who do you think is right?"

I stare at her. I've never thought about it. "The communist will say they are, the anti-communist will say they are. I guess they each have their reasons and arguments."

"I mean, what do *you* think?"

My mind goes blank. I don't know what I think, except that no one could force me to be a youth shock worker, but I'd like to be one anyway, it would be a blast and you could feel good about yourself at the end of the day.

Aisha is watching my face, still waiting for me to say something intelligent. "I guess it all depends on your values," she says. "So the real question is, why were, are, some people communists and some people anti-communists?" She's doing that teacher thing again, asking questions that are meant to suck the answers out of you.

I'M DOWNING thick black espressos at this café on College Street full of Toronto hipsters eating cheap food, drinking expensive coffee, thinking about conquering the world with art and secretly investing in stocks and the next cool uncool haircut, or whatever goes through their complicated minds. I'm waiting for Sava. She wants to meet in a real place, a place that's not school, not my bed, not someone's bedroom floor. A place with chairs, tables, waiters, drinks, food, music, like we're real people living real lives in a real city. We need to talk, she said, which sounds like bad news, something she never says. We need to talk, but I'll meet her anywhere she wants, in the street, in a parking lot, in a ditch, on the front line of life.

The thing is, last night in bed an army of fire ants drinking Jack Daniel's invaded my veins, colonized my mind, heart, hands, sad lonely cock, and commanded me to touch her, feel her, pull her to me, kiss her neck, shoulders, hold her tight for a few heart-thumping moments of sweetness before she woke up and slapped me, swore at me, grabbed her clothes and stormed out of the house. I'm thinking about what I should tell her while the hipsters flip pages of magazines, scribble in notebooks, talk softly as they look over each other's shoulders.

I pull out another letter and think what my grandfather, this man named H., would have said if Baka did the same, if she'd squirmed away from his reach. Because the letters do send me some kind of message. That the two of them, way back five hundred years ago, or fifty years ago, or whatever the fuck, were not only in love, they got it on whenever they wanted to without any obstacles in the way. Maybe that's what happens when you fight for years, when you face death constantly. You get over the idea of life, how it should be, and you just fucking live it to the max every moment of the day.

Sava is standing at the table.

Sava sits down, looks around, scowls. "Who *are* these people, Andric?"

"They're real people, living real lives. You see, chairs, tables, cutlery," I say.

"If you say so," she says. "They don't look real to me. They look like they've bought themselves off a rack in some department store."

I smile. Sava cuts, she slices, she dices, she takes people apart. I wonder what she'll be like when she's older, when she needs people, the world, to hang together.

"What do you want to talk about?" I ask her. I've decided on a tactic.

"What the fuck was up with you last night? Why are you getting weird on me?"

"What? What are you talking about?"

"Last night, you . . . you . . . Jesus. You were mauling me."

"I was what? What are you talking about?"

"C'mon, Jevrem."

"I woke up and you were gone." I say this with my most innocent look all over my face.

Sava says, "Argh," and stands up, scraping her chair backward loudly. "It's impossible to get through to you."

She's walking out the door when I'm struck with a realization. Denial is a kind of lying too, and I decided not to do that. Not to lie to her.

"Sava," I call out. "You're right. Come back, goddammit."

She's striding down the street like a bullfighter, hair billowing behind her. I see everyone else on the street turn their heads to stare at her, I see both men and women thinking secret thoughts of possession and fulfillment. Her long strides, her steady eyes and set jaw, that hair, those bones, that way she throws her hips. It's even worse than I thought, she's royalty, she's a goddess, everyone can see it. I catch up with her. I grab her arm.

"Can we grow up for a minute?" I say. "We're not kids anymore. We like each other. We have things in common. Why can't we get it on? Jesus."

Sava stops and stares at me. I think I see tears in her eyes.

"Jesus, Jevrem, what's happening to you? You're changing on me."

"So? What's so wrong with that? Things change. Life moves us along. In a year we'll be done high school, we'll be adults. We'll be out in the world living real lives."

"I don't know what you're talking about. Back off. Don't ever do that again." Sava pulls loose, begins to walk away.

I stick by her side. "You're in my bed all the time, I love having you there. Look at me. We have to get real here."

"Sex would screw up everything," Sava mutters, her eyes flashing lightning bolts. "If that's what you're talking about."

"It's my bed, and you're in it," I reply.

"That makes no sense. We stole that bed together."

"But, it's not just a bed," I say, "it's *me and you in it*. We made it out alive. Don't you see? Our bodies are *alive*." What's wrong with Sava, forcing me to say these words out loud? Suddenly I do something I've never done before. I grab her and wrestle her against the side of a building. I've surprised her, so she thuds up against the brick easily, letting out a puff of air as her lungs compress.

"I'm not just a poor boy with a body," I whisper in her ear. "I'm a poor boy who wants you." *With a heart*, I want to say, but it sounds cheesy. And I can't use the *L* word. *Love*. It's a word that you can never take back. It's a word that changes everything once it's escaped from the guarded gate of your mouth.

"Andric, snap out of it," Sava hisses, and that's when I realize why she calls me by my last name.

She slips out of my arms and disappears. I turn and walk back the way we came. I refuse to watch her striding away from me, like the last woman alive after the apocalypse, through the dark concrete valleys of the city.

IN THE bar in Kensington Market a girl wears straps. They're over her shoulders, around her neck, criss-crossing her back, clutching her biceps, protecting her wrists, holding up her stockings, pulling back her hair. I drink vodka, she drinks beer. I drink beer, she drinks vodka. I ask her if she's built a railway, she asks me if I've built a railway. She says no, I say no. We two have a lot in common.

She says that she built a footstool once, out of orange crates. I say that I've built nothing at all in my entire life. Not a thing. She says that's okay, I shouldn't feel bad about it, not many people have. We don't need to build things, she says, the world has already been built for us. And I say, what about doing good, and she says that's not so hard, you just have to help people when you see they need help, not act like an asshole, be kind. It's not that hard.

The girl's hair is raven black. It's been dyed that way and it suits her green eyes. Her plucked eyebrows make her seem wise beyond her years, *she's seen it all*, those eyebrows say, *she's seen it, she's fine with it*. She shows me her tattoos. Celtic patterns and symbols, she says, very powerful, if you want it to be. I say, are you Celtic, and she says, no. And I say, oh. And she says, that has nothing to do with it, anyone can feel the Celtic spirit running through their veins. Culture, she says, is radically transferable, that's the great thing about it. And spirit too, come to think of it. Nothing to do with biology. It's about where you live now, what you do, create, think, feel, desire, experience now. *You. Now*. That's what's real.

The girl goes to university and studies theory of something. Third year, she says.

I show her my scars.

Quite a bit later, we're doing bumps of coke in the bathroom, I'm not thinking about Sava, the girl is unstrapping her straps, the bathroom is glittering, the bar is roaring, the universe is streaming through the top of my head. It's a wonderful life if you let it be, maybe that's the message, I think, from Baka and my grandad H., and their delirious letters. Seize the day, seize the hour, seize the minute, seize every last second, all that cheesy crap's just the truth, no one can deny it. The girl drags me into a stall and locks the door. She throws me against the wall and I let out a puff of air as my back hits the toilet paper dispenser. I think, so that's how it feels to be commanded, but the thought is remote, very remote, maybe out in the stratosphere between clouds and nothingness. Closer in, I've got a mouthful of girl, her tongue, her lips, her neck, her shoulders, her Celtic patterns and symbols. She tastes, she pulsates, she hums, she quivers with life like a newborn creature. The straps are off and there are breasts to sing to, to build a whole network of railways for, they're just there, out in the open, waiting to be consumed, so I consume them like a carnivore, and I feel so much better than ever before. She sits on the toilet tank, opens her legs to all possibilities and I dive in headfirst, like snorkellers and deep-sea divers who chase after flashes of colour their whole lives. My sad lonely cock is feeling better too, way better, now that I have her ankles at my ears, her hips in my hands, the stamina of mountains. I say to the girl, do you want to keep doing this forever? And she answers with a mysterious smile. I say, why do sex and poetry and drugs go together? And she says, have some more, use my key. Time weaves, warps, stretches. There's more of time and feeling good than I ever thought possible in the little box I've been living in all these years. Outside, kids come in and out of the bathroom like waves on a beach. They do bumps of coke, they unstrap their straps, they glitter, they roar, they feel the universe sucking them into orbit. And, floating out there like dust in sunlight, they look back at our perfectly smooth glowing marble of a planet and wonder.

‡ ‡ ‡

WE SIT IN THE CAR, STARING AT THE SMALL, shabby house. Overflowing garbage can out front, soaking newspapers and torn candy wrappers in the shrubbery. Flaking paint, rusting metal, crumbling brick, rotting wood, cardboard blocking up windows, torn blinds. It's perfect. Perfectly sad and pathetic.

"Okay," I say. "Be quiet and fucking careful, this time. Don't break anything."

The others slouch across the deserted street to the house, heels dragging, chins tucked in. There's no exhilaration this time, I note. They're just humouring me. You don't deny a person crazy with grief, they're thinking. They don't realize that I'm not crazy with grief, I'm just crazy. That's how I feel. I feel crazy, like someone born again is crazy, or a person quitting drugs is crazy. The extraordinary people, the people filled with this unexpected, driving, glittering energy that allows them to do a hundred things at once, when before they could hardly get off the couch.

Zijad and Madzid haul the grocery bags. Milk, bread, cereal. A carton of cigarettes. Enough cans to feed a monster family for a month. We work for ten minutes to get into the house without shattering glass, Sava sweating over the window frame, swearing the whole time. She manages to get the frame up in one piece, and slips in silently. We wait, and then she's at the door, holding her sleeve over her mouth, gagging. The stench inside is dense, opaque. I can't read it. It has many layers, layers that have chemically bonded to each other, layers that repel each other. A tiny, skinny cat slips between Sava's legs. Sava looks at me with hard, furious eyes.

"Food in the fridge," I say. "Cans on the counter. Zijad, stay outside and clean up the yard,"

Zijad bolts off the spongy porch, garbage bag in hand, and Sava and Madzid follow him.

"I'm not going in that house, Andric," Sava hisses at me. "It's disgusting."

"Quiet," I whisper back. "Don't be such a baby." But I let them go. We thought we were tough. This takes real balls. I go in alone.

The hallway and small living room are filled to the ceiling with furniture, sagging boxes, tall piles of paper, magazines, newspapers, books. I can see this in the murky light from a grimy forty-watt bulb hanging on a high wire in the hallway. The kitchen also bulges with stacks of paper, assorted chairs, a three-legged table, two filing cabinets, boxes stained with unidentifiable seepage, empty food cartons, wraps, strewn packaging; there's only a small clearing around sink, stove, and fridge. The fridge is empty but for a carton of milk, half a bag of bread, ten empty cat-food cans, and green algae-like scum swimming in the vegetable crisper. I take everything out of the fridge, pour out the sour milk, throw the cans into a garbage bag. Then I look under the sink for cleaners. There are many, neatly congregated, all unopened, and next to them, a shiny red bucket. I fill the bucket, get down on my knees in front of the fridge. The hot water steams beside me, and I realize that this house is not heated, which is a real drag on an April night in Toronto. I scour the inside of the fridge with Ajax, then take the crisper out and let the scum swirl and slither its way down the sink's crusty drain, releasing a smell like liquid manure.

Zijad, Sava, and Madzid are at the front door.

"Jevrem, get your ass out of there. We're going."

I dump another load of Ajax into the crisper, close my eyes and scrub wildly.

Sava is at my shoulder. "For Christ's sake, look at you. Get a grip. We got her the food. That's enough."

I rinse the crisper, careful not to let the water splash.

"There's more to do," I say, eyeing the one bowl, the one pot, the one spoon, all resting primly in the dish rack. They're all crusty with a thousand ancient meals.

"We're going," says Sava.

"What's going on? Who is there?"

The voice comes from the darkness upstairs. Sava and I stare at each other.

"Who is there? Get out of my house, you bad people. Who's there?"

The voice has a piercing overtone, yet it's also unusually low and gravelly. The old lady also has a big-ass European accent of some kind. She sounds like a Nazi concentration camp guard from an American 1950s war movie. I wait for her to start barking commands and laughing fiendishly, but instead, metal springs strain and squeak. She's right above us, and she's getting out of bed.

"I will call the police," she wails. We hear unsteady shuffling footsteps, floorboards straining.

Sava laughs. This is getting more interesting for her now. I put the crisper back in the fridge. Then I fill the sink with hot water and put the dishes to soak, place the milk, bread, butter, brick of cheese, cold cuts, mayo, pickles, lettuce, tomatoes, and jam that we bought at Dominion on the top shelf of the fridge. I stare at the arrangement, then move the milk to the other side so it can all be viewed more easily in one glance.

Sava rolls her eyes. "We have to go, Andric, you've gone fucking insane. She may have a phone up there."

"She doesn't have a phone at all," I say.

I unpack the rest of the grocery bags, leaving the cans of cat food in four neat rows on the counter. Then I grab the garbage bag, turn off the kitchen light, and creep toward the front door.

The old lady is at the top of the stairs, peering down. She's a baggy ghost figure with her nightgown or something ballooning around her like a parachute during landing. Her hair, like sheep's wool, so fine, so wispy, is sticking out in all directions. She's gasping and sobbing now. "I will call the police. I will. You will not get away with this, no you won't."

I stop at the bottom of the stairs.

Sava punches me in the arm, grabs my sleeve, starts pulling me out. "C'mon, goddammit, let's go."

I want to go upstairs and reassure the woman, maybe put her back to bed. I know how to deal with old ladies, I think.

The yard looks much better, everything tidied up. The garbage can is no longer overflowing, and next to it are two full garbage bags, to which I add mine, lining it up exactly.

‡

WE GO back in a few days and put the garbage out on the curb. We bring pots of geraniums we've taken from a gardening centre and arrange them on the weathered front porch. Zijad and Geordie reinforce the porch railings with brackets and screws, Sava replaces a soft tread on the front stairs. Inside the mouldering, smelly living room crammed to the ceiling with ancient stuff, I find a rocking chair that makes my heart sing. Every old lady should be able to sit on her porch, rocking gently, contemplating flowers, clouds, birds, the past, neighbours walking by, or whatever they like to contemplate.

The others wait by the car, smoking, kicking stones, staring at the full moon flying like a dolphin through thick, foaming clouds. It starts to rain. I slink through the house room by room and find fancy stuff from fancy days long gone. It's in boxes, cupboards, closets, in amongst mouse droppings and dust as deep as snow. Silverware, china, linen tablecloths, napkins, crystal. A side table holds ancient implements I don't recognize for foods I've never seen. I set up her table for her, which has been leaning separated from its legs, up against a wall for who knows how long. I lay the table for afternoon coffee and cake, the kind my aunties and grandmothers liked in the middle of the afternoon. Then I think, who wants to eat coffee and cake alone? And there is Papa standing in the archway between the dining room and living room, a newspaper tucked under one arm, staring at me with a little smile on his face. *This is an interesting approach to life's difficult questions, Jevrem,* he says. *Highly unusual, highly suspect, but definitely interesting, definitely creative and proactive. You get points for being literal-minded.* Whatever, I say. Look at this huge silver tray. It's so ornate, and it's still pretty shiny. Nice life this lady had when life was good. There's no reason she can't get some of that back, with a little help from her friends, don't you think? Oh wait, she doesn't have any friends, that's the thing. But Papa doesn't comment. He turns and rifles through an open box.

By the time I step out the front door into pouring rain, I've made up my mind. This old lady needs some people. I'm going to call Social Services or whatever they're called. I see a gossipy gang of crones in that dining room exchanging war stories and knitting baby blankets for orphans in far-off places, or whatever it is old ladies like to do. But Sava and the others don't want to hear about it. They're sullen and insist on holding up a gas station for drinks, chips, gum, cigarettes, on the way home, which pisses me off, as we sneak through Toronto's empty, tidy streets waiting for dawn.

AT HOME, Sava and I creep in the side entrance and down to my room. Thunderous piano music crashes through the ceiling from above. I check my watch. Mama is up again at 4 a.m. She's working up her repertoire. The Romantics. Beethoven, Brahms, Schumann, Liszt, Scriabin. Now that Baka is not sleeping next to the living room, Mama says she can audition again. I don't see what Baka has to do with it, since she loved to listen to Mama play, but some story in Mama's mind tells her that this, this final death, has freed her, and so she plays all day long and through the night. No more visitors, no more Sunday dinners, no more dragging herself around pretending ordinary life is okay but hating every minute of it. "Creativity," says Mama, "is all we really have, in the end, in the final instant, when everything else has passed. And it is everything, it is the world."

"How the hell are we going to sleep through this?" Sava asks, falling onto the bed.

I run upstairs. "Mama," I say. Only the small lamp is on, so Mama is playing in shadows. "Mama." I walk into the living room and stand right next to her. Her eyes are closed. "Mama," I say. But she doesn't respond, she's listening for something other than a human voice.

I go to Aisha's room and carefully open the door. I wonder how she deals with the all-night practising. By the night-light I can see that she's squeezed herself into one side of the single bed, as she always does, leaving space for Berina. I see everything neatly laid out for the morning, clothes, knapsack, stack of books, violin, music bag, everything on her desk lined up at right angles. I walk right up close to her, listen to her slow, steady breathing, watch her chest rising and falling. Then I see her trick. She's wearing earplugs, there's a box of them on her night table.

Downstairs, the window is open. The room smells of spring mud, stormy lakewater, wind that's travelled a thousand miles over thawing farmland. I sit on the chair, which is uncomfortable, and stare at Sava. I still want to strangle her, shake her until she breaks, until she looks at me and says, *Jevrem, come closer, what are you waiting for?* Instead she says, "You're both fucking nuts. Your mom quit her cleaning job, didn't she? And you've lost it and aren't bringing anything in either. How are you going to survive? What about Aisha?"

"Don't worry, I'll look after her and Aisha, and honour Baka's last words to me."

"Oh please, Jevrem. There were no last words. There just weren't any. Why do you keep lying about that?"

I throw earplugs at her and she stuffs them in her ears and crawls under the quilt. I stare out of the window, which is a square of black. In a couple of hours the sky will lighten suddenly to neon blue, and yet another day will be upon us. Why? For what purpose? Maybe there was transcendental telepathy between Baka and me, because last words are definitely ricocheting around in my skull, causing quite a bit of damage. Last words that I can't quite decipher, that just won't leave me alone.

I perch on the torture chair for a long time, thinking, smoking, drinking my face off, watching Sava sleep. I'm exhausted, but it'd be far more torturous to get into bed with her. After our last fight about it, Sava didn't move back to her own bed, to her own house. I don't know what she wants me to do, but I'm done with that bullshit, lying there with my pathetic heart pumping blood like a motherfucker, my poor lonely peripheries itching to make a move. Finally I get up, grab my coat, and sway out of the house.

In Cedarvale Park, trees weave by me like drunken dancers.

I have no idea what they are, maple, ash, birch, fir, pine, poplar, walnut, mulberry. Wood and leaves, roots and branches. The forest floor bounces and ducks as well, and maybe I'm dancing too, because my breathing is a kind of ugly rasping and wheezing. I stagger my way up a steep hill, a heavy pack on my back, a rifle at my side, a grenade on my belt, a knife in my boot. Baka, I say, tell me what it feels like to be as purposeful as a soldier of resistance and revolution. But she's not talking to me now, and I don't find a pine tree that will keep me warm through the night, like she did when she was my age. After an hour, my dark thoughts whither and die in the blustery cold and I leave the park and walk the pre-dawn streets making random turns, edging closer to home and my bed.

On Bloor Street, I pass the old church that's never open, the Shoppers Drug Mart that's never closed. I stop in front of the second-hand bookstore and peer in the window. Dusty coffee-table books on display. Orchids. Turkey. Poor People. Chagall. Eastern-Orthodox domes. World War Two, still the most popular. And, of course, Sarajevo. Sarajevo happy, Sarajevo sad, and Sarajevo roses, all different shapes, the spray of blood on ancient stone. I think about gunshots, pedestrians running, the athletic ones sprinting like Olympians to live another day. I turn and there, a long way ahead of me, is Papa striding quickly toward Bathurst, his shoulders hunched, his hands in his pockets. He hears my footsteps, he turns, he waves. Then he disappears into a doorway.

At home, my feet aching, I crawl into bed next to Sava. She's a million miles away in another galaxy of existence, I can tell by her breathing, but her body is here, warm, heavy, unmoving. I lie an inch from her, suffering in ecstasy, soaking up her heat like a sand lizard at high noon.

‡ ‡ ‡

IT'S EVENING. I SLEPT THROUGH A WHOLE DAY, MY body glued to the place where Sava had lain. Upstairs, Mama is playing a sonata. She's on fire, bouncing around on that piano bench like Ray Charles on speed, I can tell by the tempo. Sometimes, she and Aisha play together and I stop to listen on the way to wherever I'm going, because they sound like that Ashkenazy and Perlman record we had, they sound like a freaking concert at Carnegie Hall. Aisha in her new wardrobe of performance clothes, our family's little ambassador, winning competitions, acing her classes, going on a trip to the freaking UN in New York City.

Meanwhile, in my subterranean world, Zijad is in pill-land, slumped against the wall. We watch as his eyes flutter and his head dangles next to his shoulder like it's about to fall off. Madzid is playing a game on his new computer, recently liberated, chewing his lips, scratching his neck, rubbing his bloodshot eyes until they're puffy slits. We sit around all evening, smoking, sleeping, not saying much. We start drinking coffee at around midnight and creep out of the house at 2 a.m. It's raining again. Icy, sleeting rain. One day, hot sunshiny weather will appear to sooth our souls or maybe we're cursed to live in the butt-end of winter forever, what they call spring here, as a punishment for our terrible sins. We hop into Geordie's car, but Sava takes the wheel.

Tonight we're after a man. Old, one shoulder higher than the other, yellow, waxy face. An ugly, insecure, confrontational look to him. The others are joining in because there promises to be some action, but once again I don't feel much joy from them, not much enthusiasm at all. And Papa says to me, *you may very well be entering that part of the life journey that comes just before getting totally lost.*

Sava says, "You're targeting too many from your own neighbourhood, Andric."

I ignore her. Of course, I think, that's where I watch them, that's where I see them living their lives.

"This guy," I say, "leaves that shitty bar on the corner, where the Pizza Pizza is. Bad beer, bad lighting, bad sound, fucked-up TV. So, what's the draw? Lots of other men like him. They talk and talk. About what? Nothing good, I guarantee that. Nothing fucking uplifting."

"So, we're getting him for being a stupid ass from some nasty primitive backwater?" Madzid asks.

Sava is shaking her head, rolling her eyes. She says, "There is this house I saw over by Mount Pleasant and Eglinton. Lots of big packaging in the recycling. You know, electronics, furniture, appliances. Just moved in. Just married. Wedding gifts, lots of stuff they didn't even pay for. Perfect."

"This guy," I say, "I don't like the way his wife walks ten steps behind him, carries all the groceries home from the store. He stops to talk to some guy, chest stuck out, cigarette smouldering in the palm of his hand. Stops and talks for as long as he wants, his wife just standing there a few feet away, staring at the sidewalk. When he's ready, he barks at her to follow."

"Oh please, Andric. That's lame, that's none of your business." Sava screeches around a corner. The car slides into the intersection, bucks, jerks, then straightens out. It doesn't matter. There are few cars on the road in the early mornings, not much to crash into. But we all instinctively listen for sirens.

"Right here," I say. "All the way down, south of St. Clair."

Sava slows. We look into a bar with third-world lighting. It's empty.

"I'm going in," I say. My blood is lava exploding in fiery cascades behind my eyeballs. I feel primed to do a bit of good. I describe the man to the bartender, who sighs and points vaguely at the street. "Left about five minutes ago."

I'm outside, looking both ways. The sleet has turned to snow. White flakes zigzag in every direction. I know where the man lives, but don't know which route he takes. I want to get him before he arrives home. My foot taps to some inner beat that's not my heart.

I get in the car and we drive slowly along St. Clair. We see the man lurching along the slick sidewalk, his joints rubbery and uncooperative.

"He looks pathetic," Madzid says. "A pathetic old grandpa."

"That's no excuse," I say, "there are lots of grandpas out there who are scum of the earth," and Sava nods. She understands. Maybe this will be the one that brings us together again.

We cruise beside the man, rolling down our windows.

"Hey," I say. "Hey, over here."

The man looks at the car, then points his head forward again.

"Hey, old man, I'm talking to you."

"Maybe he's too drunk to understand," Geordie says.

"Let's put him in the trunk," Sava says, a glimmer of enthusiasm in her voice.

Before she's finished her brilliant sentence, we're out of the car. We scoop the man up by legs and chest, him crying, "*Ahh ahh*," and swing him into the trunk. He doesn't fit very well, but we rearrange his limbs and force the trunk closed. And there is Papa, standing on the other side of the street, hands in his pockets, looking straight at me, shaking his head, his shoulders up in that what-the-fuck posture that he sometimes had.

I THINK the eastern horizon is paler than before. I think I can see a hint of blue. But basically, we're in darkness, except for a distant street lamp. The invisible water laps calmly. It's very relaxing to be at the lakeshore, but the ground is cold. We've been smoking joint after joint, and downing Madzid's bottle of vodka. For the last few hours, the man has stumbled around, sat awkwardly on the ground, gestured at the sky, calling out, why me, why me, why me, and babbled on about accountants, tax men, customs officials, politicians, all the people who have treated him badly.

"What do you want from me?" he keeps croaking. "What? What?"

"It's six fifteen," Sava says. "Sunrise soon."

I get up and stride over to the man. He clearly won't guess by himself why he is here. The thought will not cross his mind in a million years, which is too long for us.

"We've invited you here for a reason," I say to him. "You have to figure it out yourself."

"Are you crazy?" the man asks. "Who are you? Who set you onto me? I paid those debts. I paid them in full. Yes, I did. You ask Pickle."

"We don't know any Pickle," I say. "Like I said, we're here to tell you something about life, you fucking low-life."

"But what do you *want*?"

"We want you to look at yourself and see what a giant fucking asshole you are, then we want you to stop being a giant fucking asshole."

"But I don't understand," the man wails, and shivers and stamps his rickety feet.

I pick up Sava's baseball bat and saunter toward him. The man stares at me with incomprehension and terror. I guess he'll never see what he needs to see all by himself, maybe a little head-rattling will help.

The eastern horizon turns a glowing swimming-pool blue. Lake Ontario materializes before our eyes, moving restlessly, waiting for something to happen. The ducks push off for some other part of the shore. Birds begin to twitter all at once, a thousand cars suddenly roar along the highway behind us, and the silence of pre-dawn gives way to a raucous barrage of sound.

‡

AT SCHOOL, we trudge down the deserted, echoing hallway. Shiny floors, scuffed walls. We're late, as usual, and so tired our ears are ringing and our hearts are racing.

"That wasn't cool," Sava says, icy voice. "That was for Baka?"

Zijad takes a handful of pills and offers some around. "Anyone?" he asks.

"Torturing is for Baka?" She's not letting this one go.

"For Christ's sake, Sava, we just scared the nasty wife-beating shit a little." I flash her a wide smile, but I don't feel fully confident that she understands my thinking on this. "And it was time someone did. Apart from the kidnapping, we didn't touch him at all."

She's not laughing, not smiling. None of them are. They're staring at me in a strange way, like I'm a dangerous freak they've never seen before, like they think stealing stuff is way less fucked up than giving this dude a little talking-to for the good of society and his cringing, pathetic wife. It's a look that sinks into me like a knife, for some reason. There's a sharp little pain, then an ache that says whatever's holding things together in there has been slit apart, that it's all sliding around loose, that I'm never going to get it together again. I don't know why I'm so shaky today, but I kind of feel like sobbing my guts out, my vision is blurry, my hands are cold and clammy. Maybe it's because all the signs are there: the days of our gang are over, we're going in different directions, I don't know what the fuck I'm trying to do for Baka, and when nothing makes sense anymore, when the gang is no more, what will exist in the world for me?

I HOLD my breath, look up and down the street carefully, calculating angles and distances. It's too open, this street. No trees, no awnings, no newspaper stands, no municipal buses turned on their sides and stacked on top of each other like giant shields against the sniper fire. Only a few parked cars. What am I doing here? I spot a sheltered doorway. Two people are huddled there already. I aim for it and sprint like a greyhound with eyes on the rabbit. I crash into the door, huddle, pant. The two others, a man, a woman, stare at me, then look at each other with wide eyes.

"There's a sniper up there," I say. "I can feel it in my bones. Just wait here for now."

But they look at each other again and step quickly out into the street.

"What are you doing?" I call after them.

Sometimes it's impossible to help people. Sometimes they just have a death wish and there is nothing you can do. I watch them walking away fast, looking over their shoulders. But walking out in the open here means doom. I follow them with my eyes, and there it is, the small, glistening whale-spurt of blood pluming out of the woman's head. I wait for the rag-doll collapse,

I see the man drop to his knees shouting, *noooo, noooo*. Then the Red Cross is on its way. I hear the sirens. I hear women screaming. Someone else got it too. Maybe a whole crowd of people. Well, I'm not going to wait around for the next bullet, I'm going to take matters into my own hands. I'm going to walk up into the mountain forest, I'm done with being held hostage in this death trap of inertia and waiting.

Drops of water land on the black rock beside me. They make a small slapping sound at regular intervals, while mossy pools glisten and shiver, reflecting a brooding spring sky. I look up at the tangle of black branches, which shine and click and rustle. The forest is charcoal and brown, but I sense the coming of green. Beyond the trees are valleys, mountain peaks, moving clouds, and Croatia floats in the distance like an island. I'm happy here, in the brush, close to the earth, sheltered by trees, but I wish I could get in deeper, like an animal in its hole, to where I'm invisible, untouchable. I scrabble in the dirt and rotted leaves with my fingers, my fingernails lifting from the flesh, with my mouth, my teeth, my tongue, but it's useless, it's so cold in these parts that the earth is still frozen, it doesn't let me in. So I just lie here and let the mountain air rush over the burning surface of my skin.

Someone is slapping my face. "Andric," she shouts at me. "Andric."

The voice rattles me, my nerves are live wires.

"Jesus." I try to raise my head. It pounds with too much blood. "What the hell, Andric?"

It's Sava and her face is close to mine. It's white like a chalk drawing, lines drawn in black from nose to mouth.

"We've been searching for you forever."

"Oh yeah?" I say. My mouth is filled with a bitter taste, my lips feel brittle, burnt, about to split open.

"You're acting totally insane."

I lift my head, look around. There is no valley, Croatia isn't floating like an island in the distance.

"Look at you. You're lying under bushes in a ditch. Your eyes are completely red."

"How did I get here?" I ask her. "I was in the mountain forest."

"You're scaring me," Sava says. "You're cracking up. Get a grip."

"On what?" I say. I feel weird, like I'm impersonating someone I've never met.

"On life, Andric." She pauses. "And death. People die in everyday life. They get old. It's okay. You don't have to go crazy over it. Just cry or something."

I have no idea what she's talking about, and I wish she'd go away. The sight of her makes me sad. I try to get up, but my head really hurts. Maybe I hit it on the way down.

I sit for hours in the roti shop on Eglinton chain-smoking like Papa and drinking warm Cokes. Sava says I should lock myself up in a psych ward, that my mind is broken. I don't think she's joking. It's true, yesterday I lost a few hours, or a day maybe; it was like a crazy time-travelling speed trip, just as freaking tense and fucked up. It's stress, Zijad says, and stress does that shit to sensitive kids like us. But everything's back to normal today.

"You look rough," the guy behind the counter says. He's cooking up a storm. "Try eating something, brother, this food will do you good."

But I don't feel like eating. I'm trying to think. I'm picturing a log jam, how one log gets pulled loose, then all the other logs slowly start to move, jostling each other, finding space, how they one by one begin to flow with the river. Except for the ones at the edges, they stay stuck, they get bleached white on the top and rot black on the bottom. I'm a log on the edge, I think. I'm watching all the other logs sail by. I have to focus, get myself moving, stay with the plan, with or without Sava and the others, with or without Baka watching over the good of my soul.

"Brother, are you wanting some advice?"

The owner behind the counter is getting sick of me, he's going to get rid of me with friendliness.

"I don't need advice," I say. "I know what's what. Something's gotta give in my life."

He nods, flashes a wide smile, points at his ghetto blaster propped on a high shelf. *Sittin' in the morning sun. And watching all the birds passing by . . .*

I trudge down Oakwood, then along side streets lined with little houses no taller than their doors and windows. Even the poor, shabby neighbourhoods in Toronto are tidy, with cut grass, gardens, hedges, trees. Inside a garage with its door wide open Papa is fiddling with a small fridge. He's got the door off, and is going into the back panel with a screwdriver. Papa, I say, how's it going? Papa raises his head and looks around for the source of the voice but doesn't see me. He looks as happy and purposeful as a child with a toy as he sticks his head in the fridge again.

I let myself in through the back door and sit down at the kitchen table. It's time to move this story along. I've decided what I'm going to do, which is the only way forward for me, through the eye of the needle. There are voices in the living room, the low rumble of a man talking and a woman's laugh that's a familiar echo from a time long ago. That's Mama, the one we left behind, I think she's back.

I walk into the living room and there she is perched on the piano bench telling a story in French with both her hands and her whole body. The person she's telling it to is a man with grey hair in a hipster suit, bright blue shirt, string tie. He's folded himself into one end of the couch, he's holding a cap in his hands, he's wearing a crooked, mischievous smile on his face, and his eyes are glinting over something funny that Mama just said. Mama turns and plays a few chords and a melody line on the piano. The man says, oui, oui, c'est ca, c'est ça. He sings a few words of a song in low, raunchy tones. Then he sees me and stops.

"This must be your son," he says in French, and looks at me with interest.

Mama leans toward me on the piano stool. "Jevrem. There you are. This is Leo Colard. I'm going to accompany him at an upcoming concert in Toronto. His songs are so beautiful." She's speaking Serbo-Croatian to me as if he can understand.

"Hi, good to meet you," I say, in English. And there we are, three people in a room speaking three different languages.

Leo stands up and bows in an old-school hippie beatnik kind of way. "The pleasure is all mine, my friend."

"I'm going downstairs," I say to the empty space between us.

"Why don't you join us for dinner," Leo asks. "Your mother and I are going to sample some delectable Ethiopian food. I've been telling her about the fine Ethiopian restos in the city. Exquisite coffee served with frankincense, such a fragrant after-dinner puja. But there's also Vietnamese, Korean, Japanese, Chinese, Thai, Tibetan, Indian, Punjabi, Pakistani, Italian, Portuguese, Greek, Caribbean, Polish, Hungarian, Latin American." He pauses to smile his crooked smile that I already know means *isn't the world a beautiful array of glittering wonders*, he's that kind of tuned-in grooving old peacenik dude.

"Some of it as authentic and magnificent as you can get back in the old country. That's the kind of city Toronto is, and I say this as a proud Montrealer."

"No thanks," I say. I try to think of the last time Mama, Aisha, and I went out to a restaurant, just a regular one from wherever, and can't. I try to think of anywhere we've gone as a family in all the time we've been here but nothing comes to mind, except visits to Milan and Iva. You need money for that kind of thing, and the energy to get out of the house.

"Aisha is coming," Mama says.

She's in four dimensions today with her lily perfume on, the smell of it making me want to scream. I see the four of us sitting at a table like a family, discussing the plot of a movie, or whose turn it is to mow the lawn, or whatever it is families talk about at dinner.

"I'm busy, have fun," I say, and walk through the kitchen and down my stairs.

‡ ‡ ‡

THEY'RE ALWAYS THERE ON THE STEPS OF THE boarded-up building, garbage and rags trampled all around them like compacted earth. A main intersection, a steady flow of traffic, these people on the steps, drinking, laughing, sleeping, looking like they're about to die, everyone skirting around them, pretending they don't exist.

Tonight I'm alone. Sava and the others have given up on me, they're doing their thing in the rich parts of town. The evening is clear, almost warm. I walk up to the group and introduce myself.

"Hey, people," I say. "I'm Jevrem."

"Hey, Jevrem," everyone shouts. They are in party mode and make a lot of hosting kinds of comments. "Come on in. Have a seat. Got some smokes? Relax, have a laugh. Wanna swig?" Leather-tough hands thrust toward me holding bottles and inch-long butts.

"Is it good times?" I ask.

"Yeah, it's good times, man. It's real good times." Deep brown faces crack wide with smiles.

"Why are you here all the time?" I ask.

"Having good times," a guy shouts, "like you said."

"But you don't look very well," I say. They all laugh like happy people at a fair. "I mean, really, you guys look like hell, you've got injuries all over, you're filthy, and you don't seem to have anything to do."

More laughter, hooting, whistling. "Whoa, this guy's real perceptive."

"No, I mean, I'm serious. You look really bad, all sick and beat-up. No one mentions this when they walk by, but they're all thinking it. If it were them, if they were in your shape, they'd expect someone to call an ambulance immediately, they'd expect that of their fellow human being. It would be a high-alert emergency. So, what gives?"

"As long as the bastards leave us alone," a guy wrapped in a sleeping bag says, "what're we gonna do? Work for some white motherfucking asshole who disrespects us, for no pay, get treated like shit all day long?"

"Too much fun partying," says an old woman, a skeleton with sagging skin, no teeth, shaking hands.

"No, I'm serious," I say. "What do you want from life?"

"We want to be fucking left alone, like Buddy said." A guy

with a giant purple swollen jaw is narrowing his eyes at me. He's not smiling anymore. "You got a problem with that?"

"A hot bath," says the old woman, who might also be about thirty. "That's what I fucking want."

"So, you want a hot bath?" I say. I'm on a mission, but it's harder alone, without the Bastards and our work camaraderie. And Baka is fading in and out of range.

"Yeah, but, you know, like in a hot spring or something. A spa. Yeah, I wanna go to a spa."

More laughter. These guys are so cheery. I haven't heard this much laughing ever.

"So, you mind that you smell?"

"You got a big frigging mouth on you, boy." The man with the purple jaw stands unsteadily. "Are we gonna ask this boy to move along?"

"No, I don't mean to be disrespectful," I say. "Everyone wants to ask, they want to know how you got here, if it's their fault for being white settlers or what. But no one does. Ask, I mean. I, however, am really interested."

"We're all frigging drinkers and sniffers, boy. What do you think the story is? Mansions and butlers and private schools? We're here because we see through you. The whole big pile of shit called society, the one you're a part of, we see it for what it is. You think you live good? You're just crawling to the top of that pile of shit, slithering and sliding and swallowing the crud, you and everyone else. You think that don't smell?"

"I don't think I live good," I say. "I live bad, really, really bad."

"Oh yeah, boy? You don't know what bad is."

"Yes, actually I do," I say. "I know what bad is. I've seen bad. But the point here is that this fine lady wants to go to the spa. Anyone else?"

IT'S LATE and I'm searching for one of those big vans, like a small school bus. I drive around various neighbourhoods and up and down a lot of tree-lined streets. I finally find one outside a small bungalow off Keele Street, north of Lawrence. Maybe a bus driver's house, one who parks the bus in her own driveway every day after doing the rounds.

I park Madzid's car a few streets over and drive my hot-wired bus downtown, behaving like a good boy, stopping at stop signs, signalling every turn. When I pull up at the intersection, the mangy group is there as always, on their steps, sitting in a perfect circle.

"Oh man, it's the boy with the mouth. Hey, you, boy."

"You came back, man. That never happens, man. Wanna drink? Come on over."

"It's the pickup for the spa," I say, jumping down the steps onto the sidewalk. I feel like an actor on TV. "I have room for twelve."

"What the hell?" They point and shout and don't move from the steps for quite a while.

It takes me about an hour of chatting and cajoling to convince them that I'm for real, I'm here to take them to paradise, I'm not an asshole Indian-catcher here to cart them out of town. Finally, they pile in with high spirits, feeling safety in numbers.

I roll down the window and drive sedately along the city streets, cursing one-ways, hoping no cops cross our path.

"Are you some kind of religious nut?" asks the guy with the eggplant jaw, sitting on the seat behind mine and poking his head into the aisle. "You know that clean isn't just soap and the laundromat, boy. Clean and dirty go right down to the fucking soul, man, and believe me, we're not the dirty ones. I've got a name, by the way, it's Robert."

"Hey, Robert," I say. "I'm Jevrem and I know all of that, you don't have to lecture me like I'm some freaking little kid. I don't care about cleaning you up. I see a need, I try to fill it, that's all, I try to spread a little joy. I'm, you know, changing my ways."

"Where you from, Yvy? You speak like a fucking Kraut, man."

"A Kraut? Jesus, no way," I say. "I'm from Bosnia. Very different than Kraut."

"Oh yeah, Bosnia, man? You guys finished killing each other yet?"

"I don't know," I say. "We have to wait and see."

"Fucking white guys, man. Slaughter on the mind all the time. Just wanna kill, kill, kill. You should think of socializing instead, hanging out with your friends, partying, having a good time, live and let live, to each his own, exist in the moment. It's healthier that way, man, way healthier, way less deadly."

He's got a point, I guess, in his lecturing I'm-down-and-out-therefore-I'm-a-wise-man kind of way. Drinking, sniffing, shooting up, living on a Canadian street probably is healthier than a civil war.

The bus scrapes through a narrow alleyway and I pull up to the butt-end of the community centre I know for certain has a fine new swimming pool, saunas, steam bath, the whole deal. I did my research. In the back of the van are two garbage bags full of good clothes and towels that Sava has collected from houses in the last weeks. Annex clothes. Forest Hill clothes. Even Bridle Path and King City clothes. I haul these out and tell the revellers to be quiet. They're staggering all over the place, shouting, laughing, singing.

"We're going in there," I say. "I don't know about the security system. It may go off, but I don't think so."

I aim my beat-up handgun at the lock in the metal door. My group stands around watching warily, less chipper now.

"Whoa, who the hell are you, man? This is too fucking intense. I don't know. Don't like guns, they're wicked, they're white-guy stupid."

"Just getting the door open, nothing to worry about."

The lock shatters with a godawful bang. But the door swings open and I don't hear an alarm. I look around the frame and along the baseboards and can't see any kind of security wiring. There are no cameras.

We're inside, walking along murky utility corridors in single file.

"Jesus Christ, man. What kind of fucking loser spa is this, man?" One of the guys falls down and seems suddenly to be in deep sleep.

"Just leave him there. We'll get him on the way out," says his buddy, crossing the guy's arms over his chest to make him comfortable.

After about ten minutes we find the right door. In the gloom, we hear the stirring and rippling of water, we feel humidity circling around us then grabbing hold of our skin and sinking in. Echoes tell us we're in a big space and everyone piles through the door, stepping carefully on tiled flooring to where the pool begins. Exotic bird calls erupt, the fluttering sound of a flock landing on open water. *Helloooo there*'s shoot up into the rafters to float back down like the honks of fogbound fishing boats. I walk back into the hallway and start hunting behind the scenes for lights. I find the switches in an unlocked closet and turn on the hallway lights, leaving the pool room dark. When I re-enter, I can now see the large swimming pool shimmering dark blue in the half-light, like a lake on a windy day. All my wretched of

Canada's earth are crouching at the water's edge, hands submerged, looking down into the sparkling depths. Then we all strip down and plunge into the tepid water.

For a few minutes, there's complete silence except for the lapping of water against the tile edge. We glide around each other like water animals, otters or dolphins or beavers maybe, everyone as agile and whole again as small children, eyes skimming the glowing surface, mouths opening and closing like fish, long-buried lake-memories forcing their way to the surface like tiny, sparkling air bubbles. We float on our backs and watch faint water reflections flicker on the ceiling.

I drag myself out, lie on a towel on the pool deck, and drift off. Splashing and laughter are the sounds of my dream, like they're the sounds of childhood, and we all had one of those, we were all playful, trusting little creatures once, at least to begin with. Soon I'll look around to see if I can find and turn on the saunas and steam baths. Every good spa needs that kind of thing, hot after cool, cool after hot.

‡ ‡ ‡

THE COPS COME FOR ME ON A TRUE SPRING DAY, gloomy clouds and cold rain in the morning, bright hot sunshine in the afternoon, steam rising in puffs from soaked lawns. They come right to our front door. I feel so relieved that I stretch and sigh like a cat. It's a strain holding things together without Sava and the others, without much certainty that I'm making Baka proud.

When they knock, I'm sitting on the living room floor listening to Mama's Emperor Concerto, which she plays like it expresses everything there is in the world. Aisha is sitting next to me on the couch with her rulers, sharpened pencils, protractor, calculator lined up like surgical tools on the coffee table. She's making a blueprint of our apartment back home, mapping every wall, door, window, all the furniture, accurate to the last millimetre, perfectly to scale, and beneath that is the building that was there before our apartment building was built, and beneath that, what was there a thousand years ago, and beneath that, a million years ago. This isn't a drafting project, it's for her history class. We think of time like a road we move along through space from one place to the next, she tells me. But it isn't like that, history piles up on top of itself in the same place, it doesn't move forward, and you can't look backward at it either. It's always right here. Think of it as a fixed camera shooting time-lapse film, time transforms the scene completely but the scene itself always stays put, it's always right here. And the camera is our own mind, she says. History is something that exists only in the mind of whoever happens to be alive on planet Earth at any given time. It's a vision of the present. These are the things that my thirteen-year-old sister thinks about while I'm about to be taken to jail. She's very precise, stacking her history in layers, giving space to Papa, Dušan, Berina, Baka, and all the others she only sort of knows about who aren't here, our djedica, the other grandparents, the Ilidža uncles, Ujak Luka, friends of the family, great-grandparents, great-aunts and -uncles, cousins she's heard about once or twice in stories. Ancestors, tribespeople, wild animals, vegetation, geological rock formations, she gets it all on the page.

There are two police officers, and like cops on TV, they say they're going to drag my ass downtown. And they do, but we're not going downtown, we're going up to 13 Division, by the Allen Expressway, that building we drove by so many times, the Bastards and I, checking it out, wondering what it was like inside, snickering at its fortress bricks and mortar as we sailed by free as scavenger birds. We even mooned it once, Madzid and I, those were the days, when we were as high and ridiculous as frat boys.

I slump in the back seat of the cop car, in the cage like the animal I am, and watch Oakwood go by, that functional uninteresting residential city street with its big trees on some stretches, its run-down shops on others, which told me every day how far from Sarajevo I was, with its ancient, narrow, cobbled streets, its sticky layers of world history on every corner. I say goodbye as our school slides by, its serious facade reminding me of how little I did with all those teachable hours, sleeping and dreaming, what a waste that probably was. Already my time in Toronto, this flat city beside the lake as large as a sea, with all its trees and peaceful neighbourhoods, its leafy parks and one thousand cultures, way more than Sarajevo ever had, has slipped into the past tense in my mind. Easygoing, ambitious, pretty, ugly, shambling, friendly, irritable, young, and all the other good city qualities I've ignored.

I think of the look on Mama's face, when she finally stopped playing, when she turned and saw the cops. She was waiting for this too, but the uniformed officers still shocked her into silence, still drew that veil of suffering over her eyes, the one that had just lifted. It was Aisha who tried to talk to them, tried to explain who her brother is, why he's crazy, why he's fragile. "He's got post-traumatic stress disorder, he's a war refugee, be careful with him, you can't blame kids for the trauma adults inflict on them," she said. And all kinds of other things that surprised the hell out of me, talking like she's a social worker, a lawyer, a fighter way beyond her years.

The division is a maze of narrow corridors, and small square windowless rooms where they do different things to me: search me, interview me, show security tapes featuring me as the star. As I well know, a house I did a week ago was conveniently located opposite a bank and its security camera. So, there I am centred perfectly in the frame, hauling items off the porch at 3 a.m., the light of the street lamp giving me a radioactive glow. There I am a few days later, breaking in through the front door, carrying boxes of groceries and five giant chocolate Easter eggs, since that silly little bunny didn't come to this house this year.

"So, what are you doing?" one of the cops asks. "Who are you? I don't get it."

There I am fixing busted hinges on an outside window shutter. There I am carrying away broken stuff, replacing it with new stuff. This woman, all alone with five snotty, pale, exhausted kids.

"I was drawn in by the junk on the porch, in the yard," I say. The cops stare at me without expression. "Soggy boxes. Two bikes. A coat stand. An easy chair. Two tennis rackets. A skateboard. A swing set. All broken. It's not right."

There I am screwing down loose porch planks, levelling the walkway, setting up porch chairs. I like porches. I wish we had one where Mama could sit peacefully in the summers watching the world go by.

"We're either doing bad or we're doing good," I tell the cops. "There's no neutral in between. But it's not always clear which is which, that's the thing."

They leave the room and are gone for what seems like

hours. There's nothing to do except think too much or sleep and dream. When they come back, they bring a bottle of water.

"You know it's still a B and E even if you're doing that shit," says one cop.

"You know that people don't like strangers messing with their stuff, even if it's crappy junk," says the other. "You know that do-gooders, interfering people, are our worst headache. They're the crazies doing creepy shit, you know? So what we're going to do for you is we're going to send you for a little psych test. How does that sound?"

"My school social worker at school thinks I'm a total write-off," I tell them.

"You're a piece of work, that's for sure, son," says the other. "What's the accent?"

He really does use the word *son*.

Part Three

Spring 1998

———

Ready for a Brand New Day

6

THE DOOR SLIPS SHUT BEHIND ME. NO CLANG. Just a tight little click and then quiet. Cinder-block hallways, shiny floors, faintly buzzing lights, no clouds racing by, no green sprouts bursting out of moist soil. As soon as the door closes, I feel dizzy and breathless. Water, food, electricity, phone, books, TV, fresh air, movement, all these will be rationed again, just enough to keep me alive. I have a sudden fierce need to be in the wet weather, walking through crocuses, purple and white, an icy rain slapping my face. I remember this feeling: you'd kill like an animal to be outside in the open, going wherever you want to go.

A woman is directing me to a chair in the hall, she's asking me about something, drug use, illness, medication, diet, pestilence, famine, fire storms, failed states, massacred peoples, I don't know, I can't focus. My idea was that getting caught would save me, that it would straighten me out, rein me in, make things clear, but I hadn't counted on feeling terror all the time, terror of rooms, walls, shut doors, of being inside twenty-three hours of the day where the air never moves, the seasons never change. I can't help myself, I get up and walk back toward the door. The woman follows me, trotting like a pony, saying that I have to calm down, look on the bright side, that I can turn this time to my advantage. Then there's a commotion behind me. Two big men wearing guns are charging down the hallway toward us. It's completely futile, but I just keep walking toward the door anyway, without looking right or left. They grab me before I reach it, they throw me to the ground, they bind my hands behind my back.

"I'm your youth worker," the woman says. "And this is not how we like to do things." She's crouching next to me, my cheekbone crushed against the glossy floor, little flecks of coloured stone catching my eye. "We want this to be beneficial. It's up to you."

A lot of time has gone by since the cops arrested me, one long year in remand in Mimico, where kids forced each other to eat shit out of toilets and got beaten into comas on a regular basis. Where I waited in vain for swarms of friendly social workers to tell me what was what, where I fought for my life like a dog each day, where I thought too much about all that had happened. Every bad deed I'd done burned inside me, the terrified homeowners, the tied-up housewives, the screaming, shouting, sobbing citizens, how innocent and oblivious they'd all been in their comfortable houses until we showed up. And the family's sacrifices to get me out, Mama begging acquaintances for money, Aisha studying the law like the freakishly proactive kid she is, trying to find some loophole defence involving victims of crimes against humanity, or some such crazy piece of genius logic.

Sava, Madzid, Zijad, and Geordie rolling their eyes at me in the courtroom. *Why get caught*, their eyes said, *why confess to all that stuff they could never prove?* Because they knew I got caught on purpose. They knew I told stories about weapons, duct tape, broken bones, that I confessed all. But I never gave names, that's one thing I can hang onto, I didn't cave on my Bastards. The thing is, Mama couldn't raise the cash for bail while I was waiting for trial, and she wouldn't take it from the Bastards. How would I account for it all, she asked them, when I bring your dirty bundles to the police station, or to the teller at the bank? Mama, finally, playing concerts again, which reviewers called stunning, uncompromising, passionate, the essence of humanity. But it didn't make her rich, she still couldn't get her shit-for-a-son out of his cell. She begged the judge, tried to find strings to pull, got psychiatrists involved. They talked about war children, about post-this and -that, but I guess I seemed pretty solid to them. Everything I said was rational, maybe even more rational than usual, the experts reported. We're the canaries in your dust-filled coal mines, I told them. You should thank us for drawing your attention to the hypocritical bull-shit that glues society and nations together. For my lack of remorse, they sentenced me as an adult, and I got four years of detention, minus my year done in remand. Structure and safety, Mama said finally, when she had no more moves, at least you'll get that. She said it with forced optimism, the same way she sent me off to school all those centuries ago. Lots of people make this mistake about jail.

ORIENTATION is a lecture, then another lecture. The rules say, Obey the rules whatever they are, and whatever they are they are for your own good.

Night comes after day, even in here, and sure as the world turns I am welcomed to detention by some of the crazy boys, the stupider ones, while the guard reads a magazine, his ears unhearing, his gun lying flaccid on the security table. Sure as the sky goes black when the sun goes down, they saunter into the bathroom behind me and lay me flat on the floor again, but this floor is rough and wet, there are no colourful pieces of stone, and they are taunting me with their dangling penises, their honking laughter and poetic curses. They're a skinny-assed jailhouse gang, I can tell by how they all move the same way, their walk, their gestures, the tilt of their shorn heads, like they're dancers with parts choreographed for them, dancing the musical of their own sad fucked-up lives, some in the front, the leaders, some in back, the followers.

"Get the fuck down," they hiss. "Fucking pussy. Lick the fucking floor for us, show us you love us, you fucking Euro-trash piece of shit, you cocksucking motherfucker. Fucking crawl before us, you bitch-fuck, you cunt."

They gather round, they poke at me, they grab their skinny-ass balls, they say I'm their bitch, they tug on their puny little dicks, they say, bitch, suck on this. It's just skin and tissue, I say to them, spitting in their direction, and a small amount of blood from time to time. Who's scared of that, that small amount of flesh and blood? And when they try to show me who should be scared, when they push their hard little faces into mine, when they throw me onto my stomach, when they kick me and try to strip my shorts off, when they start slapping my ass with their nail-bitten hands. When they say, submit bitch, we're gonna fucking do you like the bitch-girl-next-door, I spring up and fly at them with so much fury, arms punching, legs kicking, claws out, teeth bared, that they back right up. They get kind of scared by how I'm frothing at the mouth and barking like a dog, how I'm trying to jab my fingers into their eye sockets and actually pull out their eyeballs. They stand in a wider circle around me, they take aim at me from a distance, they beat me up at arm's length. They see they'll have to kill me before they can fuck me up the ass like drunk, coked-up soldiers in UN-patrolled safety zones, oily red faces, alcohol breath, jerking back and forth and grunting like wounded animals. And I suddenly remember it so clearly, that time I crossed the river. There I am, running, I've been running forever, I'm trying to catch my breath, it's dark, but still the footsteps of the unknown soldier, thug, killer, are closing right behind me. I see an open door, a dim light. I run there, I go inside, I sprint up the stairs, I open the door at the top of the stairs. And there they are, the soldiers in uniform partying and laughing and yelling at each other, trousers around their ankles, raping three teenage girls. Rape, I know what it is, I was right all those years ago, it's not sex, it's total war, scorched-earth policy, firebombing body and mind and the will to live all in one go. I see the whole scene, I walk through it, I check out the soldiers' faces, I smell the sharp smell of their alcoholic, drug-sour sweat. I tell them, I see you clearly, I recognize your faces, I'll know you for the rest of my life, so you watch out, you sad, fucked-up losers, you broken specimens of humanity, you lowest of the low. Then I'm looking at the crazy boys again, how their faces are kind of blank, how they're just a skinny-assed gang of neglected, loser kids in an Ontario juvenile detention centre, and I wonder about the raping soldiers, about their skinny asses and their pathetic lives and dismal stories and everything makes sense. I see how the whole world works, this circle of violence and pain and violence, on and on, down through the generations, that old saying, you reap what you sow.

So I say, you don't scare me, you can't hurt me, I've seen a lot worse, you have no idea. And I begin to laugh high and crazy at the obviousness of it all, how we all just react to shit in our lives so predictably, so stupidly, then pass it on to whoever is closest. I begin to jump around like a deranged baboon. I say, it's so clear, you idiots, you're doing exactly what you're set up to do, look at yourselves. And they look at each other and make weird faces, they say, you're fucked in the fucking head, you crazy little bastard, and I don't stop laughing and jumping until they slink away into the dark hallways like urchins into alleyways, like shadows into shadows, and the guard can suddenly hear again and comes and kicks my ass back to the dorm, me trailing blood from my nose.

The bottom bunk is narrow and hard but enclosed and protective like a cave. I fall asleep with my teeth chattering and dream of everything that exists beyond walls, fences, trenches, basements, enclosures of any kind. On this first night of three more years, I crave things I've never paid attention to on the outside, like a thunderstorm over a lake, a meal at dawn, trips to the corner store, the smell of cigarette smoke in sunshine. I wake in the murky brown darkness to Dušan hovering over my bed. *Come on*, he says, *what are you doing here? Come with me.* And I get up and see that there's a door next to my bunk that I hadn't noticed and he's opened it and is waving me through. *This dump*, he says, *why are you hanging out here, it's so stuffy and smelly with a bad vibe, come with me, we're out there where the weather is wild, where we can explore.* And together we walk out into moonlight. In the park, the wind is loud, branches creak and moan above. I lift my face to the wind then look around. I notice Papa, that he's waiting for us out here, lying on his back, his hands behind his head, staring up at the wild, restless movement all around. He says, *Oh, Jevrem, there you are, why are you wasting your time in that place, you should see this. Look up, the branches are dancing to the music.* So I lie down next to him and look up. Mama always told us to

listen when we went for walks in the mountain forests. Listen
to the music that the elements make, she said, and I wanted to
hear that nature music more than anything. Sometimes I did.

When I wake I'm still listening for it, but there is no music,
no door, no moon, no Dušan, no Papa, no wind in trees, just the
sound of boys breathing.

‡ ‡ ‡

BREAKFAST IN THE CAFETERIA IS LOUD AND GLIT-
tery. The tables glare and the metal trays catch light like
mirrors. I eat a mound of soft, greasy, salty food and watch the
boys, who swagger, slouch, scrape their chair legs, and don't say
a word, it's too early. Later on, I will deal with them, one by one.
But now my attention is on the doors. On the windows. On who
is in charge, how many, how they carry their keys. I pay attention to the walls, I ask them to tell me where they are weak.

I'm in the office with the youth worker, who is a butterfly,
flitting here and there, sorting papers. I think, why is she nervous, I'm the one locked up, but then she sits very still at her
desk and stares at me. She says her name is Ms. Ghorbani. She
says, you can also call me Dr. Ghorbani, if you feel more comfortable with that. I say, it doesn't matter to me that you're a
doctor, if that's what you're trying to tell me. I know doctors
who have murdered, I know doctors who have ugly, ignorant
ideas, who have ranted about blood bonds and cockroaches. Just
because you're a doctor doesn't mean you're good. She looks at
me with interest, then studies the contents of the file.

I ask, "What does it say about me? What do those papers
say? Tell me."

"It just gives me your history, Jevrem," she says.

"Oh, my history," I say. "In such a thin folder? My history wouldn't squeeze into a thousand folders. A million. It's the story of invasion and rebellions going back hundreds of years. It's the story of empires and freedom fighters."

"I mean *your* story, Jevrem. Not your 'people's'." She indicates quotation marks with two fingers of each hand. "You know that, I'm pretty sure."

"Whatever," I say. I'm shocked to feel my face contort strangely and I have to hide it in my sleeve like a child.

Dr. Ghorbani says, "It's okay, Jevrem, I know you've been through a lot. I know you've seen horror first-hand."

Then she's onto her broken record again. "The past has happened, we will try to help you deal with that. But it's important you ask yourself how you want to handle the present and future. What do you want to get out of your time here? It's up to you to decide."

I raise my face and look her directly in the eyes. "A lot of dick up my ass," I say.

She says, "Really, be serious for a moment, Jevrem."

And I say, "I don't mind dick up my ass, it's just a small bit of flesh and blood."

"I've read your file, I see that you got creative with your energy. We'll talk more about violence, Jevrem, but you know that your intention doesn't matter, even the best of intentions, if you're breaking the law and behaving violently."

And I say, "Yes, it does, anyone knows that from history. If you're the U.S. of A. and it's an inconvenient law and your intention is making the world safe for democracy and Coca-Cola."

Dr. Ghorbani sighs. "Okay, Jevrem. I read you loud and

clear. I know you're not here because you don't care about any-thing. I know you're here because you care so very much, and so much is so very flawed."

I make a sad face, roll my eyes. Poor, hurt little boy.

"Rebels and delinquents and even nihilists," she continues, "are fierce moralists, contrary to popular understanding. They see what's wrong with the world and react with their own forms of outrage."

"Hardened criminals too? Sadists and warlords?" I say. But I check her out again, carefully, when she's looking down at my life on paper. She too knows that all the crazy boys are here because they spot bullshit a mile away, just like I do. And they hate it, it makes them sick.

"'When the leaders speak of peace . . .'" She looks up, pauses. "That's part of a poem. Do you know what the next line might be?"

Of course I fucking know what the next line is, it's totally obvious. "Everyone prepare to die, because an unholy mother-fucking war is about to be unleashed on your heads," I say. It slips out before I have time to think if I want to take part in her little lesson.

"Yes. Well, it's actually, '. . . the common folk know. That war is coming.'"

"So?" I say.

"So," she continues. "This poem, by Brecht, a great German playwright and poet, is about hypocrisy. Hypocrisy, Jevrem. I know that it's this, of all things, that makes you angry, that makes you feel entitled to go rogue."

Here we go with the psychobabble. Were you disappointed by the world when random adults tried to kill you over and over again for years when you were a kid?

"Hypocrisy enrages smart people, Jevrem, as it should, since it's about lying, about hiding one's true nature. Doing one thing, saying another. Committing injustice, then hiding this commission. Expecting something of others, but not of oneself. And it's fairness that we yearn for the most, it makes life livable wherever we are. People your age still know this, you still expect it, you still get angry at its absence. Brecht created a book called *War Primer* that I'm sure would appeal to you. Beside a photo of children maimed by war, he wrote a short verse, only four lines. Something like . . . all you warriors out there fighting this or that battle under this or that difficult circumstance, see who you've conquered, hail your great victories."

She looks at me with her eyebrows raised, waiting for me to hit the ball back. But I say nothing more, because why be drawn into a serious conversation about teenagers with stars in their eyes and sleazy bullshitting politicians and hero soldiers who slaughter children by the tens of thousands because they can't be bothered to find a better solution. As nice as it is to shoot the breeze, this is not a university classroom or a shrink's office, this is my life in jail. I can't stay in here, not for another week, I won't survive it, I will be possessed by the monster, I will become the monster. No matter how many philosophical ideas she throws my way, no matter how many German poets she recites to me, this place is a place of violence that creates more violence. Hypocrite yourself, Dr. Ghorbani, why can't you at least be honest about that?

Sometimes you just have to remove yourself from the muck, that's what I've learned. And anyway, every cell in my body is already outside, roaming the streets and up in the treetops shouting to the racing clouds high above.

‡ ‡ ‡

I SIT IN LISTLESS CLASSROOMS, I STARE OUT OF smeared windows. The days are a blur. The colours on the walls are deadly pinks, rotted greens, filthy whites designed for suicide. And the shabby carpets, meant to make things more homey, are matted and foul, like the coat of a terminal dog.

When night comes and lights are switched off with an abrupt flick, the crazy boys slip quickly away into sleep where they float free and high in the moonlit sky, but I wait in murky corners of the bathroom for hours until I am so cold I shake like an epileptic. Eventually one of my attacker boys shows up stumbling with sleep and I take him down with a quick blow to his temple with the side of my hand. As he lies dazed on the gritty concrete floor I strip his pyjamas off him and grab his little sluggish penis and I hold it up, and I say to the boy, look at this thing, this bit of flesh and blood, well, mostly flesh now, and tell me something. And he cranes his neck, tries to focus his eyes, bares his teeth with fear. And I say, tell me why this little thing is used as a weapon of war? And he looks up at me, I see his shiny eye-whites, greasy eggs over easy, and he shivers long and hard but doesn't say a word.

I smack him across the face and see that he has blood on his lips, that he's licking it off with a glossy, plump young tongue. I say to him, what's your gang? Tell me about your gang. And he just swallows and blinks his eyes, and I say, tell me or I'll have to smack you some more, but harder, for real. And he groans and gags, and I say, tell me. And so he says, we're the Portuguese. And I say, what? And he says, we're the Portuguese. And I say, you're not fucking Portuguese, even I can hear that with my second-hand English. And he says, we're the Portuguese, yes. What's your name? I ask him. And he says, we're one of the posses, like the Indians, the Jamaicans, AK Kannan, you know, the Sri Lankans, Tamils, Vietnamese. *What. Is. Your. Fucking. Name?* I say directly into his ear. We're the Dovercourt Boys, I mean, a few of us are in here, that's all. We're the Portuguese. And I think, that's pathetic, all these gangs based on where their parents and grandparents came from so many years ago trying to elevate themselves out of the gutter, how sad that's all they can come up with for a reason to do shit and hang together. And then I have a blinding revelation: ours was a gang from the old world too. From the inside it was so mixed, all the nationalities together, but from the outside it just looked like plain old Yugo.

So I tell him about my gang, what crazy motherfuckers we are, and I can see his mind working hard, because even he's heard about the Croats, Serbs, Muslims, all the young militiamen who swaggered around so tough, with beards, without beards, slaughtering and raping without hesitation for their leaders, who would stop at nothing for the map-makers. He shuts his eyes and winces. And I say, do you want me to hurt you some more or do you agree to never touch me again? Never touch me and show some respect? He nods vigorously, his eyes leaking fluid. Yes, yes, he squeaks. Because, I say, tonight I am being very lenient, but next time I will make my mark.

IN the morning, in her small, paper-filled office smelling of the rubber that holds things together, Dr. Ghorbani marches me through my life. Yes, I lived through four years of war, yes, my father and brother were killed, and my sister expired like a little caterpillar on an icy winter day, yes, I immigrated to Canada, yes, I did B and Es, yes, I put the heat to a few people, only to do what was necessary, only for the sake of justice in this unjust world, yes, I did some guerrilla social work, got caught, and yes, now, after the legal aid lawyer tried this and that, after a year of waiting in remand, of Mama visiting twice a week, sometimes pale and despairing, sometimes perky and reassuring, of Aisha writing a dissertation on refugee populations, post-traumatic stress, crime, rehabilitation, that somehow made it into my file, here I am. I am in this place.

Dr. Ghorbani leans forward. She says, "Tell me about your father."

I just stare at her, because there's no way in hell I'm going to talk about Papa to this stranger. She'll just ask me what he was like, or some such bullshit. As if a list of things describing him could ever be more than a lie. I could tell her that he's pretty close by all the time, that he likes to stand in doorways and walk through doors, get into elevators, that sometimes he gives me advice, but she'd think I was talking about some weird thing happening in my mind because I miss him so much.

"Okay," she says. "Tell me about your brother. Older brothers are so important to boys."

Older brothers, older brothers. Important to boys. I'm feeling hot and antsy in this room. I want a cigarette. I want a breath of fresh air. I want to be outside.

"You can speak to me, Jevrem. That's what I'm here for."

Older brothers. I didn't think of Dušan that way. He was just Dušan. He was Dušan down to every last cell of his body. I knew the feel and smell and touch of every cell of his body like I know my own. If he'd made it out alive, he'd be the one in jail, not me. And he'd be scoffing and making a joke, he'd be laughing his head off at Dr. Ghorbani's questions. And I'd laugh with him, I'd honour his jokes, I'd be happy that he was on top of his world. It's exactly what this moment needs, I think. Dušan and his jokes and fooling around. I suddenly miss him so hard it's like I'm being electrocuted. I look up and scowl at Dr. Ghorbani. The scowl is how I really feel.

"Leave me alone," I snarl.

"Okay," she says slowly. "Okay, I understand. If you don't want a conversation, I encourage you to use this time to your own benefit, whatever that means to you. That's what we want here. It's up to you."

She's repetitive, this one, with her turtleneck sweaters and clicking shoes. I notice a plain gold ring on her finger and wonder about her marriage, her husband probably a professor who wears designer glasses and linen suits. She has a nice watch too, and small gold hoop earrings that are very thin, very fine. But I make sure to keep my mouth shut. My mind is on the outside anyway, it's a trick I've learned from a year of lock-up. For the whole year, I travelled our vast country on air currents like a bird, exploring thousands of miles of unpopulated terrain, me and the atlas they let me have, cursing how I'd ignored its endless possibilities before, tethered to one small place, eyes down, head up my ass, when I should have been on the move. For a whole year, I went on road trips with Sava, waking at dawn with her, watching the sun rise over mountains, lakes, winter fields, endless bush. Standing on glaciers, the cold of twenty thousand years under our feet. Right now, as the doctor goes on some more about wonderful imprisoned opportunities for education and training, I'm racing over the bush of northern Quebec toward craggy, glowering Newfoundland, and, rising with the ocean air, I see the Atlantic Ocean, steel grey, solid as matter, crashing into rocks that crust the shore.

‡

AFTERNOON comes and twenty-five boys and I are in the locker rooms, bodies bumping into bodies, roughhousing, or whatever they call it. When they are done pushing, shoving, getting naked, sauntering, swearing, insulting each other, they throw on track pants and shirts and burst outside like a single body, football in hand. But I invite myself into the stall where one of my skinny-assed ball-breaking boys is crouching down by the bowl puffing fast on a joint. He says, get the fuck out of here, punk, and I kick him in the face with the second-hand running shoes the detention centre has found for me. His head cracks against tile and he slides between wall and toilet and lies there for a bit, then moves like someone waking from sleep. He tries to get up and I kick him again. Then I repeat my little performance with the friendly request to be left alone, I tell him about my vicious, psycho, old-world gang outside. Understand? I ask. Next time I will wreck you. And not a whining word to the others, except that I am supremely untouchable. You can tell them that. He nods and swallows and bolts out of the stall like a horse at the races, and I slump against the toilet, breathe hard, feel dizzy, feel nauseated, and more tired than a third-world mule. Intimidating crazy boys really takes it out of you.

But on the field it is do or die. The rule is no tackling, but no one obeys and the guards don't care. They stand on the sideline and crack smiles when boys go down, bones crunching and ligaments stretching like bubble gum. Farther down the field stands Papa, hands in his pockets, watching the game with a small smile on his face, which I know means he thinks it's stupid but he's really enjoying it anyway. The muscle boys, the hard-as-rock boys, they are fit and strong and have been taught how to play. I am soft and skinny, and don't understand this game that stops and starts like a stutter, but I remember my childhood days when winning the game was staying alive. No one can take me down, zigzagging like I do, running for my life, legs remembering their soccer-playing days, with the pointy ball clutched to my chest like it's a bag of rice on my sprint for home. Zigzagging is not a technique taught to these peacetime boys. They think it's ridiculous and frustrating, but it's my sniper-survival specialty and it's foolproof. And then, at the end, a sudden stop, a quick turn and a fist in the neck of my pursuer, with Papa shouting, *Hurrah*. I score several key touchdowns. I live to see another day.

"So, you're a fighter, Jevrem," Dr. Ghorbani asks me the next morning.

I say nothing to her. I look out of the window, which is too high for a view.

"You're a fighter because you're a survivor."

She can tell me about myself for a hundred years and I'm still not saying a word to her because I won't be here for long. What's the point of getting into a deep, meaningful conversation, it's always a trick to get you to do what they want. I'm already outside, my mind is circling over vast blocks of city, counting chimneys, antennas, trees, cars, basketball hoops, mingling with the spring breeze that cajoles the dead to rise again.

Then, after lunch, we sit in a room in a circle and the group counsellor gets us to talk by making outrageous, provoking statements, like, what is the most violent thought you've ever had and why did you have it? All around me the boys grunt out their pornographic fantasies and laugh like louts. But I still don't say anything. I won't be seduced by language into this web. This web is not sticky enough for an insect like me.

I get the next boy in his bed at four in the morning. Unfortunately for him, he's in the same dorm as me. I shove a toothbrush in his mouth like it can do some damage, and I say, why is it that objects and orifices are tools of war, but he has no answers, he just gags a few times and agrees to my proposition of an armistice. Peace, that's all I want, I say, and hum a little communist tune I learned from Baka.

And then I'm in Dr. Ghorbani's office again, because that's how time works in this place. She sits in front of me and stares at my face for minutes, hours, days, centuries, her eyes moving over its peaks and valleys, its perfections and imperfections, and into its pools and voids. I feel my heart pumping faster and faster and sweat springing out of every pore in my body. I want to cry like a widowed woman. I'm tired of the fighting, I'm tired of the surviving. *Make it stop*, I ask the universe silently. But I don't say a word with my breath, my mouth, my tongue. My face is a rock.

THE LAST skinny, gangly boy has survival instinct, but my hunting instinct is sharper. I get to him in the lineup of the cafeteria, and what better place, I figure, than surrounded by all the crazy boys and their beefed-up arms and chests and their spindly twig legs, they all need to see what I can pull out of my sleeve when I have been wronged. I stand behind the boy, whose blondish hair grows down his neck like peach fuzz, who hangs his head on a long stem to hide his open-book face. You allied yourself with the wrong boys, I say, the losers, the weaker ones, and now you must be punished. This is the law of the world, look anywhere on our globe.

The boy turns quickly to face me, his mouth a thin line, his eyes two cosmic black holes, expressionless with an emotion beyond fear. And in the moment that I let the pen slide out of my sleeve and I gouge his skinny belly with its sawed-off end, I see that he's already been sliced open a thousand times in the course of his short, panicked life, that my incision isn't teaching him anything new. So, there he is bleeding on the cafeteria floor, holding his skinny ribs with shaking hands, eyes blinking rapidly, his face blank as an animal's, and there I am standing over him looking at all the crazy boys in that pale green cafeteria, showing them my invincibility, my mad martial heritage, feeling not too good about it all, that it wasn't really fair to that skinny little kid, and wondering, suddenly furious, why is he in a fucked-up place like this, anyway? I slip away just as the guards turn their heads and peer like startled chickens in our direction. I wash off the blood on my hands in the bathroom sink. I gag, I shiver, then I walk quickly to the library. That boy will bear his wound without complaining. He will nurse it alone. He doesn't know any better, doesn't expect anything else, that's how it's always been for him.

The next morning, Dr. Ghorbani asks me if I did the stabbing and I sit in front of her with a small smile on my face, feeling defiant and like a monstrous villain both at the same time.

"Nobody would give up your name, someone else even confessed, someone else is in solitary today. That's not a good thing, Jevrem. It means they're scared of you. I know things can be tough in here, but it's not the answer. It's not a good way to live, people fearing you. It never ends well."

I wonder how she knows for sure it was me, and what she really knows about fear and intimidation and the need to survive. But I'm not about to start asking questions, since conversing is no use to me.

"Anger management," she says. "Anti-criminal thinking, life skills, cognitive therapy, anti-gang education, relapse prevention, family therapy, substance abuse treatment." She stops, and lets these options sink in. "Mental health treatment, including PTSD, high school education, vocational training. You get the picture, Jevrem? Like I've said, I know you've got a sharp brain in there. All these and more are available to you. You are seventeen, so can choose not to go to school. But, of course, I would advise very strongly against that. Education is the key to every new beginning."

I think, but what kind of education? They were educated back home and what good did it do us? All those communist apparatchiks turning into fascists at the drop of a hat for a bit of power, they all went to school, they all read books. It didn't make them good people. Everyone knows that, but everyone still sends their little children to whatever school happens to be on the block. But I don't say anything. I can't have a conversation with someone if I'm not here.

"You can continue grade eleven, starting on Monday. The teacher will assess your level with a series of tests."

Dr. Ghorbani looks at me; I look at the window, the wall, the ceiling. The window, the wall, the ceiling have no eyes to look back.

"And you and I will continue to have sessions, during which we will work together to identify your issues and struggles at the individual, family and community levels. I know you are a special case, Jevrem, and I know that child refugees and children suffering war trauma are underserved in our schools and health-care system. I will work with you to help you focus on your strengths, help you gain your feet . . ."

I stop listening to Dr. Ghorbani. She makes it sound like it's me who's got the problems, it's me who needs fixing. She goes on for quite a bit longer about steps we're going to take together. The sound of her voice isn't bad, it's quite friendly and soothing and I take the time to think about who I need to see before I make my move. Mama, Aisha, Sava, and the Bastards.

"But whatever you decide to do or not do, Jevrem, everyone here helps run the centre together. It's a good experience for the future. I'm putting you on pots in the kitchen. Work is good therapy."

Great, I think, it's like the brigade cookhouse, all of us pitching in selflessly to build an incredibly useful thing for the whole of society. I think about suggesting this to her—put us to some good use, let us build your roads and bridges and city halls. But I guess that wouldn't go over so well in this day and age. Child labour and exploitation, and all that. Better to keep us locked in cages.

Dr. Ghorbani walks me down echoing hallways, nodding at each guard we pass. They look like giant savannah animals next to her, enormous, slow-moving hippopotamuses. She's thin, tense, formal, a gazelle with sleek coat, quick movements, alert face. In the kitchen, the crazy boys are sauntering and strutting, trying not to look panicked. The kitchen boss, an old biker dude with a walrus moustache the colour of ash, bangs a spoon against a metal garbage can. "Speed things up, ass-wipes," he screams, then stares at me like I'm a hairball in his drain.

"Okay, Jevrem," says Dr. Ghorbani, looking around the kitchen coolly. "I will see you on Wednesday."

I realize then that she doesn't usually escort her boys around the joint, that she's doing me a favour.

The sink closest to the ovens is where you sweat the hardest and that's where I go. They're cranked high to heat food made of plastic waste shipped in from Chinese factories manned by too-skinny humans with small hands and bony cheekbones, or that's how I picture it anyway. I scrub pans, sweat, swear, splash water. And think and scheme and plan for what is to come.

THE guard doesn't forget to dig his powerful sausage fingers into my neck before he shoves me into the visitors' room. The room is a dead-man shade of beige. There are tables with chairs arranged neatly around them, two squat windows showing clouds dark grey with rain, a red-brick wall, part of the fence that curves inward at the top, a playing field, a basketball hoop. Like a high school but with barbed wire.

I spot Sava right away. She's slouched at a table and looks more like a juvie than the juvies, hard face, hunched shoulders, not like a visitor at all, the mothers with their toxic halos of perfume, the freaked-out siblings, the awkward, shifty fathers in their dress shirts, collars undone. But I know it's an act. I see all of her revealed in her shining eyes, and she looks different than before, less hard, less hostile, closer to the surface. When she sees me, Sava stands up fast and lunges at me, kissing me, her lips mashing into mine, tongue sweeping the inside of my right cheek. The guards shout, Sava pulls away, and I'm left with a mouthful of plastic that I gag on for a moment, then cough into my hand. Out comes a large lump that my palm can barely conceal. I want to do that all over again with her, I want to merge with her bones, her heat, her breath, but the guards are watching us closely now, and Sava wouldn't agree, anyway.

"Hey," I say. "You look great."

"Thanks," Her voice is low, she sits again. "I'm sleeping more."

An image of Sava in some other guy's bed sears itself onto my mind. I miss those nights of torture with Sava more than any other part of my life outside.

"Are you seeing anyone, Sava?"

"Don't be ridiculous, Andric." She scowls at me.

Relief is sweet, it sort of floods my mouth like I'm salivating. And then I think, why not? She's hot, she's not religious or anything, and she can get whoever she wants. But she's never had a boyfriend.

"Andric," she says. "Drop it. Men are pigs, all of history proves I'm right, that's all I'm going to say. More importantly, I want you to know that's all I'm giving you. I'm not muling for you again. It's a stupid risk. Ask one of the others next time."

"Sava, don't worry, there won't be a next time. I'm getting out of here." I'm happy she thinks men are pigs, she has a right to, she had all those nightmare images in her head when she was a kid, and it'll rule all the others out. But maybe one day, when I've worked on becoming exceptionally un-piglike, she'll give me a break.

She gives me a look of pity before she scans the room, studying the guards studying us.

"You have to finally accept reality."

"What does that mean? Reality is a motherfucker." I speak loudly. The guards don't care what I say.

"I mean, Jevrem, that you should stop fighting the wrong battles. Use this situation to your advantage, don't just keep banging your head against the same wall. What's the point of that? Just step around it, step around the goddamned wall."

"I'm going over," I say, dropping my voice. "Not around, over. It'll work." The guards might be interested in this news.

"The wall I mean is in your head, Jevrem."

"I know what you mean. But the wall I mean is just over there." I point to the window, to the fence beyond it, so unguarded, so climbable. I change the subject. "So, what's new?" I try not to stare at her too hungrily. She looks different on many levels, more impatient, not so angry. She moves in her chair as though she's an athlete warming up for a race. She's pumped like I've never seen before.

"I'm moving out," she says.

"Yeah?"

"Yeah. It's time to get my life going."

"Yeah?" I say.

"I'm going to do it fast, I've wasted enough time. I'm going to get all my degrees by the time I'm twenty-five." Sava coughs, looks over her shoulder, leans in toward me over the table, looks into my eyes. "You could too. Get started in here, without any distractions."

"Why?"

"You can do things with an education," Sava says. "You can make things happen."

"You don't understand. After this year here, I go on to do two more years in an adult jail full of vicious, fucked-in-the-head hardened criminals. I can't do that, enclosed, buried, caged, too many people in small spaces, waiting. It gives me nightmares, it makes me insane, don't you see? There will be no hope for me at the end, I know it. I will end up the meanest motherfucker Canada has ever known. Or dead."

Sava doesn't say anything. She knows what I mean, our survival instincts are too good, our ability to adapt, to keep going in shitty circumstances until the day the sniper meets his mark or we become the sniper. We sit without talking. I study every detail of her. She looks out the window, letting me get my fill.

"You see," she says after a while. "One day, I was sitting in Madzid's car just before doing a house and a thought dropped into my head, you know, all by itself. I realized it takes just as much energy being a pointless badass victim scurrying around in a shit-pile as it does being a rebel with a cause."

She sounds exactly like Baka, it's a conspiracy.

"What are your plans for your future, Andric, besides breaking out of this place? I mean, years down the line? You could start by writing it all down, what's happened so far. That's what I'm doing. It's pretty fucking clarifying."

A future? I think.

"You could call it 'The Difficult Springtime of My Life,' or something cheesy like that."

I get the pills to the crazy boys and a layer of friendly feeling piles onto their new-found respect for me. They give me *yo-nigga* punches in the arm, they get me my tray at lunch and say *it ain't no thing* like American corner-boys. And I have cash in my pocket, which is important for breaking free.

Early in the morning, I lie awake, my head turned to the square of grey moonlight on the wall. I think about Baka, the night she died, how it felt like time stopped for a while. Mama and her piano, how I used to lie on the couch looking out of the apartment window while she played, how I didn't see much, a bird passing, a cloud floating, the flash of an airplane, how my daydreams became one with that small patch of sky while Mama's notes filled the room with other worlds. I think about Sava and her body and her face and her eyes and her hair and her voice and her movements and her smile, how I wish she was beside me like always, sleeping close, pushing me away. I wait for Papa to show up, to pace beside my bed, to tell me what he thinks of NATO bombing the shit out of Baba and Deda in Belgrade, the new money called the Euro, Clinton's bent penis, important news that makes its way through bars everywhere, or whatever else is on his mind. But I fall asleep before he does.

In my dream, Dušan grabs me by the hand and we fly down the stairwell of the apartment building and burst out onto the street, but the street is nothing like a Sarajevo street, it's like a Toronto street, wide, straight, with tidy concrete sidewalks on each side, and he says, *look, isn't this great, I love it here, so much space, so few people, thank Christ we moved.*

When day comes, I have no appetite. I eat no breakfast, I drink no coffee. I sit at the cafeteria table and grip its edge hard with both hands. In our session, Dr. Ghorbani tells me that violence, substance abuse, inconsistent parenting, weak attachment to family and school, poverty, bad housing, and under-resourced neighbourhoods are why the crazy boys are in this place. She says that this is what the youth workers and therapists think, but that the guards and detention managers think the boys are bad seeds, defective kids rotten from birth.

"Why is this, do you think?" she asks me, raising her eyebrows, the way she does. "Why do some people see that violent kids are the result of violent backgrounds, and other people think that violent kids are just wilfully bad?"

I think about this question for a while, and then I answer. "Because you youth workers are here to heal us and the guards are here to punish us, so you invent boys that can be healed, and they invent boys that need to be punished." Then I put my hand over my mouth, turn my chair away. I see her sneaky game, I see how clever she is in baiting me with questions.

She floats other questions like balloons and bats them gently my way, while I think about food, supplies, garbage, sewage, repairs. Things that come in and out of this house of rehabilitation and retribution, things that could carry me with them.

"How are your classes so far? Maybe we can talk about that."

They're for infants, as usual, I think. Don't they know that we crazy boys are smarter than other kids? That's why we're here, we get what's really going on, we see through everything. They should teach to our level. I slouch lower in the chair, let my head fall forward, close my eyes, fold my hands over my stomach. Time goes by. I hear Dr. Ghorbani moving around. Then, when my breathing gets deeper and my body thinks it's asleep, I feel her standing next to me.

"I understand that you're angry and cynical," she says very quietly, her head close to my ear. "That's a normal response to the abnormal events you've experienced. But at some point you'll find it to your advantage to take the leap beyond reactive feelings and put yourself on the road to your own freedom. For yourself."

Baka once told me that famous men used their time in prison to educate themselves and prepare to change the world. Tito, her hero. Gandhi, Malcolm X, Nelson Mandela, Trotsky, and so on. Hitler, too, of course, got a lot of preparatory work done in jail. But I'm with Dr. Ghorbani. I'm going on the road.

I DREAM that I am high up in the Yugoslav mountains with a view of other, distant peaks and a pale blue horizon that curves down on either side, like I'm seeing the shape of Earth itself. I have the feeling that I'm at the top of it all, at the highest point on the planet, where I can see every approach, where no one can creep up on me unexpectedly. In my dream, the sun, the wind, the banks of white clouds rise up in me and I become the mountain, the sun, the wind, the clouds. This high up, there is only thin air and green rocky pastures speckled with small, tough wildflowers that have a strange scent, like daisies, and mountain goats climbing upwards, always upwards. Lower down, there are narrow rivers that flow fast through deep crevices, and slower, wider stretches too. There, the deep waters appear dark olive green. They hold fish that quiver and dart and sometimes splash upwards, breaking the water's surface. It's a dream I never want to leave because the forests are full of bears. When I was little, Papa told me we had the largest concentration of bears anywhere in the world, except Canada.

In the morning, I attack the pans like they've personally wronged me. I listen to gangsta rap with the cooks, sweat like a boxer, flood the floor, splash the walls. And I watch, I observe. Prison is alive like a beast, it takes nourishment in through one hole and lets waste out another hole. Nothing on this earth stays alive if it's completely sealed off from its surroundings. Always, there's a way in and there's a way out. Back home we had our tunnel.

In the group session, the counsellor talks some more about violence, but he's a soft man with soft hands, soft face, soft voice, soft ideas. His violence is from textbooks, it smells of paper.

"But the violence in your life was different, wasn't it, Jevrem?" he says. "Would you like to share your story?" He's reading from Dr. Ghorbani's notes, I can hear her voice.

I decide not to share, not today. I have other things on my mind. The rest of the boys look away, shuffle their feet, cough into their hands. No one puts me on the spot by looking at me, they know better. There's a pause, a brief moment when the room is completely silent.

"Well, I think it's okay to reveal that you lived through a terrible war," the counsellor says.

The boys' faces remain expressionless, they make no signal that they've heard. This isn't news to them, they've never cried a river for me.

"That's something to think about," he says. "What we're dealing with generally is immediate caregivers letting you down, sometimes due to their actions and sometimes through no fault of their own, but in this case it was the whole society. The whole society broke down, turning on each other, this is a different phenomenon. It must be tough seeing violence like that, not just your dad or your uncle or a teacher letting loose, but all men being compelled to fight, and to fight each other."

No, I think, you're an idiot, it's all the same thing, in the living room, on the battlefield. It all comes from the same place, the struggle for survival, power, place, someone to love you for who you really are, all that shit. Where do you think all those badass militiamen and macho soldiers come from?

The counsellor keeps going with a deep vibrating voice about cooperation, trust, conversation, empathy, working together for the benefit of the family, the community, the society, the whole. I feel sorry for this earnest dude, almost sorry. All his education but no brains, it's very sad, one of those guys who thinks you're agreeing with him when you don't say anything. And all the boys are quiet, not a word from them. But we're all thinking, the benefit of which family, which community, which society, which whole? The corrupt ones? The fucked-up ones? Why would we want to benefit them? But I fast tune out of this inspirational monologue. Instead, I think about the fence, getting over it, and alternatives, the possibility of expelling myself from this noble place of healing and rehabilitation in the garbage truck at 5 a.m., of escaping on the way to hospital with a broken arm purchased from a kick-boxer.

‡ ‡ ‡

WHEN I COME INTO THE VISITORS' ROOM, MAMA and Aisha are sitting at the same table where we sat, Sava and I. To me this feels like a sign, but of what I couldn't say. The room is empty except for one guard, who doesn't once look in our direction. Instead, he files his nails with a small piece of sandpaper and sucks lunch out of his teeth with a squelching sound.

Mama looks more like I remember from the time before than she's ever done on this side of the Atlantic. Her hair and face and eyes are shining again, the way she moves smooth and sure and relaxed. She's wearing her coat for Sarajevo winters, grey and tailored, and her favourite silk scarf, the one she brought back from Paris and wore all the time back home. But everything else is new, bright, unfamiliar. She's dressing for a fresh life, I can see this clearly, and smell it too, she has a new perfume. Aisha is fresh too. A whole new person has showed up in the past year, taller, curvier, as composed as an adult. It's the way she sits, her hands folded on the table, her eyes focused without wavering on whatever she's looking at, which right now is me. She jumps up and rushes over, saying my name like it's a spell. She's wearing a necklace around her neck that says *Berina* in curved writing. Berina is no longer inside Aisha, she's moved out to the surface of her skin.

"Hey, Aisha. How are you?" I give her a hug.

"Hi," she says, smiling with her eyes and whole face. She holds onto my hand with both of hers, pulling it tightly against her chest.

Mama stands also, slowly, looking at me with her motherly eyes. "Come here," she says. She wraps her arms around me. She keeps me there for a while, until it's awkward, until we can no longer pretend we're not in a jail. I sit down opposite the two of them, my eyes on the table.

"Jevrem," Mama says. "Please look at me."

And I try, I want to do this right, but they both seem so happy and I feel even more like a huge fucking loser in my overalls and this ragged brush cut they keep giving me. I stare over Mama's head, out the window, at the walls, the clock, the ceiling, anywhere but into those familiar eyes looking at me from the past.

"Jevrem," Mama says, leaning forward, "I know you feel ashamed. Can you get past that? Please? I want a real conversation with you. You're seventeen now."

"I don't feel ashamed," I say, reading the graffiti on the side of the table: *S.O.S. You're an asshole, Dad I love you, girl, get me out of here.* "I've told you that." I glance at her face, but there's something about her that disturbs me.

"The only time you didn't look me in the eyes was when you felt ashamed," she keeps going. "From the age of two. Ashamed about the trouble you made."

I didn't make trouble back then, I think. That was Dušan, Mama is confusing us. But I'm not surprised, he's living through me.

307

Aisha smiles some more. She says, "Kids who make trouble are the most creative."

Mama says, "Shh, Aisha. This is serious."

Aisha winks at me. She's even sweeter than I remember, which somehow makes me sad.

"I'm with Aisha on this one," I mumble.

"Jevrem," Mama says, looking at her watch, then at the guard. "We don't have time for this."

So I look directly into Mama's eyes and see what's bothering me. She looks just like Baka. Baka's back, her old chipper self, full of opinions and energy and ideas about how I should be, out there saving humanity. For a moment I feel disoriented. I look around the room and wonder where I am, what the hell is going on. I think, I was the dreamer of the family, maybe I'm hallucinating this whole second half of my life, maybe I'll wake any moment in my bed back home, the sounds of Sarajevo coming in my window.

Mama leans toward me. "Jevrem. Tell me how you are." And time keeps piling on top of itself with its idea of an interesting plot.

"How are *you*?" I say. I really want to know. I want to know that she'll be okay when I run away. I want her to be inside her own life, to stop thinking about me. I want to be sure she won't fall apart when I'm gone.

"I'm fine. Everything is coming together," she says.

Mama puts her arm around Aisha's shoulder. I can see in this moment exactly how their life is, how they've made it work, how the future has finally arrived to greet them with open arms.

"Life pulls you forward," Mama continues, "and when you finally let it, when you decide to go with it, it rewards you well. My music is always there for me, Jevrem, and Aisha will be going to a private high school in September, one that can meet both her musical and academic abilities. She received a full scholarship, isn't that wonderful? It's in Montreal, and I'll be moving there too. But this doesn't mean we won't visit, Jevrem. It's only a little farther away."

Oh, I think, of course Aisha got a full scholarship, she's going to rule the world one day, and thank God for that, maybe we'll all get some peace and quiet for once. And then I have a realization. That man who took Mama out for Ethiopian food, the French musician, Leo Something, he lives in Montreal. In my mind's eye, I see a glossy full-colour image of Mama and this guy sitting at a sunny table eating baguettes and drinking strong coffee, like it's a memory of a moment already lived, or a photograph I saw stuck to Mama's fridge door. They're leaning in toward each other, they're laughing, his fingers are circled around her wrist. I feel dizzy seeing all of this and I know it has happened, our past is no longer our present, it has finally gotten away, it has jostled free. I see our Sarajevo life floating downstream, Papa, Dušan, Berina, and all our relatives and friends perched on a little raft, getting smaller and smaller by the second. Papa is standing up, a barge pole in one hand, looking back at us, waving. He's so far away I can't see the expression on his face. Is he sad, is he angry, is he glad to be moving on? Papa, I want to cry out, Papa, Mama still loves you, I know she does. But Mama and Aisha are staring at me, and I don't want to worry them with strange behaviour right now.

"It's good, Jevrem, things are really improving for us. But with you in here, well . . . I want to know, how is it? How do they treat you? Do you get enough food? Enough sleep? Are you in school? Please tell me. I know how hard our first year here was. I wasn't myself, I wasn't present, you thought I didn't care. I do care. I care very much." Mama pauses, looks at her hands, smoothes her hair. Then she whispers, "I'm your mother and you are on my mind every minute of every day."

I want to say, *I'm happy that your life is better, I really am, it's the most important thing.* And I want to let her know somehow that I'm going to be leaving, that she shouldn't worry. But Mama is suddenly shaking. She grabs my hands and pulls them toward her, she bends her head and kisses my knuckles, her eyes pouring saltwater tears onto them. I try to get my hands back, but Mama is strong, she won't let go. And I can't help it, I start to lose it too. Then suddenly I'm sobbing, crazy and wild, listening to animal sounds coming from my chest. It feels strange, like I'm in a storm and there's a tidal wave hitting me from behind. I'm knocked down, flattened, and the room fills with water, rising fast right up to the ceiling, and I feel Mama's hands slipping away, I see her reaching for me, calling out to me with a silent underwater mouth, but it's too late, she and Aisha are floating off in slow-motion, twisting slowly around each other, swimming in slow circles, the guard is drifting with them like a whale with no concern for small fish like us, and then they're at the far end of the room, hair undulating like rubbery seaweed in a tropical ocean. In a flash of light they're sucked out of the door upward to the surface of the outside world.

‡ ‡ ‡

WOUNDED BELLY BOY IS CROUCHING NEXT TO MY bed, at the very top where my pillow is. I walk silently toward him, my hair wet from the morning shower, and see that he's got my roll of bills in his hand, that he's fished it out from under my mattress, that his trembling fingers are trying to work the elastic off. I know that I am going to kill this skinny, shivering, squinting boy who is challenging me so pathetically, right out in the open, that I am going to enjoy it because I've caught him red-handed disrespecting me. Barefoot, silent, I slide up close and stand behind him for a few seconds until he feels my heat. He turns, flinches, then covers his face with his arm and squeezes his eyes shut like someone who knows the drill. I say, "Are you out of your fucking mind?" and throw my granite fist at his temple, but right in that moment, when my bone hits his bone, I have a realization. He knows the drill, that's the deal. I'm his tormenter and he wants my attention, that's how it works when that's all the attention you can get. Well, he's got my attention, he invites my fist against his temple, he doesn't care about money, he doesn't care about getting hurt, he doesn't care about crawling in the dust. So I hit him again in the mouth, just to be polite and give him what he needs. He crumples, he moans, he curls into a ball at the foot of my bed and lies there without saying a word.

"Who sent you?" I say, to give him some shred of dignity. "Is it those ridiculous brothers of yours, your so-called gang? Are they trying to send a message?"

He nods his head, then shakes his head.

"Yes, no? Which is it, you fuck?"

He just lies there, cringing, shivering, waiting for more blows, hoping they never stop. Contempt is lava through my veins, scalding my tissues. I could keep hitting his pathetic, sorry face forever like all the billions of downtrodden losers in the world and their contemptuous overlords and he'd never stop me, he'd not even try. This makes me want to smack him harder, that's how this works. Then I remember what I've learned about reacting like an idiot to every little thing even when I know the real reason why those little things are happening. I'm playing a role, and this boy is playing his. But we could stop it, we could just fucking play some other game, there are so many to choose from.

"Who sent you?" I say again.

"Not the gang," he whispers, his head turned away, eyes staring up at the ceiling.

"I know," I say, stepping back, sighing, "you're here just to say hi," and the world swings on its axis and what was down is now up. It's quite easy to do the opposite of what you always do, if you take a moment to think. So I kneel beside him, take his bloody face in my lap, wrap my arms around his head, hug it tight, very tight, and I put my hand on his forehead and I kiss his temple, and that's just how it is.

"My name is Eddie," he says.

He gets up and I get up and we look at each other for a moment, really look.

"Eddie," I say. "I'm Jevrem."

The other crazy boys come into the room and see us, eyes locked, and shout, "Fight, fight, fight," with taunts and gestures, performing for each other, and Wounded Belly Boy ducks and turns and runs from the room. "Faggot," they cry after him, and laugh. "Fucking loser, cocksucker."

DR. GHORBANI sits behind her small desk like a sprinter waiting for the gun, she has that kind of energy. She writes something down on her notepad. Her fingers drum the desk. I sit back in the chair and study the empty patch of blue sky that the small, high window reveals.

"I've taken note, Jevrem, that you're on strike," she sighs, shifts in her chair. "But you know, your story is more common than you think. No human calamity in history is inevitable; it happens because not enough people prevent it from happening, and this is going on all around the world. So, instead of feeling sorry for yourself, put your energy into preventing the next calamity. That will provide enough meaning and direction to last you a lifetime, starting right here with the programs we offer. It's really that simple."

I sit there with stinging cheek, my ears ringing. I realize I've just been slapped in the face without the use of hands, and I'm shocked, I didn't see it coming. I squeeze my head between my palms, I breathe like a boxer. Then I finally look Dr. Ghorbani right in the eyes and say something.

"Stop feeling sorry for myself?" I say to her. "That's what you have for me?"

"Yes, Jevrem. That's it, in essence, distilled. It's not complicated, but it changes everything. We can go the long way round with hours of talking and analyzing, but you've made it clear that you don't want that. You want someone to tell you the way it is, not feed you lines, so I will."

I'm about to feel furious at this woman who is sitting so pretty on the other side of the desk where it's easy to talk about shit in the world, when it hits me once again, the exact same thought as this morning with Wounded Belly Boy Eddie, exactly what she's trying to tell me about myself. I'm a dog that barks pointlessly at every freaking little leaf that rustles in the grass. And as I'm thinking about this, another thought flashes into my mind: she has an Iranian name. I know because they came flooding into Sarajevo during the war, Muslim brother-hood, Islamic solidarity, with weapons and fire in their eyes, and all of that. She's been through it all too, that's what she's telling me with her eyes. She lived through civil war too. I suddenly see why she's kept going with me even though I've been a total fucking sullen asshole. She's had her own fascists and crazies who ruined everything just at the moment when everything was possible.

She's on a roll. "Your cynicism is not unique."

She's decided to change tactics with me, make me feel like we share something, and it's working. If I weren't leaving this place in a matter of days, I might even let her know a thing or two that's on my mind about heroes and villains.

"Many of us in the field know that this system of detention is lousy. I disagree with a lot about it. It causes additional trauma and it's not set up to bring about healing. Why lock up society's disaffected, abused, poor, broken, marginalized, neglected, addicted, ill, which is the bulk of the prison population? It's only different in degree from all the other repressive systems of incarceration in the world, where they round up dissenting voices as well. That's why I'm here, Jevrem. To study it. I'm doing research, I'm here for a reason. I know what my role is in society. What will your role be?"

Dr. Ghorbani squints her eyes. She's scrutinizing my soul to see how many of her words have sunk in.

I CARRY my tray to a table. The plate is piled high with mush. Powdered potato mush, canned pea mush, stringy chicken-leg mush. And a carton of milk. I don't look at the others sitting there, I don't care who sits where. I create space with my legs, with my elbows, I force myself in, and no one says a word because I'm the man, that's how it is in a place like this. I turn and signal Wounded Belly Boy Eddie, hanging off the end of a bench at a back table, allowed only six inches for his meal. "Hey, Eddie," I yell. He looks up, sees me, raises his eyebrows, gets up, walks over, and then he's standing behind me. "Make some space," I say, and the crazy boys do, and Eddie sits down beside me, hunches over, and directs his eyes at his bleeding fingernails. The crazy boys continue to slurp, burp, shout insults, snigger at nothing. They shovel food in their mouths, I shovel food in my mouth, Eddie shovels food in his mouth, and we all know what's just happened. Power has shifted. Eddie is with me now, inside and outside, he's going to make it, he's going to survive, that's how it works because I'm the man and I've decided. But it doesn't make me happy. This isn't a moment to feel warm and fuzzy about, this fucked-up way that people stay safe, this game of thugs, all over the world. It's how wars start, and I'm sick of it, I'm done. Goodbye, everyone, I think, I'm moving on, in the simplest way I can think of, after thinking of all the complicated ways. Minimum security is the clue. A fence, a few guards slouching around, lots of distractions. I'm not playing warlords anymore

After lunch, we trudge through the door one after the other. Outside, the sky has cracked open, the sun is everywhere. The crazy boys turn their faces to the south. They blink, they joke, they do their deals, they look at the trees beyond the fence with veiled eyes. Maybe they have springtime memories of longer days, open jackets, curbside games, loitering twilights, but they don't show it. Their eyes reveal no regret, no yearning, nothing to show their captors their souls are still alive.

Half an hour goes by, then I move like I know how to move. No thinking, just acting in the here and now, calculating, man- oeuvring, hunting the goal like a predator. In this moment, in the middle of this afternoon, I'm as alert, pumped, primed, high as all those times before when I was young, running from snipers, running from cops. I just go for it, ploughing into a huge Jamaican posse boy with rasta hair, ploughing into him, saying, sorry, this dude pushed me, and I point to a giant Indian crazy boy with missing teeth and bulbous muscles. Like in the movies, they challenge each other, chests out, chins up, moving slowly as mud, throwing ugly stares, and the guards turn their heads, make grim faces, saunter over. And I, skinny boy from Bosnia, back up, sit on the table, move to the wall, skulk behind a huddle of boys, slip around the corner, crouch next to the electrical box, run to the fence and just climb it.

I pull myself over lightning-fast, clothes tearing, skin slicing, like I used to go through windows in the old days, like I used to whip through houses to get to doors to make it to the car with the cops four minutes away, no hesitation, no looking back, my body like an animal knowing what it must do to get what it needs to survive on this earth. I am over the fence and running so fast I don't feel the ground at all, just a strong breeze against my scalp and blood pounding in my eyeballs. Now it is me and time bartering for a good deal. I think of snipers and I think of a million shells raining down on my head and I turn into an Olympic sprinter to cover the open ground and soon I'm in the trees, I am crashing through the forest like a deranged bear, panting, spit flying, thinking of nothing but moving for- ward. Then I slow down, stop, listen. There is silence, but this doesn't make me safe.

I don't know where I am exactly except that it's near a small town north of Toronto. I start walking fast and lightly through the forest, thinking about police dogs and heat-sensing helicopters, which they probably wouldn't waste on a skinny-assed refugee kid like me, but I don't know that for sure. What I want is a road, and a truck driving to the other end of the country. Soon I'm standing at the edge of someone's backyard. I see an empty pool, a large house, acres of lawn. And beyond that a country road. There is nothing to do but just walk out of the forest toward the road, and I do, feeling like a giant bull's eye, a clear shot for a thousand sharpshooters. My shoulders hunch, my fists clench, but I don't run, I walk, and then I'm on the road watching cars and trucks go by. Cars with moms and kids in them, old men out to buy a litre of milk, ordinary folk going about their ordinary day. And small local trucks, guys driving home from fixing a toilet or sealing a foundation. And I wonder what kind of man would pick me up with my detention clothes, my flushed face, my sweaty hair, my black eyes and hungry mouth. A decent man, I think, who will call the cops, or a crazy man who'll fuck me up, that's what kind of man. So I cancel the plan to catch a ride in broad daylight. I don't stick out my thumb, I don't wave a truck down, I dive into the nearest culvert when the road is clear, I cover myself with rotting cardboard and last year's leaves. I coil up into a tight ball and lie as still as I can with my blood crashing through my veins.

For hours there is nothing but graveyard cold, heartbeats, pulses, breathing, blinking, twitching. Centuries go by while I think of dogs on the prowl, sniffing through the forest, of police on the hunt, probing my people, my places. I think of Mama's face, its lines and creases, its glow when she's happy; I think of the Bastards, their musty rooms, their cagey, clever ways; I think of Sava like I always do and wish she were lying next to me like she always did, how she'd love this, how she'd challenge a hundred police forces to catch us, how she'd know exactly what to do next. I wait for Papa to show up, but he's not close by anymore, he's still floating down the river of the past that Mama and Leo the French dude put him on. I want him to lean into the culvert, to whistle, to chuckle, I want him to say, *interesting place to find yourself, Jevrem, in a dank culvert in the countryside outside a small Ontario town on the Canadian Shield, it's definitely a long way from the Jerusalem of Europe, maybe as far away as a person can get.* I pray for sleep so Dušan can grab my hand and lead me to a safe-house that he knows about, a bunker or trench, where we can lie side by side smoking and talking about things, all kinds of things. That would kill quite a bit of time while we wait for the darkness to come.

But finally darkness comes without anyone's help, and I'm out, standing in the infinite night, inhaling the black fresh air, clear and sweet as water in a desert, observing the car lights sweeping the road, listening to the trees having conversations with the wind. The wet ground, the chattering branches, the dark blue fog, the road leading to the horizon, they're all welcoming me to a world without walls, doors, locks, basements, streets, rules, bullshit, stuff, conflict, outrage. I turn in one direction rather than the other, and I start walking.

I follow the road until I meet another, bigger road. It has two lanes with wide gravel shoulders and ploughed fields on either side. I turn right, hoping it's south, toward the Trans-Canada Highway and thousands of miles east and west. It takes me two hours to get to the nearest gas station, me fading into every tree along the way when car lights appear. At the gas station, I avoid the pumps, their blinding lights, their crisp red and white markings. I avoid the kiosk, its stoned attendant and tinny music. I have no cash, anyway, to buy cigarettes, coffee, chocolate, I left it all with Wounded Belly Boy Eddie to buy more important stuff. Friends, for example. Security. The chance to make it through. Instead, I walk along the row of transport trucks parked on the murky off-ramp to the highway. I sit behind a tree, staring at my knees, getting ready to spring into action, my stomach knuckling into a fist, my head itching with foreshadowed triumph. Then I hear the sound of an engine revving, a truck coming to life, slowly, light by light. I hear it sigh and suck air and fart toxins out its fat exhaust pipe. I stand, stretch, look around. There it is at the head of the pack, creaking into movement, beginning to roll, and suddenly I'm a rodent scampering madly in the tall grass, then I'm a blind man plastered to the truck's back end, scrabbling and clutching and tapping its hooks and handles, anything for a solid grip. It takes four minutes for the truck to pick up enough speed to kill me if I fall.

And then, nothing but black roaring for unending time, a lethal, frothing highway below me, my hands and feet vibrating like jackhammers. My brain cuts electricity and there is no more thinking, no hoping, no wishing, no dreaming. Just hanging on. Nothing looms all around, and that's all there is.

‡ ‡ ‡

THE TRUCK DRIVER STOPS HIS TRUCK, GETS OUT, walks slowly but purposefully to the back. He stands, hand on hip, head cocked to one side, staring at the creature attached in several places to his vehicle. He stares as the creature moves its head an inch, tries to shift its limbs.

"Well, I'll be damned."

"Ow," the creature says. "Ow. Help."

The truck driver moves closer, but hesitates, doesn't know what to expect. He puts out one hand while holding his head back in case of snapping teeth or a Vise-Grip to the throat. Finger by finger he pries the creature's hands off the handle, then steps back and watches as it falls to the ground in slow-motion, like a dead lizard from a cooling wall.

"Jesus Christ," he says.

The creature lies on the dust and pebbles of the shoulder and praises the universe for inventing the earth's crust, for giving it the illusion of motionlessness.

"What the hell do you think you're doing?" the truck driver says, finally. "It's illegal to catch rides like that. Are you're crazy? You'll get killed."

The creature notices that it's still night. He's happy about that. The highway is empty. The sky is a cocoon. He wants to crawl into the gutter with April's weeds and sleep there until the world has stopped existing.

"Where are we?" he asks. He tries to get up, but can't. "I can't feel my arms or legs."

"We're just past Montreal," the trucker says.

"Where?" the creature mumbles, spitting exhaust out of its mouth.

"Past Montreal."

"That's good." The creature attempts to get up on his hind legs. His body is an alien object he's trying to control with his mind, like a telepath. He makes it to his hands and knees in a few crablike moves.

"Jesus Christ," the trucker says again. "You know I should call the cops. Another driver radioed me about you, otherwise I'd be going another few hours and you'd be . . . I don't know, maybe the other driver called the cops already. He didn't say."

The word *cop* jars me into my body. I feel my skin like a burning shirt. I pull myself up and stand swaying in a new province far away from my pursuers.

"Are you a mechanic or something?" the trucker asks, but he's distracted, he's wondering what to do.

I look down, see that my detention clothes are smeared with thick, oily dirt, that my hands are black. I look like a mechanic, it's true.

"You should know better, then," the trucker says.

I understand his logic; mechanical types have a healthy respect for machines.

"You could have been killed. You could have been killed off the back of *my truck*. Goddammit." He's angry, he's shaky. "Well, there's not much to be done about it now." The trucker wipes his forehead and shrugs his shoulders like he's given up on trying to understand life. He strokes his moustache with thumb and index finger while he decides what to do with me.

"I'm going to take you to the nearest service centre. Next time, just knock on the cab door and ask for a ride. Jesus."

The trucker trudges to his cab, I follow behind, a hobo mumbling thanks, pathetically grateful. Just ask for a ride, I repeat in my mind. It sounds so simple. The cab is warm inside. I sleep, my head tapping the window, my hands tucked into my underarms. The service centre is deserted. At Tim Hortons, an older woman, grey hair, tired eyes, is wiping down surfaces. The Wendy's counter next door is bright as a casino but empty. I go to the bathroom and sit on the toilet for a long time, thinking about what to do next. Footsteps jerk me awake. I've slipped sideways, I'm sleeping with my head against the toilet roll.

"'Allo," a male voice says. Then something in French. A hand shakes the door of each stall, one at a time. He's moving closer.

"Yes," I say. My voice is hoarse, too high.

"Oh, 'allo, sir? I'm gonna clean now. You okay?"

"Oh, yeah," I say. "Just fell asleep sitting here. Tired."

I charge out of the stall, suck some water out of a tap, walk fast out of the bathroom to the nearest exit. I don't turn, I am a forward-moving machine, I can afford only what is in front of me. Outside, there's a feathery early-morning mist. Tall sodium vapour lamps light a giant parking lot that doesn't hold a single car. I walk to the far end, I sit on a derelict picnic table, I contemplate the signs around me. Cracked pavement, anemic weeds, flattened cigarette butts, shredded ice-cream wrapper, highway going two ways, and all around me bush and forest and farmers' fields. I spot a pay phone and think of people to wake from sleep with my voice. Mama. Sava. But I know it's too soon. They'd both give me up, for my own good, of course. And the rest of the Bastards, I can't think of what they could say to me to get me to see what's coming next. Only the wind in the branches of the tall trees behind me has a say in my life now. I think, will I have to walk into the forest, burrow in the underbrush, exist there for days, or maybe weeks, months, years, foraging for roots and berries, diving the service centre Dumpsters at the crack of dawn, disappearing myself until no one remembers me?

I sit for a whole day. Cars and trucks drive in and out, but I'm not motivated to move. I think about directions to travel, west back to Toronto, hiding among its neighbourhood streets, friendly alleyways, tidy corners, Saturday markets, leafy parks. Under the bridge near the harbour and ferry, in full view of islanders and happy tourists. Looking over my shoulder, wearing hats, avoiding recognition on streetcars, in convenience stores, while eating roast duck in Chinatown, and every single other place I can think of to go. Hell, that's what it would be, going underground, not contacting Sava, the others, and a thousand cops breathing down my neck every minute of the day. Montreal, avoiding Mama, Aisha, and their brand new lives. Calgary, Vancouver too, where could I work, where could I live, without some do-gooder giving me up? And in Halifax and every other little town between here and there, I'd open my mouth just one time to order a black coffee, no sugar, and every motherfucker in the diner would be on the phone to the RCMP in a minute reporting a skinny, shifty-looking boy with a prison haircut and a crazy-ass accent. And south, that's a whole other scene I think about shrouded in ignorance. I don't know anything about it, what state is south of here, where would be a good place to go? There's Ujak Luka, but what would he do with an illegal refugee delinquent teenage escapee relative like me?

When the sun begins to set, I still don't know why I'd go in one direction not another, so I let chance take over, or whatever it is that's going on when one thing happens and not another. The sky is neon pink as I watch two cars glide to a stop at the pumps. Two guys climb out, in mirror-image, unhook nozzles, stick them in their cars, stand staring at nothing. I get up, stretch, walk slowly toward them. They both turn their heads and watch me without curiosity until I'm right up close.

"Hi," I say.

One nods. The other guy says, "Oh, hello there, fellow road-jockey."

"Any chance I can get a ride?" I ask, trying to sound like a nice boy.

One looks in the opposite direction, then walks in to pay, careful not to make eye contact.

"Shit, do I look that bad?" I mumble.

The other guy laughs a long, savouring laugh. "Does a pig say hi to a cookbook?" he says. "Or a carrot to a carrot peeler? Or a baguette to a breadknife, for that matter?" He laughs again, high and broad. Then he looks me up and down. "Yup. You look like you have some rough-and-ready recipes in you. Old-world and new-world recipes."

"What?" I say. "How about a ride?"

This guy is solid, with a tanned face, scraggly grey hair down to mid-back, eyes shining autumn-brown like chestnuts.

"If you're a wolf in sheep's clothing, what am I?" he asks.

"What?" I say.

"If you're on the run from the zoo, what kind of animal am I? My name is Jim, by the by." Jim is fiddling with the pump. He's got his wallet out. "I have to pay," he says. "Always a downside to this procedure."

"Jevrem," I say. "My name is Jevrem."

"Well, wait for me here, Yevy, and we'll see what we see when we see it."

When he's back at the car he looks me directly in the eyes. "The mother bird welcomes her chick back into the nest if it falls or jumps out, especially the ones ruffled by gales, the ones injured by eagles. This is the truth of the natural world." He pauses. "But the world humans have invented has different rules, doesn't it?" He laughs his huge melody of a laugh. "When human chicks fall out of the nest, for one reason or another, they often have to fend for themselves. Sometimes they're even punished for getting mangled out there, poor sons of bitches. Get in."

My brain feels soft, I don't understand a word this guy is saying. His car is a shitty old Toyota. It's packed full of stuff, but is surprisingly neat. I move CDs, a blanket, a couple of sweaters, a flashlight, and six jars of preserved tomatoes to the back seat, where I see a sleeping bag, shoes, a pile of books. Then I get in.

"Practical kind of boy," Jim says.

"I have no money," I mumble. "I left it behind."

Jim looks across at me, says, tsk, tsk, tsk, like Mama sometimes does. He shakes his head. "Do fast-moving clouds haggle about expenses? Do sunbeams worry about the cost of tea in China?"

"I don't know," I say, "do they?"

Jim roars with laughter, spins the steering wheel, and skids around the pumps toward the exit.

On the highway, Jim cranks Neil Young, even I know who that raggedy hippie dude is, coaxes the car to the speed limit, then carefully presses it up to a bone-rattling, law-breaking cruising altitude. He sings along with a high, breezy, intricate voice, he harmonizes, he strums air guitar, he talks his own words over the instruments, over high-singing Neil. I watch the road, feel tranquilized by the vibration, wish we could drive forever, then, weirdly, begin to shiver and shake like a junkie. Jim turns down the music, looks over at me.

"You're in fine shape," he says, then scrabbles around behind his seat with one hand, in quick succession pulling out a bottle of water, a banana, a box of Timbits, a blanket. He passes them to me.

"This pigeon," he says, pointing at me, "has flown its coop.

Eastward across Quebec, I'm assuming, and then where? Will it ever turn back? Will there be a message to bring home?"

"What?" I say.

"You haven't asked me where I'm going," he says. "It's a rare individual who has no opinion about his location on our fair Turtle Island."

"Oh, yeah. I guess, I just assumed you're going . . ." I look at the sky, then in the side-mirror. The sun has set behind us. "East."

"Okay, I smell fish, so tell me your epic story, my trembling young European. A man, i.e., me, should know what laws he's breaking. And why."

I'm having trouble following this Jim. It could be my state of mind, or my English-as-a-second-language, but I'm pretty sure it's him.

"What? I don't know what you're saying. Are we both speaking English?"

Jim laughs again, takes deep breaths in, lets vibrating trumpet calls out.

"There are many Englishes, my lean Caucasian. Your English," he says, "is like fragrant, flagrant champagne around a late-night fire." He reaches for the glove compartment and pulls out smokes. "Do you want a smoke? And I'm going as far as Rivière-du-Loup, if such trivial space-time info is of use to you."

We both light up, he turns up the radio. He sings a loud burst of song. *Come a little bit closer. Hear what I have to say . . .* He drums the dashboard. Then he turns the radio down again. The highway is empty of trucks and cars. The sun has set, the eastern horizon is black as night. We are in a tin box hurtling through a far-off galaxy devoid of stars.

"Okay, let's try this again, down at ground level." Jim inhales from his cigarette as though smoke is beneficial to the soul. "You're on the run, I can smell it. You have the scent of the hunted, the haunted, the wanted. So tell me from what and to what. I am a fair-minded sinner, songwriter, storyteller, and dreamer, so I'll give you a fair, wax-free listen. Do you understand me now?"

After a genius escape, I think, now this guy is going to pull the story out of me with nothing but words. But I have no choice. He has fox ears, and a feather in his breast pocket.

"My baka was a partisan," I begin.

"Oh really? Is that so? Is that the truth? Is that what matters to you?"

He says this with interest. So much interest that his words feel like a prayer, and I feel, for the first time in a long time, like a fascinating little piece of creation.

"Yes," I say. "She and I spent a lot of our war together in the basement."

"Isn't that something," he says. "A miracle of miracles. Basements are very important at certain lunatic times in human history. It all makes so much sense. What war would that be? Chechnya? Yugoslavia?"

"Bosnia," I say. "They—the leaders set the militiamen on each other, and there was nothing the rest of us could do."

"Oh yes." Jim nods. "'When the leaders speak of peace . . .' Well, they are the kind to do that, if you think about it. They are contracting when the universe is expanding. They're contracting into deadly vortexes of death in a way that sometimes happens, unfortunately for the rest of us. Like lockjaw at a singalong, like penny-pinching at the charity ball, like salt in the birthday cake."

"My mother stopped playing. She was a concert pianist. And my baka, tough freedom fighter, began to lose her communist faith in humanity. Her heart gave out, she stopped wanting to live, she was disgusted by the next generations."

"And so the light that lights up the firmament was extinguished."

"Yeah," I say. I've never heard it put so well. "And we moved to Canada."

"*And* you moved to Canada." Jim cradles his jaw in the palm of one hand and rubs his nose with his forefinger. "Hmm," he says. "So, this is the beginning of your story? A grandmother, a basement, deaths in a time of contraction, the end of music, a broken dream for a better world, and a migration to a vast unknown land."

"Well, no. There was a before of that."

"A before *of that*. I like it. A before *of that*."

"Yes. It wasn't bad before. For me, anyway. I have to start with World War Two, and the liberation of our country—many stories start there."

"Yes, there is always World War Two. Many stories do start there. So true. So true."

"Or maybe World War One, I don't know."

"Or you could go back to the dinosaurs, to fallen angels." Jim looks over at me and winks. He's steering with one finger. "You should start your story where you think it starts. But you are aware, my dear Yevy, that all stories are connected."

And this is how I tell everything to Jim like it's a story, while we drive eastward through the night at hair-flattening speeds. I throw in everything I can think of, plus a whole bunch of Papa's ideas.

Jim murmurs, mutters. He nods. "Yes," he says. "Empires,

Cold War end-games, economic collapse, geopolitical interests, expanding capitalist markets, cheap labour, access to natural resources, power grabs. A familiar tale to a creature like me, too familiar. The angels weep for us, yes they do, and also wonder why humanity, so well-endowed with brains and hearts, puts up with the same BS over and over again like a glut of brainless, heartless jellyfish."

And I keep going. Half of our family killed, I tell him. *Killed.*

"My papa," I whisper, "is more than a name, a place he came from, a list of things that he did in his life. He has this smell, sweat, cigarettes, soap, cologne. And a laugh, warm hands, a voice. Do you understand?"

"I do understand, Yevy," says Jim. "I understand perfectly."

"He was around for quite a while, but now he's floating away. Down that river."

"Down that river," Jim repeats and nods his head like he knows what I'm talking about, like he's had people float away too.

"And I had a brother. An older brother. We did a lot of things together."

And after that Jim lets me sit without saying anything until I fall asleep. Hours go by, I sleep, I dream. In my dream, Jim is a general disguised as a peasant. His hair is feathers, his nose is a beak. We're back home, and he's riding his cart filled with sweet-smelling apples along a narrow, winding track, he's asking me how to get to the top of the mountain. That way, I say, and I point to a white peak glinting in sunlight. When I wake, we're driving straight into a pale, unavoidable sunrise. I sit up and blink at the wild landscape on either side, empty bush spreading around us like it's taken over the world, like it's decided to crowd out human pests like us, like we've died and are driving through the unpopulated part of heaven to get to the gate. I see hints of colour washing over the brown branches of winter, light green, yellow, pink, orange. The trees are wearing the palest of their spring halos, I remember this from home.

"We came to this country in an airplane, we came here like tourists with suitcases, like people who decided to go somewhere, who planned and bought tickets, but that's not really how it felt. It felt like running blindly into the dark and ending up anywhere, any random spot. It's a nice, good place, I know that, it's obvious everywhere you look, but for some reason I just couldn't act like a normal boy when I got here." I feel like I'm confessing to Jim. "I just couldn't do it. Things *weren't* normal—why was everyone pretending they were?"

The sun climbs free of the trees in front of us and I see nothing but glaring white light. Jim drives with a hand shielding his eyes, a knee steering the wheel.

"Thank you, my friend," Jim says, "for telling me your tale. So, here's a simple observation for you. Our world suffers from unnecessary, intended scarcity, my boy, which leads to submission, which cultivates fear and insecurity, which leads to suggestibility and suspicion of others, which leads to cruelty and lack of compassion, which engenders all the rest of the terrible messes we humans get ourselves into. But none of that has to happen, none of it is inevitable. Remember this, it's important, it will affect how you live the rest of your life. You, yes, *you*, can avert world-historical catastrophe. A tidbit of advice. Learn, explore, be curious, be open, be playful, fall in love with humanity and the universe, be more open, be more playful, notice the connections, then learn some more."

This is the truth, that's really what he says. I think of everything that's happened in my life, and how I don't know a thing about it all, not really. Not enough to understand. The highway keeps unravelling, we keep driving. Then I'm asleep again, and wake when the sun has risen properly and is hanging overhead. We've stopped, and Jim is standing beside the car, smoking a cigarette, meditating on the new day. I see now that he wears a flowing Jesus shirt and several necklaces with colourful stones, he's a real original hippie from back in the day.

I get out and stretch, rub my eyes, brush my dirty fingers through my bristly hair.

"Where are we?"

"This be the place, Yevy. This is it, my fork in the road, where I turn one way and you go the other." Jim's voice has no sleep in it. It's as high and bright as ever.

He pulls out a cigarette, lights it for me. "Smoke," he says. "Not good for the lungs, but good for the spirit. The thing is, all the terrible things you've experienced, all the terrible things you've done, *learn* from it, draw the conclusions, help to make things right. It's a plan, at the very least."

I smoke, I nod. I feel like a character in a movie, important enough to run into saints and seers, important enough to have wise words chanted in my ear. I want to keep going with Jim for the rest of time, I want to meet the people he knows, but he says no.

"I have fish to fry," he says. "I have fateful promises to keep. I have cosmic errands to run."

"I could do that stuff with you," I say. But I know he won't give in. After only a few hours together I know he's the most steadfast person I've ever met. Jim looks closely at me to see if I'm going to burst out crying, crumple to the ground in despair, or anything like that.

"Do you have people to go to?" he asks quietly.

I stare over the hood of the car at birds on a wire.

"People?" I ask.

"Anyone who will say, 'Oh, there you are, Yev, my friend, I've missed you,' when they see you?"

I think for a moment. "I have an uncle," I say. "He's in Hollywood or something, producing movies. Or maybe he's a businessman or a thug for the mob. I'm not too sure."

"An uncle on this continent, occupation unknown. Well, that seems like a definite destination possibility." He hums a tune, sings a few words, "*Every song I sing, I'll sing for you,*" looks up at the sky, tests the wind with his forefinger. "Yevy, my friend, I am proud of you. You are a true traveller. Many do not travel the path of their own life, and that's the sad truth. They do no wrong, they make no noise, no dust is stirred up by their feet, but they don't go anywhere either, they don't do a damn bit of good to anyone. You get the direction of my tongue? You see where it's pointed?"

Jim grabs my hands and holds them between his, which are huge and dry and warm.

‡ ‡ ‡

I SIT IN THE SHRUBBERY ON THE HILL OVERLOOKING the gas station. Cars and trucks drive in, pause for a few minutes, drive out again. Fat people and thin people and mid-size people walk into the station, stay for a few minutes, walk out again. Coffee, chips, chocolate, Coke, cigarettes, window-washer fluid. It's a constant stuttering stream, like widgets on a conveyor belt.

I'm waiting for a sign.

Every minute is a thousand centuries, but the day goes by anyway. A breeze blows in all directions, clouds stand still in the sky, grasses scratch against each other, the dirt is hard and dusty. And I'm hungry, but I don't get up to hunt for food. I keep sitting, like a boy looking out to sea for ships, until hunger goes away and I'm nauseated and that goes away and I'm dizzy. Then come crazy visions and weightlessness. I'm a wraith up on the hill. I hear voices, right up close, beside my head. They tell me stories and remind me of memories. I re-dream dreams, I rethink thoughts, I hover six inches above the ground while the sun drills sunbeams into my forehead. I can live here forever, I think. I can float tall and raise my arms and a vapour-bright light will appear all around me, and I'll be the sign I'm looking for, a roadside attraction, like the Virgin Mary who appears all over the world giving directions to the end of time. The Virgin Mary, who I don't know any-thing about, or Mohammed, or any of the others. My family wasn't religious. Baka said, they're a fantasy and a spectre, the kind that people believe in to feel better about their hard, senseless lives. She said, Jevrem, the war taught me, Tito my hero taught me, it is much better and easier to remove the cause of suffering for all and be happy and contented than to change nothing, suffer, fight each other for crumbs, kill each other over pride, then plead with phantoms in the sky for forgiveness.

I watch the grasses flutter, I stare at my hands, I imagine drifting high into the sky so I can see the whole of the land, so I can spot arrows that will show me where to go, and little message-bubbles that will tell me why. The sun sets. The sky is purple, then blue, then black. Stars really do appear one at a time, until they're suddenly all there like a curtain has lifted. I sit in the dark with the people of the planet, I think of the lives they live, I wonder why they live them. I think about happiness, what it's for. I see ordinary scenes of work and learning. I watch my life flow backwards. I'm a newborn on my mother's belly. I watch it flow forward, but my mind won't be tricked into reading my own future like a psychic at a summer fair.

I sleep. I wake.

I keep watching the station as people arrive and leave, walking an identical path through the station's white cloud of light. They move without thinking, life is easy for them, they're travelling from A to B and they know where B is. They never look up to where I'm sitting. The moon rises, the sky goes milky grey, the stars fade one by one, there is no curtain now. Traffic stops and silence takes over, with its hollow echoes. I hear dogs howling, or maybe it's coyotes, or the wolves in my dreams, or the animal that lives in my mind. Warmth seeps out of the earth. The ground is an arctic surface, it has no sympathy for me. So finally I stand, my knees, my back, my ass burning, I rub my belly, sagging like a hammock between my ribs, tight and cramped with hunger and its nightmarish memory. I stretch like a man risen from the dead. Then I pace back and forth like a thinking man, but I have no more thoughts or memories, I'm sending and receiving static.

BAKA is next to me. *It's going to be a cold night*, she's saying. *Are your clothes dry?*

"Yes, they're dry." My jaw is tight, it's hard to talk.

Good, she says. *Dry clothes win the war. That and gasoline.*

"There is no war anymore," I mutter. "It ended."

Baka slaps me on the shoulder. *You were always such a rascal, Jevrem.*

"But," I say.

As long as your clothes are dry, you can survive the cold. It won't go below freezing. Baka has her hand in the air as though it's a barometer. *We survived for three years in the mountain forests,* she says. I mouth the words along with her.

"I know," I say. "You told me about fifty thousand times."

And it was because we knew what we were doing there, and we worked with the forest, not against it.

"I know," I say.

When I was young and I walked up into the mountain forest to begin the rest of my life, I was waiting by the side of the road for my guide. When the sun set I heard footfalls. I listened with anticipation. I was told to expect a man when night fell. I knew what he would say to me once he came upon me. I knew how I would respond. I stood before he arrived and shuffled in small circles, letting blood circulate to my legs and feet. Then the man was at my side. I sensed him as much as I could see him. He was a dense breathing presence undulating in the blue and purple night. Do you wish to continue with me? he asked.

Baka stares down at the glowing gas station but she's in a completely other outdoor nighttime of her life. *Do you wish to continue with me?* she repeats, her voice quiet and serious, like she's reciting an epic poem that reveals the meaning of all life. Then she shakes her head and gets back to giving me survival advice. *So, if you think you'll be cold, look around you and see what you can find to keep you warm. It's all here. Everything you need is always right in front of you. Always.*

I look around half-heartedly. The shrubbery is ragged, dirty, highway-swept.

Look farther back, Baka directs.

I stare in the direction of her pointing finger. "It's dark," I say. "I can't see a thing."

You don't have to see, she says. *Just walk in that direction. Half a mile back, beyond the fallow field, is a forest. There are pine trees, and also deciduous trees, their branches still naked except for seed-size buds.*

"I'm not eating things I pull out of the ground," I tell Baka, but she's not here anymore, she's wandered off. It's just me and icy gusts of wind.

I STARE at the floating gas station in a huge expanse of cosmic blackness. The temperature keeps dropping. The moon sets. I tremble, I vibrate. Finally, I do what I should have done hours ago, I listen to Baka. I turn, push through the brush away from the station and the highway, and walk into nothingness. The field, the forest, are invisible. But I can feel the ground rising to meet my feet, and cold air pressing up against my face like water, thick strong-smelling, of grasses, earth, manure, worms. I walk for some time, my ankles twisting on crumbling, lumpy furrows, and then I run into the forest as into an impenetrable wall. I push forward with all my might, and cracking, splintering, the forest reluctantly lets me in. I bend down and feel the fallen branches and twigs, how brittle and light they are, and below that a spongy, springy layer of pine needles, just sitting there ready to burn. I'm inside, I stand and listen. The forest is hushed but alive with scurrying, rustling, running, and climbing. I hear sniffing and snorting. I hear flapping, and licking, sucking, chewing. I know I'm hallucinating with my ears, that my mind is inventing, taking me places, that it's brought me back home, to the forest of our vacations, to my overnight adventure, when the dark was like moth wings caressing my face, my hands, neck, wrists; crawling into my ears and nostrils. I let myself believe, for one moment, that I could walk out of this place and back to Papa, Dušan, Berina, Aisha, and Mama, all sleeping soundly in their hostel beds until morning and another ordinary day.

In the dense, breathing forest, I drag branches, whole trees, into a clearing. I blunder, I swear, I let the forest know I'm human. Animals and spirits have speed, instinct, sharp teeth, claws, invisibility. I have matches, courtesy of Jim. I light a roaring fire. Tree trunks undulate gold and orange, small branches shiver in the rising heat, thick white smoke plunges upward, fountains of sparks spray into the void.

It was wonderful, glorious, a dream, Baka says, telling her story about the golden time, the one I missed by being born too late. *We had joy, we had fun, we had seasons in the sun,* she sings. She must have heard it on the radio. *We were young, we were free, we were Marxists on TV.* Baka giggles. Sometimes she's just a girl again, she can't help it. The girl who built a railroad. *But the country that we made, was just dreaming out of time.*

She sits cross-legged near the fire, poking a stick into the hottest part, her face weathered and creased, her eyes smiling as they look into the past. *The most wonderful communist nation on the planet. Dear Tito took everything that was good from both the capitalist and communist systems and put them together.* She lists off the pros by yanking on her fingers. *The borders were open. We carried our own passports. We read foreign literature and newspapers. We had consumer goods. The factories were owned by the workers. No fat-cat got rich by stealing the value of people's labour. Everyone was looked after. Jobs, health care, education, cultural life. We were Yugoslavs, religion and tribe didn't terrorize our lives . . .*

She goes on and on. I know the list by heart. The fire is a

creature, I see how it dances with itself. Baka talks and I follow her words like they're shapes in the coals, remembering all the good things of my life before, soaking in the heat. It's so nice to have her here by the bonfire, the two of us happy and cozy side by side, she having a field day summarizing the past.

"Yes, I know all that," I say finally. "But I want to know what comes next, what's ahead. Tell me that story."

How should I know, Jevrem? What's ahead is up to you. Nothing is fated. That is what's so nerve-racking and exciting about being alive.

I jolt awake, see only black all around me, except for a patch of glittering starry sky so close to my face I panic, turn my head, scrabble to my hands and knees. Baka? I say. The sky is falling, the fire has gone out except for a few glowing embers. My hands and feet have disappeared, my skull has no shape, my mind bleeds into tree trunks, catches on crooked twigs, runs down along roots into the densest earth and rock where humans end and the universe begins.

I stumble around on frozen stumps, trying to find my way out of the forest to open space where I can pull myself together and think like a domesticated animal. Instead, my palms, my face, press against the bark of trees that stand in my way, their dead tissue holding wastes and toxins, protecting against insects, animals, disease, fire, bad weather, cracking with growth, preventing evaporation.

And there he is. Dušan is waiting for me, and he says, *c'mon, Jevrem, let's go,* and he disappears into the trees and I scramble to follow him. I can hear branches breaking as he goes, and him shouting, *c'mon, Jevrem, there's this place we can go, you'll see, it's perfect.* And then I'm there and it is better than out in the open, it's a nest in the hollow of a tree, lined with pine branches and needles and dry dead leaves.

I wake as the eastern horizon brightens, a streak of yellow, a streak of pale blue. I stand up like an old man, teeth rattling, spine fused, ribs collapsing. I'm too cold to walk. I stare at the sky. All I can do is wait for the sun to rise.

AND the sun does rise. It sweeps upward, that's how it feels to me. Precise, certain, unwavering, quick, and then it shines right on me. My head opens like an exotic flower and light pours into me and right through me into the spinning earth, way down to the fiery core.

7

I WALK BACK ACROSS THE FIELD TO THE GAS STA-
tion. In daytime, the distance is nothing and the lumps of
earth aren't treacherous at all. Five trucks are lined up in
the parking lot. The pumps are busy with cars. I look for U.S.
plates, because I've made up my mind. I've decided.

I head into the station to pick the shelves for edible food.
I grab a couple of sandwiches out of their plastic boxes, several long thin salamis, a few packs of peanuts, and shove
them all down my overalls into my filthy underwear. I push a
small carton of milk up my sleeve. Then I walk out the door.
Everything is fine for twenty-five paces, then I hear shouting
from inside and a disturbance, the kind made by a running
adult male, objects clattering to the ground, the thudding of
heavy footsteps. The door bangs open and he's yelling, "Stop
him, stop that boy." So I pull my loot up to my chest where
I can hold onto it with both hands and take off at a sprint for
the bush behind the station. The lumpy slacker from behind
the counter doesn't have a hope of catching me, but what I
don't see coming at me from the side is a guy in a black car.
I'm running, and then I'm not. I'm running and then I'm flying
over a hood, I'm rolling along the asphalt, I'm lying winded

several feet from the edge of the parking lot. I have a sense of a car braking a few feet from my head, of a car door opening. I hear more shouting, many voices, countless running footsteps from all directions. A hubbub. And I'm on my feet again, I'm tearing into the brush, I'm running for my life, I'm up over the embankment. I sense something alive and snorting behind me, I feel arms around my legs, and I'm down again. I'm on my stomach, face in the dirt.

The rest is a blur of flailing arms, flying spit, wild-animal grunting. Then I'm in the forest again, way deep in the forest. I'm lying face up, I'm panting, my lungs are burning, white clouds are sailing by above the treetops. I try to sit up, but I can barely move. I lie back, I watch the clouds. I close my eyes. When I open them again, my right hip is a vortex of pain, my right hand is swollen to twice its normal size. The knuckles are bloody.

Walking is hard, but I walk for hours through forest and fields parallel to the highway. I get as far away from the gas station as I can, keeping my eyes open for an abandoned building of some kind to lie low in for a while. Barns and sheds are all close to houses, so I pass those by. Then I see a high wire-mesh fence. Behind it are two long low buildings with a series of large orange roll-up doors. I climb the fence and nose around, looking for cameras. The garages are padlocked. In a large firepit fifty feet away from the end of the buildings, I see pieces of charred metal. I find a piece of a bedstead strong enough to lever apart the cheap padlock on one of the doors. I roll up the garage to find a whole home inside, all stacked up on itself. There are chairs, lamps, tables, a couch, a bedstead and mattress, rolled-up carpets, cardboard boxes and plastic containers. It takes only fifteen minutes to set up the bed, complete with damp pillows and musty blankets. I roll down the door, fall into the bed, and sleep.

I WAKE with parched mouth, racing heart, crashing headache, burning face, nostalgic symptoms of siege dehydration. It's night when I leave the storage locker. I head east. The moon is up and almost full, transforming the highway into a river of glowing silver. I jog along the yellow line, tuning out the pain, gazing up at the vast domed sky, the pale stars, like I'm a ghost on a planet that's sighing with relief to be rid of its number-one pest. Occasionally a car or truck appears on the horizon with lonely headlights and a mournful roar to break my illusion, and when it does, I step down into the ditch and wait for it to hurtle past. After about half an hour, I see a gas station on the opposite side of the highway but it's not open. It doesn't matter, gas stations are no use to me now. Just beyond it, a rural road crosses the highway on an overpass and I scramble up the embankment and walk north along it for about a mile looking for a promising house. Because, there's no way around it, I once again have to do what I have to do to make it through. I spot a rundown bungalow with a shabby porch and two derelict cars on the front lawn. Not much of a cash prospect, but it'll have some food, and no lights are on, no car is parked in the driveway. I break a window at the back, the glass tinkling, as always, in the high notes of the piano on the stone below, and pull myself in slowly, carefully, trying not to twist my hip. It's the same MO as always, but I feel no thrill, I feel no charge. It feels wrong to be in this house, depressing and grim, nothing more.

The house smells of cigarette smoke and air freshener and something else I can't identify, something salty and greasy. Pet food maybe, or unwashed pots. I find a poker by the wood stove, then creep along the hallway eerily illuminated by a Snoopy night-light at the far end. I silently open the doors to each bedroom, but find no one. The house is empty. I stoop over the sink and drink water for a long time, then I look in the fridge. It's a mess of crap, but I manage to collect enough to keep me going for a few days. A packet of wieners, a packet of cheese slices, hamburger buns, mayonnaise, pickles, dip for chips, old pizza in its oily box. In the cupboard I find packs of juice crystals, peanut butter, jam, cans of meat, crackers, tuna, marshmallows, Campbell's soups. I take a can opener from a drawer, then check the basement, which is a crawl space with junk in it and a small cat that's cowering behind a stinking litter box. I find some cans of beer, old plastic bottles to fill with water, and a mouldy knapsack for the food. I search the house for a space heater and an extension cord but don't find either. I take a winter coat, scarf, hat, and boots from the front hall closet and am looking around for a sleeping bag when I hear the unmistakable rattle of a Harley in the driveway. I feel true fear deep in my bones at that sound, so I throw the clothes in the bag with the food, haul the bag over my shoulder, my right hand fat and bruised and useless, and slip out the back door. I hear a woman talking and a man laughing loudly as they walk to the front door. I hear the front door open and slam shut again. I stand behind a tree until they've been inside for two minutes, then I walk into the moonlit countryside, heading west again, back to my nest in the locker.

THE cinder-block walls and concrete floor hold the night's icy temperatures all through the day. I sometimes open the door when the sun is shining, but mostly I bury myself in blankets, shiver, sleep, dream. Dušan takes me by the hand and leads me to the city-end of the Sarajevo tunnel, a house on a street. We sit side by side on a trolley and someone, maybe it's Papa, maybe it's Leo, maybe it's Ivan or Mr. Duff, rolls us along the rails all the way through the cramped suffocating darkness to the other end, where we emerge, outside the city, next to a lonely bush, in the midst of open space, free to go where we want. We walk into the empty field. No one is around. I turn to ask Dušan, what next? But he's not there. It's just me in that field, looking in all directions, searching for clues.

Sometime during the afternoon people show up. I hear a car, a truck, voices, but I can't tell what they're doing. When they're gone after several hours and silence reigns again, I emerge and crouch over the glowing coals of the garbage fire they left behind. I feed it with wood from the surrounding trees. I begin to warm up, I begin to feel my hands and feet again, and my face stings with the heat of the flames. I sense life beyond the circle of light, noises that belong to animals, and I stand facing out, holding a smoking stick, looking for the shimmering discs of reflected light that are their eyes. Then I hear wolves howling, or think I do, somewhere close by and get back in to the locker. I twist and turn on the bed, focus on the hot aching of my hand and hip, listen to mice scratching, think about how to find my way to a future I can't yet see. Other kids just do what's coming next, the next grade, university, a job. I try to picture one thing after another, in some place, any place, a job, any job, finishing high school, in any school, going to college in a nameless town, sitting next to nameless kids, studying whatever for a long life of doing whatever. And every scene I come up with has danger lurking in it, a shattered window, a soldier with a rifle, cops knocking on the front door, wolves congregating in the park. Three days go by with me recreating those scenarios, over and over again, trying to imagine the danger away.

WHEN I leave the storage locker for good, it's early morning. The sun has just risen, and a wispy mist is floating among the trees. I'm wearing the coat, I'm wearing the toque, I'm carrying the bag, so I'm in disguise as I walk along the shoulder of the highway with my thumb out. At this hour, there aren't many cars so I just keep going, shoulders hunched, head low, trying to get into a rhythm, a flow, accepting the pain, keeping my mind free of police cars and red alerts.

Hours later, a car stops in front of me. It's one of those cars that looks like every other car, and I walk up to it expecting a middle-aged dude in a tie and a rain jacket, but find a young guy in his early twenties looking wrecked and strung out. Worried frown, slit eyes, flushed cheeks, oily skin.

"Get in, bro," he says, barely looking at me.

He accelerates hard off the shoulder, pebbles flying high behind us, and drives slumped down in his seat, chin resting on his chest. He doesn't say a word, so I take the coat off, I settle in. The car is pristine, a small bouquet of straw roses dangling from the rear-view mirror, a box of tissues wedged between the seats, individually wrapped mints in one cup holder, change filling the other. This is a mother's car, and the son looks oversize and sloppy in it, like he's about to crush something delicate. At my feet is a dog-eared notebook, splayed open, the pages covered with cramped, smeared boy-writing and doodles. I pick it up.

"Sorry, I stepped on this."

"No worries. Studying for an exam." He grabs it and tosses it onto the back seat, then faces forward wordlessly again.

I'm happy to stare at the highway just before it disappears under our wheels, thinking about things like walking, how it doesn't keep pace with reality at all, about how good it feels to be moving forward, straight forward at a fast, steady, motorized pace, that this is how I want my life to be from now on, not stuck in some accidental place doing an accidental thing, but me at the wheel steering where I want to go. This is when I notice that the guy is swerving out of our lane, then back in again, that we're weaving all over the place. Suddenly we swerve into the left lane and head for the concrete blocks in the middle of the highway.

"Hey, Jesus." I grab the guy's shoulder.

The guy snorts, jerks his head up, rights the wheel.

"Holy shit," he gasps. "Goddammit, this isn't working. I drank, like, six cups of coffee this morning but I can't keep my eyes open."

"Okay," I say. I notice that he smells faintly of vomit. "Late night?"

"No night. We stayed up till I had to split this morning. I promised I wouldn't, but you know, once you get going. My exam is at two, and I need to do some studying."

We say nothing more for ten minutes but I notice that the guy is slipping down so far in his seat that he can barely see over the wheel, that he's pinching the skin of his right arm, that he's throwing his head back and grimacing with fake yawns, the kind you make to get extra hits of oxygen, then shaking his head like a dog.

"You drive," he says finally. "I need to sleep, then I'm gonna study. Okay, d'you mind?"

"Okay," I say. "I don't mind at all. Where are you going?"

"UNB," he says and pulls the steering wheel hard to the right. We skid to a stop. I assume this is a university. "Fredericton."

We switch places. "Turn in to the city at the first exit when we get there. Thanks, man," he says, then throws the seat back and pulls his sweatshirt hood over his eyes.

He's asleep before I pull off the shoulder, his breathing erratic and ragged. It feels great driving a car, how fast you can go on a perfect highway like this. I check to see how full the tank is, I check the side pocket, the glove compartment, I fumble behind me in the backpack on the back seat, find his wallet and riffle through it. His name is Brad, he was born in 1977, and he's got forty-five dollars in cash on him and a debit card and two credit cards. I see a sign for Fredericton, still hundreds of miles away. I could just keep right on driving till we hit the east coast, or try to cross the border into the U.S., since Brad could sleep all day without moving an inch. I could pull over, open his door and push him out. It would be that easy, he'd fall, and wake only when he landed on the gravel, when his car was pulling away from him, when it was too late. He'd lie there for a few moments, bewildered, then he'd swear like a loser and get up slowly, brushing gravel off his palms, staring at the disappearing car.

But then I find his pack of cigarettes. In it, wedged between the cigarettes, are three joints so lovingly rolled that it's like a sign from his guardian angel. I look at him sleeping so trustingly beside me, believing that nothing bad will ever happen to him besides this last inconvenient exam of the year, that he has to somehow bullshit his way through so he can get back home to a summer of partying. And I think of Dušan, I can't help it, it's the lovingly rolled joints, and how close in age they are, and how Dušan used to sleep the same way, still high, still drunk, putting off the work and bullshitting he'd need to do when he woke up. How having a good time with his friends was also the most important part of his life. How Dušan took me for granted and ignored me and assumed I'd always be on his side and would never squeal on him or take his stuff or screw him in any way, just like this Brad is doing. I think, how good it was that Dušan grabbed all that time for himself, how right he was to live selfishly for the moment, not doing his math homework, not doing any homework, not worrying about his bad attitude or making it in the world or any of the things he was constantly nagged about. How wrong everyone else was, Mama and Papa, his teachers, the responsible ones, about his pointless teenage fun, how sur- really, horribly wrong.

For the next four hours I drive, watching Brad with one eye as he snores and tucks his hands into his armpits, as he wriggles his large frame to get more comfortable, as his head tips back and his mouth opens and he looks like a fat-cheeked baby in a crib. And I debate his fate with myself, his fate versus my fate, how perfect it would be for me to have his car for a solid day and night so I can make some good time, how shitty it would be for him to tumble headfirst out onto the shoulder. And the whole time, in my mind's eye, Dušan is also asleep, also trying to get comfortable, also trying to stay warm, but he's lying on the floor in a trench somewhere, or a gutted house they used as a bun- ker, it's never clear where. His head is tipped back, his mouth is open, just like Brad's, just like an overtired child who can't take any more of this world. And I watch him as he twitches and babbles from time to time, as the innocent slackness of his face is troubled by a grimace, which sometimes happens when people sleep and dream. And then a brief scene unfolds that I haven't been able to watch until now. A soldier with a gun shows up in the trench, in the house, wherever exactly the two of them find themselves in this fateful moment, and without pausing for an instant aims his gun down at sleeping Dušan and shoots him in the face.

SHORTLY after I turn onto the first exit for Fredericton, I pull over and cut the engine. The silence of the stationary car does not wake Brad. I take a twenty out of his wallet, and ten smokes, two joints, and the lighter out of his pack of cigarettes. Then I get out and close the door quietly behind me. I trudge back to the Trans-Canada and walk far enough along so that Brad's car is out of sight. I turn and stand waiting for the next vehicle to come speeding along. When cars pass by I stick out my thumb, but no one picks me up. After about an hour, I start walking.

I STAND outside a service centre inhaling the food and sipping the coffee that I paid for. I also bought smokes, and that's it for Brad's cash. Then I watch the trucks that are idling in the parking lot, wondering if I should travel as far east as I can get in Canada, St. John's, Newfoundland, which is still several small European countries away, or whether it's time to turn south then travel west again, to attempt the border, to cross the continent, to find Ujak Luka. He's way on the other side of it, at least a week away. That means a week of open road, staring out of windows, thinking, dreaming, figuring things out.

I walk up to the nearest truck with U.S. plates, knock on

the passenger door, pull myself up, and look in the window. I'm amazed by what I see. The cab is a home. There's a quilted blanket, tasselled pillows, dog-eared photos stuck to the dash, magazines, books, clothes on hangers, dangling amulets to keep road-death away. The driver is reading a magazine, smoking a cigarette, sipping coffee.

"Hi," I say. I motion for him to lower his window.

"What's up, kid?"

"Where are you going?" I ask direct, like the other driver said.

"Pittsburgh," he says. "Via the Houlton border."

"Okay. That's it, then. Can I get a ride?"

"What's your destination?" He puts his coffee down carefully and turns to look at me closely.

"California," I say. It sounds really sweet coming out of my mouth. I have to say it a few more times. "California. I'm going to California. Los Angeles, California."

The driver is short, with bulky arms and neck. His skin stretches taut over a mighty, grizzly face. He rolls his eyes.

"That's where they all want to go," he says. "Know someone there?"

"Yeah, I'm going to visit my uncle. He's some kind of Hollywood star, or producer, or businessman, or something like that."

"Oh yes." He sighs. "Everyone knows someone there, someone who's just about to make it big. You got a passport?"

I shake my head. "I'm not worried about that kind of thing."

The driver laughs and puffs smoke in my direction.

"Oh, to be young again. What's the accent? Something from Europe, I'd guess."

"Where do you want me to be from?"

"Oh, anywhere outside of this continent will be good. I can tell you, I'm up for some fresh words and ideas. I've heard most of the ideas in the heads of North American kids, I know what they're thinking about, pretty much, and it's got flaws, I tell ya. It's got flaws."

"I'm from Bosnia," I say.

The driver claps his hands. "Bosnia? Well, I'll be damned. Hop in, I can take you as far west as I'm going, and if you've got a brain between your ears, some good stories, a few jokes, a decent way of eating, no one likes a slob, I can maybe pass you on to some brothers from there."

I haul myself in. It's a soft sofa kind of seat, and there we are sitting nice and high off the road like thin-skinned aristocrats.

"My name is Samuel L. Jackson. Not Sam. Samuel. Like the actor, but short, fat, white, and one-hundred-percent teamster, Local 299. That's Detroit, son." Samuel smiles a flashy smile. "The city of rusty champions."

Samuel does some bustling around before we get going, then turns the key, presses a series of buttons and levers, and the truck picks itself up and charges up the highway on-ramp. Samuel drives it like it's a high-strung prize horse, clucking and crooning to it, saying, *whoa there, girl, giddy-up, back, walk, gallop, step, easy.* He tells her she's a good girl; he says, you can do it, girl, pass that pathetic short-strided pony, go on, pass that son-of-a-glue-pot. I ask Samuel if he's a horse guy, does he like to ride, and he looks at me like I'm nuts. I get comfortable with his pillows, I feel my muscles go soft, I feel my skin burning from exposure to the cold and the night, I feel sleep filling my head. We're heading west on Highway 2, still the Trans-Canada, nothing but brush on either side.

"We're going to cross at Houlton in about an hour," Samuel says. "Then we'll be on I-95."

I let myself be carried along like a bundle of cloth, adding no energy or thoughts to the process, just letting the exploding gas, pistons, axles, wheels do all the work. And I feel so relieved I want to cry. I stare out at the monotonous brush, I stare into car windows at shoulders, laps, car interiors. I know there's no other place on the planet that I'd rather be but on this road, pointing in this direction, so many thousands of miles ahead of me to get lost and found in.

At the border I join the boxes of office supplies in the back. If you get nabbed, Samuel says, I've never seen you before, you got that? But his truck rolls right through after a short stop, paper clips, binders, desk accessories and all, and me with it, one skinny-assed Euro-fugitive from an imploding past lying flat on his back with the smell of cardboard pressing into his lungs. I say ciao to Canada, the giant, friendly land at the top of the globe, with its mash-up of people from all over the world living together pretty well, considering. And I think, I didn't get to know you much, or at all, really, you tried your best, thanks for all the cigarettes, weed, stale doughnuts, sorry about the mayhem. Maybe one day I'll make you proud. Who else would let in a screwed-up motherfucker like me?

‡ ‡ ‡

THE U.S. OF A. IS A BIG PLACE, JUST LIKE CANADA, this is the first thing I notice as I look at the map Samuel's given me as he chases down the miles with unwavering focus, like a hunter following his dogs. It's a real physical country, that's the second thing I notice, as I look out the window, with earth, rocks, soil, plants, trees, rivers, towns, cities, people. It has farmers' fields, cows, barns, orchards, fences, silos, small towns, gingerbread houses, a church on every corner. It has industrial wastelands, dingy down-and-out towns, low-rent strip malls with low-rent chain stores, rusty railroad bridges, highways that cut through shapeless scrub, three hundred million flags, one for each person, give or take. It has foggy foothills, winding roads, deep ravines, rushing gorges, pounding waterfalls, small lakes with sandy beaches and rocky shores. That's what I've seen so far and we're only halfway through Maine. I laugh at my foolishness quietly as I watch it unrolling in front of my eyes. In my mind, Canada was the wild land full of natural wonders. America was a huge perfect golf course decorated with plastic palm trees and twenty million cruise missiles sticking out in all directions.

And that's not all, Samuel tells me, his eyes shining and alive, there is marsh, prairie, desert, badlands, giant mountain ranges craggier than anywhere, canyons you can fly helicopters into, distances that dwarf the European mind.

"It's better live, in person, on the ground, than it is as an idea," he says, "that's for certain."

In the middle of Maine, we heave off the I-95 and come to a standstill at a truck stop that Samuel declares is passable. There are other, really swanky ones, he says, like spas and resorts and vacation stays where you can get rested, fed, bathed, entertained, fucked, fleeced, and shop for your kid's birthday, all in a few hours' time. Samuel says I need a shower. And I need new clothes. I wander inside to the shower room.

I stand under the hot jet and feel all kinds of places on my body sting like a motherfucker, my scalp, my mouth, the backs of my hands, my asshole. Soap makes it worse, then better. My fingers slither over my body, but nothing is as familiar as it should be, something feels different now that I'm a free man, sort of, out on the open road. My sad lonely cock is an unfamiliar append- age too, but it gets hard and jizzes after only a couple minutes of attention, of thinking of Sava, alive and breathing and doing something ordinary and sexy and smart back in Toronto, that's all it takes, and I get out, dry myself off, feeling so much better, light, bursting with energy. I roam the corridors full of polite heavy-set men in baseball caps, looking for Samuel.

Samuel is waiting for me in the restaurant. He loudly and slowly reads out all the breakfast and lunch options on the menu, as if my accent means I'm illiterate or something, then tells me exactly what I should eat to get healthy. He's so motiv- ated he offers to pay for the whole deal. He's decided that I'm a sickly kind of Yugo, a boy who must devour kilos of bloody, fatty, patriotic American cow every day, helped down by buck- ets of milk and bushels of mashed potato. He orders me a steak and when it comes it's the size of Sarajevo.

"Do you ever wonder why things happen?" Samuel asks, when we're charging down the highway again. I was hoping he'd be the tough silent type, but he's got a few things to say.

"Yeah, I guess—doesn't everyone?"

"No, I don't mean *why is the bus late?* or *why did my teacher give me a bad mark?* I mean, don't you ever find yourself really wanting to know why certain big events happened, you know, in history and politics. Why the course of the world is as it is?"

I look over at Samuel to see if I can tell from his face what kind of answer he'd like.

"I do wonder," I say.

"You see, a European education!" Samuel proclaims. "Here kids just swallow and regurgitate, no thinking, no wondering, no asking questions."

"A European education," I repeat. "You could call it that, I guess."

I wish Papa would show up in the cab, he'd love to sit up here watching America slide by, talking about why things are as they are. And Dušan, he'd lie on the narrow back seat wearing his headphones, sleeping and smoking the whole time, pretending he didn't give a shit where he was or why what is, is. The truck roars down the highway at a steady pace all the way through Maine, New Hampshire, Massachusetts, Connecticut, and I feel like I'm in a trance that will never end, staring out the window at trees, fields, the edges of towns that go on forever. I love the highways that run through cities, when you're so high up and sail by buildings right up close and have clear views of the streets and shops and factories and even into backyards and windows and can see people walking on the sidewalks doing their shopping and kids cycling and hanging out. I imagine what this ordinary day is like for those people, how they live in their city at different ages in their lives, through the seasons, how they think about it, and I get this feeling that maybe I could settle down in a city and live some ordinary days too, in between learning everything there is to know about the world's crap and taking down the hypocrites and bullshitters.

By the time I'm dizzy with hunger, when Samuel finally pulls into a big service centre complex for dinner just beyond a city called Hartford, dusk has fallen. Samuel has talked on and off in a drowsy voice about conspiracies and mega-conspiracies and convinced me that the whole world is connected in creepy ways down to the last mayor in the shittiest little town, down to the dirtiest whores in the slimiest port, right up to the Pope, every head of state, every secret service, every arms manufacturer who drums up wars, every contractor who goes in after to rebuild what was destroyed, all just doing business. With each other. In secret. It's kind of like religion, Samuel's logic, everything has an explanation and it all makes total sense, especially the parts that are most unbelievable.

We eat half an animal and a field of corn and potatoes and watch the light dim away to nothing outside the restaurant window. We sleep in the cab, Samuel on the back bench, me on the front, my stomach straining and painful, while the clothes I've grabbed from the centre's Lost and Found dry in the laundromat. I dream about Mama on her hands and knees scrubbing the floors of our apartment back home, of militiamen packed into our kitchen cooking up a stray cat, of Dušan waiting at our local barber to shave his head monk-style, of Wounded Belly Boy Eddie trapped and terrified in a basement filled with swinging cow carcasses, all kinds of crazy weird shit. And there is Papa in the distance, on the river, in a kayak, shooting down whitewater rapids, his paddles like windmills, water spray glistening like jewels high in the air.

When Samuel wakes me, it's four in the morning, the night has not lifted, a fine rain is falling, but I'm happy to get moving. In the laundromat I dress like a trucker, in denim and flannel, but none of it fits. Everything flaps and drags and makes me look small.

"We'll get you a monster breakfast in a few hours," Samuel says when he sees me. "Don't you worry."

We roll past early-morning towns, our lights plunging through fog, our roar heard by no one. I sense people asleep in their beds, I imagine the shape of their lives, I sip coffee. We say nothing until day has come, grey and drizzling, until we've stopped at a diner and eaten breakfasts that could feed a family back home for a week, bacon, sausage, steak, half a dozen eggs, a pile of pancakes, a pile of French toast, hash browns, a plate of toast, butter, jam. And for dessert, hot chocolate with whipped cream, five cigarettes chain-smoked together standing under the awning, as we sniff the sweet smell of the fields beyond the parking lot.

‡ ‡ ‡

S AMUEL STOPS JUST OUTSIDE PITTSBURGH AND I climb down from the cab like an ancient bowlegged cowboy. Two days, one night in that tiny rolling living room, with Samuel interrupting his stories about capitalist-secret-societies-that-run-the-world to blurt out newsflashes for tourists. Sailing off the coast of Maine, mountain climbing in New Hampshire, whale watching in Massachusetts, fly-fishing in Connecticut, fields where bloody battles took place in Pennsylvania, every nation has had its civil war, that kind of thing. And New England autumns. The colours. He has no words for those. It's nothing like old England, Samuel says, which he thinks I must have visited since in his American mind it's extremely close to Sarajevo.

He's going north, I'm going west. I wish I could keep going with him, but there's nothing for me up there but more skulking around in cracks and crevasses. As I shut the door, he shouts, "The biggest conspiracy is that there are no conspiracies. Do the research, do the research." And there I am, standing blinking in the vortex of giant highways as they collide and tangle around each other on their journey to somewhere else. A million tons of steel roars in every direction, racing to get stuff to where it needs to go just-on-time, America's vast gas-guzzling warehouse on wheels. The sun is a small white dot in a clear blue sky. Samuel has told me to wait until this time tomorrow. A friend of his will pick me up, a friend going all the way to L.A.

Wind and dust, a huge wasteland of tough weedy grasses, this is where I am. I flutter like a puny flag on a spindly pole as I figure out what to do. I can't stay here, I'll be blown high into the air like garbage thrown from windows, like fumes sucked into the ozone from a thousand shiny exhaust pipes. I'll never find my way back down again. So I pick an off-ramp and walk along its soft rutted shoulder. It takes half an hour to get away from the massive four-leaf clover, over an hour before I'm out of range of the high-pitched whine of tires and pistons, before I smell manure, leaves, standing ditch water containing frogs, reeds, fallen branches.

Then, it's just a quiet country road, one that farmers use to get to their fields with tractors, pickup trucks, hay wagons, combines, manure spreaders, maybe even the odd horse-and-wagon to entertain the kids, or at least, that's what I'm imagining. It makes me calm. I picture haystacks, piglets, mud ponds, apple trees, warm, sweet-smelling milk, grass-stained eggs. But I see no farmyards around, only a house every now and then, with clapboard siding and flowering bushes.

I sit down at the side of the road like a kid waiting for the school bus. I know they do that here, drive all around the countryside picking children up one by one. I listen to birds, to insects, to frogs, the breeze, a lawn mower in the distance. This spring day is acting like summer. I try to think about my life in a clear way, the lessons, the advice, the experiences so far, to see what they say about this moment. I'm tired again, and hungry. I don't have any money. As always, I think about Baka and how they starved in the mountain forests but beat the Nazis anyway, but it seems different here, without all that group camaraderie and possibility of death and glorious triumph to urge you on. If there was a pay phone I'd make a call to Mama. I'd tell her that I'm okay, that I'm not doing anything bad, that I'm on a path to good, or whatever. I'd call Sava and say, we'll meet again maybe when the time is right, maybe we'll go to university together like my baka and djedica did. Maybe we'll even study the same thing. I'd call Dr. Ghorbani and tell her, it's true, I was having a conversation in my head with you the whole time.

I walk a few feet from the road, into high grasses and budding bushes. I find a sunny patch, I curl up, I fall asleep. When I wake it's dusk, the sun is just a streak of purple on the horizon. I sit up and listen for the sound that woke me. I hear a car racing fast along the road, I hear voices laughing and shouting, and loud bangs, the sound of violent impacts at high speed. I get up, brush myself off, step out into the road to see what's going on, and there is a pickup truck barrelling straight toward me. It squeals to a halt just a foot away and five teenagers jump out. One of them is holding a baseball bat.

"What're you doing here?" the boy asks me, sauntering into my space. He's jittery and aggressive, I recognize the state. For a moment I think he wants to whack me in the head with his bat, so I stand my ground, put my fists up, fire back at him with a snarl.

"What are *you* doing, a-hole?"

He steps back fast, and I feel the old power thrill. "Hey, no disrespect, man," he mumbles, "it's just mailbox baseball, man. It's the best."

"Oh yeah?" I say. "I've never tried it. Any of you guys have a place where I can crash tonight?"

The boys stare at me for a moment. "Where are you from?" Bat-boy asks.

"I'm just trying to get across the country. I've got a ride tomorrow. I need somewhere to crash."

"Nah, can't do it, man. Parents."

"Nowhere you could sneak me in? Someone's basement, a garage?"

"You might rob us or kill us in our beds, man. We don't know you."

"Hey, look at me. Do I look like I'd do that?"

"You can't tell that shit just from looking at someone."

"A car. I'd sleep in your truck here. I'd be gone early."

"It's not going to happen, man. Get a hotel or something," Bat-boy says, then gestures at the others. "Let's go, c'mon."

"Please, guys. I'll take whatever." I can't believe I'm begging from these ridiculous brats. I really want a place to sleep, I really want them to give a shit. I feel shaky, it's strange, kind of like I'm going to fall to pieces.

The kids don't care, they pile back into the truck and race off up the road, one of them hanging out of the window, the baseball bat cocked over his shoulder. They disappear around a corner and I hear another bang, the sound of wood splintering, loud shouts and whistles. At least they don't have guns, I think.

Darkness suddenly envelops me. There's no moon, there are no street lights or house lights, I can't see anything except the very last of the day glowing in the western sky and a few jagged tree silhouettes. I stand shivering for a moment, then force myself to keep walking, eyes strained for a porch or garage light. But there's nothing, I'm completely blind, every footstep forward is into a black void, and sounds of snapping branches and rustling leaves start to freak me out. I have a strong feeling of presences on the road in front of me, mangy, starving animals or giant humans with hulking shoulders and wild, unnatural faces. I think I can see them, darknesses in the darkness, and I stretch my arms out to ward them off. I cringe and duck as paws come at me, as huge heads loom above me. I light my lighter, but all it illuminates is my grimy fingers. Soon I'm standing totally still; I can't get myself to move in any direction. And, for the second time in my life, fear possesses me completely, a primeval demon devouring every last shred of rational thought. It takes over in sharp jolts to my heart, electrocution-style, and spreads out through my veins to every cell of my body, until I'm slippery with sweat, until I'm vomiting bile, until I know I'm under attack, I'm being tracked by the sniper with his night-vision goggles, by the soldier with the loud footsteps who won't ever stop following right behind me, just a breath away, by the packs of rabid wolves who've taken possession of the world, in a perpetual night that contains nothing but danger and dread and death. I sit down on the freezing gravel, there's nothing else to do, running away has never worked. I cover my face with my hands, I fold my head to my chest, I squeeze my eyes shut, I try to breathe slow and steady. And I wait to die, shot in the head, strangled from behind, ripped apart by rabid teeth, whatever my fate has in store for me.

BUT nothing happens except that time goes by, it could be half an hour or three hours or a thousand years, and then I hear a car. Fear surges again, but it's countered by a small, shiny gleaming of hope. There is only one option left when you've given yourself up to the worst and it doesn't come: prepare

for something better. Humans, I think. Humans are unpredictable, but any human driving from somewhere to somewhere
in a warm car is better than enduring this night and this dark
alone. So I stand up and turn to face the headlights coming
toward me. When they're close, I raise a hand like I'm hailing a
cab, and in that moment the car swerves and bucks, then skids
to a stop and stalls. It starts up again and rolls toward me.
When it stops beside me, a man shoves a big shaggy head out
of the window.

"Jesus Christ," he shouts, "what the hell are you doing out
here at this time of night?"

"I got caught by the darkness," I say. My voice is quivering
like a little boy's.

A woman's voice calls out, "You scared the bejesus out of
us, standing there like a zombie."

"Can you give me a ride?" I try not to sound like a
demon-possessed crazy boy.

"Where to?" The man opens the door and gets out. He's got
massive arms, a huge gut, and he towers over me like a fairy-tale
giant. "Who are you?" he asks.

"I'm, um, I'm just travelling through."

"You don't have a bag."

"Yes, where are your bags?" the woman calls from the car.

"To where?" the man asks.

He has crossed his arms over his chest. Is he a cop?

Feeling desperate, I begin to bullshit. "Hey, guys," I say.
"It's been a long day. I was riding with a friend and his car broke
down. I tried to hitchhike but wasn't getting rides. I left my
bag with the car . . ."

"What's the accent? Where are you from?"

"Um, the east coast," I say.

"Oh, the east coast," the huge man says, sounding more suspicious. "Well, what do you want us to do about your troubles?"

"Can I get a ride . . . that's all."

"To where?"

"Um, well. The closest town?" My teeth start to chatter.

The man suddenly relaxes. "Well, I suppose we could do that for you. Jump in, what're you waiting for? It's about five miles down the road, won't take any time at all."

I get in the back. The car smells of candy, and it's warm. Sitting pertly next to me on the seat is a tiny dog. It looks me up and down, then squeals and scrabbles forward onto the woman's lap.

"That's He-Man, he's our little baby goochy-goo. What's up, baby-buttons?"

"How about a motel?" the man says. "That would be the best option at this time of night. Nothing is open in town now." He's driving cautiously, high-beams muscling bravely into the dense darkness. "Animals jump out at you like they want to commit suicide. You have to drive slow around here."

The woman laughs. "We thought *you* were a wild animal at first. Just for a split second. A deer or a coyote. Didn't we, goochums?" The dog looks up at her and licks its tiny black lips with a miniature pink tongue.

"Your face and neck and hands glowed very white in our beams," the man says. "You looked a bit like E.T."

"Yes, that's right, Hank." The woman laughs again. "He did look a bit like E.T., like an alien creature, but also very lost and lonely, like a human kid."

"That's it, hon. An alien creature and human-kid hybrid, that would be weird."

"Yes, that would be weird. Anyway, we haven't decided where we're going to eat. We did Arby's last week. Let's go to Wendy's. I'm really in the mood for their chocolate malt."

"Oh, not Wendy's, hon. I'm sick of that place. I don't like their fries."

"Well, I'm sick of Arby's. Very sick of Arby's. We always end up there."

They go on like this for quite a long time and I sit back and taste the bitterness of relief in my mouth and listen to my stomach rumble. So, this is what normal people argue about in normal times in normal little towns all over this normal country, and it's depressing and comforting at the same time.

"Well, what do you say to a motel?" Hank says, when they've decided to compromise over someplace called Hardees. He looks back at me, eyes squinting into the rear-view mirror.

I pull myself forward so my head is hanging in the space between them. I see that Hank's belly is pressing hard into the steering wheel, that his ruddy face is bristling with grey day-old stubble. The woman has long hair, it's up in a ponytail like a girl's, tied with a fuzzy purple ribbon, but her face is as wrinkled as a dried-up peach.

"Is there any chance you've got a garage or a shed or something that I can sleep in? Just tonight."

"A shed?" The woman sounds alarmed immediately. "Sleep in a shed?" She lights a cigarette.

"Do you mind if I light up too?" I whip a smoke into my mouth and light it fast.

"Where did you say you were from?" Hank asks again.

"The east coast," I say.

"The east coast? But what's the foreign accent?" The woman half turns and stares at me with one thickly eye-shadowed eye.

"We don't have anywhere for you to sleep," Hanks says. "Unfortunately."

Something's shifted. I feel fear emanating from both of them like body heat. Oh no, I think, I've passed it on like a virus. I wonder if I smell, if my breath reeks of the chemistry of life-and-death emotions. I know how terrifying that can be.

"I'd be very quiet, just sleep and get moving early."

"I'm real sorry," Hank says, his head ducking into his neck. "It's just not gonna happen. We have no space at all."

"You know, no extra beds," the woman sing-songs. "Sorry about that."

She leans toward Hank. "Faster," I hear her whispering. "Go faster."

"We should have extra beds," she continues, more loudly and slowly than before, because murderous hitchhiking psychopaths are known to be hard of hearing, "we're thinking about it. But here, look, we're almost at the motel. That's your best bet."

"Okay," I say quietly and sit back. It's a fucking tragedy that everyone is afraid of everyone all the time. "I'd be happy to sleep on your floor," I say, trying one more time. "I don't need a bed, just shelter."

"I'm very sorry, young man," Hank says, his voice trembling a little with the effort of being firm. I know he' sweating. I know that her heart is racing. "We don't have any floor space, we live in a very small house, no sheds, no space in the garage. You'll have to make do with the motel."

He's rocketing down the road now, and I bounce gently behind him on the car's soft springs. "It's not like I'm going to rob you or anything," I say. I'm feeling sad now, really fucking depressed, because I can suddenly see so clearly how this whole web of emotional connectivity works. Fear begetting fear begetting more fear, endlessly, until the human race has destroyed itself out of fright. Because I feel it happening right here, in myself, how their fear is making them cold, unfriendly, and their coldness and unfriendliness is making me antsy, confrontational, furious at all of existence. How their grovelling and refusal make me more crazy boy, and the more crazy boy I become, the more scared they are, the more heartless and bad-ass that will make me, on and on, to a bad end.

"I mean, who doesn't have a few feet of floor space to offer a kid?" I sit forward again. I just can't let it go. I watch Hank white-knuckling the steering wheel, I watch how the woman clasps the little panting dog to her chest. "A kid with no money."

"Here it is," Hank sings out. He overshoots the driveway, steps on the brakes, stalls the car again, and there we are, the three of us sitting in silence on a country road, a motel sign blinking on and off behind us. The windshield wiper is going, turned on in Hank's panic to stop the car. For several seconds, we watch it scraping back and forth.

"The motel, it's just back there," the woman whispers, finally. "Please, there is the motel. We brought you here. Please, go."

I get out slowly, reluctantly. I want to beat some generosity of spirit into these two, with their greasy hamburger and chocolate malt fetishes. My fists are itching for it. After all, all I want is a warm place to sleep, just for a few hours, is that really too much to fucking ask? I want someone to say *yes* to me, *what can I do to help*. I leave the back door open so they don't drive off, then lean into Hank's window as he scrabbles for the window power button. In his terror, he's forgotten where it is.

"Thank. You," I say slowly. "I. Really. Appreciate. Your. Help."

They stare up at me with wide glistening eyes. All they want to know is that they are free to go. I step away from the window and close the back door slowly. The car pulls away and I watch the tail lights until they're out of sight, cursing the two inside but also forgiving them. What have I done to instill confidence in humanity?

I turn. The hotel's neon Open sign is on, the letter O flashing on and off at regular intervals, but there are no lights in the office. There's one car in the parking lot. I walk quickly to the end of the building and around to the back where the property is wild and overgrown and black as a cave. I discover by feel that each room has a small window in the back wall, about shoulder height, that several are boarded up. I scratch around in the weeds and find a rock, pick a window, break it quickly, brush the shards away, pull myself through the opening into the stuffy, smelly gloom within. I drink from the rusted tap in the bathroom for a long time, then open the curtain of the front window a sliver and sit in the broken-down armchair watching my knees appear and disappear in the light of the defective sign. I think about a hot shower, about an unhurried cigarette, about lying on the bed and closing my eyes for a hundred years. But I'm too tired to move.

I'm still sitting when I wake to foggy morning light filtering into the room through the crack in the curtains and the feeling that Dušan's been here, that he crashed on the bed, that he lay there all night telling me a long story about a wolf pack that found a newborn baby on the doorstep of a church in a small village high up in the mountain forest. This wolf pack discussed among themselves whether they'd eat the baby then and there or take it with them and save it for a later meal. They made their decision and picked it up gently by the blanket knotted around its tiny body and carried it into the forest where a wolf-mother nurtured it with wolf-milk alongside her seven wolf-pups. Dušan told me how the wolf pack watched the baby thrive and grow, how they fed it meat scraps when it was old enough to chew, how they brought it along on hunting trips when it could run fast enough to keep up. How each year they licked their lips and dreamed of the day when the baby would be a large, healthy man and they could all eat their fill.

I step into the shower and stand there until the hot water runs out. As I dry off, I turn on the ancient TV and flip through the channels, looking for a news bulletin on local stations warning about a menacing teenager from the east coast with a foreign accent. But the news flash is about a basement fire in a town called Harmony. Dressed, I slip out the front door into the dawn gloom and trot fast across the parking lot. I ache with hunger and instantly feel frozen as I walk along the road back toward the highway. The sun is rising behind the brown haze of tree trunks, painting swaths of pink and pastel blue across the eastern horizon, and birds are beginning to sing. After walking for half an hour, I see a light blinking at me through the undergrowth. I turn off onto a dirt driveway and follow its curves until I see a house in a small clearing. Lights in several windows, downstairs and upstairs, glow deep yellow in the surrounding forest gloom, and smoke spirals up to the treetops from a metal chimney on the roof. I walk closer and see a man in a housecoat in the kitchen, pots hanging from a rack behind him, a potted herb on the windowsill. He's moving back and forth, passing the window, head down, concentrating, and steam is rising from a pot or a kettle to one side of him. In an upstairs room the head of a child appears briefly in the window, then the flash of a white towel. I need to get in there, I think, looking around for a fist-size rock. I yearn for the morning they are having, waking slowly in warmth and quiet surrounded by their own things, sensing each other moving in different parts of the house. I want to get in there right now and take it from them.

Instead, I crouch down in the bushes and wait patiently, shivering and breathing on my hands. Nothing is inevitable, Jim says, which I guess also includes what I want and what my wants make me do. After the family, a man, a woman, two small kids, gets itself together to face the world, after it trundles out the front door, dragging knapsacks and briefcases, after it drives off in the family hatchback, I enter the house as gently as possible, forcing the back door, no tinkling of broken glass, no smashed window frames. So I go in just for the food and drink, just to keep me going, and I find that the kettle is still warm and leftover porridge is still in a pot on the stove. I eat the porridge, as well as two bananas and an apple that are in a bowl on the counter, a whole slab of cheese, and a pack of sliced ham from the fridge. Then I make myself a giant egg-and-tomato sandwich and a pot of strong coffee. While I eat the sandwich I wander from room to room and poke at the scattered early-morning artifacts of a peaceful life.

I wait in the windy vortex of interweaving highway ribbons for Samuel L. Jackson's friend to pick me up. Hour after hour he doesn't show up at the very centre of this buzzing continent, so I sit cross-legged like a half-starved Buddha who's out of smokes, trying to focus on my next move. I visualize the west coast, I visualize Ujak Luka and his crew of hoods, how I'm going to fit in with that, how I no longer feel the urge, the itch, for that kind of life. The sun says it's early afternoon when I spot a cop car circling around the ramps for the third time, and I feel totally exposed. I'm a skinny kid from another country in someone else's clothes, no ID, no luggage, no money, an accent. I make myself small and sink low into the dirty grass. It's no big challenge to turn myself into a pile of garbage, rags, bones, crap hurled out of car windows. I lie still, my head down. But when I look again, the cop car has stopped, the cop is getting out, he's looking right at me, and I'm thinking of stories to tell him. If I knew where I was, what local town I could say I'm from, just a stupid high school kid being stupid, that would help. I think of Harmony. I could mention the basement fire and chat to him about that. But the cop isn't walking toward me. A large transport truck has pulled over and he and a tall, thin, beak-nosed trucker in a Leatherman cap are discussing something and pointing in my direction.

I stand up and walk toward them, there's nothing else to do. I feel like cursing them and begging at the same time, the usual mix. I can't and I won't go back to detention, that's one thing I know for sure. The cop stares at me with cold eyes.

The trucker yells, "Git your ass in the cab, boy." And I do.

The cop struts off, the trucker hauls himself in, and we're roaring up the gears to a wild vibrational speed, and there I am sitting high and dry again, looking down on the world of little vehicles and the little heads and torsos going about their day. I let my body relax a notch or two. We drive in silence for a while, then my saviour asks me if I want a cigarette. Yes, I say. In that moment I want a smoke more than anything else in the world.

‡ ‡ ‡

TWO THOUSAND FIVE HUNDRED MILES DRIVING into sunsets from the middle of the continent to the west coast and you're still in the same damn country. I wonder how our war back home would've gone if our own collection of united states weren't so small. If they were as big as this, it would've taken forever for the militias to move around, standing for days and days in the backs of trucks, too exhausted to wave rifles in the air and shout slogans, the drugs and alcohol wearing off long before they got anywhere to do their fucked-up shit.

Samuel's friend is named Big Red. Another movie name, but then, this is the U.S. of A. I say, you're tall but you're not big, and he tells me about losing two hundred eighty-one pounds in the past year, how he did it by learning to meditate. This explains why he looks kind of baggy around the face and neck, but his eyes are bright, icy blue, the whites clear icy white. You can live on light and air, he tells me, pulling on his cigarette like it's the source of life itself. You can eat the sun with your eyes. It's very nourishing, believe me. I ask him about the Red part of his name, and he says it's from a long time ago when he used to go to the same bar every night on the same street in the same small town. This was in the days when he worked in a factory that made metal bits for another factory that made tools for another factory that made many different things at different times for different factories. In the bar, every night, he and his so-called friends would have drunken discussions about the way people in this country live their lives. Everything that came out of my mouth, Big Red tells me, seemed red to those guys, yes, red as in communist, but they weren't exactly students of political science, if you know what I mean. I'd say, it's too bad that Frankie got fired after he mangled his hand in that faulty machine, and they'd turn on me. I'd say, wouldn't it be better for employers if their employees had enough income to cover expenses and lead healthy, happy lives, and they'd turn on me. Every night they'd hound me out of the place, tell me to get my fat ass to Russia, and every afternoon after work they'd welcome me back and tell me to buy a round for my sorry-ass working-class friends, too poor and exploited to do anything but drink and act stupid. You know what's interesting to me, boy, is when people think and act against their own cause.

But other than conveying this little bit of his history, Big Red doesn't talk that much. I tell him my baka was a committed communist, Death to Fascism, Freedom to the People, and he looks at me, nods, but doesn't ask any follow-up questions. So I slide down in the seat and close my eyes, and the combination of sitting still and rolling through the landscape puts me into a deep, peaceful daze.

I wake from deep dreamless sleep to see a sign for Dayton sail by. I sit up and stare out the window.

"Where are we?" I ask.

"Almost through Ohio. Two-and-a-half days to the coast."

I look carefully at the fields, the stands of trees, the subdivisions that pass us by. They seem so innocent, so ordinary. Somewhere around here is the air force base where Bosnian fate was decided, signed by our three tribal warlords and some random European and American politicians. I think of telling Big Red how weird it is to be passing by this place just when I'm escaping to a new life, something different. I think of asking him to find it on the map so we can drive by and I can see what it looks like, this place that produced such a fucked-up new country. It made Mama so depressed she could hardly breathe. *So many died for this? No democratic citizenship can arise out of it. Not for anyone.* But I feel exhausted just thinking of talking about it, so I don't say a thing. I let the truck carry me away from it and all the sad, suffocating memories.

Big Red is solar-powered. He gets his energy from nuclear fusion, just like a plant, and doesn't ever seem to tire. He drives straight all day and into the night, through flat farmland, past huge brown fields ready for planting, North American barns and squat fat silos just like in Canada, small towns with churches of all different shapes and sizes, peasant farmers in carts and buggies pulled by horses like back home. When the sun goes down and the vast sky is streaked with the red and pink of an ending day, I settle in for the night with a blanket and a pillow Big Red pulls out from behind his seat for me. The temperature is falling, he says, but I hear him from my dreams. I'm already asleep, my mouth is open, my bones are humming, my legs twitch like a dreaming animal's. When I wake again with drool on my cheek, it's already another day and I know I haven't slept this well and long and uninterrupted since I was ten. We're charging through Oklahoma, that's what Big Red tells me, vast and flat, overarched by the biggest, palest dome of a sky I've ever seen.

Heaven is roadside diners at regular intervals. Big Red doesn't mind sitting opposite me while I cram in the food as fast as I can, giant hamburgers, the ribs of half a pig, mountains of french fries, soup bowls full of gravy, though he eats almost nothing himself, an apple, a few spoonfuls of yogourt.

And he pays for my meals too, like benevolent Samuel, without asking why I have no money, where I'm going, where

I've come from, what I'm doing on the road. Back in the cab, legs stretched out and head on the pillow, I imagine saying hi to Ujak Luka, saying, I'll just crash for a few days, a week maybe, and I imagine him asking me to become his side kick gangster, pimp, movie star, drug lord, or whatever it is he's up to these days. I picture guzzling drinks with him by the pool, snorting eight-balls in backrooms, flirting with porn stars and their giant straining tits in Hollywood mansions, and being a badass whenever he needs me to be one. But as I think of these things I don't feel a fizzing rush of adrenaline, I don't feel a bursting gust of excitement. I feel a cramp in my gut and flashes of white in front of my eyes and greasy sweat all over my face.

‡ ‡ ‡

BIG RED IS A GOD OF A MAN, I KNOW THIS NOW. HE can sit in the same position for days, staring at the infinite highway with the alert attention of a tennis player who's just served, who's waiting for the return, who's relaxed and in position, who knows he'll win the point, who doesn't care who wins the game. As the endless hours go by, I twitch and fidget, I chain-smoke, I pass out and sleep for who knows how long, deep but on guard, like a drunk man on a park bench over a subway line.

I wake up groggy, with a million shards of rainbow jumping all over my body. I sit up fast, peer around, and spot a triangular bit of glass hanging from the rear-view mirror.

"Refracted light," Big Red says.

He's still there at the wheel, motionless as a statue, eyes on the vanishing point.

"And I've also wanted to ask you about how you live with what's stored in your unconscious," he says to me, as though we've been talking for hours about the state of my mind. The truth is, we've hardly said anything to each other at all.

"What are these lights?" I ask, mesmerized by the jittering brightness of the cab. It's like we've taken off and are cruising at thirty thousand feet, or maybe higher, climbing toward heaven.

"It's my prism," Big Red says. "And the desert light. Colour is refracted light, did you know that? Buried within the physics of that phenomenon is the answer to the question."

"What question?" I reach out and steady the prism.

"Whatever question you feel the need to ask."

Oh, I think, he's one of those Zen guys, where nothing is something and something is everything and everything is nothing. But as I'm thinking this, I look outside and my eyes pop wide, my mouth cracks open, and my head is suddenly clear of everything. We are in the desert and it's something I've never seen before, not even in my mind's eye. My mind's eye, which has seen quite a lot of things, hasn't even tried to come up with something like this, a landscape without stuff in it, no clutter, junk, buildings, people, just a vast, hot, gold and lavender open space, with red jutting rocks, scraggy grass, and peaked mountains as serene as monks on opium in the distance. Our truck speeds along its surface like a tiny metal beetle voyaging outside of time.

". . . and it lives on in your body, that's what I've learned from meditation. So, how has witnessing life and death occupied your body, Jevrem?"

"My body?" I ask. I hold up my busted hand, but I see that it's better now, the swelling almost gone.

"Trauma stays stored in the body unless it's intentionally released," Big Red continues.

But now I'm distracted by what I see outside the window. "Where are we?"

He laughs quietly. "Oh, we came into New Mexico a while ago. Spiritual landscape, takes your breath away, and all the garbage in your head with it. You Europeans don't taste that kind of spiritual much. Maybe ever."

"Can we pull over for a minute?" I ask.

I think I'm going to explode, I'm so shocked that life has given me this astounding sight. I guess I've stopped expecting to be impressed.

"I want to feel the heat," I say.

Big Red likes this idea, he's going to be my tour guide into the landscape of the soul, or some such thing he talks about as we stop and get out and crunch away from the truck past brittle scrub into the baking, shimmering emptiness.

"This is Native land," he says.

We walk and walk. It's hot and dry and dizzying. After some time, we stop in front of two beat-up car seats sitting by themselves facing west in the middle of nothing, and we sit on the car seats, side by side, and look out at the desert. We're in front of a monstrous piece of rock, red and jagged, lunging all by itself out of the desert like a whale flinging itself out of the ocean.

Big Red doesn't seem to be in a hurry, in fact, he's turned into a rocklike entity himself, maybe enjoying a fresh meal of sunlight, his face tilted, his eyes wide open. I lean back and let the sun shine down on me as hard as she wants. It feels so good I tingle and shiver and shake all over, it's that strong, that complete, without shadow feelings of any kind. My muscles untwist, and my head opens its petals for the second time in my life like a flower on a magic mountain.

Big Red sits. I sit. Hours go by. The sun travels her arc, then sets.

WE roll through the night desert, a big half moon riding right beside us in the clear sky. I see my dead people, they're all here, in this moment, drifting about like breezes and dust clouds. Here, they have space, or maybe my mind has space. I watch them out of the window, I think about them, I go over memories with them, the details of moments and places I don't remember noticing, and we're swinging past Santa Rosa, Moriarty, then Albuquerque, and I'm sure I'm in some kind of sun-trance watched over by the moon, and I sense that Papa, Dušan, Berina, and Baka don't worry about this planet anymore, all the terrible things that can happen here; they just eat light, like Big Red, and sway around the cosmos as much as they want, feeling the bliss that exists beyond time and space, wishing everyone on earth would just freaking relax and feel it too. I ask Big Red if he slipped something in the bottle of water he bought me, and he shakes his head like he might have but didn't this time.

"The desert is like that," he says, "you think thoughts you haven't thought before and you feel feelings that you've always believed are someone else's feelings."

I daydream, doze off, lose track of time. I wake and see the sign for Flagstaff going by. And I let the landscape flow through my eyes and mind and imagination and out the back of my head.

"We're in Arizona," Big Red tells me at some point. He lights me a cigarette. "We'll stop at the next service centre for feeding and watering, and then we're in the final stretch to the coast."

"That's good," I say, and I really mean it. I'm feeling excited, even cheerful. And if I look back through the second chapter of my life, it's true, these feelings were almost always someone else's feelings.

In the service centre, I find a pay phone and stuff it with coins. I dial Mama's number and wait for her voice. For once, I don't feel nervous, angry, depressed or crazy. I'm getting used to this parallel universe, the one that's always on the move, where everyday life is daydreaming on the open road. As I listen to the dial tone, I eye the panel of pop machines against the opposite wall humming like a giant U-boat getting ready to dive. So much extra of everything here, on this continent, I think, that twenty huge lit-up machines run all through the night in case one thirsty driver with a giant gut wants a Coke at three in the morning.

"Hello?" Mama answers. She's so close she's inside my head.

"It's me," I say.

"Jevrem, Jevrem, Jevrem." Mama sings my name like it's a jingle she can't get out of her head. "Jevrem, Jevrem, Jevrem."

"Yes, it's me."

"Oh, Jevrem! Jevrem, Jevrem."

"I'm okay," I say, in case that's what she wants to ask me. There's a pause, I hear her snuffling.

"Where are you, Jevrem?" Mama asks, finally.

"I'm really okay. I think everything will be better."

"Where are you?"

"I don't want to say, Mama, in case the police try to torture it out of you."

"They don't do that in this country, Jevrem."

I can hear a smile in her voice, and I feel so relieved my eyes suddenly sting with tears.

"How are you, Mama? How is Aisha?" I'm wiping my face with my sleeve like an exhausted street kid.

"We're fine, Jevrem."

"Did they come and ask you questions?"

"Yes, of course."

"What did you say?"

"What could I say?"

"Have they bugged your phone?"

"Come on, Jevrem. They don't want you back that badly."

"Soon, I will be where I'm going, Mama. Maybe you and Aisha can come and visit."

I don't know where that idea came from, it popped out of my mouth without asking my brain. I think of Ujak Luka and his glamorous outlaw lifestyle and can't see how that will ever work.

"Oh, um, Mama? Can you give me Ujak Luka's phone number?"

"Luka? So." Mama's voice has that tone.

"Yes." I know it's a risk, but I'm sure he'd be unlisted.

Mama goes off to find the number and I feel my pulse picking up speed. What if the cops were waiting in the house with Mama until I called? What if they're letting time go by so they can trace the call?

Mama recites a number. "That's what I have for him. I don't know if it's still good. When will you go to him?"

I repeat the sequence of numbers five times, since I don't have pencil or paper, with Mama patiently following along.

"Mama, I have to go but I will call again."

"Jevrem. Where are you now? When are you planning to be at Luka's? Give me something to work with, please."

I can tell she's starting to crumple, that she's filling up with the old despair. I squeeze my eyes shut and force words out that need to be forced out. "Mama, listen to me for a second. Three things. One, I am sorry. Two, I love you. Three, we will see each other again, soon."

I hang up quickly, slide down the wall to the floor, sit there trying to get my breath back. I'm still sitting when Big Red comes by and drags me to the restaurant. He asks me short sharp questions while he sits opposite me and I eat as fast and messily as a starving kid in one of the world's stinking slums. He doesn't seem to mind how I eat, he doesn't seem to mind much. He's looking into my eyes with his laser beams.

"You're carrying something heavy in your unconscious mind, Jevrem. What is it?"

"What?" I ask him, since he's looking at me like he's expecting a response.

"Like rocks under water, completely invisible, people bury traumatic experiences so well they're completely unaware of them. Except they keep capsizing as they try to paddle along the river of life."

"Okay," I say.

"For example, you killed someone," he says, sipping from a huge glass of water that's mostly ice.

"No," I say slowly, feeling my face burn. "No, I didn't."

Big Red smiles like a fisherman who feels a tug on his line. He doesn't answer, just keeps staring me down with those light-beams of his.

"Did I kill someone?" I repeat, trying to understand the question.

"You said that you killed someone."

"I did? No, I didn't say that."

"You spoke in your sleep, Jevrem, over and over again, as hundreds of miles sped past. You called out names, you sounded distressed. You killed someone—two people, maybe?"

Big Red is crazy, all the sunlight has fried his brain. I feel annoyed, I turn away, I try to get up. But he reaches over and pins my hands to the table. He's surprisingly determined for a man of few words and surprisingly strong for a fat person who went skinny.

"It's okay, you can tell me," he says, and I know I don't have a choice.

"I was a motherfucker," I say. "I admit it, I terrorized totally clueless Canadian citizens in their houses. I feel bad about that, I really do, spreading that shit around. It wasn't fair on them, they have no idea about the world out there and how totally ignorant and lucky their lives are."

"No, no, there's something more. Someone named Konstantin?"

I can't breathe. The room keeps fading in and out. Because he's right. It's true. There is something else.

"Yes," I say. "You're right."

"Who?"

"Who?"

I stare at a little gaggle that's formed at the buffet, how they're edging slowly around the salad bar.

"Who, Jevrem?"

"Who what?" I'm confused. I don't understand what he wants from me.

Big Red leans forward in the booth. He pats my cheek with a heavy, warm hand.

"Jevrem, look at me."

I try to look at him, but I can't focus. He's a blurry mass.

My eyes are drawn away and up, and I'm looking at the corner of the room, high up, where the wall meets the ceiling. I can't pull myself away from that spot, though there's nothing there but dingy shadows and dusty spiderwebs. Then I'm up in that corner, in a tight ball. I am the spider and my web trembles around me.

"Stay with me. Here, on your chair," Big Red commands.

I'm in the chair again and wonder what the hell we're talking about, and where all the food went. My plates are empty, I feel nauseated. Big Red pats my cheek again, he wants me to say something. In the next booth, two kids are jumping up and down on the seat while their parents eat pie. This is why truckers have a separate section for eating, I guess, though Big Red doesn't seem to mind.

"Two kids. Konstantin and Galib, they were friends," I say.

"What happened?"

"They were hit by a shell. Nezira was screaming, do something, do something. So I went up to them and crouched down next to them. Konstantin was mangled, so was Galib, there was blood everywhere. Konstantin was crying, help, help. I picked up a paving stone with both hands, I raised it over my head. I really wanted to do something, to make it all go away."

"And what happened then?"

I look at Big Red but can't hear what he's saying. His mouth is moving, but there is no sound. I am sitting in silence. Suddenly I see it playing in front of my eyes like a movie. There I am, this skinny kid with bony wrists and mushroom cut, kneeling over a child who's been thrown to the ground, who has blood seeping out of him, whose eyes don't see anything anymore, with a paving stone held high over my head with two hands. I look determined and cringing at the same time, I'm biting my lip, I'm gritting my teeth. You can see my jaw muscles tensing, you can see my eyes squinting, I'm getting ready for the impact, for the blood to spray, for Konstantin's final cry to ring in my ears forever. I command myself to bring the paving stone down hard on Konstantin's head…but nothing happens. I stay frozen like this for a moment, then lower the stone and burst into tears.

This is what I see as I review the scene. I burst into tears and I howl like a little boy, snot flying everywhere, veins in my neck and forehead standing out, my face bright red. Between howls I call for Mama and Papa, I call for them over and over. Then, suddenly, I stand up and walk away, in the direction of my apartment building. I stop crying, I don't look back, I pay no attention to Nezira, who is still screaming high piercing notes. I stick my hands in my pockets, I kick a bit of rubble in front of me, and if it weren't so noisy, the screaming, the moaning and begging, the shouting from balconies, the sirens, the shells going thud and boom, the guns going gak-gak-gak, I think it would be possible to hear me whistling.

"I didn't kill them," I say to Big Red, looking at my grease-smeared plate. "It's much worse than that. I fell apart, then I just stood up and walked away."

Big Red sits there. He seems to be almost asleep, his eyelids are lowered, his eyeballs are moving behind his eyelids, his face has no expression on it at all. I watch all the people at their tables eating yet one more meal in this endless feeding-frenzy called life. Then finally he speaks.

"I'm going to ask you to look at that scene one more time, Jevrem. What do you see?"

I shut my eyes and look again. I see those bloody lumps, how they're so strange looking, how they hardly look like anything at all, and I see a child kneeling with a rock raised over his head, I see children running around screaming.

"Children," I say.

"Yes," he says. "That's it. Just children, all of you, trying to make it through."

‡ ‡ ‡

THERE ARE MOUNTAINS BEFORE YOU GET TO THE coast. They form a spine down the western edge of the continent, as big as or bigger even than our mountains back home, but they're smaller around the city of L.A., more like big foothills, I don't know, Big Red goes on and on about them, about bigger and smaller mountains with oak, pine, and cedar trees, with streams and gorges, waterfalls and small lakes, and about foothills that are grassy not barren, but I can't pay attention, I can't even sit up. I have to lie back in the seat, I have to lie down as flat as I possible, I feel tired beyond life and death. Big Red says, it's okay, you were a child, there was nothing you could have done, it wasn't your responsibility, it was the adults and those who call themselves leaders who failed to protect you, forgive yourself, let it go. War is a criminal failure of fathering, plain and simple, if you ask me, all the fathers, the presidents, generals, foreign ministers, peace negotiators, men mostly, who make decisions that put their and other people's children in the line of fire, because there's always another way, you know that, no matter what anyone tells you. Shitty, immature, selfish dads, that's the only way to think of them, they should all go to jail forever, the war heroes and the war criminals, the diplomats, negotiators, all of them together. He grumbles on and on, patting my thigh in a fatherly way with that heavy warm hand of his, putting me to sleep.

I wake to Big Red shaking me. It's dim, and perfectly still. The truck is parked.

"We're here," Big Red says.

"We're where?"

I look out the window and there in front of me is the glittering ocean, so close I wonder for a moment if Big Red has driven right in. The moon got here before us, and it's hanging proudly in the southwestern sky like the ocean below is its own clever invention. We climb down from the cab and lean against the bug-smeared grate. We try to light cigarettes in the breeze, we feel salt on our cheeks.

"That salt smell," Big Red says, and he chuckles. "The ride across the whole country is worth this one moment, every time."

"Do you need a trucker-helper, or something?" I ask.

"You've got a plan," Big Red says, because he can read my mind. "Stick to it."

"I do?"

"Somewhere in there you're feeling your way home."

"What home?"

"Exactly. That's the blessing. I'm at home everywhere I go."

And so it's goodbye to Big Red too, to his questions, his Zen mind, his sunshiny X-ray eyes. We're south of L.A. and he's going farther south still, down to San Diego to deliver to a warehouse on its outskirts. After staring at the water for a while and listening to it roar and sigh, we get back into the truck and drive a few miles before he drops me off in a place called Huntington Beach. Before I slide off my high seat onto the unmoving ground, Big Red hands me a roll of twenties, like the one I left with Eddie. Just take it, he says, as I'm opening my mouth to say no. Thanks, I say, I climb down and walk to the water without looking back.

I sit next to the embers of a dying fire abandoned hours ago, listen to the waves, steady and powerful, run coarse sand through my fingers, smoke, think about life-changing moments. When the sun rises I watch surfers climb into their suits and throw their boards into the water. I stay on the beach until late afternoon, sleeping, smoking, broiling my skin red, watching the beach people lounging through another day. When I get hungry I find a snack bar and buy three foot-long hot dogs, eat my first meal next to the thundering Pacific with skin stinging and salt in my eyes.

When the sun is a giant pink ball close to the horizon, I walk up to a group of surfer boys drinking around a truck. I ask them if they'll sell me a pair of shorts and a T-shirt. They stare at me with stone faces and I can see in their eyes that I look strange to them, like a stray, a street kid, a refugee from another time, and I say, my knapsack got stolen but I've got money. They look at each other, shrug, ask how much I'm willing to pay. I say, I'll pay whatever it is you want, and they ask, what's the accent? I say, I'm from Europe, and they say, that's cool, that's tight, that's real. They hand me a beer and tell me about their trips to England, Germany, Switzerland, France, the hotels, the powdery snow, the girls who put out, the drinking, the motor scooters, gambling, ganja, beaches, sailboats. Yes, yes, I say, that's it, that was the life, and one of them goes off and comes back with a T-shirt with *Quicksilver* written on it, baggy shorts in blue and grey, a pair of black flip-flops. I give him three of Big Red's twenties but he shakes his head and smiles a perfect, glistening, American-boy smile, and another boy goes to his car and finds me a baseball cap and a hooded sweatshirt, also dark blue. I strip down in front of them, letting them jeer and slap each other, point and shout. And then I put on all their gifts to me. I strut, they whistle, and I know I'm in perfect disguise. The surfer boys build a huge hissing bonfire and I sit with them for a while. They joke like crazy boys, talk waves, equipment, girls, blow jobs, ask me questions about skiing in the Alps and surfing off the coast of Spain, Holland, Scotland. Before I leave, they say, stay out of the boneyard, and I say, you're friendly and generous, not like your a-hole politicians. They laugh, they boo, they stand up and yell, *U.S.A. all the way, U.S.A. all the way.*

I find a pay phone and call Ujak Luka's number, the number that I memorized with Mama's help. As it rings, I think about Baka's children, how she built a whole world for them with her bare hands, how they got separated by war, how they ended up on far sides of a foreign continent not speaking to each other. As it rings, I look down at myself, feeling nervous, antsy. I hope that Ujak Luka doesn't mind that I'm still kind of scrawny, just a kid. I'll tell him not to worry, I'm fast and ruthless, I get in and out of places like a ghost, I take what's necessary, I carry heat. After many rings, a kid answers and says hello in a high, steady voice.

I say, "Is . . . um . . ." and choke.

"What?" the kid says.

"I want to talk to . . ." I say. "Is your dad there?"

The child says, "Yes, just a minute," drops the phone and rushes off shouting, "It's a man from the old country."

"Hello, Jevrem?" Ujak Luka's voice is very familiar, as if I've heard it every day of my life.

‡

I WAIT on the road by the water, staring at the sailboats and yachts moored to the docks and the tall skinny palm trees that wave in the breeze. The sky is pink, the clouds on the horizon yellow, orange, purple. When Mercs, BMWs, and Jaguars approach, each one has Ujak Luka in it with two of his toughest bodyguards, two of his hottest girls falling all over him. But each car passes me by, leaves me standing like a fool with a forced grin on my face. I pace up and down, I chew my nails, I scratch my sandy scalp. I wait an hour, two hours, and then the sky turns electric blue and some stars come out. I think about taking off up the highway, going all the way to Alaska, over to Russia, back to my torn-up country.

The road is suddenly completely empty. I'm looking for a place sheltered from the accelerating breeze to lie down for the night, feeling pissed off and relieved both at the same time, when a beat-up old VW van races up, stops, and two small girls jump out and run toward me.

"Jevrem," they call out. "Jevrem."

It's Berina and Aisha all over again, at three or four years old, the same fine dark hair down their backs, the same huge eyes and mischievous smiles.

"Jevrem, it's us," they shout.

And there is Ujak Luka standing by the open door of the van in dusty clothes, bushy beard on his face, straw hat on his head, worn sandals flapping on each foot, two barking dogs on the seat behind him.

"Jevrem," he says. He's smiling a wide, delirious smile. "There you are, you crazy boy. I'm so glad you called. I was expecting you."

"Jevrem's here, Jevrem's here," the girls sing.

I walk to the van, one girl hanging on each hand. When I

get there Ujak Luka grabs me and hugs me like I'm his long-lost relative or something, squeezing me, kissing my cheeks, my forehead. I feel his whole body shaking like he's on spin-cycle and he keeps spinning and my shoulder is getting wet and the girls are singing, Daddy's crying again, Daddy's crying again.

"Okay," I say.

"Yes, it is," he says.

It's late, so there's not a lot of traffic on the coast highway. We fly along it like we're all in the same surreal dream. The two dogs pant in the back with the girls, a small poodle-type dog and a large shaggy dog, and every now and then I turn around and look at the four of them squirming in a pile and I'm confused. These aren't the girls I expected, this isn't the car I imagined, Ujak Luka isn't the dangerous motherfucker I was working up the nerve to meet. Maybe Ujak Luka is in a witness protection program, or maybe these are his fake kids, the kids of his body-guard, a way to throw his underworld pursuers off his scent. Because I don't remember any cousins, I don't remember being told about their birth. I look down at the worn mat at my feet and see straw, clumps of dirt, a little wooden car, a granola bar wrapper, a paper cup, some CD cases. Ujak Luka keeps looking over at me and smiling his huge face-splitting smile. He's nothing like a gangster or Hollywood heavy-hitter. He's more like a Mexican singer on his way to a country wedding, like he's about to haul out a battered old guitar and sing about peasants and true love in a field of dust and dry grasses.

"Your mama called a few days ago," Ujak Luka says, finally. "The first time since your baka died." He pauses, but I don't say anything. "She said, *my boy is coming to find you, be there for him.*"

He looks over at me again, waiting for me to jump in and add something, but I have nothing to say.

"And I said, yes, of course." Ujak Luka speaks slowly, crisply in accented English, then very fast in Serbo-Croatian. "I said, of course, I'm here for him, I was here all along, I tried to be in contact with him but you wouldn't let me. That's all I got to say to her. She said, *goodbye, Luka,* and hung up the phone. I called her back but she didn't answer. What more can I do? If someone's heart isn't open, there's nothing you can do. But she'll come around, she'll realize someday that everyone has their own path, that there was more than one right way to respond to that fucked-up situation. She'll find a way to forgive me for leaving. Now, with you here, she has to be in touch, right?"

He grabs my thigh so hard with his gnarly hand that I jump and swear.

"I'm not here for Mama or the family or the past," I say.

"I know," he says. "I understand."

‡ ‡ ‡

I'M SITTING AT A LONG WOODEN TABLE IN A LARGE farm kitchen, listening to a dozen men and women shouting over each other in Spanish. They're so into it, whatever they're saying, they sometimes stand up when they speak, they sometimes bang their fists on the table, intense as revolutionaries or drunken gamblers. I follow the debate around the room like it's a beach ball in a seaside game, even though I don't understand a word, and I forget why I'm here. There's a plate piled with food in front of me, real food, homegrown and home-cooked, but I can't eat any of it, not even a bite.

Rosario, Ujak Luka's wife, says, "Oh, poor Jevrem, the sun got you good. Look at your burnt nose."

She brings me a glass of water with ice cubes and lime and sugar, tells me to drink, drink. And it's true, I'm burning up, light-headed, trippy. The debate goes on and on and I sag in my chair and finally Rosario signals to Ujak Luka and he leads me upstairs.

On the second floor, I sense breathing, dreaming children tucked away somewhere close by, the two girls who stroked my hair and sang into my ear all evening, the two-year-old boy with his "no's" and non-stop running, and the boy baby they say looks exactly like I did when I was small. I hear the twitching and snoring of the animals, two cats and two dogs and a rabbit that sleeps in a doll's cradle, which they showed me before they went to bed. We climb another steeper staircase to the attic, and Ujak Luka leads me into a small room with slanted walls and narrow bed covered with a patchwork quilt, a small lamp beside it.

"Here," he says, "you will get some peace and quiet." He leans against the door frame staring at me like I'm some kind of exotic animal. "It's so nice to see you," he says. "It means a lot."

I sit on the bed. "Are you a farmer?" I ask him. It sounds ridiculous, but I have to ask.

He laughs hard when he hears my question. It's so funny to him that he dabs tears off his cheeks with a handkerchief.

"I'm sorry, Jevrem," he finally has the breath to say. "I'm sorry." He looks at me. "Yes, I'm a farmer."

"Why are you laughing?"

"Because you look so amazed."

I shrug my shoulders and smile. "I don't know. We all thought you were a crime boss or something."

"You and the rest of the world." Ujak Luka turns to leave.

"Will you stay?"

"Stay?"

"Here, in California? Or go back?"

"Go back?"

"Yes, go back home."

Ujak Luka turns and comes to the bed. He grabs my shoulders. "Jevrem, Jevrem. I am at home. Home is here."

"But they need people to build things up again over there, it's not going so well."

"Humanity needs people everywhere. Things need to be built up everywhere. We're all just nomads of existence until we die, and humanity is our people."

I stare at him.

"Our war wasn't regional, Jevrem, it was global. Everything is linked and we're all in the same matrix of causes and effects and consequences, all of us, the whole world over. Who cares where your ancestors came from, it doesn't matter. I've got important work to do here, for my people here. They're all the same issues, anyway."

After his little speech, Ujak Luka gives me another of his fierce bone-crushing hugs and ducks out of the room. I turn the light off and get into the bed. I lie staring up into the darkness and listen to the creaking of Ujak Luca's house and the voices from downstairs rising and falling and the humming of the land outside the window.

I FEEL normal when I wake up. My head is clear and I'm no longer burning up. I look out of the attic window and see a large yard with swings and a pile of logs for climbing, I see a barn, a barnyard with chickens, a tractor, some trucks, a pile of manure, a bunch of goats, three cows, two ponies. I see green planted fields rolling in every direction over small hills.

The kitchen is still filled with the Spanish-speaking shout-ers, as if they'd been talking all night long. They cheer and say *hola!* when I come in. They tell me to sit and eat, they tell me I'm too young to travel across the continent all by myself, they tell me California is best, they tell me all the places I should visit. And they say they can see I'm Ujak Luka's nephew by the way I come into a room, the way I sit down at a table, the way I turn my head to listen, the way I nod and smile when I don't under-stand, the way I stay silent when everyone else is talking, biding my time. All those things. I eat scrambled eggs with tomato salad mixed in, I eat spicy sausage, I drink a hundred cups of black coffee, I smoke a thousand raunchy cigarettes along with the rest of them. And they continue to debate, making their points, scribbling notes, agreeing and disagreeing, as focused and on fire as last night. Maybe there is no need for sleep on this coast with its crystal-clear light and warm velvety nights.

Ujak Luka comes in carrying a bag of rice, followed by Rosario with the baby and all the kids, who swarm around me, climb me like a tree, and ask me a hundred one-sentence questions.

"They're discussing strategy and tactics, in case you want to know," Rosario says, shushing the kids, pointing at the debaters, putting food on plates.

"For what?" I ask. I actually want to know.

"The usual issues, decent housing, a living wage, docu-mentation, the end of pesticide poisoning, NAFTA," she says, swinging the baby up to her shoulder.

"And right now," Ujak Luka says, sitting down next to me, "there's a special campaign. In places like Chiapas, Guerrero, Oaxaca, Veracruz, Nuevo León, Baja California, Tabasco, Morelos, militant peasants are continuing to rise up and we are with them, doing what we can on this side. You see, the Mexican

acknowledgements

My deepest gratitude to Jackie Kaiser, Chris Casuccio, Jane Warren, Phyllis Bruce, and Andrea Griggs.

after you've read this and given it some thought.) Of the Bastards, our nights of fevered action and days of floating about without a clue.

The radio blasts thrashy Euro-punk and I see Sarajevo, a grey day, when the clouds are heavy and thick as smoke, when they hang so low they brush the roofs and cars and pavement of the streets. The kind of day when Dušan and his friends would drift through the streets smoking and joking and looking for a laugh. And I think about how you go on when life has been wrecked, how you build a new one, who you blame, who you forgive. I take in the concrete-box stores, the hut-houses and tiny bungalows, the large chain-link-bordered yards, the grassy alleyways, the tangles of phone wires, the pink walls, the turquoise window frames, the giant bulbous graffiti. I search for colours and territories, spot Korean convenience stores, Ethiopian jazz clubs, Mexican grills. The palm trees give that vacation vibe, the cypress trees make me feel at home.

surreal, just when you're hoping to wake up, it turns into a nightmare more mean and fucked-up and savage than anything you could have thought up in your own twisted imagination. Then you're doing things you never knew you could do, and you're seeing things that shouldn't be in this world, and you're escaping to places you never knew existed. You're fighting for your life, basically. That's what I tell them, but it doesn't really describe the runaway-train feeling of terror watching everything good being forsaken right in front of your eyes.

WHEN everyone's asleep, I take Ujak Luca's beat-up van like they said I could and drive into L.A., into the basin full of cities, looking for angels and devils. It's heaven to be at the wheel and I cruise the streets of South Central, searching for their city of flames, their militias of unemployed, their spring of rage and riots, their tribal deceptions, Crips and Bloods, Latinos and Asians. To understand, to make the connections, that's what everyone's telling me to do, between here and there, then and now, my history, their history. Because the people here were divided and conquered too, set to battling among themselves, their power destroyed. I think about Baka and her idea of righteousness, and take in the wide sprawling roads, the low, flat buildings, the towering street lamps and electrical poles. I cruise along slowly, I light up a fat organic spliff, I think about Dušan and his smoky room, the twins, how they moved like one little creature, Mama and Papa, how they fitted together perfectly when they argued, when they talked, when they laughed and worked hard, the family acting like life would be normal forever, like families do. Of Sava, my comrade-in-arms, how I love her even if it's doomed, or maybe it isn't. (*Tell me, Sava,* capitalists and landowning classes who exploit Mexican cheap labour are supported by powerful interests in the U.S."

I nod. All of this reminds me of Baka, this sitting in farm kitchens organizing the resistance.

"Do you know why the Mexican poor are kept that way?" Rosario asks, settling the kids in front of their food.

I look at them and calculate in my mind. Ujak Luka and Rosario must have had one every year or so since they met.

"Do you know what would happen to the American economy if cheap labour no longer came north searching for a decent life?" Ujak Luka answers with another question, that teacher thing.

Rosario points at the baby. "His name is Jevrem, we named him after you." She smiles at me and the baby smiles at her. "But we mostly call him Javier, it's more common around here."

"Industry on every continent needs its pool of cheap labour," Ujak Luka says.

The girls look over at me and nudge each other as they eat their food. They don't seem to be listening to a word, but I know that someday they'll remember these moments and what was said in unexpected detail.

Rosario turns to me. "You must be a student of history and politics and economics if you're serious about building a just world. Are you serious about building a just world, Jevrem?"

"What?" I say.

"Here." She gives the baby to me. "Hold Little Jevrem."

The baby is a hot little ball of muscle. He jerks his head around powerfully, paying attention to every bright shiny object in the room, responding with a contraction of limbs to every raised voice. He clutches my hair with steel-trap fingers, he gnaws on my nose and chin with hard little gums, his breath hot and sweet-smelling. I'm happy he's named after me, but

I feel tired when I think about his life to come, how he will spend his childhood trying to understand this crazy world. And underneath the tiredness there's something new, a little sprout of excitement for him, all the things he will touch and see and taste for the first time, how good and blissful that will be.

Ujak Luka finishes his toast and grabs my arm. "Let's go out to the fields," he says. He takes the baby from me and passes him to a woman wearing a red T-shirt with a black clenched fist on the front.

We wander in the hot sun through carrots, spinach, strawberries, squash, beans. Straw-hat-wearing American teenagers are weeding, debugging, hoeing, wheelbarrowing. They smile and say *hiya* when we pass them by, looking superhuman with their big frames, plump muscles, even tans, shiny hair, damp T-shirts, can-do attitudes.

"Good kids," Ujak Luka says. "Local high school kids and WWOOFers from other states and Europe. Canada as well. The Mexicans on this farm are busy with something else, let me tell you." Ujak Luka bends over to inspect a plant. He picks a leaf and shows it to me.

"Organic," he says.

It does look especially perky.

"You see?" he asks, tearing off a piece and offering it to me.

I nod, put it in my mouth. It tastes dark green. Earthy, mossy, like the forest floor back home.

"So what do you want to do with the rest of your life?" Ujak Luka looks at me hard. "I'm assuming you've left your previous activities behind. I'm assuming that you'll never do that bullshit again." He crushes a leaf between his thumb and finger, then smells it. "I'm assuming that you've repented and suffered some internal agonies for the suffering you caused."

"Yes," I say. I feel my sunburnt cheeks with my fingers. The one thing I didn't worry about when I worried about coming to stay with Ujak Luka was a lecture about repenting. But he's right. I deserve internal agonies for passing my shit on, it's the number-one problem in the world. "I guess I want to do a bit of good for once, you know."

Ujak Luka laughs, slaps my back, and does a little dance in his sandals.

"Good old Baka," he says. "Did she give you the why-don't-you-boys-do-some-good-for-once speech? Did she tell you about the railways they built with their bare hands? For free?"

I nod, swallow hard.

"Well, it worked," Ujak Luka says, totally serious now, grabbing my shoulders with both hands, like he does. "My whole childhood all I heard from her were stories about the peasants feeding the partisan fighters and in that way subverting fascism. My early dreams and visions were of produce and chickens, that was my idea of moral perfection. I'm not joking." He turns and looks out over the fields beyond the barn. I nod my head again. I know exactly what he means.

"It's all connected, what we do here and now, what happened back then. It's up to us. What we do with those experiences. Do you know what I mean?"

I don't say anything. I'm not going to be a farmer, I can tell everyone that right now, including Baka up in communist heaven. In this moment, I wish more than anything that she was here, standing with us in this field. She would be so happy, Ujak Luka and me discussing the good life.

‡

AT THE farmhouse, I finally call Sava. The girls stand very close to me, hold my hands, whisper long sentences into each other's hair.

"Andric," Sava says. "I've been waiting for you to call. Jesus, what took you so long?"

"I'm at Ujak Luka's," I say. "He's an organic farmer, his wife is a labour lawyer, and Mexicans are planning a revolution in their kitchen. Baka is a fucking genius, that's all I can say."

Sava laughs into my ear. I feel her whole body taking up space beside me, I feel her moving and breathing like she's in the room.

"You should come out here, the light is amazing," I say. "We could go to university together or something. I'll write all my shit down, like you told me to, and get clearer about things. Whatever it takes. It's paradise, I promise you."

‡ ‡ ‡

THE OFFICE BUILDING GLITTERS INSANELY IN THE sun, like a giant blood diamond thrown carelessly into a desert wasteland. I sit in the car, waiting for Rosario to come out. I watch shiny limos go by with tinted windows, I watch the red-bloomed bushes sway in the ocean breeze, I flip through radio channels, landing on PBS shows that explain the world with complicated words, religious shows that bury it in hot-headed warnings, country and hip hop for eardrums of various colours, Mexican drug ballads with accordion combos and full brass bands.

Rosario opens the back door, dumps a kilo of paper on the seat, swings in beside me. She's very athletic for a lawyer.

"Drive, Jevrem," she says. "Get me out of here. They just don't care that their employees can barely get by. They would let people starve to death to protect their profit margin." She sighs, takes off her sunglasses, rubs her eyes.

We drive five minutes, then get out of the car, and Rosario skips around on the beach, calling out to the ocean birds and shouting at me to relax, to open up, to get my heart pumping in my chest.

"That's what California is good for," she shouts at me. "You need to *moooove*. Come on, let's run for a bit."

"I can move, if I want," I say. "When cops are chasing me."

She shakes her head. "You and your uncle, so tough."

We're running side by side on the sand and she's calling out, *isn't this amazing*, and I'm nodding, trying to catch my breath, wondering what happened to my soccer lungs from childhood, hearing Pero's and Mahmud's sharp high cries for the ball all around me. It's the birds. Rosario grabs my arm and pulls me toward the water.

"Hey," I say, "I've got clothes on."

"Oh, who cares? Come on, Jevrem, live a little."

Then I'm tumbling under foamy waves, every part of me going in a different direction, all my cells and molecules shifting around. The sun and Rosario's face appear and disappear, I go limp, I learn to breathe bubbles.

Sitting on the hood of the car, we watch water pool around us then run in narrow rivulets down the slope and over the edge. Rosario tells me about meeting wild Ujak Luka, a crazy man, a tornado in his own skin, a jittery mofo who did everything hard, liquor, coke, women, running from nightmares. And then one day, from one moment to the next, he went sane.

"He went through the eye of a needle, I don't know which

needle, but on the other side he was a fine specimen." Rosario smiles. "Ask him about that," she says, "how that's possible."

I stop at a hundred stop signs, I make a thousand turns, Rosario shouting directions at me as we race through a maze of neighbourhoods with squat bungalows, ornamental shrubs, stubby palm trees, open-air carports. Brakes smoking, gears grinding, anything to avoid L.A. highways. We get home to buildings on fire with sunset light. Baby Jevrem-Javier is shrieking for dinner, the young globe-hopping farmhands with wise baby-faces are walking off the fields. In their quarters a bonfire is being lit. Tonight, like every night, they'll sit around, smoke weed, strum guitars, sing folksongs from the tune-in-drop-out give-peace-a-chance days, have serious and informed discussions about how to save the world, lie facing up at the stars, asking each other how to think about a hundred billion galaxies. In the kitchen, Ujak Luka is feeding thirty academics from Mexico City with produce and chickens. A think-tank, Ujak Luka tells me, is not only something for right-wing business magnates and cranky ex-generals. If Papa weren't rafting on the river of time, he'd love it here, talking all night long with people just like him, obsessed with a better life for the poor bastard underclasses of the world. He'd learn Spanish for that, for sure.

When I've finished eating with them, I wander outside and join the farmhand kids and smoke and toke with them, sitting on an orange crate. They ask questions like, what's it like living in a socialist country? And I reply, I don't know, I was born too late. And, what's it like living in fascist times? And I say, it's like a dream that starts off okay then slowly turns strange, with normal people acting bizarrely, letting their fear be turned into paranoid ideas, and just when you think it can't get more